FLAT WORLD

The Arrival Part 2

IVOR KOVAC

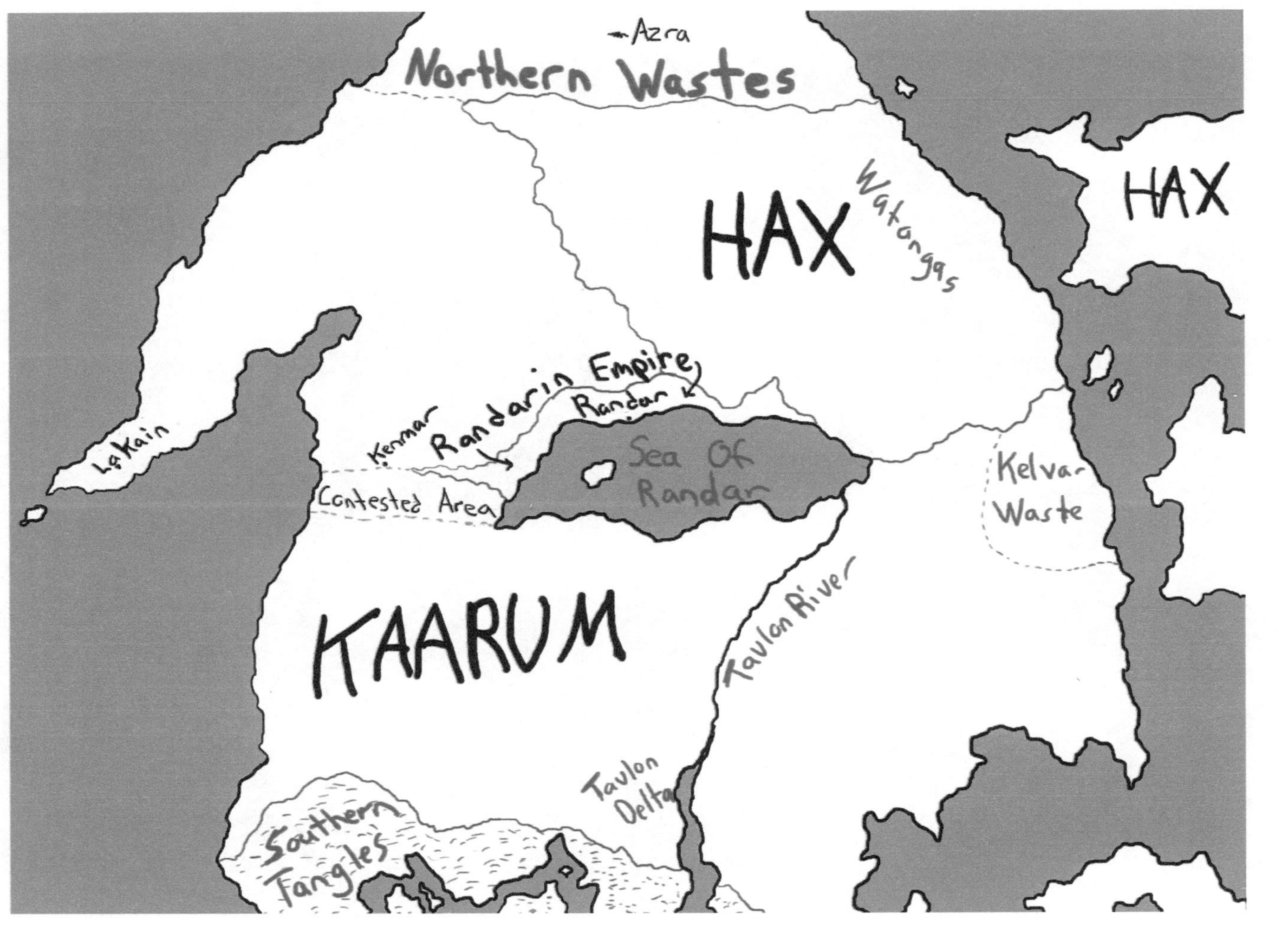
Azra
Northern Wastes
HAX
Watongas
HAX
Randarin Empire
Kenmar
Randar R
Sea Of Randar
Kelvar Waste
Contested Area
Lafain
KAARUM
Tavlon River
Tavlon Delta
Southern Fangles

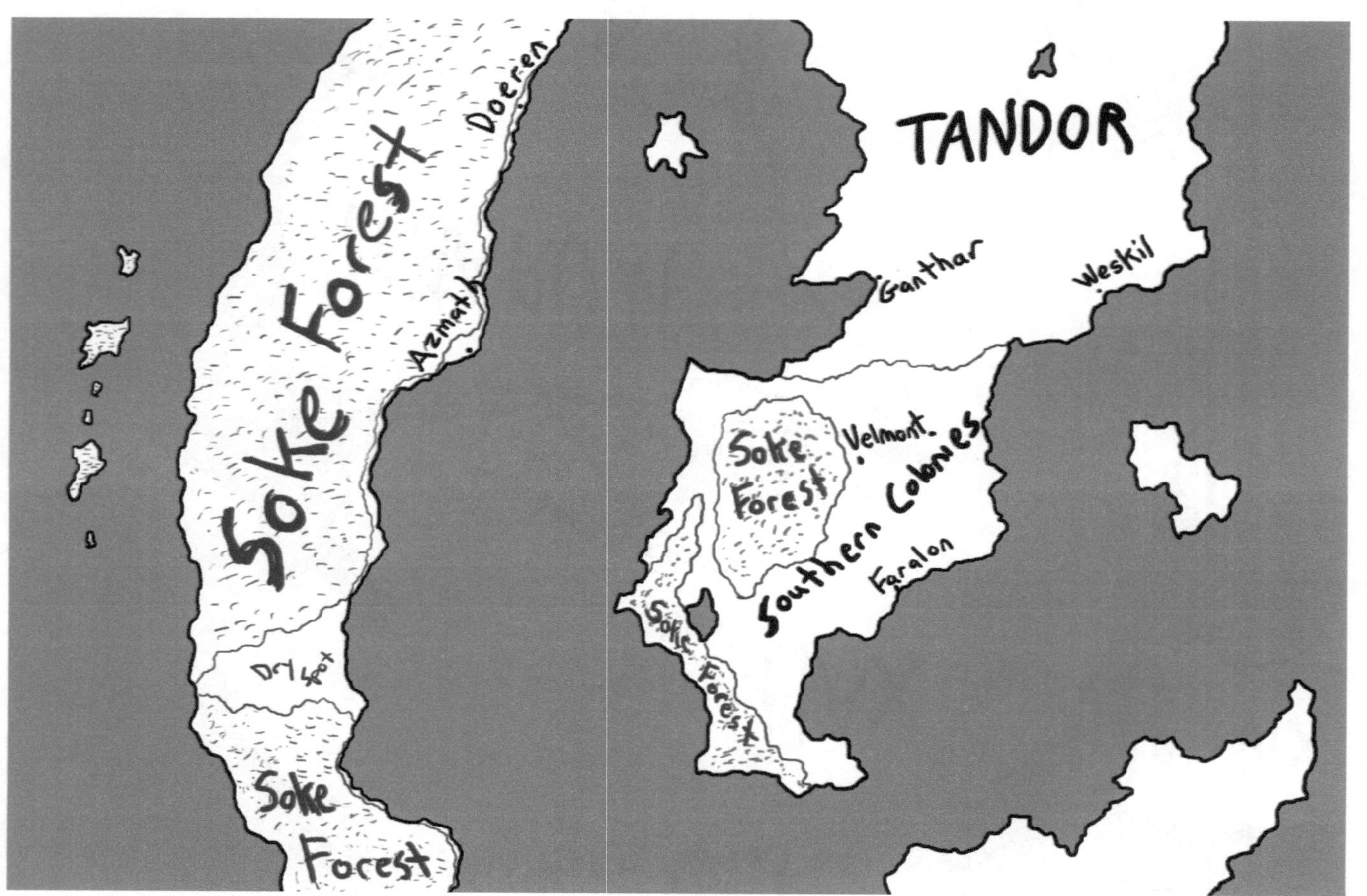

Soke Forest
Doeren
Azmath
Dry spot
Soke Forest
TANDOR
Ganthar
Weskil
Soke Forest
Velmont
Southern Colonies
Faralon
Soke Forest

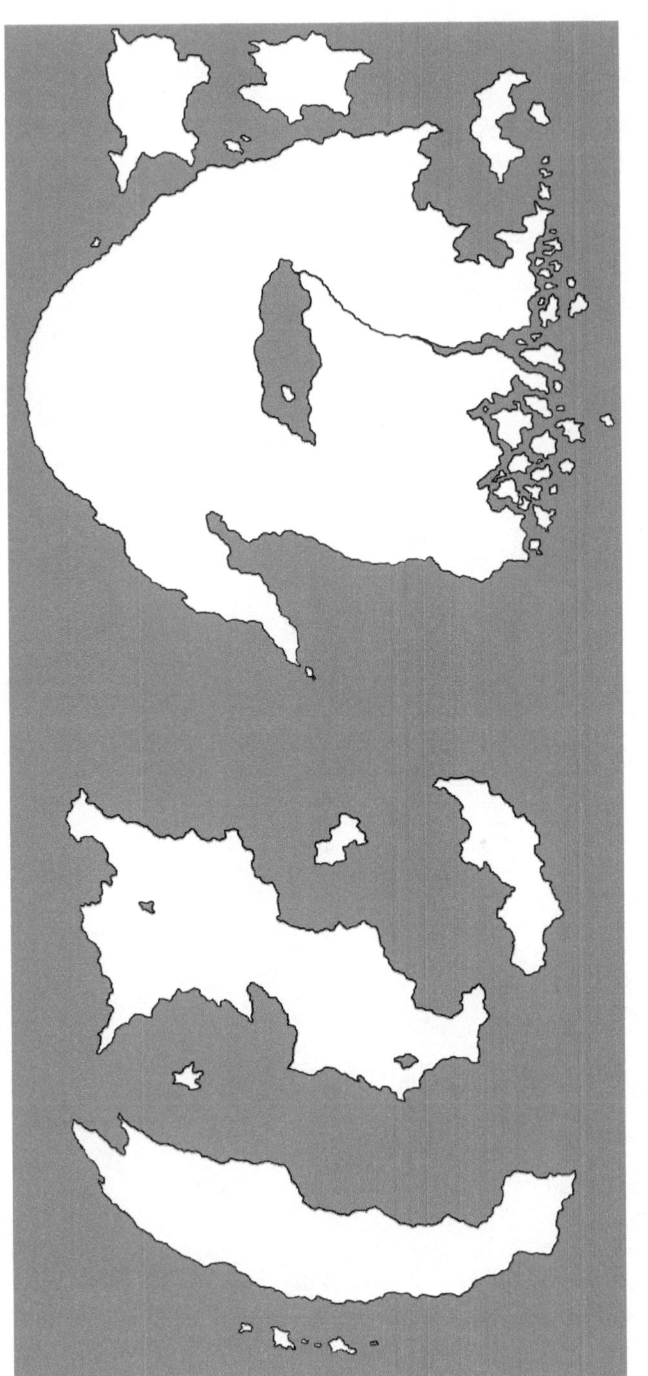

CHAPTER 1

The Randar Stone

ROGER STOOD IN THE MIDDLE of a crowd people, mostly men, and all of them Kaarumites. The majority of them were shirtless, covered with tattoos, and had haircuts which Roger found to be in poor taste. Most of them were tall southerners but those closest to him seemed to be white Kaarumites from Randarga, and there were other white Kaarumites interspersed throughout the crowd.

The crowd stopped about ten feet in front of Roger where the tallest man Roger had ever seen in his life stood on a platform. His facial features, pigmentation, and build were consistent with those of the southerners, but his size was such that he made the largest of southerners look small by comparison.

Looks like he's about 14 feet tall, give or take...

Behind the man were what passed for buildings in a Kaarumite city. They were made of poorly carved gray stone, and had an open design to them. There were long windows on the sides, and in many cases there was not even any glass. The tops of the buildings were covered with domes which were sometimes transparent. There were many tents and shacks interspersed about the bases of the great buildings. Everything looked filthy and dirty. There appeared to be open sewage in the streets and pools of collected filth, and there were wrecked bits of stone, metal, and machinery cast about.

"People of Kaarum, followers of the Truth of Kaarum, the time of our victory is nearly upon us!" the giant shouted with a deep voice.

The crowd cheered, but the giant held up his hands and they fell silent.

"My father, Kaarum, has given us all the lands to the north," the giant said. "He has stricken them with affliction and weakness. He has grown weary of their rebellion against his truth. He closes the wombs of their women so that their children are few and weak. He afflicts their minds with cowardice, so that they have no will to resist us. Kaarum has shown me that the Empire, our oldest and strongest enemy, no longer has the ability to resist us."

The crowd cheered, and this time the giant allowed them to silence themselves before he continued.

"We will wash over the Empire like a tide, and bathe our hands in their blood!" he continued. "We will ravage their women. We will tear down the lofty towers of Randar. I will personally kill the Emperor and turn his skull into a drinking goblet. I will shatter the crimson doors of their temple and desecrate their shrines. I will sleep in the Imperial Palace, and make a concubine of the Emperor's wife!"

The crowd cheered once more, and when they fell silent he spoke again.

"From there we will take all the lands of the heretics to the north, and we will put their men to the sword, or enslave them, and take their women as war booty!" the giant shouted. "When the time comes you must all follow me. Are you with me?"

The crowd roared with approval.

"Do you want the blood of heretics on your hands?" he shouted.

"YES!" the mob shouted as one.

"Do you want to tear down their cities and destroy everything they hold as valuable and precious?" he asked.

"YES!" they shouted again.

Then the crowd began to chant, shouting "Atuskus-Var! Atuskus-Var! *Atuskus-Var!*

The name startled Roger into wakefulness. He sat up straight in his bed and looked around the room.

"I was wondering when you would wake up," Aneme said.

She was sitting on the couch reading her holy text, but she was entirely dressed and ready to go. Her hair was completely black and her skin white.

After the incidents of Tandor and the contested area she made certain that both of their disguises were thoroughly intact. She closed her book and quickly tied up her hair as she rose to her feet.

"I had a dream about Atuskus-Var," Roger said as he got out of bed and began to dress himself.

"Do you want to talk about it?"

"No. Right now I want to go out and get something to eat. Maybe after that we can talk about it."

"Very well."

Most of the people they passed in the streets were westerners, but there were also people with varying degrees of southern admixture. They were individuals who were taller and had some color to their skin. Sometimes they had facial features that almost looked northern as they struck a balance between the western and southern features.

This is a good place for us. Easier for us to blend in.

There actually seemed to be more individuals of southern ancestry in the Empire than there were in Tandor. As Roger scrutinized Imperial citizens more closely he determined that about one out of every ten showed some sign of southern ancestry.

"I wonder where the southern influence comes from?" Roger asked. "They don't allow Kaarumites in here."

"We both know that not all southerners are Kaarumites," Aneme replied. "Back when the Empire was at the height of its power parts of it extended deep down into southern territory. As the Kaarumites started taking over some of the southern citizens ran north and mixed in with the westerners over time."

They came to a restaurant which had a dining area shaded from the sun by a patio with arching columns. Roger said little as he ate. He had some kind of meat that he tore from the bone with his hands. He was not sure whether it was a bird or reptile, only that he was hungry and that it filled him. The vegetables were served as some kind of stir-fry. When he had finished most of his food Roger paid and got up to leave.

Before he left the dining area he refilled his disposable cup with whatever liquid they had poured in. Imperial cuisine was considerably more complex than Northern, so half the time he had no idea what he was eating, and the other half was only theory.

He held hands with Aneme as they walked.

"I think the Empire is in serious trouble," Roger said. "I don't think they can survive without our help."

"Oh?" Aneme replied. "Did you learn that from your dream?"

"I saw Kaarumites stretching off into the horizon, and cheering this Atuskus-Var guy while he talked about how he was going to kill them and sleep with the Emperor's wife."

"Did the dream tell you that we should help them?"

"Well not specifically, but listen... You remember when I told you about the Roman Empire?"

"Yes, but I also have ancestors that were Romans."

"I remember. You're like me. I have ancestors who were Azrans, and others who helped destroy Azra."

"But I don't think I told you that in my world, my people are called 'westerners.'"

Aneme cocked her head and gave Roger a puzzled look.

"Yes, and the people in my world who look the most like your westerners are actually easterners."

"Then who are the northerners in your world?" Aneme asked.

"There aren't any. Our arctic region is a big ocean covered with a huge floating iceberg. I know it's weird, but just bear with me. The Roman Empire started out as one city: Rome. They started expanding, mainly to protect themselves, and ended up expanding around an inland sea and taking over parts of three continents."

"Wouldn't that make them a lot of enemies?"

"Yes, and it did, but they also had fear and respect."

"Alright."

"The Roman Empire brought civilization and protection to most of my people, and to others as well. They provided roads, libraries, running water, and sanitary facilities. People thought the Roman Empire would never fail, but over time it was attacked by barbarians from the north, and barbarians from the east.

"Piece after piece of it was taken away, until only a small part remained in the east, and then that was also destroyed."

"Didn't they also have some civil wars?"

"Well, yes… There was that, but the point is that since then, my people have tried again and again to revive the empire but no one has been able to do it. Most of our civilization is based on it, but we can't bring it back.

"Why not?"

"Once the egg is cracked then there is nothing you can do to uncrack it."

"That's a good metaphor but it doesn't answer the question."

"Because the original conditions that set up the Roman Empire can't be recreated. Things have changed too much since then, and it's hard to artificially mimic things that happen organically."

"I understand."

"So then, you see why we have to help the Randarans?"

"No. I mean, I understand why your empire can't be rebuilt."

Roger sighed and felt suddenly tired.

"It reminds me of the Humpty Dumpty rhyme taught me to help me learn English," Aneme said. "Once he fell all the king's men and horses cannot put him back together, but the pieces will remain and remind everyone of what was lost so that future generations can share in the sadness. I'm understanding your culture better, but I still don't see what it has to do with Randar."

"I'm making a comparison between our old empire and the Randarans."

"But what point are you trying to make?"

"What I'm saying is, when the Randaran Empire is destroyed it will be a huge and permanent loss to the western race of your world, just as it was to mine. They are going to suffer for a long time, especially with these Kaarumites running amok. I know your father doesn't think much of westerners, but since we have been in Randar don't you get the impression that this culture is worth saving?"

"Yes, but not at the cost of giving them our secrets. I won't feel comfortable sharing our secrets until you are absolutely sure that it is what the Great Maker wants you to do."

Roger and Aneme reached a narrow street designed explicitly for walking, which was lined with columns, arches, and balconies that contained a wide variety of flowering plants. Before they turned down the street Roger stopped walking and faced Aneme.

"You know some of my dreams seem to be showing me things that happened, or will happen, in other parts of the world, and others show me things that I will experience directly," Roger said. "The last kind are like mile markers to me, letting me know that I am on the right track. The dream about saving the Emperor was of the last kind. The dream about Randar sort of fell into both categories. Randar said "protect my heirs." I already saved the Emperor. So was that it, or is there someone else I need to save? Do I need to save the Emperor again? Do we need to stay here and act as the Emperor's bodyguards? What do we need to do?"

Roger started walking again and took a sip from his straw. Suddenly he heard a scraping noise coming from the walls somewhere higher up, and someone dropped down from about 15 feet in the air and landed on the ground in front of them. He quickly rose up and turned in their direction in one swift motion, colliding with Aneme.

It was a young man. He appeared as though he were still in his teens and growing. He had light brown hair which was almost yellow, and icy blue eyes. After colliding with Aneme he muttered an apology and tried to run, but Aneme grabbed his arm and held him. He jerked violently but it was futile.

"Don't let him go yet!" Roger exclaimed, remembering his dream about the young man.

"I said I was sorry, there is no need for this," the teenager said. "If you wish I can make reparations for whatever damage you might have suffered. There is no reason to turn me in."

"Who are you?" Roger asked.

Something about the young man's face struck Roger as peculiar, as if something were out of step with the established native phenotypes.

"Is that a trick question?" the teenager asked.

Roger leaned in and studied his face closely, and he finally understood what was out of order. The eyes were not completely blue. There were spots of purple and pink around the edges of his irises which protruded inward slightly at various points.

I've never seen a thing like this before. Is it some kind of deformity? There has to be a story behind this…

"Who are you?" Roger reiterated.

"You really don't know?" the young man asked. "Ah, I can see that you don't. Why, this is wonderful! I think the better question is, 'who are you?' Are you Haxians?"

"No, we have come here from the Western Lands."

"Quite so! You are very far away from home then, and the lady is very strong," the teenager said. "A quality which is both remarkable and attractive in a woman. Would you like to see a trick?"

"What sort of trick?" Aneme asked.

"I will show you," the teenager said.

Aneme tightened her grip on his arm.

"You can hold onto my arm if you want, I only need one hand for this trick," the teenager said.

He extended his other hand toward the side of Aneme's head and was about to touch her ear when she grabbed his other hand by the wrist and held it tightly.

"I don't just let anyone touch me," Aneme said.

"I have no intention of harming a hair on your lovely head, but for this trick to work I have to touch something beautiful," the teenager said.

"Consider yourself warned," Aneme said as she let go of his wrist.

The teenager turned the back of his hand towards her and lightly touched the side of her head. Then the teenager rotated his hand and clenched his fist in one swift movement. He held his fist out in front of Aneme's face and slowly opened it, revealing a blue flower in the palm of his hand.

"A flower, for an even more beautiful flower," he said. "I think blue is your color."

"What is your deal kid?" Roger asked. "A flower for an even more beautiful flower'? Come on, you can't be legally old enough to romance an adult."

"I am an adult. I just turned 17 three weeks ago," the teenager said.

"What?" Roger exclaimed. "That's not an adult!"

"In northern culture one is an adult at 16," Aneme said.

"She is married," Roger said.

"Ah, how unfortunate," the teenager said. "I mean, my mistake. I meant no disrespect."

"For a kid you're acting awfully smart."

"Does she have a sister?"

"No!"

"A pity," the teenager said. "Well in any case, what did you think of my trick?"

"It was well executed, but in some parts of the world people perform far more complex slight of hand techniques," Aneme said.

"So you have seen northerners in action then?" the teenager asked. "I take it you are from one of the Tandoran colonies? Somewhere in Velta? What are your good names?"

"My name is Roger, my wife is Aneme," Roger said.

"Demekus, at your service," the teenager said with a bow.

"Do I know you from somewhere, Demekus?" Roger asked.

"I don't know. Do any of us really know each other?"

"I have seen your face before."

"Well, I can only guess where that might have been. But if you like mysteries there is one artifact which might interest you, and since you are from far away you have probably never seen it before."

"What is that?"

"It's called the 'Randar Stone'," Demekus said. "In his later years Randar carved an inscription on a stone in an alien language, but would not tell anyone what it meant. It is written that only one from beyond the Empire would be able to understand it. There are some people who believe it is just gibberish."

"I have heard of the Randar Stone before," Aneme said. "But why do we need you to see it?"

"The actual Randar stone is kept under guard for most of the year," Demekus said. "What you see in the museums is only a replica. But I can take you to see the original stone, and I may even be able to arrange for you to touch it."

"Why would you do that for us, and how?" Roger asked.

"Let's just say that I'm pretty well connected," Demekus said. "As for why, it's because of the lady. I have always wanted to be with someone like her. Yes, I know she's your wife, but I have a feeling that she could connect me with the person I need. I have always had a strong interest in northern culture, and I find the women absolutely stunning."

"What does northern culture have to do with us?" Aneme asked.

"We are all as we are, and you are close to it," Demekus said.

"Alright, take us to see the stone," Roger said.

"Very good," Demekus said. "If anyone asks, you two are my escorts."

"How can we be your escorts?" Aneme asked.

"Because, you're escorting me," Demekus replied as he began to walk. "By the way, you two have some very northern looks. I could easily believe that you are full blooded northerners on a skin changing drug."

Roger did not like the direction that the conversation was going in, and he had no way of knowing whether he could trust this strange teenager, or what he was driving at. He could not let the conversation continue in that direction because if Demekus suspected they were northerners he would take silence as an affirmative.

"You can think of us as northerners if you want, but it would not be entirely accurate," Roger said.

"I see," Demekus replied. "Well I would like to go to the Northern Wastes sometime, and the Kelvar Waste as well."

"What draws you to such desolate places?" Aneme asked.

"Different reasons," Demekus said. "I would like to live among the northerners and immerse myself in their culture, learn their fighting, and marry one of their women."

"That's not very likely to happen, the northern people are very much closed to outsiders," Aneme replied.

"Yes, well… maybe they will make an exception for me," Demekus said.

"On what grounds?" Aneme asked.

"I hear there is an advanced fighting art for people gifted with agility, and that's me," Demekus said completely ignoring Aneme's last comment.

Demekus suddenly veered right and ran straight for a nearby wall. He ran up the side for a few feet, flipped in the air, and landed on his feet facing Roger and Aneme. He bowed and resumed walking in the direction he was leading them before.

"I also want to go to the east," Demekus said. "There are supposed to be great secrets there. I want to find out what causes the interference. I learned the Watanga language a few years ago. I'm fluent in the northern and southern dialects of Watanga. Yes, it's true that the Watangas attacked our Empire in the past, but today they are not so wicked. They stopped worshiping Gro-Sho-Var thousands of years ago. Today they are more like… noble savages."

"Wait," Roger said. "Hold up. What interference are you talking about?"

"Don't you know?" Demekus replied. "There is something in the Kelvar Waste that causes most forms of technology to shut down. It's a complete power blackout zone. That's why no one bothers to go in there and take the land from the Watangas. It's the last part of the world where the Watangas live in their fully traditional lifestyle and have full autonomy."

"Yeah I heard something about that place, but no one said anything about any interference. Who would be interested in taking their land?"

"The Haxians. They already took over most of the Watanga territory in the east. The only thing that stopped them from going further south was that none of their equipment would work. So they decided it wasn't worth it. There are also some nations of southerners in the east who never converted to Kaarum. They would also try to take it, if they could, but their technology won't work either. They don't much like Watangas, lots of bad blood between Watangas and southerners."

"Why?"

"An ancient war, no one really knows who started it. Some people say it is a holdover from something that happened in the Eastern Lands in the ancient days. My father could probably tell you more."

"Who is your father?" Roger asked.

"We're here!" Demekus said gesturing to a building with a pale blue exterior.

There was a set of stairs leading up to the patio, which was lined by pointed arches. Armored guards in blue and white stood next to each arch and on either side of the doorways leading in.

"The Imperial Museum of Antiquities, made out of imported northern stone," Demekus said. "You will probably not find such a large museum anywhere else in the world."

Roger looked up and felt dizzy. The part of the building directly in front of him appeared to be about 100 stories tall, but it was tiered and contained domes on multiple levels. The shorter parts of the museum appeared to stretch on down to the end of the block on either side for a good distance.

"I thought you said it wasn't in a museum?" Roger asked.

"I said it was not on display in any museum, not that it wasn't in a museum," Demekus answered. "Come on!"

Demekus bounded up the stairs and Roger and Aneme followed.

"We don't have to pay to get in?" Roger asked.

"Not while you're with me," Demekus said.

"Why is that? Does your father run the museum or something?"

"In a way."

The interior of the museum was vast, and filled with a multitude of relics as far as the eye could see. According to the inscriptions many of the items and relics were older than any human civilization back on Earth.

Either this world is way older than mine or time just moves faster here.

"Will you be wanting an escort sir?" asked a very official looking older man.

On Earth the man would have been taken for someone in his 50's, but given what Roger knew about his new home the man was probably closer to 800. People did not age outwardly to the same degree as people on Earth. In all likelihood this man would probably look almost exactly the same if he lived to 1000.

"No thanks," Demekus replied. "These two are my escorts today."

Demekus pointed a thumb over his shoulder toward Roger and Aneme.

"Very good sir," the old man said as he turned away.

"Come on," Demekus said to Roger and Aneme.

"So… What?" Roger asked. "You can just go anywhere?"

"Yes and no. It's complicated…"

Demekus led them through rooms and hallways. Roger wanted to stop and examine many of the artifacts but he stopped himself because he had a feeling that the Randar Stone was more important. As they traversed the museum they gradually went lower and lower. Eventually they came to a door which was locked, and a guard was standing nearby.

"Hello," Demekus said to the guard. "I want to go inside."

"Sir!" the guard said with a salute.

He walked away and returned with a small group of guards. One of them opened the door with a key, and Demekus passed through followed by Roger and Aneme. They stepped into an empty room, passed through a heavy metal door that the guards also had to unlock, walked down a flight of stairs, and found themselves in a room full of artifacts in sealed containers. In the center of the room was a transparent cube containing a stone about the size of Roger's torso.

"Behold, the Randar Stone!" Demekus said as he spread his arms as if he were giving a benediction. "Go and feast your eyes upon it my friends. Let it speak to you."

"It does look like there is something written on it," Roger said.

"Yes, carved right into the stone," Aneme added.

They both stepped closer to examine the stone.

"It's definitely writing," Roger said. "Actually it's... it's..."

"He's down this way!" said a voice.

Aneme turned to look just in time to see Demekus run towards a stone column just as a new set of soldiers came down the stairs. Demekus ran up the side for a few feet, then leapt to an adjacent column. He leapt back and forth going up as he went. At the top of the columns the stone ended and metal bars connected with metal rafters overhead.

Demekus grabbed the bar and leapt to a crawl space near the top of the wall, where he quickly scurried out of sight.

"I can catch him," Aneme said. "I have the agility to get up there."

"No!" Roger said as he grabbed her by the wrist. "Let him go."

"Adimnor's blood!" one of the guards grumbled.

"Find all the service exits and head him off!" another shouted.

"Aneme!" Roger said. "This is impossible. There is no way anyone could have faked this. Is there?"

"What is it?" Aneme asked.

Roger felt his skin crawl, and for a moment he became light headed. The inscription on the stone was written with Latin letters, and in plain modern English it said, "Protect my heirs."

CHAPTER 2

The Decision

Once more Roger found himself locked in an Imperial security room surrounded by guards. In spite of Dekemus' ability to get them into restricted areas of the museum, and in spite of the fact that museum guards allowed them to get as far as they did, they were still locked up and held for questioning.

The guards asked Roger and Aneme about their relationship with Demekus, how long had they known Demekus, what was the nature of their association with him, where did they come from, etc. The fact that Roger and Aneme had no Imperial ID's made the situation even more difficult. They took Roger's sword, and Aneme was patted down by a female security officer who discovered many of her hidden weapons.

Roger and Aneme could have easily dispatched the guards and probably gotten away, but they both felt that it was better not to undermine their relationship with the Empire.

"I want to see the Emperor," Roger said.

"Oh you will," said one of the guards. "He has received a report of the situation and has taken time out of his busy schedule to interrogate you himself. He is on his way right now."

"Good," Roger said.

"What do you mean 'good'?" the guard asked as his eyes narrowed and focused on Roger.

The door swung open and the Emperor Adinis Maxelis entered the room with two elite guards on either side. When he saw Roger he raised a hand and ordered all the guards out of the room.

"Sir?" the chief of the guards asked.

"These people are not prisoners, they are my friends, and I would like to speak with them alone," the Emperor said.

The chief of the guards shrugged and left the room, followed by his men and the two guards who came with the Emperor.

"Well, Roger," the Emperor began when the guards shut the door behind him. "Did you enjoy looking at the Randar stone? It is one of our most ancient and mysterious artifacts."

"Actually… it's not really that mysterious to me," Roger said.

"Oh? Do you have some special insight that allowed you to understand the purpose of the stone?"

"I couldn't believe it when I saw it, at first, but I have seen so many strange things in this world, and I have experienced things that I never thought possible. I have seen light run like liquid and fall to the ground, I have seen constructs made out of pure energy, and I have had dreams that came true. So I can accept that someone from your world might know how to write in my language."

"What?"

"The inscription on the Randar Stone is in English, my native language," Roger said. "I have been teaching my wife my language, but I haven't taught her any of the text yet. Barring a miracle there is no way Randar could have learned my language over 20,000 years ago. I know that time moves differently in your world but the technology to cross the barrier of the universe did not exist in my world until the people I was working for developed it. There is no way anyone could have gotten here before me."

"Are you sure about that?"

"Are there any records of aliens visiting your world?"

"No, just the prophecies of one whose ancestors were created in a different garden. One who would come to reunite sokes with humans and tavlons, and take the world into a new, and better, era. We have discussed all that before."

"And I don't know what the exact time difference is between your universe and mine. In my universe modern English is only about 400 years old, and there is nothing in my world that is 20,000 years old. I can definitely believe that Randar was a prophet."

"He was. Without a doubt. Now tell me, what did the inscription say?"

"It said, 'protect my heirs.'"

"Do you think the message was intended for you?"

"Definitely. When Randar spoke to me from the ancient past, he said 'protect my heirs.' When I had a hard time believing what I was seeing he hid a crystal for me to find. He probably wanted to leave some additional concrete evidence to help with my decision making process. I got the impression that he knew a lot about the future."

"Your decision making process?"

"Yes. When I had my first dream about Randar I didn't know what he was talking about, or even if the dream was a true one. Then after I saved you I realized it was a true dream, but I figured that he was probably talking about protecting you. But now I know better. Randar didn't say 'protect Adinis,' and I'm sure he could have if he wanted to. He said 'protect my heirs.' I understand what he meant now. You see, I already saved you before I saw this message, and I also saw that teenage kid who led us here in a dream. I have put everything together now. It's not just you, or even your family, but all the people of your Empire who are the heirs of Randar. What he founded here has lasted over 20,000 years, and I think if we move quick we can save it."

"So you will help us then?"

"I will."

"And what of you?" Adinis asked as he nodded to Aneme.

"If my husband is satisfied that it is the will of the Great Maker then I am satisfied," Aneme said. "I will help."

"Excellent!" Adinis said. "Let us return to my palace and we will have a feast. We can discuss plans over dinner."

"Sounds good, I'm very hungry," Roger said. "What I had for lunch wasn't really anything to speak of."

They followed the Emperor from the security room and were joined by the two elite guards on the way out. The Emperor removed a small communication device and ordered food to be prepared for them before they arrived.

They boarded a small aircraft which was parked in a secluded courtyard in the center of the museum and took off. In less than five minutes they were back at the Imperial Palace. They disembarked and followed the Emperor down the hallways until they came to a set of large golden doors with relief carvings of a man wrestling with a giant fish.

"The prophet Esak" Adinis said when he noticed Roger staring.

The doors slid aside and they entered a large circular room with a long table in the middle. A woman stood by the table and watched them as they entered the room. From the door she appeared to be a full-blooded westerner with light brown hair, but something about her seemed unusual.

All around the wall was a series of what looked like paintings, but as Roger took them all in some images changed and were replaced by others. Roger guessed that the images were artistic depictions of famous heroes and events. He could not help wondering if there were any images of tavlons in the Imperial database.

There really ought to be given the great age of the Empire.

Roger was about to ask the Emperor about the matter when his thoughts were interrupted.

"My wife, Lanicia," Adinis said. "Lanicia, meet Roger and Aneme. They are the ones I told you of."

Lanicia held out her arm with the palm of her hand facing straight out toward Roger. Roger was uncertain how to interpret the gesture.

"I apologize," Adinis said. "This is the classic gesture of greeting and agreement among Imperial citizens. There are very few who use it today, but my wife is very conservative. The proper response is to extend your own arm and briefly touch palms."

Roger did as the Emperor instructed and Aneme followed his example.

"It is a pleasure to meet you both," Lanicia said. "My husband has told me so much about you."

Roger realized what it was that struck him as unusual about Lanicia. Her eyes were mostly brown like her hair, but the edges of her irises were green, and a few streaks of green ran further in toward her pupils like randomly discolored spokes on a wheel. Near the edge of her right iris was a speck of red which penetrated in a short way, blending with the brown as it went.

Roger wanted to ask about her eyes, but he did not know enough about the Imperial culture and etiquette to determine whether such a question might be considered rude. In the northern culture, with which he was significantly more familiar, questions about unusual aspects of a person's physical appearance were not considered rude if the person being questioned was a guest or new to the area. Under those circumstances a refusal to answer such questions was considered taboo.

When Roger first began to move about the northern village and socialize he received many questions about his skin and hair color. Asking questions of hosts was not considered rude, but a host was under no social obligation to respond.

Then a thought occurred to Roger, since Demekus had similarly colored eyes it was unlikely that the multicolored eyes were a unique feature or deformity. In all the time Roger had spent in the alien world, he had not seen a single individual with a natural deformity. Roger had to know the truth.

"I am curious," Roger began. "Earlier today I saw someone else with eyes a lot like yours. Is there a specific part of the world where those traits are common, or is it that they are common among a particular bloodline?"

"It is the second," Lanicia replied. "Over half the people belonging to the Maxelis family have multicolored eyes. It comes from our great ancestor Larella, who was a tavlon. Surely my husband told you of Aleric and Larella?"

"He did, but he never mentioned anything about multicolored eyes," Roger said. "So wait, are you telling me that you two are... related?"

"We are related going back three generations," Adinis said. "Her great grandfather was my great grandfather's brother. I do not have the eyes because for the last three generations my ancestors married women from non-Maxelis families. The family of Maxelis is large. Aleric and Larella had 20 children, and following Aleric it became the custom for each Emperor to have five sons. Since the extended family of Maxelis is so large many Emperors have married other Maxelis people, which causes the traits to become accentuated more in the next generation. Both of Lanicia's parents were from the Maxelis family."

"So then, that kid who got us into the museum was able to do that because he was a Maxelis?" Roger asked.

"No. Demekus was able to get you into the museum because he is my son. My youngest son in fact. He always had an interest in history so I granted him special access, but apparently he has little respect for it."

"Demekus is your son? When he first stumbled into us I suspected that he was running away from someone, but when I didn't see anyone following him after a while I just dismissed the idea."

"He was running from his guards."

"Why does he have guards?"

"Normally he does not, but after the assassination attempt on me I placed guards on all my children, especially Demekus, and I attempted to restrict his... activities."

"I take it he does something you disagree with?"

"He likes to run through the streets like a madman, and climbs on monuments and buildings as well. It is an old sport called 'streeting.' It was allegedly invented by the Emperor Aleric."

"The same guy who married the tavlon?"

"Yes. He used to go streeting when he was young, and later on he did it with his wife, all the way into his old age. When he broke 1,000 he took a tumble down the side of a building, and received injuries. After that he deteriorated rapidly. Streeting started in Randar at about the time that Aleric was a child, but there has been no concrete evidence to tie its origin to Aleric, and he never took credit for it."

"To engage in streeting one must be fairly agile," Aneme said.

"Well yes, incredibly so," Adinis said. "But please, let us all be seated."

Shortly after they were seated the food arrived, and after Adinis said a prayer they began to feast.

"I wanted to thank you for all you that have done for us, Aneme," Adinis said.

"Why me?" Aneme asked. "I was the one who delayed Roger."

"Precisely, and you had good reasons. Roger never would have agreed to train my people without your consent, and without you we never would have discovered the meaning of the Randar stone, or discovered the third Randar Crystal. Your conscientious objections helped us confirm beyond all doubt that we were on the right course."

"Hmm... I agree, but I doubt if many of my people will see it that way. You must also not forget that even at peak efficiency your best men will be only a third as strong physically as the northern soldiers. War with full blooded northerners would be inadvisable."

"I agree, and I have no intention of going to war with your people. No Emperor ever has."

"So far none of my people have ever considered the Empire an enemy, but after this some of them will consider you a threat. If even half the northern race decides the Empire is a serious existential threat to them, then there probably isn't anything you could do to stave off their onslaught."

"I hope that does not happen. Perhaps if we can deal with Kaarum decisively we can turn our attention to the north and help your people with their enemy."

"That's getting ahead," Roger interjected. "First we have to decide how we are going to deal with Kaarum."

"Agreed," Adinis replied.

"Aneme and I have been discussing, and what we would like to do is train a handful of your men as instructors, which will in turn instruct your regular army trainers, who will then bring all your troops up to speed," Roger said. "We think it would be best to put those men on the learning drink until they are proficient."

"I cannot agree with that," Adinis said. "The learning drink has dangerous addictive properties."

"Northern children spend their life training," Aneme said. "They begin as little children shortly after they learn how to walk, and when they are in their teens or twenties they begin their advanced training. I don't care for the learning drink either. My husband almost became addicted to it. But there is no way your troops will be ready in time for the Kaarumite invasion without it."

"Very well, but I want all of the men free of it immediately after their training, and I am going to institute substance checks to make certain that they stay free," Adinis said.

"A wise precaution," Aneme said.

"I will send you my top commanders," Adinis said

"Actually, I had something else in mind," Roger said.

"What is it?" Adinis asked.

"I think that all the men who watched me dig up the Randar Crystal should become the first instructors," Roger said. "Since they were the ones who witnessed that my dream was a true one, they would probably be glad to be a part of it, and they would be very devoted instructors."

"A sound plan, it will be so," Adinis agreed.

"I would like to add another person," Aneme replied.

"Who?" Adinis asked.

"Your son, Demekus," Aneme replied.

"You cannot be serious," Adinis said. "Demekus is a child, and he has no sense."

"According to your laws he is legally an adult, and according to northern tradition as well," Aneme said. "Training him will help keep him out of trouble and make him more capable of defending himself. In addition, my specialty is the school of agility, and your son is quite agile. He would be the perfect student."

"I don't know... That is a lot of responsibility for Demekus..."

"Having more responsibility should make him more responsible," Aneme replied.

"I agree," Roger said.

"I think it would be good for him," Lanicia said, speaking up for the first time since they were seated.

"Very well, but we will tell him tomorrow," Adinis said. "I don't want it to appear as though he is being rewarded for his foolish actions today."

"Roger and I will need to examine and test your armor and equipment in order to suggest modifications," Aneme said. "Normally northern armor comes with a blade on one gauntlet and a way to mount interchangeable blades on the other. But your armor does not include accessories like that."

"No," Adinis replied.

"I have noticed fan like blades fixed to one side, but they don't look sharp enough to cut anyone," Aneme said. "What are those for?"

"They are part of an apparatus that generates a type one forcefield," Adinis replied.

"Can you refresh my memory on what that is?" Roger asked.

"A type one forcefield is derived from the earliest forcefield design created by the tavlons eons ago," Adinis replied. "It lets nothing in or out, regardless of how slow a thing moves. We cannot wrap a man's entire body in a type one forcefield because he would suffocate, but they can use it as a shield in combat and no blade can penetrate it, no matter how sharp. It is powered independently of the standard forcefield generator which only blocks fast moving objects and strong bursts of energy."

"That is a design worth keeping," Aneme said. "Perhaps it would be best to adapt our combat techniques to include that aspect of your armor. In the meantime we could still modify the other gauntlet to allow for mounting blades for backhand strikes."

"Yes, I will have you coordinate with my engineers to make whatever modifications you deem necessary," Adinis said. "I would also like to make the both of you members of my military council. It's highly irregular to promote foreigners to such a position, but these are dangerous and extreme times, and since you have chosen to help you should be fully aware of the situation as it develops."

"Any way we can help," Roger said.

"Do you both wish to continue to hide your identities?" Adinis asked.

"Yes," Aneme said.

"Then I shall give you both new names," Adinis said. "You will be Mattis and Vaila Maxelis. You will each be assigned the rank of Commander General, which is the highest military authority one can have without being Emperor, and no one will question you. Still, I would like both of you to avoid any contact with the media, and try not to be too much of a public presence."

"You don't have to tell us," Roger said.

"Among all of my subjects you will be known as Mattis and Vaila, and I will only refer to you as your true names when you are in private," Adinis said. "If the world ever becomes a better place then perhaps you can reveal your true names, and you will be known in the Empire by your original names for the rest of time."

"Hope for the best and plan for the worst," Roger said.

"I would like to begin instructing the men right away," Aneme said.

"I will supply you with a studio and anything else you need," Adinis replied. "After dinner I will show you what precisely is available. We have some of the most advanced three-dimensional real-time simulators in the world, which should allow you to convincingly duplicate any enemy. It is my understanding that your people train with such facilities."

"Yes, many of us do, but the technology in the northern dens is quite limited, so I cannot speak for all of my people," Aneme said.

As the Emperor and Aneme conversed Roger decided to let her handle the technical aspects of the equipment and training times since she knew a good deal more than he did. They did not seem to notice his silence either, so he focused strictly on his food. He was eating some meat which struck him as some type of bovine, and a round vegetable about the same size and shape as a baseball. On the outside it was brown and had a thin crispy shell, and on the inside it was orange like a sweet potato. But the taste was somewhere between that of a sweet potato and pumpkin pie, and the texture on the inside was like a mashed sweet potato.

When Roger finished one he took another, and another. After a short time he began to feel drowsy, so he leaned back into his soft red chair to relax for a moment while the server took his glass and refilled it. The Emperor and his wife were still completely focused on Aneme when Roger shut his eyes.

"What do you think?" someone asked.

Suddenly Roger snapped fully awake and found himself sitting at the table in front of a plate with four round thin empty shells on it. He turned to look in the direction of the voice and found that it was the Emperor's wife Lanicia who had spoken.

"Well?" Lanicia asked.

The Emperor's wife was looking at Roger, waiting for an answer to a question. Roger blinked and shook his head.

"What do I think about what?" he asked.

"Did you fall asleep?" Lanicia asked.

"I may have dozed for a second."

"You ate four gava puffs. They have a chemical compound in them that can make you drowsy."

"What are they made of?"

"Gava."

"Which is what exactly?"

"You really are from another world! The gava puff is a fungus. When it's raw it's spongy and toxic, but when you boil them they get soft and sweet. You have been eating spores."

Suddenly Roger felt queasy. He did his best to keep from throwing up.

"So you didn't hear any of their conversation then?" Lanicia asked. "They have been arguing and talking in circles for the last two minutes."

Adinis and Aneme were indeed arguing about something.

"But you don't understand," Adinis said. "Most people in our country are non-military, and labor is specialized."

"Labor is specialized among us as well, but we are all prepared to do our part in defense," Aneme replied.

"But you have a somewhat tribal culture, do you not?"

"Yes."

"That is not how it is with us, different people have different jobs, when it comes to war some will serve the country by fighting, while others will serve in tactical support positions, and others will serve by keeping the social and economic machinery running. We can't just have everyone drop what they are doing and fight."

"I am not suggesting that, but everyone should be able to defend themselves. Now that we have committed to help, you should let us go all the way."

"What are we talking about?" Roger asked.

"You weren't listening?" Aneme asked.

Adinis cast a glance at Roger's plate and noticed the hollowed out shells.

"He was eating the puffs," Adinis said.

"Yes I was eating the fungus puffs, because you two were talking all this technical stuff and I thought we were good," Roger said. "But what is this argument about?"

"Your wife would like to have everyone in the Empire trained to fight as soldiers," Adinis said.

"That is how her people do things, and that is how they managed to survive all these millennia," Roger said.

"Yes but, we have a regular army," Adinis said.

"Just because someone doesn't know how to use a sword doesn't mean they can't die on one," Roger said.

"That is what I said," Aneme added.

"I can agree with that position, but how can we train everyone and have them ready?" Adinis said. "That would be making heavy use of the learning drink, because as you said before, northerners spend their entire childhoods to become proficient under normal circumstances, and the tactics might get leaked to our enemies."

"Well I definitely think the top priority ought to be preparing the military," Roger said. "As for the average people, maybe we could set up some optional classes to give them instruction in basic techniques. They don't need to know the advanced schools, but they could take the basic training, and take it at their own pace, and without the learning drink."

"That seems sensible," Adinis replied.

"That's a start…" Aneme said.

"We could also make sure that everyone is supplied with weapons and personal forcefield generators," Roger added.

"Many are already, but I will see to it that everyone is," Adinis said.

"Sounds good," Roger said. "This way we give people some level of readiness without causing too much of a disruption to society."

"Yes, we work for victory but be prepared for an invasion," Adinis replied. "I see the wisdom in this."

"Aneme?" Roger asked.

"The compromise is sound," Aneme said. "I do wish everyone could be trained, but I understand that we need to prioritize."

"I am glad we are agreed," Adinis said. "Let us enjoy our feast then, and tomorrow we will begin the preparations."

"Here, here," Roger said.

Training the Trainers

Roger stood in the foyer next to his grandfather's dogs, Brutus and Cassius, and watched as his grandmother pulled all the curtains and blinds shut. It was dark outside, and past his normal bedtime.

"Roger, did you check the front door to make sure it was locked and bolted?" his grandfather asked as he walked past Roger.

"Yes," Roger said.

Roger's grandfather walked past him and tugged on the front door, then flicked the bolt with his finger just for good measure.

"Hm," his grandfather grunted. "You know when I was your age no one had to lock any of their doors. Everyone left their houses unlocked all the time, and there was a lot less theft. But these days you never know what might happen. Our society has just gone completely down the tubes."

"Which tubes?" Roger asked.

"Eh, it's just an expression. It means that things have turned really bad, like garbage. It's unbelievable the stuff that's going on these days, the stuff they have on TV… Anyways, come with me."

Roger and the dogs followed as his grandfather locked the door leading out to the back patio, and another door on the side of the house which led out of the laundry room.

"Grandpa, why do we need to lock the back doors?" Roger asked.

"You always lock your backdoor, Roger," his grandfather said. "That is the first door that a thief is going to try. Everyone can see what is going on in front, including your neighbors. If someone wants to do something criminal they are usually going to go for the back, because it's less guarded, or so they think. You always lock your back door. Protect yourself on every side, and it's good to have an early warning system. That's half the reason why we got these dogs. If someone tries to break in they will go crazy and wake me up, and if they don't scare away the thief then I still have time to get my guns. Remember that."

I will always remember…

The images melted away but the memory remained fresh in Roger's mind, as if it had just happened. Roger originally had that conversation with his grandfather when he was nine, and he always remembered it, but he had not thought about it for years.

Roger sat up groggily in bed, and noticed that his wife was already awake and dressed. She stood in front of a mirror wearing a simple black outfit consisting of pants and a sleeveless shirt. The outfit was not lewd or immodest, but it was form fitting.

And Aneme's perfect form is distracting. She's got to know that…

"So… you're looking good today," Roger said.

"Thanks," Aneme replied.

"Aren't you worried that you're going to distract the men?"

"It's the closest I could get to a basic training outfit. I'm not trying to distract them. My only concern is efficiency, and a loose outfit with lots of folds isn't the proper thing to train in."

"That doesn't mean that they won't be distracted."

"I don't see why they should be. The westerners have no shortage of beautiful women. I'll be wearing this outfit until we start training with armor."

It was decided that Aneme would bear the primary responsibility of training the men since she had the greater knowledge and skill, and Roger would spend more time planning with the military council, but overall the responsibilities would be shared.

"Are you ready to begin?" Aneme asked.

"Good to go as soon as I get dressed," Roger replied.

"I am glad we decided to help these people. I feel like we can really make a difference in the world, and how often does the Emperor make foreigners Commander Generals?"

"Probably not very often, but we are probably going to catch some grief for it."

"Yes, jealousy is always lurking inside people, waiting for an excuse to be let out."

"But with our new names people will probably think its nepotism."

"Well, we will just have to show them how qualified we are."

After Roger was finished dressing he opened the door to their apartment and stepped out. Roger and Aneme were given an apartment suite in the Imperial Palace and allowed access to the Emperor any time they wanted. They were provided with guards and servants as the need arose.

When Roger stepped out into the hall the guards saluted.

"Commander General," said the chief of the guards who was dressed in blue and white armor.

"We're ready," Roger said. "Take us to the training grounds."

They were taken from the Imperial palace to a complex next to the river and toward the northern end of the city. It was a high security compound with walls, guards, and security dogs. The compound was made of white stone, and it appeared to be a new building, although Roger knew that it could easily be over 100 years old. Most of the buildings in Randar were far older than one century.

The guards saluted as they approached, and led them on across the lawn to the building. When they reached a blank white wall they stopped. The wall was completely smooth.

"Now what?" Roger asked.

The guard placed a hand on the wall, and rectangular cracks suddenly appeared around his hand and portion of the wall sunk in beneath his touch. When he removed his hand the section rose back up and the cracks disappeared, but a much larger section of the wall sunk in, split down the middle, and slid back into the wall on either side.

"I didn't see any cracks or anything, and now there's a door?" Roger said. "Is it new tech?"

"Actually sir, it is very old tech," one of the guards replied. "This building was constructed by tavlons as a warehouse about 7000 years ago. It was one of the last things they built here in the Empire. There are many buildings built by them in Randar, and our people have done our best to maintain them, but as you know Sir, tavlon constructs are built to last."

"And now it's a training ground?"

"Yes sir. It was repurposed about 600 years ago and it has recently been equipped with the latest energy projection technology, so that any environment can be simulated with 99% accuracy."

"I am intrigued."

Roger looked through the opening, and he noticed that the light was just as bright through the door as it was outside, and the tone of it was identical as well. It seemed like he was about to step through a wall rather than enter a building, but once he entered he saw that it was indeed a building, and that the roof was glowing.

"Conductive lighting?" Roger asked.

"Yes, sir, many of the larger buildings have it, especially the ones built by tavlons," the guard replied.

"It's rather bright, can it be turned down at all?"

"Yes, sir. Everything in the facility is at your disposal."

As Roger stood looking around an officer entered the room and saluted.

"Greetings Commander Generals, sir and madam," he said. "I am Weapons Officer Valis Nicis in charge of this compound. I am at your command."

"Are the men here?" Roger asked.

"They are sir, and they await you in chamber 36. The Emperor has informed me that he is on his way, and has instructed me to ask you to wait for his arrival before confronting the men. But if you wish, I can give you a tour of this facility as we wait."

"Uh, very well. Make it so."

The weapons officer led them around the compound, showing them room after room. The larger rooms had all been repurposed with energy emitters capable of reconstructing any scenario or environment known to man, as long as the pressure and temperature conditions were not too extreme. The officer stated that the rooms were used both in combat training and espionage.

There were many smaller rooms that served various purposes, from offices, to store rooms, to sleeping quarters. There were computer rooms for running the simulation, and there was also a large dining area and lounge.

As Roger was scrounging around the kitchen and lounge area for food the Emperor arrived.

"Greetings, your majesty," Aneme said, bowing slightly as the Emperor approached her.

"Well met, Vaila," Adinis replied. "Where is your husband?"

"I'm over here!" Roger shouted from the kitchen.

As he stood up his back struck against a large cooking pot, upsetting it and causing it to fall to the floor with a clatter.

Adinis turned to face the weapons master.

"I wish to speak with my friends alone," he said.

"Sir," the weapons master said as he turned to leave.

"Are there any last minute questions or concerns before we address the men?" Adinis asked once they were alone.

"Yes," Roger said. "I know you didn't want anyone to know or use our real names, but those men who watched me dig up the crystal already heard you say my real name. So maybe we should allow them to address us by our real names in private, and only in private?"

"Very well," Adinis replied. "It is appropriate, and since they have already shared in your vision they should be able to respect what we are trying to accomplish here."

"Great," Roger replied. Then turning to Aneme he said, "Do you have anything you want to add, babe?"

"No," she said. "I'm ready to get started."

"Let us go then," Adinis said.

They passed through the hallways until they reached a simulation room where the men were waiting. There were ten soldiers waiting for them, plus Demekus. When the Emperor entered the room they all snapped to attention, including Demekus.

"I greet you in the name of the Great Maker," Adinis said. "You have all been selected for a very important mission. You are to become the most powerful and valued guardians of the Imperial realm. Aside from having proven good character, bravery, and devotion to the Randaran Empire and the Great Maker, most of you have been chosen for having shared in the vision of this man."

The Emperor gestured toward Roger.

"What I am preparing to say next is confidential," Adinis continued. "Therefore, if there are any among you who do not wish to undertake this assignment I must ask you to leave now. I want only volunteers for this, and I want men who are committed 100%. If there are any among you who does not wish to participate you may leave now without facing any disgrace or ridicule."

None left.

"Very well," Adinis said after nearly a minute of silence. "I shall take your silence as assent. With the exception of Demekus, you were all present when this man located the third Randar crystal, and you bore witness to its excavation. Even now our scientists are working to find a means to play the Randar crystal. Once they succeed, you shall all be allowed to watch. Our Empire is facing the gravest threat ever, and that calls for new and bold action.

"This man, Roger, comes to us from another world, a world that is rounded into a ball, and which circles around its sun. I believe this man is the man whose ancestors were born in another garden, who will come to reunite the three kindreds of our world. I may be wrong, but time will tell, and I believe it will tell soon. We are preparing to enter a crucible, and when we come out we will be changed forever, for better or worse.

"Roger is married to Aneme, a woman of our world and of the northern race. She has agreed to share the fighting techniques of her people with us. Once each of you become masters, you will be sent to different parts of the Empire to train our armies. That is the purpose of your presence here.

"You will not reveal the true names of Roger and Aneme. I have given them citizenship, and in public, and among anyone other than those present in this room you will refer to them as Mattis and Vaila Maxelis. Their identities must be kept secret for now, as must their origins. Understood?"

"Understood sir!" the soldiers shouted.

"Here, here," Demekus said.

"Then after a brief prayer, I shall turn you over to the care of my Roger and Aneme," Adinis said.

Adinis spoke a benediction and when he was done he nodded to Roger and Aneme. They looked at each other for a moment, then Roger thumbed toward the men.

"You should at least say something first," Aneme said after seeing his gesture.

"Alright," Roger replied.

Roger stepped forward to address the men.

"At ease, men," he said. "My name is Roger, as you know, and I have dreams which show me the future and the past sometimes. It actually started in my world just before I left. Even though what we are doing here is very serious, I would still like for all of us to be friends. You can call me Roger, but when we are out in public you will have to call me Mattis. My wife is the real northerner here, and she is going to be doing most of your training. I'll be in and out but she is going to be your main instructor. So I'll let her have the floor now."

Aneme stood forward and put her hands behind her back.

"Greetings, soldiers," Aneme said. "My name is Aneme Strauss, and I am a full blooded northerner, and a master of the Northern Arts. There are four different advanced schools of the Northern Arts. Those are strength, agility, speed, and perception. Since I am a master of the school of agility then that is what you will learn. Roger is trained in perception, so he will come in from time to time to teach you what he knows, but I will be your main instructor.

"During training you will refer to me as 'master' and follow my instructions. Over the course of your time here you will be making heavy use of the learning drink. Time is of the essence for us, but as soon as you become masters you have to quit the drink.

"I have read each of your profiles and I am familiar with your specifications. I know how strong each of you are, how much you can carry, how much you can lift, how far you can run, how fast you can run, and what sort of training you have had. But the best way to understand what a man is capable of is to test him directly. You, come here."

Aneme pointed at one of the men, and the man immediately stepped forward.

"Your name is Saiven," she said.

"Yes, madam," he replied.

"Master," Aneme corrected.

"Master," he repeated.

Saiven had black eyes, black hair, and no facial hair. To Roger he looked very much like an Earth type human of east Asian background, except for his skin being completely without color.

This guy looks the most like an Earthman out of anyone I've met since coming here. Is that why Aneme picked him?

Roger found himself beginning to feel a connection to Saiven.

I guess not. She hasn't seen any of the other Earth races. She probably has her own reasons for singling him out.

"Strike me," Aneme said.

"Master?" Saiven said.

"Do what I say."

Saiven threw a loose punch toward the side of Aneme's face, and with a casual motion of her wrist she flicked it away.

"What was that?" she said. "I said hit me. You aren't even trying."

"But, master, I cannot hit a woman," Saiven said. "It is an evil thing to do."

"A noble sentiment, and normally I would agree with it, but you can't learn if you don't follow instructions."

"Very well."

Saiven cocked back his fist and struck with more force and speed, but he struck in an easily predictable fashion. Aneme simply leaned to one side, and swiftly struck Saiven with two fingers in the ribs just beneath the armpit. Saiven lurched and stumbled away in a clumsy fashion.

"Better, but still terrible," Aneme said. "Your heart is not in it yet, but I can fix that."

She struck him with her fingers again, not hard enough to do any serious damage, but just hard enough to cause discomfort. Every time the man tried to dodge or block Aneme went around and struck in a different area. Everyone watched in silence. Her movements seemed completely random for the purpose of irritation.

Then suddenly Roger understood the pattern behind Aneme's attacks. She was hitting pressure points and nerve clusters that would cause his body to rapidly produce adrenaline.

Saiven was clearly becoming irritated, and just as his irritation peaked Aneme slapped him across the face with a resounding smack, and then went back to poking him. Adinis took a step forward but Roger held an arm out in front of him.

Aneme slapped him again, but from a different direction this time. Saiven grunted with displeasure and attempted to grab Aneme, but she stepped aside and slapped him even harder. Then she immediately followed the slap with a second slap from her other hand.

"She is toying with him!" Adinis said.

"She is teaching them all a lesson," Roger said. "Just let it play out. There's a reason."

Aneme raised her hand to slap him again, but this time Saiven saw it and attempted to dodge. He was unsuccessful, but following the strike he took a hard swing at Aneme with clear intent to do harm. She deflected his swing and grabbing his arm, pulled it into a leverage behind his back, and forced him to the ground.

"You can relax now," Aneme said.

Saiven gasped and slowly rose back up to his feet. He stretched his arm and shook it out.

"Thoughts?" Aneme asked.

"You bested him with very little effort," one of the men said.

"Yes, and I could do the same with any of you at this point," Aneme replied. "Do any of you know what mistakes he made?"

"I… I tried to hit you…" Saiven said.

"Yes," Aneme said. "If you had followed my instructions from the beginning you could have been spared the pain. When we are on the battlefield you cannot just do whatever you want. This is all very serious, you have to follow instructions. In an actual battle situation you might receive an order that you don't understand, but if you don't carry it out then more people could end up suffering.

"When you refused to actually try and hit me I began stimulating your adrenals, and I induced a fear and anger reaction in you after a short time. That was your second mistake. In battle you cannot give in to your emotions, you have to be an efficient combat machine, dealing with each situation as it arises with your full intellect."

"I understand," Saiven said.

"Also, you thought that because I am a woman I would be weaker and more fragile than you," Aneme continued. "Normally you would be correct, but in this case you were wrong. Always try to know your opponent, and if you don't know what they can do, then take some time to test them."

The soldiers nodded and voiced agreement.

"Now I want Lysandrus to step up," Aneme said.

A large man stepped forward. He was clearly the most powerful man in the group, and was in fact the same size as Roger. His upper arms were nearly as wide as Aneme's head.

"Computer, generate a small round table for two, with two chairs," Aneme said.

Suddenly a small round table appeared with chairs on either side.

"Have a seat, Lysandrus," Aneme said as she gestured toward one of the chairs.

The man sat down and Aneme sat down across from him.

"Arm wrestle," Aneme said.

The man put his arm on the table and held up his hand. Aneme grasped his hand and they began.

At first both of their faces remained expressionless. Their hands moved slightly one way, then another for the first few seconds, but after a short amount of time the skin on Lysandrus' white face began to flush somewhat pink. His eyes began to squint and his face started to show evidence of strain. Aneme's face remained expressionless.

Then it happened, Aneme began to slowly push the large man's arm down to the table. He grunted and ground his teeth. He looked down at his arm and gasped, while Aneme sat completely still and silent except for the steady motion of her arm and her cheeks remained colorless.

With a thump the back of Lysandrus' hand struck the table, and he let out a moan.

"Saiven felt sorry for me because he thought he was striking a weaker opponent, but the fact is a fit northern woman is just as strong as a strong western man," Aneme said. "This is why it is important to have complete knowledge. Now does anyone know what mistake Lysandrus made?"

"How can there be a mistake?" one of the men asked. "There was no technique involved, you were simply the stronger."

"His face showed what he was thinking and how he was struggling," Aneme said. "You do not ever let your opponent see your emotions or sense your struggle. Whatever you give them, they will take. The Northern Arts are about discipline. Now everyone spread out. I am going to show you some basic stretches, and then we will begin our warm up activities."

Roger and Adinis stood some distance back, watching as Aneme trained the men.

"I did not wish to say anything when your wife was listening, but she does appear to have a draenock wound," Adinis said.

"What makes you say that?" Roger asked.

"She has a line on her neck, it is barely visible, and only visible up close."

"She does have those symptoms, but she has never been attacked by a real draenock. She spent most of her life in Velta."

"Her people did not try to treat it then?"

"They did try, and they failed."

"But it is only the draenock wounds that cannot be repaired by them, is your wife absolutely certain that it was not a draenock?"

"Has anyone ever heard of a draenock looking like a southerner?"

"Never. As far as I know there is no humanoid variety of draenock in this world."

"I still don't know much about this world, but if my wife says it was a southerner then it was a southerner. But, yes, she does have all the symptoms of the draenock touch, and we think that the southern woman who cut her might have been in league with the draenocks."

"Well perhaps I can have my doctors look at her. We have healed draenock injuries before on northern expats who chose to settle in the Empire and never return home."

"Could you? That would be great. I'll be sure to tell her."

The Sign of Kaarum—by Ivor Kovac

CHAPTER 4

Strategies

"I would rather not," Aneme said.

"Why not?" Roger asked.

"Because I don't need it, I'm fine."

"But doesn't it bother you?"

"It's not hurting me."

"But it bothers you."

"I'm fine with it. It mainly bothered me before because it kept me from getting married, but now that I am married it doesn't matter."

"It's not going to hurt anything to have the doctors fix your scar."

"It's dangerous."

"How is it dangerous?"

"Who knows what they will do?"

"You don't trust the Emperor? He's been nothing but good to us."

"I don't like it. It would be a violation of my body."

"At least let them look at you. They don't have to operate, but they can at least give us an idea of what might be wrong, and then maybe later your people can fix it."

"I don't know…"

"I'll go with you and be with you the entire time."

"Well… I guess we can do that much. But I don't want to get an operation from them."

"Good. That's a step in the—"

Roger sudddenly heard an odd sound like a combination of a shriek and a hiss, and the room went black around him, while the image of a hideous face with grey skin, bugged out red eyes, and dripping fangs flashed before his eyes. It blinked on and off again in under a second, then it reappeared and sped toward him snapping with its fangs. It all happened in a second, and then it was gone but Roger gasped and stumbled back.

"What's wrong?" Aneme asked.

Roger shook his head.

"I think I blacked out for a second," Roger said.

"Are you alright?" Aneme asked.

"I'm fine," Roger said.

Aneme said nothing further but she continued to look at Roger and her eyes were full of concern. Roger smiled at her.

"Really," he said.

Roger took her face in his hands and began to kiss her. It was a method he often used to put her mind at ease when he had nothing effective to say, or to change the subject, and of course he also enjoyed himself.

After some time they stopped and held each other by the arms. Roger stared into her medium blue eyes and reflected that her beauty would last the rest of his lifetime, fading only a little by the time he died, and they would both live the equivalent of many lifetimes, assuming that they found a safe harbor to live out their lifespans in.

"I never get tired that," Roger said.

"Me neither," Aneme replied. "I don't think there are many men who kiss like you do."

"Glad you think so. Are you ready to get going then?"

"Ready."

"Will you be training the men at all today?"

"I will be training them every day except for the rest day."

Aside from the occasional holidays, northerners normally only took off one day a week, while the people of the Empire normally practiced a two day weekend. The men wanted to have a two day weekend but Aneme overrode them, stating that time was of the essence and they could not afford to let an extra day go by each week.

"You were kind of hard on them yesterday," Roger said. "My first lessons weren't so rough."

"We have less time," Aneme said.

Roger and Aneme left their suite in the royal palace and made their way toward the military headquarters of the Empire, from which all military activity was coordinated. Today they would be spending time in the war room, and discussing logistics with the military council of which they were both members. The Emperor would be there as well.

Aneme planned on staying no longer than necessary as training the men was her top priority.

"What do you suppose Garek is doing?" Aneme asked as they drove down the roads in their personal hovercraft.

"Probably drinking with his buddies, if he they can find any booze in this place," Roger said.

"We should tell the Emperor about him. He needs to know that we did not come here alone, and that there is one person here who knows our true identities."

"Alright."

"And we should try to find him."

"We will. We can always go to the Haxian hang out spots and ask around for him. But first we need to get to this war room."

They arrived at a multilevel parking facility and went inside. The buildings surrounding the facility were not particularly large or assuming, in fact the area seemed more like a transition between a commercial area and a city park.

"Are you sure we are in the right place?" Aneme asked.

"This is where the guidance system told us to go," Roger said.

When they stepped out of the vehicle they were approached by soldiers who saluted them.

"Commander Generals, they are waiting for you below," the soldier said.

"Below?" Roger asked.

The guards led them to an elevator, which they entered, and once the doors were closed it descended for some time.

When they stepped out of the elevator they found themselves in a hallway of black mirrors with red and purple running lights in each of the corners. They were the only source of illumination at the time.

They passed many doors and a few intersecting hallways, until eventually they came to a large round metal door resembling a safe.

"Remain still for identity verification," said a soft female voice which Roger took to be the computer.

"Commander General Mattis Maxelis confirmed," the voice said after a few seconds. "Commander General Vaila Maxelis confirmed. You may now enter strategy room one."

There was a hissing sound like a sealed container decompressing, followed by the door sinking in and rolling to the side. The opening was crisscrossed by red beams of light, which caused Roger and Aneme to hesitate before entering.

"It's safe for you to step through," one of the guards said. "The grid allows authorized persons to pass through. But if I tried to pass through things would turn out ill for me."

"Well… no one lives forever," Roger said.

"Tavlons do," Aneme said.

"But we aren't tavlons, so here we go…"

Roger took a step through the beams and felt nothing. He found himself with a clear and unobstructed view of the strategy room once he was on the other side. The room was massive, and there were three different levels descending toward the center. There were terminals and glowing consoles ringing around the room at every level, as well as tables with holographic displays hovering in the air. Most of the light came from the monitors and holographic projections, the overhead lights were quite dim.

The overhead lights consisted of glass constructs which glowed purple or blue around the edges, and the edges of the stairs and the edge of each terrace were highlighted with glowing strips of red light.

Aneme stepped through behind Roger a minute later and came to stand so close to him that their shoulders touched. Her facial expression was unreadable, and she said nothing.

"Mattis, Vaila, come down here," the Emperor said from the lowest level of the room.

Roger and Aneme walked down the stairs for each level and approached the Emperor, who stood in the lowest level next to a tremendous display screen showing a realistic map of Kaarum, the Empire, and the lands immediately adjacent. Smaller images of different maps hovering nearby.

There were three other men with the Emperor, and they appeared to be having a discussion prior to Roger's arrival, but when the Emperor called to Roger they all looked up.

When they reached the level with the Emperor he introduced them to his associates, and ordered them to resume the briefing.

"As I was saying, sir, we have reason to believe that the actual numbers of the Kaarumites are about twice what we previously anticipated, and those are the conservative estimates," said a man named Savion. "There are some in my department which believe that there could be three times as many."

"You are certain of this?" the Emperor asked.

"We are certain that our previous population estimates were based on faulty data, and are much less than the actual total population of Kaarumites. We also know that the population density in Kaarum is far more varied than we thought, and that our previous estimates of the total population were calculated based on numbers taken from the lower density regions."

"Dire news."

"Look at the map, sir. I will set it to display relative density based on current estimates."

The area of Kaarum turned mostly orange and red, and after pressing a series of buttons the image zoomed in over the southern part of Kaarum.

"As you can see it is completely red, and some parts are in the black," Savion said.

"What is that strip of gray just beneath the red?" Roger asked, pointing to a strip of land at the very bottom of Kaarum.

Savion gave Roger a strange sideways look.

"Answer his question," the Emperor said.

"The grey indicates that we have no data on that area," Savion said. "That is the great Southern Rainforest, also known as 'The Southern Tangles.' As far as we know, the Kaarumite presence there is minimal at best. The topography and weather make it next to impossible to build or farm there, and that is with modern technology. The technology available to the Kaarumites is considerably less. The land is punctuated by mountains and gullies with sheer drop offs, and marshes in many of the low places.

"For all intents and purposes, the land is useless, and southerners have never bothered to colonize there as a result. At least, not much. Some of our sky-eyes did photograph a stone building, which bears a resemblance to old style open air Kaarumite temples, but there is no evidence of current habitation around it. It appears to have been abandoned some time ago."

"What about Kaarumite movements?" the Emperor asked.

"Evidence indicates northward movement sir, they are massing against us," Savion said. "I believe it will be the heaviest assault we have ever weathered."

"Terrible, but not unexpected," the Emperor said. "We all knew this had to happen eventually. We have been quarreling with them for years, but now it has come down to our final blows, under which one side must break forever, never to rise again."

"The Great Maker will not allow the city of his Temple to perish," said an advisor named Gaemus.

"You don't know that," Roger said.

Roger had not yet visited the Temple of the Great Maker in Randar, but he heard many things about it. He heard that the innermost chamber of the Temple was believed to be the footstool of the Great Maker on Avramis, as far as the people were concerned. It was one of the few scripture passages Roger had memorized from their holy text.

"I will make the city of Randar my place of habitation in this world, the innermost sanctum shall be a stool unto my feet for all time..."

The words seemed to echo through Roger's head as he closed his eyes.

Can the "Great Maker" really be there in some form? I really wonder how much of this religion is true.

Roger had also heard that the doors were originally crafted from the blue northern crystal, which was the same material the northern women make their jewelry out of, but at one point a wandering prophet laid hands on the doors and the red color spread out from his hands until all the crystal of the doors was transformed. They turned a blood red color, and so they have stayed since then, the only northern crystal in the world to be red.

The change of color coincided with a new revelation announcing that it was now acceptable for anyone to enter the innermost chamber, although in general access to the inner chamber remained limited for pragmatic reasons.

What he heard about the Temple reminded Roger of the Temple of Jerusalem back on Earth, and the current conversation brought to mind how it was ransacked and destroyed in 70 AD, never to be rebuilt again.

"If the Great Maker wants the Temple to be destroyed then it will be destroyed, along with this city, regardless of our best efforts," said another advisor.

"Yes, but there is no reason to think he does," said Gaemus.

"Oh yes?" said the other advisor. "The numbers would indicate otherwise."

"That's a useless thing to say," Roger said. "All we know is that it's our job to defend this place, and if we sit around and do nothing then it will definitely get wrecked."

"We are in desperate need of allies," Savion said.

"Suggestions?" the Emperor said.

"Look," Savion said, and the map changed to show the Empire and its borders with Kaarum and Hax. "Most of our mercenaries have come from Hax historically. Some parts of Hax are very crowded. I suggest that we try to bring in at least two million Haxian mercenaries."

"How will we pay them?" the Emperor asked.

"With land," Savion replied. "In addition to any parts of Randarga we take, we also give them the southwest corner of the Empire, the Island province of Kavros in the Great Central Lake, and the eastern province of Kamna."

"Give them parts of the Empire?" the Emperor said. "That will remove nearly a third of our territory."

"Yes, but it will put the Haxians between them and us, assuming we survive," Savion said. "We have used Haxians as shields in the past, and allowed them to take Imperial territory for their own."

"That was a pre-invasion Hax, and as I recall, the reprieve it offered us was only temporary, and we never gave them territories that were still under our control and full of our people," the Emperor replied.

"But if this is our final battle with Kaarum then it should be a price we only have to pay once," Savion said.

"This is a terrible idea," Roger said, thinking back to the late Roman Empire back on Earth and how it accelerated the barbarian invasions by giving territory to German tribes.

"Well what is your enlightened suggestion then?" Savion asked.

"Let's get the Haxians, but offer them the Contested Area along with whatever Kaarumite territories we take."

"The Contested Area is worthless! Have you ever been there?"

"I have."

"They will be insulted by the suggestion. The land is decimated by war. There are so many places where the ground was literally melted and reformed as solid rock, and aside from that there is extensive debris from wrecked vehicles, not to mention land mines. It will take a thousand years to make the land fit for agriculture and ranching again."

"Sokes could do it in a year."

"And where will you get sokes from? How will you make them cooperate, or understand, or even care? How do you know they even have such power?"

"I have seen what they can do. When they put their minds to it they can eat away at buildings and pavement. They make the trees grow faster, and use the roots to bust up the pavement a bit at a time, and they use moss to break the smaller pieces. They could make the Contested Area into a viable place again, and the southerners would be scared of them because they are sokes. Of course, we would also have to offer the sokes something as well, maybe divide the Contested Area and whatever we take from Kaarum between them and the Haxians?"

"Garbage and rot!" Savion said. "Everyone knows that no human can relate to sokes. Short of the Great Maker, it would take a man from another world, no, another plane of existence to even make them listen. Much less care."

"I think I can do it," Roger said, turning to the Emperor.

"What makes you think they would be willing to help us?" the Emperor asked.

"Sokes are hemmed in, and their numbers are growing," Roger said. "One thing they need is more land."

"We will make the attempt, you have only to tell me what you need," the Emperor said.

"Sir," Aneme said speaking up for the first time. "There is a man we were traveling with when we came here. He is from Hax, and his family is well connected there. Perhaps he can help procure some additional Haxian mercenaries?"

"Yes... I would like to meet with this man," the Emperor said.

"I will arrange it," Aneme replied.

"Vaila, what is the timeframe on the training?" the Emperor asked.

"I believe that I can have them ready in a year with intensive training, and after that they will be prepared to train other masters," Aneme said.

"Is there any way you can cut down on that training time?"

"If you let me have them for ten hours a day I can have them ready in half that time. I also need to be able to work with them uninterrupted. After that they can take over training the army, and can host classes on a mass scale. The mass classes will be less efficient, which means more time, but I think in half a year with heavy use of the learning drink they can teach the army basic northern arts. It will take another half year beyond that to teach them an advanced school and make them all masters. But again, that is with heavy use of the learning drink. The need for allies remains."

"What about northern allies?" the Emperor asked.

"Unlikely," Aneme said.

"We will speak of it later," the Emperor replied.

"What about Tandor?" one of the men asked. "Can we expect any help from them?"

"If I may?" Gaemus said.

"You have the floor Gaemus," the Emperor said.

"There has been a lot of unusual activity from Tandor lately," Gaemus said. "First they positioned many of their troops along their east coast. Then a few months later they began to deploy troops and secret police into the Central Lands. We have no idea why, but Hax is concerned that they might be trying to escalate a conflict. They are avoiding areas occupied by the Kaarumites, or contested by them, so it could be that they are trying to instigate or defend against Hax."

"An odd time for a move like that," the Emperor said.

"I don't understand, Tandor has always been an ally of the Empire," Savion said.

"But how much real help have they offered us?" Gaemus replied.

"I don't think we can rely on them," Roger said.

"I tend to agree," the Emperor said.

"But we should try all the same," Savion said.

"I have already attempted to contact the office of the Chancellor for help," the Emperor replied. "The Chancellor has pledged to give us his moral support."

"What a useless man," Gaemus replied.

"Still, we should ask them of the purpose of their troop deployments in the Central Lands," Savion said. "At the very least we might be able to convince them to station some along the border of the Contested Area."

"I certainly intend to confront them on it," the Emperor said.

46

Negotiations

Marvis Skoranthor was a man in distress.

That blasted Olgrim! Why is he leaning on me so heavily these days? And what a lot of guts he has to treat me like an underling? What if I just went north and roasted the whole area with earth scorchers until it becomes a molten sea?

Marvis felt as if he were being pushed and pulled in different directions, as if he were just along for the ride rather than being a man in full control of his affairs and circumstances.

Olgrim demanded that he negotiate with Doeren Kand in person, but first he was diverted to a small island off the west coast of the Central Lands for an emergency meeting of the Brotherhood Council.

The Brotherhood Council was a meeting of the highest ranking members of the Brotherhood, many of which Marvis had never seen before, and some of which he had never heard of, but a surprising number of the council members were Koshantai. Marvis had never seen more than one of those mysterious and powerful beings in a room before. For a brief moment his mind wandered.

The leaders of many other western countries were there as well. The Premier of Hax was conspicuously absent, but there were a few mid ranking Haxian officials present. There was no representation from the non-Kaarumite nations of southerners to the east, which remained completely closed and insular, and as usual there was no representation from the Empire.

The most intimidating presence in the room was Atuskus-Var, the leader of the Kaarumite nations who claimed to be a son of their god. Most of the westerners seemed to be afraid of Atuskus-Var, and even the arrogant Koshantai seemed to treat Atuskus-Var with deference.

It was the first time Marvis had ever seen the man, if he could even be called a man. He was at least twice the height of a normal man, and he could barely fit inside the building. As he walked by the place where Marvis was seated he paused and turned to face him. Marvis realized he had been staring and quickly averted his eyes.

"You should bow down," he said in an unbelievably deep voice.

The way he said it was not a recommendation or a command, it was simply stated as a cold fact.

His voice sounded almost as unnatural as those of the Koshantai, but in a different way. When a Koshantai spoke it sounded as if two or three different voices were speaking at the same time, sometimes the pitch was disconcerting, but in the case of Atuskus-Var the voice was far deeper than anything in the normal human range. It was almost like listening to the rumbling of a volcano put into words.

It was hard for Marvis to organize his thoughts on Atuskus-Var, but his overall impression was that the man was as different from normal humans on the inside as he was on the outside. He felt even more alien to Marvis than did the mysterious Koshantai.

"Kaarumite," Atuskus-Var rumbled.

He was still there!

"What?" Marvis said. "I'm not a—"

"Kaarumite," Atuskus-Var stated again.

It was a statement that did not leave room for argument. Marvis' father was a Kaarumite, and many of his sympathies were towards Kaarum, in fact he felt more of an affinity for Kaarum than he did for Tandor, so perhaps the giant was correct. Yes, the more he thought about it the more reasonable it seemed.

"Please be seated Atuskus-Var," one of the Koshantai stated.

Atuskus-Var glanced at the Koshantai for a brief second, then he went to sit down in a large chair which appeared to be designed specifically for him.

"Let us get right down to business," the leading Koshantai began. "You have all been brought here because we are in a crucial phase of history. The time has come for us to formally establish our dominance over the world. To that end, there are certain powers in this world which must be broken. The Empire has long been a nuisance to us. Atuskus-Var is preparing to attack but it will take him some time to mobilize."

"It will take at least a year or two to bring all the men and animals at my disposal there and to have them arrayed for war," Atuskus-Var rumbled. "But I can send preliminary attacks against them in the meantime to keep them from having time to rest and regroup."

"Very good, our master will be pleased," the Koshantai said.

"Of course he is!" Atuskus-Var shouted.

His response was so loud that Marvis had to cover his ears for a moment.

"In the meantime, the Empire will likely turn to Hax for aid, and our control over Hax is rather tenuous," the Koshantai said. "That is where you come in Marvis."

"W-what?" Marvis blurted.

"They will certainly ask for help from Tandor, you must deny them help without making it obvious that that is what you are doing," the Koshantai said. "You will order more troops to the Central Lands and place them in locations that will appear menacing to Hax. If all goes well we can induce a state of panic, keeping them from sending any significant amount of aid to the Empire.

"Once the Kaarumites obliterate the Empire, they will begin to focus their attention on the isolated nations of free southerners to the east. Once the leader of every nation is a member of the Brotherhood we will go forward with our goals to restructure humanity. In the meantime, we want you to work on the rebellion of northerners in Velta. Until you receive further notice from us, you are authorized to use only diplomacy, and we want you to make a show of it. We want media coverage, and sensationalism."

"I... I think I can do that," Marvis stammered.

"Even though it is likely that most of the northern race will have to be obliterated to make way for our new world order, we still do not wish you to escalate tensions with them at this time," the Koshantai said. "Am I clear?"

"Wait, I thought our official position was that there is no such thing as race or differences between people groups?" one of the human leaders asked.

"It is, but what you are to say in public has little to do with what we actually believe," the Koshantai said. "It is all a show, we manipulate the public for our purposes. Under our new world order the public will eventually become Koshangar, after they have been sufficiently thinned, while you human elites will be given the honor of becoming Koshantai."

Murmurs of approval and speculation spread through the room, but after a minute the Koshantai put a stop to it.

"Enough!" he said,. "Marvis, do you understand what you are supposed to do?"

"Yes," Marvis said. "I'll do it."

"Excellent. Get it done and you shall be richly rewarded by the Koshantai, fail, and your usefulness ends."

A few weeks later Marvis found himself in Azmath, the biggest city in the far western continent, and the home of his headquarters there. The office was too small for his taste, and the selection of food was meager. He had grown up eating Kaarumite and Tandoran food primarily. It seemed that northerners had little to no taste for seasoning, aside from the use of salt.

To make matters worse, there was also no chance to play soven.

What do northerners even do for fun? Don't they have an upper class?

It seemed that no one in Velta was even remotely interested in soven, and he could not figure out what it was they did for entertainment beyond attending religious services in cathedrals laced with northern crystal.

Can they even be considered civilized? Bland food, dull clothing, no plays, movies, or sports, other than brute tests of strength! Music is all either religious or about killing things, and the women don't even clomp when they walk! They've got no taste for the finer aspects of civilization!

He felt he was beginning to understand why the Koshantai deemed that the bulk of the northern race would have to be obliterated.

Stubborn and needlessly intractable people…

Since his arrival in Azmath, Marvis made many calls to Doeren, but the man refused to meet with him in person under any circumstance. When they spoke over the communications channels Doeren repeatedly told Marvis to take all of his people out of Velta and go, he was unwilling to negotiate.

In spite of the difficulties Olgrim kept checking in on Marvis and insisting that he try again. His wife Laena was also harassing him on the matter, and not giving him a moment's peace. Eventually Laena told him that she would create a list of questions and responses for Marvis to go through with Doeren, as well as possible actions.

She came back later and slapped a computer panel on his desk in front of him, interrupting him while he was heavily engaged in watching a soven match being broadcast all the way from Hax.

"What is this?" Marvis asked.

"A guide for how you can deal with Doeren," Laena said.

Marvis picked up the panel with a sigh and began to read it.

"Well this is a terrible plan!" he exclaimed. "'Offer to make Doeren governor of the entire continent'? Seriously? What a garbage idea! What would Olgrim say?"

"Look at me," Laena said.

Marvis looked up and found that Lania's hair was pushed to the side so that her chilling black and blue eyes were fully visible. The whites of her eyes were black and glossy, and glistened like freshly melted tar, and her blue irises appeared to glow slightly with an electric blue light.

Marvis shuddered and immediately looked away.

"I said look at me!" his wife demanded.

She grabbed his head with both hands and forced him to look into her face. Normally Marvis found her violence both awkward and strangely pleasurable at the same time, but at this point he was entirely unsettled by it.

"You obey Olgrim, and we will be rewarded," Laena said. "Do you want that?"

"Y-yes," Marvis stammered.

"Then listen up, here is what we are going to do... We are going to engage in one more attempt to negotiate with this man Doeren. It is going to be by holographic communications, and it is going to be in front of your top officials. It is also going to be recorded, so that the whole world can see how generous and kind we are, versus how intractable and boorish your opponent is. We are also going to try to make him look racially prejudiced and narrow-minded. He must appear as though he is motivated by an irrational fear or revulsion of others rather than out of some esoteric desire for political autonomy. Do you understand?"

"I think so…"

"I want you to study that list, but just in case you have any problems, I am going to have a small ear bud placed in your ear so that I can tell you what to say in some places. Understood?"

"Yes."

"Good," Laena said as she pushed Marvis' chair back and sat down in his lap.

The next day Marvis sat in a chair in positioned in a large round circle on the floor, and directly in front of him was another circle. Outside of the range of the circles was a group of high ranking Tandoran government officials.

Laena sat in another room watching and listening through hidden cameras, and she wore a communications device so that she could tell Marvis what to say if he got stuck. The whole proceeding would be recorded, and the recording would be edited later to make it more suitable for the public.

The circles on the floor lit up, and a three dimensional projection of a powerful northern man appeared in the circle in front of Marvis.

"Greetings, Doeren, and well met," Marvis said.

"Greetings, Marvis," Doeren said. "What is it you want to talk about?"

"Ah yes… Straight to the point…"

"You called me for a reason."

"Yes. I want to know what it is you want?"

"I already told you what I want. I want you to take all of your people and get out of Velta, and in 'all of your people' I am also including anyone who is a member of the Brotherhood."

"I fail to see what your fixation on the Brotherhood is. They are nothing more than a friendly social club, not a religion, and not a political organization."

"Don't waste my time with those lies and empty rhetoric, I know what they are, and I know what you are. You are part of a shadow organization that is trying to take over the world. You want to do away with independent countries and nations, and replace them with a world government."

"I guarantee you that there is no such conspiracy in place, and I would never support such a thing if there was. I am a patriotic Tandoran."

"How can you be patriotic for Tandor when you aren't even one of them?"

Marvis felt an adrenaline rush, brought on by very genuine fear.

How much does he know about me? Does he know about the Koshantai?

"Perfect, now we have some race prejudice!" the voice of Laena proclaimed in a celebratory tone in his ear.

"Perfect, now we have some race prejudice," Marvis repeated.

"What?" Doeren asked.

"Idiot!" Laena hissed. "Use your brain a little. Why would you repeat that?"

"I… uh…" Marvis muttered.

"It has nothing to do with race prejudice or whatever other biases you want to pin on me," Doeren said. "The fact is, we do not want to be part of a one world government, and even if there were no such conspiracy, your government is corrupt and we no longer wish to be under you. Tandor is already big enough. If you want to expand more, then expand out into space. You don't get to rule the whole world."

"We aren't planning on 'taking over the world.' But the world is getting smaller, don't you know, and we all have to learn to deal peacefully and orderly with all the peoples of Avramis."

"You have dealt falsely with both us and the sokes, and you have ordered us to attack an inoffensive people who have done nothing to us, or anything to merit any sort of hostile act. You have been caught in your own treachery, and we wish to sever all ties with you."

"But suppose you became a separate nation—"

"We have always been a separate nation, it's just that you had the political power over us," Doeren interrupted. "Your government has tolerated us because we were useful, but neither you nor the Tandorans have ever respected us or viewed us as equals."

"Very well, suppose you have your… er… political independence," Marvis replied. "What would you do if you had a problem like a major disaster or a massive foreign invasion? We would not be there to help you."

"Tandor put us here to guard this land from foreign invasion, so that aspect of your point is moot. As for handling other disasters and international relations, we are willing to take our chances alone."

"But what about your people? Don't you think that a major decision like that should be up to them? Have you put this to a vote?"

"We northerners do not vote. We are regulated by the moral values of our culture and religion, and we behave accordingly."

"So you have not and you don't plan to either…"

"We have decided as a people that your government and its sycophants here need to go. I want all of your people out of here. We are a sovereign nation now, and we will no longer obey you or serve you."

"Wait, Doeren, be reasonable. I am prepared to make you governor of the entire continent of Velta if you will cease this rebellion. I am also prepared to give you a high level of autonomy in all things. Let us discuss."

"I do not trust you Marvis, and I doubt that you are willing to give up on your genocidal plans for the sokes. There is no reason for me to accept your yoke, without you I already have autonomy and rulership of Velta. You have nothing to offer us, and we do not want you here any longer. You have until my people reach Azmath to get out. Any who do not leave by then will be forcefully evicted. That is all."

The communication switched off, and the government officials murmured among themselves once the image of Doeren faded away. Marvis was so flustered that he was shaking by the time the dialogue was over.

"I need a drink," Marvis said.

He got up and left the room. He returned to his office and gave the order that he was not to be disturbed. He took out a glass and poured himself a drink, but some of the liquid spilled on his desk because his hands were still shaking. He sat down in his large soft chair and swiftly drained the glass, then he poured another.

Suddenly he felt hands on his shoulders.

"Well done my husband," said the voice of Laena.

"I gave orders that I was not to be disturbed," Marvis said.

"Everyone is smart enough to realize that those orders do not apply to me."

"I am in charge here!" Marvis shouted.

His voice cracked.

"You are in charge because Olgrim and the Koshantai put you in charge," Laena said. "You answer to them, and so do I. That makes us equals."

"Whatever," Marvis grumbled.

"That's right, husband. But as I was saying, the negotiation went perfectly, aside from your one blunder on the race comment. Even so, it was a useful blunder because we can spin it to make it look like he refused to deny his racial bias."

"How can you call this a success? We failed completely to make that man see reason, even though our offer was beyond generous. Doeren should be executed for treason!"

"He was going to die either way. What he's done has bought him a little more time."

"He was going to die either way? So you had me negotiating under false premises?"

"Of course! Do you really think people like Doeren are capable of existing in the kind of world we are creating?"

"No, but you could have told me that we weren't sincere."

"We needed it to seem sincere, and it was a great success. The whole world will know how unreasonable and prejudiced Doeren is, and the media will spin it in such away that the regular mindless people will agree with us."

"I wonder though… is he really prejudiced against other races, or is it that he just knows what we are doing and doesn't like it?"

"What do you mean?"

"I mean to say, these northerners are very zealous for their religion. Maybe they know that we plan to abolish their religion, so they want to separate from us because of that? They don't seem to have any form of entertainment other than their religion."

"You think that religion is entertainment?"

"Well… sure. If it weren't fun for some people then why would they bother?"

"Ah… my husband. Just when I begin to think you might be clever you find a way to show me again that you're stupid."

"Excuse me? I'll not tolerate such brazen disrespect."

"You'll tolerate whatever you have to tolerate. Now listen, it doesn't matter whether or not Doeren hates us for our race or because of our plans for him. We are using race and culture as wedge issues to drive people apart. If can reduce his positions down to race prejudice, then the common people won't bother to listen to him or assess his arguments based on their merits."

"But—"

"Eventually the Koshantai are going to thin the common herd; but if we can get them to fight each other then some of the work is already done, and the tattered remnants of the once strong peoples will be easier to conquer and subjugate. Now, Doeren; if he has any inkling about our plans and connection to the higher powers then he just needs to die all the quicker."

The next day the story, along with excerpts from the original negotiation footage, was released around the world. The issue instantly became a hot topic for debate, with people becoming increasingly divided and hostile as they took sides in the matter.

Two days later Olgrim appeared in Marvis' office, along with another Koshantai who he had never seen before.

"Well Marvis, you did well, thanks largely to your wife," Olgrin said. "But in spite of our best efforts the government of Tandor has not been vindicated as far as most people are concerned. We need to show how savage and brutal the other side truly is."

"What do you want me to do?" Marvis asked.

"You have outlived your usefulness as far as being the Chancellor of Tandor is concerned, but there is one more thing you can do for us."

"What's that?"

"You can die."

Marvis felt a thrill of horror run through his body. He began to panic.

"Wait!" he shouted as they took a step forward. "Die? No please! I am loyal! I never did anything! I… I thought you were going to make me into a Koshantai? Remember? You promised that you would make all of us into Koshantai?"

"And you were foolish enough to believe us," Olgrim said. "Some leaders will indeed become Koshantai, but you were never anything more than a useful idiot with a below average IQ."

"Oh no! Please! Guards! GUARDS! Help me!"

"No one can hear you. We killed the guards outside of your office, and the people in the security room are loyal to us, not you."

The two Koshantai stepped into the light, and much to his horror their hands and clothes were splattered with blood. To Marvis' surprise, the Kosthantai were dressed as northerners. As they took another step closer the black markings on their skin faded away, and their skin turned to a northern blue color.

"This is for Doeren, for the sokes, and for the northern people you half-breed scum!" Olgrim shouted.

His voice sounded completely human. In a flash of insight Marvis realized that they were going to kill him and blame it on Doeren's people.

I've picked the wrong side!

"No please!" Marvis shouted as backed away from his desk and toward the wall.

He began to weep uncontrollably.

"Someone help me!" Marvis screamed. "Anyone! Please! Kaarum help me!"

Marvis suddenly found himself begging to a god he had never prayed to or believed in before, and that god did not answer.

Have I picked the wrong side?

Olgrim placed a hand on the corner of the large desk which stood between them and flung it up against the wall with one push. Marvis screamed and attempted to rush out the window, in the hopes that Kaarum and whatever people might be outside would save him. But it was no use.

Strong hands were laid on him from behind and he was dragged into the center of the room where the men pushed him back and forth between them as he shrieked in fear.

"A quick clean death is too good for you, Kaarumite halfbreed!" Olgrim shouted. "You will suffer for your crimes against our people, and anyone else who stands in our way will follow."

***

Laena thought she heard something as she sat in her office typing responses to different special interest groups. She stopped what she was doing for a few seconds and just listened, sitting completely still. Then she sensed him in her mind. Olgrim wanted to speak with her.

"Laena," his voice rumbled through her mind.

"I'm here," she replied.

"We have just killed your husband. You will soon be notified by security. I want you to get up and go to his office when they come, and if they try to prevent you from going in I want you to force your way in. You must act as a normal human woman would react to seeing her husband killed. Make it convincing, the cameras will be recording."

"I understand."

"We want this blamed on northerners in general, especially those belonging to Doeren's rebellion. We are going to use this incident to put you in charge of Tandor."

"But, master, it is highly irregular. The normal procedure is for the first speaker of the senate to take over, or the next highest ranking official in the office of the Chancellor."

"That is the law, but it will be you who takes over. After this incident there will be a major shift in public sympathy toward your party. You will have a good deal more leeway to bend or even break the law. The media will help promote you. You can then go after Doeren and impose martial law on his people, and then you can get down to the matter of the war with Hax. We want the standard of living in both Hax and Tandor to be drastically reduced, and neither of them should be strong enough to give us any resistance."

"I understand. It will be as you say, master."

CHAPTER 6

Laena

After a short time an alarm was sounded and the office of the Chancellor in Azmath was put under a security lockdown. It would not be long before the guards came for Laena to tell her what happened. Some of the guards were in the know, as was the chief of security, but most were not.

She decided to put on her sunglasses before the guards came, but as she reached across the desk for her sunglasses she disturbed a shiny silver plate with her arm causing it to clatter across her desk. The plate had previously held fruit, but she picked it clean some time ago. She caught the plate before it fell, but before she placed it back on the desk she paused to look at her reflection.

The black and blue color of her eyes was entirely inhuman.

Even the disgusting sokes do not have eyes like this. In fact, as far as the majority of the world knows, no one does, and until the masters to reveal themselves these eyes would have to stay hidden.

Her hair had grown longer in front so she could not simply comb it over her eyes without also covering her mouth anymore. She had grown tired of that look. She enjoyed it for a time, but it made it more difficult for her to see when others were around. The color of her eyes could not be disguised except by covering them up in some fashion or another.

Fortunately she was well known for her edgy looks ever since she came back from the trip to the north, so wearing dark glasses inside would seem like a small thing compared with her metal clothing and the unusual hairstyles she occasionally sported.

Once more she thought to reach for her sunglasses but was captivated by her own reflection. She had always been vain, but since her upgrade by the Koshantai she no longer cared about adhering to the traditional basic beauty standards that most of the world adhered to. She was partly inspired by her masters, but she also enjoyed making her own way.

I do remember how she used to think before the change, but I can't remember why I thought the way I did.

Suddenly a guard burst into her office. Immediately she turned away from the door and put a hand over her eyes.

"Madam!" the guard exclaimed.

"Fool!" Laena shouted. "How dare you intrude on me unannounced and without permission? Get out!"

"Yes madam, my apologies! I'll be outside waiting for you."

Once the guard was out of the room Laena put on a pair of dark blue glasses, which allowed people to see the basic shape of her eyes but not their colors. She made some small adjustments to her hair and clothes and stepped out of the room with confidence.

"Now, fool, tell me what is so confounded important that you would interrupt in such an abrupt fashion without permission?" Laena asked.

"Madam!" the guard said. "It… It's the Chancellor, he's…"

The guard choked as he tried to explain, while Laena rolled her eyes behind her glasses, then after a peculiar choking sound he said, "He's been… He's been killed! Murdered!"

"What?" Laena shouted, pretending to sound shocked. "Take me to him at once!"

"But madam, I don't think…"

"Of course you don't think, imbecile, but I want to see my husband, take me to him!"

She forced her voice to crack and waver a little in order to sound distressed, and the guard seemed to think it genuine.

The office of the Chancellor was surrounded by guards, and as Olgrim predicted they tried to prevent her from going in but she forced her way passed them. Once inside she saw medics stooping over what was left of her husband. He had clearly taken a severe beating. All of his arms and legs were either broken or dislocated, and his head was smashed flat as if it had been stomped on.

Well… he was more of an inconvenience than anything else, but I wonder if this level of violence was really necessary? Maybe there is a subtext to this… They wanted it to look like he was savagely murdered by northerners, but might this also not be a message to me? Maybe they are reminding me that if I get out of line… this is what happens…

The guards watched as she stood looking down on the body of her husband, and it occurred to her that she had better show some sort of emotional reaction soon or the guards might begin to suspect something was amiss. She tried to recall how she felt about her husband before the change, but it occurred to her that she never actually felt anything for him other than a desire for what he represented, which was wealth and power.

He's pathetic and nothing compared with the Koshantai. Why be with a puppet when I can be with the master?

Before her change she had been a person of low intellect. Although she had been a full blooded northerner, with superior strength, speed, health, and a longer lifespan she never had an interest in the Northern Arts or her heritage. She wanted to live a soft life of luxury, and to be admired and respected by everyone. She knew that she was beautiful, so she decided to mimic the western women who sometimes use their looks to attach themselves to men of power and influence.

In the early days of her career as a flower she received many proposals. It was very rare for a full blooded northern woman to become a flower, or to marry outside of their race, so she had a natural advantage over the western women who acted as flowers. She attached herself to the wealthiest most well connected man she could find, and that was the entire basis for her interest in Marvis. Not what they could have together, but what he could do for her.

When she met Olgrim for the first time it was as though he saw straight into her soul and read what was there. He offered her a chance to have true power independent of her husband. She accepted, and that was when she was taken to one of the secret dwellings of the Koshantai.

At first she found them strange and unnatural, with their larger sizes, unusual coloration, unnatural voices, skin markings, and strange clothing and hairstyles, but she got the sensation that each and every one of them was brimming with power. That was what caused her to press on in spite of the strange looks they gave her, and the unnatural things they were doing right before her eyes. They did things that most of the world would not only consider unnatural, but also unspeakable, and they relished every bit of it, as a rebellious child might relish smearing himself with mud to spite his parents.

She thought about turning back at one point but Olgrim was right behind her. Her journey was a one way trip, regardless of how it turned out. First they made her watch things she had thought were ghastly and abhorrent until she became hardened to them. Then they interrogated her and took her into a chamber and placed her into a metallic pod.

"We are not making you into a Shantai, we are releasing the Shantai which is already within you," Olgrim said. "It is a great privilege. Not everyone is fit to be a Koshantai, but those who are will become one in body, and those who are not will perish or will be made into Koshangar, the slave class. It is the way of the future."

The lid of the chamber closed, and suddenly Laena was restrained by wires which shot out and wrapped about her body in many places. Some of them pierced down beneath her skin. She screamed and writhed, but there was very little room for movement as the wires wrapping about her body constricted to hold her more tightly.

Then it began. She could feel things moving down into her body, piercing through skin and muscle tissue. Fluid was released into her veins, which burned at first and then caused her to go numb. She could feel herself begin to change, and it hurt, but in a short time she blacked out and felt nothing except distant and muted pain.

When she woke up it was like she had truly woken up for the first time. She had definitely entered into a higher state of consciousness. It was like she had gone through her life in a drowsy state, never fully awake and conscious. She also felt physically energized, and stronger than ever before.

The pod opened, and Olgrim stood waiting for her. He took her by the hand and stood her in front of a mirror. She had grown taller, and her eyes had also changed so that the whites were now black. After that everything was different.

Her mind was so much more clear and quick than it ever had been before. There was nothing that she could not understand. She could perform complex math problems in her head, and recount every step in the calculations later. Olgrim explained that her mind now had many of the properties of a computer, and that she could perform most of the same functions as a computer if she wished.

She could also think about more than one thing at a time, or listen to multiple conversations or musical tracks simultaneously without any problems following and understand them all. She was a genius, and many new thoughts and perspectives boiled in her mind. She reveled in her new abilities and did things with the Koshantai in an orgy of exultation which most humans would not even dare to speak or imagine.

She discovered that all of her senses were sharpened, and she seemed to have a sixth sense that she did not have previously. It was a sense of awareness of her surroundings, which allowed her to know the shape of things that were around her and their distance from her even if her eyes were closed. Of course that ability did not allow her to make out colors and details, but it did allow her to know where everything was and what it was, for the most part.

She was also a good deal stronger than she was previously. As a northerner she had been about three times as strong as the average normal human woman, even though she did not exercise or work out. But now she could bend raw iron with her bare hands, and she could easily crack marble and granite tables or counters if she wanted to.

But she was still not full Shantai. Olgrim promised to upgrade her further if she served them well, but he told her that it was impossible to make her into a full-fledged Shantai because the differences were still too many and too vast to make in one lifetime. However, he did promise that any children she bore would be full-fledged Koshantai after her next upgrade, and that she would be enough like a full-fledged Shantai to be treated like one and to enjoy the lifestyle.

She was satisfied with the arrangement, and she fell in love with the Koshantai culture and way of life, which she found freeing in its complete shunning of traditional values and morality. Values which she now felt were small and outdated. There was no action she dared not do, no thought she dared not have. Nothing was sacred or off limits, and there were no transgressions except for going against the plan. Her husband's only mistake was that he did not work hard enough to fulfill the plan. He had not taken it seriously, but had he cooperated fully then the rewards of his cooperation would have been far greater than the normal human wealth and vices he enjoyed as Chancellor.

She was thoroughly committed to spreading the Koshantai culture and way of life across the entire world. But the old ways of thinking were not all that she felt was small and outdated. She also felt the same way toward her husband. He seemed so small and foolish to her now.

Before her upgrade she was in awe of him because of his wealth and power, which she thought he had sincerely merited and earned, but after her upgrade she found herself getting frequently exasperated with both the time it took him to understand things and his level of knowledge. He was so limited, and stupid.

None of the wealth and power he had was earned, it was all inherited from his father, and much of that acquisition was secretly guided by the Koshantai, who had their feelers almost everywhere in the world. Marvis was nothing more than a useful idiot, and now he was dead.

Due to the superior speed of her thought process all of this flashed through her mind and was pondered by her in a second, but the emotional awareness necessary to generate an authentic reaction still escaped her. Since her transformation all she felt was lust, ambition, and anger.

She stood silent and still, with her back to the guards. Then an idea occurred to her. She had seen funerals before, as well as normal human reactions on the news, and every image remained fresh and perfect in her mind, preserved with 100% accuracy. She decided to synthesize a reaction based on what she had seen from other women.

She let out a wail and crumpled to her knees, then she bent over and buried her face in her hands. Even though her eyes were closed she could still make out all of the physical details of the room with near perfect accuracy, and she could tell from the movements and facial expressions of the guards that they appeared to find her reaction convincing. She kept it up for a few minutes, and the first few times they attempted to touch her or help her up she slapped their hands away. Then after a time she got up and allowed herself to be lead out of the room.

She gave orders to find the men responsible, and asked to watch the security footage. As she watched the Koshantai beat her husband to death she again wondered for a split second if such a violent execution was really necessary. Then she wondered why she even wondered that.

Is it possible that I actually cared for my husband on some level?

It seemed impossible to imagine, and even if she did feel anything for her husband the fact of the matter was that he was afforded more dignity dying as a human than living as a Koshangar.

He would have certainly been transformed into a Koshangar once our full dominion was established. No more luxury, sports, fine clothes, music, or wine. Only grinding slavery and subjugation, and living on in a gross parody of the human form.

She saw a few of the Koshangar when she was living among the Koshantai. They were dull lumpish beings that were in many ways subhuman. The Koshantai and the Koshangar were the ultimate expressions of man, the Koshantai being those with superior vision and ambition elevated to their full potential, and the Koshangar being the dull thoughtless majority that could not help but be followers and slaves, preferring to live their lives rather than think about why and how things work. The way it was explained to her was that the Koshangar were as equally refined as the Koshantai but in a different way. All inhibitions which might mitigate their natural slavish tendencies were removed, as was their ability to think about the state they have come to. But that was another train of thought entirely.

As excessive as it might seem, she still recognized the necessity of Marvis' death and the manner of his death. He had to be killed in a violent fashion that would both vilify the northerners and instigate a strong emotional reaction of indignation and anger from the people of Tandor. That reaction would secure both public sympathy for her for her, and loathing for her enemies.

Of course, not all Tandorans are going to change their minds. Some of them hate our policies so much that nothing will ever bring them over to her side. Some of them might even celebrate Marvis' death as a good thing, and they will still want me gone. But after this there will be less of them and they will be easier to eliminate. Such people are not even fit to be made into Koshangar.

As she watched the footage she feigned a reaction of anger and indignation, and ordered that all of the security guards be investigated. Of course only those in the know would be in charge of the investigation, but as far as everyone else was concerned everything would appear as a normal and logical reaction. Some guards would be charged with negligence and dismissed, and others might even be falsely accused of having taken part in the assassination. Laena would also see to it that the footage of the murder was "accidentally" leaked to the media.

At the end of the day she went into isolation, and when she reappeared she wore traditional western mourning clothes. She decided that for the sake of political expediency it would be best to appear as a traditional western woman, even though she was neither western nor traditional.

Since most of the people of Tandor were westerners she wanted to establish the appearance of common ground and make it easier for people to sympathize with her. That would mean no more unusual clothing or hairstyles for some time, at least, not until the Koshantai had achieved absolute victory over the world.

Traditional western mourning attire was blood red, and for women it was usually some sort of dress which covered most of the body, and often included gloves. A hat with a thin mesh veil was also quite common. Red was worn because of a scriptural passage which said, "The life of the flesh is in the blood" and when one wore the red mourning clothes it indicated that they were meditating on the passage of life. It was a common practice in western countries.

Of course, I don't believe in that garbage or care for western culture, and I'm not sorry that Marvis is dead, but appearances are everything.

Over the next few days everything unfolded the way that the Koshantai wanted and predicted. She sat in on the senate meetings, and she was allowed to participate even though she had no official legal authority because of the sympathy that existed for her, and because of the support from key politicians who were members of the Brotherhood and thus under the sway of the Koshantai.

She was allowed to speak in the Senate, and she used every opportunity to shame them over the assassination of Marvis, and the lack of concrete results produced by the investigation. It was not long before the first speaker of the senate stepped down under pressure from Laena's supporters and from the media. Soon after that Laena was made acting Chancellor.

Propaganda posters of Laena were circulated all over Tandor, some of them were produced by her political party, while many others were produced by media outlets that supported her party. They all showed her in traditional mourning clothes, and some of them showed her with tears in her eyes or flowing down her cheeks. In most of the pictures she was wearing red sunglasses or a veil, but for the illustrations which showed her eyes, they were drawn as normal human eyes. Very few people knew her secret.

Laena was depicted as a suffering saint, and in some of the more liberal temples she was officially classified as one and icons of her hung on the walls. Although she remained externally composed, she was laughing on the inside at their depictions of her. She knew she was anything but a saint. In fact, she prided herself on being the opposite of the patriarchs and saints of ancient times, and had nothing but disdain for their religion and the behavioral limits it imposed.

When the video footage of the murder of Marvis was accidentally leaked public outrage and support for her side reached a new high. She could now do almost anything she wanted, so she chose to pass laws curtailing freedom of speech.

There was only one thing that did not go her way. She sent men to arrest Doeren and take him by force, but they were all either captured or killed. Again she sent more men, and in greater numbers, but again they were all either captured or killed. Although the violence against her law enforcement officers increased the anger and indignation the public felt toward Doeren, she was still stymied in her efforts to actually eliminate him.

She called to Olgrim and asked for permission to wage total war on Doeren and his followers. Olgrim granted her permission, and he also told her to move against the sokes.

"Wipe them all out, all the northerners, all the sokes, anyone in the Western Lands who stands against our agenda," Olgrim said.

Unfortunately for Laena and her supporters, Doeren and his people were one step ahead. They took Azmath, and drove out all of the westerners and northerners who were loyal to Laena and the Brotherhood. Doeren loaded them all up onto large sea-going ships designed for carrying cargo, and ordered them to return to Tandor or be sunk along the way.

Laena was enraged. She ordered her entire military force to descend upon Velta, but she encountered a problem. There was some kind of energy field in place over the land, so that when her airships and hovercraft came within about 100 feet of the ground all of their electronic systems failed and the ships crashed. She tried to have them fly over and drop earth scorchers and other detonating devices but the energy field also deactivated the devices.

Laena had some large ocean vessels outfitted with steam engines and oil burning lamps, and using these she transported a large portion her army to Azmath, where they fought a long and difficult battle. She had hoped to overwhelm the northerners by sheer numbers but it appeared that her people were suffering heavy casualties, while there was no word brought to indicate that any northern soldiers had been killed. But they were not fighting only northerners.

It seemed that the forest itself attacked her people in some places. Those who went into a forest never came out, and there were reports of vast numbers of soldiers of a type the world had never seen before which were working with the northerners.

Laena studied the reports intently, looking for anything that might indicate a weakness in the enemy. Her people had managed to secure some beachheads but they were able to do little more than hold out. She could not even communicate with the men who were deployed except by messengers using boats propelled by steam or manpower.

Every time a report reached her it detailed nothing but death and loss. In rage Laena slammed her fist down on her desk, and it broke in two. She flung the pieces aside and stood up. Then she grabbed her chair and flung it into the wall where it stuck going halfway through to the other side.

Destroying Tandor was part of the master plan, but it was no good to take out Tandor if Hax was able to remain intact. The plan called for goading Tandor and Hax to destroy one another, taking both out of the picture at the same time. That could still be done, but then Doeren and his rebellion would be left on the loose. Doeren had to be crushed first, but she did not have the ability to crush him.

But in spite of her fit of rage her mind continued to work, and an idea began to form. She decided to completely surround Velta with her air and sea craft, so that nothing could get in or out. In the meantime she would have her people analyze the energy field and send the data back to the Koshantai so that they could come up with a solution.

Alright… the plans aren't ruined, just postponed. I can hold off until a way is contrived to break through. Those disgusting northerners… What can they possibly be doing to nullify our technology? Since when do backwards northerners have technological breakthroughs?

She contacted Olgrim and proposed a change of plans, which he agreed to.

"They are using some kind of forcefield to wreak havoc on your electronics, but they obviously have some means of protecting their own equipment from the effect," Olgrim said. "So it can be done, we just have to find out how."

Olgrim was not physically present, but he was somewhere in Tandor so he could communicate with her by the private transmission that Koshantai used to communicate over long distances or to exchange information more rapidly when they were close.

"When do you think you will have something that will overcome the effect?" Laena asked.

"I cannot say. If we had a spy in their territory we could find out what they are using and smuggle it out, but since Doeren has expelled all of our spies we will have to develop it through observation and experimentation. In the meantime, I want you to leave the troops that are deployed against Hax in the Central Lands. Do not move them against Hax, or bring your troops back, but just keep them there for now to keep Hax wary. The attack on the Empire by the forces of Kaarum will go as planned. They cannot hold out."

"But what if Hax intervenes on their behalf?"

"No one will be able to stop what is coming. We have a special surprise planned for the entire world, which will crush the Empire and Hax regardless of anything else. Even though we did not anticipate this problem with Doeren, we never operated by gambling on one resource, or putting all our resources into one place. Plans within plans, my beautiful one."

"I live only to serve you, great one."

Although she knew she was not the equal of Olgrim, she relished whatever nugget of affection or sexual flirtation he threw in her direction. The fact that she was not his equal and yet he sometimes deigned to talk to her as one served to inflate her ego. Of course Koshantai did not love in the traditional sense, but they still burned with passion, and sometimes certain individuals among them would keep favorites who they would return to for pleasure more often than they would turn to others.

"Good," Olgrim said. "Do well, and you will be rewarded well. We will speak again later."

Laena gave the orders to establish the blockade. She abandoned the men who were struggling to hold out on the coast of Velta, and watched the progress of the retreat through multiple viewing monitors. She found herself curious to see how the northerners would treat the soldiers she abandoned once they saw that her troops were no longer supported.

It did not take the Tandoran soldiers in Velta long to realize they were being abandoned. Some dropped their weapons and ran into the ocean, stripping off their armor plating as they entered the water and attempted to swim toward the retreating boats. But the bulk of her troops simply surrendered to the enemy, and to her disappointment the northerners and the strange soldiers who were with them seemed to be sparing their lives.

A shame. Had they massacred those soldiers they would have provided me with some useful propaganda. Still, if I know northerners, they won't keep those men indefinitely. If they don't kill them, then they'll try to return them to me at a later time.

Once more Laena began to feel secure and confident, but then something happened that ruined her day. She received a call from the Emperor.

CHAPTER 7

Alternatives

Roger sat in the Emperor's office on the other side of his desk, waiting. Aneme was not there. She spent most of her days training the men, while Roger divided his time between the training room and the war room.

As Roger waited, his mind went back a few days to when he had found Garek in the city, and the state that Garek was in. Garek had been spending his time in a district of Randar in the southeast called "Little Hax." It was known as Little Hax due to the large concentration of Haxians in that area, most of which were mercenaries, but some of which were businessmen or immigrants. Garek had managed to find a Haxian vendor who provided him with alcohol and other mind altering addictive drinks, and in the time they were separated had managed to engage in a variety of disreputable activities.

At the time Roger found Garek he was drunk and seated at a table with a woman in his lap. The woman wore a fluffy dress and a tight leather blouse fastened with metal buckles in front. Roger guessed her costume was Haxian, it was certainly no Imperial style. The woman had white skin and dark brown hair, but her facial features were mostly northern in appearance.

"Roger!" Garek blurted loudly. "My good friend! Where did you people go? I was looking for you for days! Pull up a chair and tell me what's happening."

Roger was nervous. Not only had Garek used his real name in front of others, but being drunk as he was there was no telling how much sensitive information he may have leaked to random people. Fortunately everyone in the tavern seemed to be Haxian, and they did not seem to notice Garek's outburst or care about it.

"Garek, I need to talk to you," Roger said.

"So pull up a chair, man, there's plenty of booze and women to go around," Garek said. "Shandra here has a sister. You want I should call her?"

Garek's speech was sloppy and slurred together. Roger reached inside his pocket and took out some currency.

He slammed the money on the table in front of the woman and said, "Here's 50 sivers, now let me have some time with my friend, alone."

The woman looked down at the money and then back up at Roger.

"Now," he said, adding emphasis.

The woman shrugged and pocketed the money, but as she got up to leave Garek grabbed her by the arm.

"Let her go, Garek, we have things to talk about," Roger said.

"What gives you the right to spoil my game?" Garek demanded.

"Just shut up and come with me," Roger said as he rose up and grabbed Garek by the arm.

"And if I don't want to?"

"Then I will make you come. On a good day you still cannot beat me in a fight, and now you're drunk. What is it you think you will do?"

"Fine. But this had better be important."

"Oh it is."

As they made their way through the streets Garek stumbled about in a drunken stupor. Roger reached inside his overcoat and removed one of the vials he had taken from the training facility. The red liquid seemed to churn of it's own as he held it up to the light, then he handed it to Garek.

"What is it?" Garek asked.

"It's a shot of the learning drink," Roger said. "I need you sober. I can't talk to you when you're drunk like this, and there is no way you can go to the Emperor while you're all sloshed and groggy."

"The... what? The Emperor?"

"Drink!"

Garek opened the vial and drank. A few seconds later he held his head in both hands and moaned. He began to slouch, and Roger thought he might fall, but suddenly he stood up straight and shook his head quickly, then he focused on Roger with clear eyes.

"Alright, I am clear now," Garek said. "What is it you wanted to discuss?"

"I have decided to help the Empire," Roger said.

"What? Great! That is the best news I have ever heard in my life!"

Roger filled Garek in on the major events of the last few days, telling him of the situation the Empire was in, how they were helping, and stating that they would still need more men.

"Well I do have some good contacts in Hax, but we will have to offer them something, and there is a limit to the Imperial budget," Garek said.

"About that," Roger replied. "I have an idea…"

Roger brought Garek before the Emperor and they discussed how they intended to bring in sokes to make the Contested Area habitable and suitable for farming. Then they received news of the events in Tandor, and found out about the blockade around Velta, the far western continent.

"Well that kills our plans for the sokes," Garek grumbled.

"Can you still get us more mercenaries?" the Emperor asked.

"I can, but they will all need to be paid," Garek said. "You might consider making an appeal to the Premier of Hax for formal help."

"We need to find a way around the Tandoran blockade," Roger said.

"If we can, yes, but I do not wish to provoke Tandor," the Emperor said. "We have enough problems at present with the Kaarumites hammering on our front door."

"What do we do then?" Roger asked.

"I thought you might tell me," the Emperor said.

"Your majesty," Garek said. "If you will give me a budget I will get as many Haxian mercenaries as I can as soon as I can."

"Very well, I will have my war ministers draft a budget and I will call you as soon as it is prepared," the Emperor said. "I thank you, Garek."

Garek bowed.

"Go with the Great Maker," the Emperor said.

"And you as well," Garek replied.

Garek stood up and walked out of the office. Roger also rose up from his chair and was about to follow when the Emperor waved him back down.

"Not you, Roger," the Emperor said.

Roger seated himself again.

"I want you to see what comes of this," the Emperor said.

"What comes of what?" Roger asked.

"I intend to call Tandor to find out what they are doing and to formally ask for help," Adinis said.

"You think they will care? Those are crooked people, and according to the news we read that S & M looking woman is in charge now."

"Esandem?"

"Uh… sorry, I used an English word."

"I see."

"Probably the less said about that the better."

"Very well."

"But really. Those people are crooked. You can't seriously expect them to help. They are the ones hunting me."

"Even so, they have always been a close ally of the Empire and have helped us in the past. We must try."

"Alright."

"You stay on the other side of the desk out of visual range, and remain silent while I speak with Laena. We have to at least try to reach out to our allies, even if they are no longer interested. After we try her we will try Hax, as Garek suggested."

"Alright let's do it."

"Initiating communication."

A holographic square appeared in the air over the desk between Roger and the Emperor. Roger could see everything the Emperor saw, but on his side the image was inverted.

The Emperor called the office of the Chancellor in Tandor. He had to go through a few functionaries but was soon routed to the Acting Chancellor Laena, who swiftly appeared on his screen. Roger's brow furrowed as he saw her.

She was no longer wearing her strange metallic outfit. She was dressed in fairly normal looking western clothes except that they were entirely red. Her hair was combed to the side but now she wore red sunglasses which made it possible to see the basic outlines of her eyes but not the color.

It's like she's trying to pass herself off as normal, but it seems so fake and insincere. She still comes across as an unnatural and twisted freak putting on an act which is obvious and contrived. What idiot will be fooled by that performance?

Roger took another look and narrowed his eyes this time as he leaned closer to study the image.

But that red does look good on her, compliments the blue skin. Who would have thought? I'll have to ask Aneme to wear red sometime, once her normal skin color is restored.

"I greet you, my lady, in the name of the Great Maker, the Watcher of Kingdoms," the Emperor said.

I haven't heard that one before.

Roger supposed it was an ancient type of formal greeting between sovereigns.

"I greet you as well, your majesty," Laena replied.

Her reply did not sound as formal, and Roger noted that she left out any mention of the Great Maker.

"My lady, you have my condolences for your loss," Adinis said. "I grieve with you. Even though I did not know Marvis as well as I would have liked, it is always a great tragedy when a young woman becomes a widow."

"Thank you, your majesty," Laena replied.

"Please, call me Adinis."

"Very well, and you may call me Laena."

"As you wish, Laena."

"What can I do for you today?"

"I wanted to ask a favor."

"Ask on."

"Normally I would not disturb a woman while she grieves, but you are the Acting Chancellor, so you are the one I must come to. Have you seen the reports on Kaarum?"

"That depends on what reports you are referring to."

"Any of the reports dealing with their numbers and movements."

"I have seen a few."

"Then you know our situation is dire."

"Not necessarily. Your people have held off those barbarians for years, and you have a massive technological advantage."

"Even so, their numbers are such that we are like a drop compared with a pond."

"I understand your concerns, and under normal circumstances I would help, but right now I am dealing with a major rebellion in Velta, and I have to devote my resources to that."

"There must be something we can offer each other."

"Actually… If you could spare some troops to help me deal with the rebellion then we could solve that problem quicker, and the sooner my problem is solved the sooner I can help you with yours."

Roger frowned and shook his head. He motioned with his hands in order to quietly express his disapproval of that suggestion to Adinis. Adinis looked up at Roger for less than a second and looked back down.

"I cannot afford to spare any of my forces given the current state of emergency and the shortage of troops, but if you wish I could send people to act as mediators between your side and the rebellion in order to come to a peaceful resolution," Adinis said.

"I thank you for the offer, but we are not interested in legitimizing the rebellion," Laena replied. "It appears that we are at an impasse."

"Not necessarily, I have noted that you have placed some troops in the Prominence and among many of the other western nations of the Central Lands. If you could divert some of those…"

"I cannot. We are dealing with a state emergency."

"What emergency?"

"That information is classified."

"Does it have anything to do with Hax?"

"I cannot say one way or another. The information is classified."

"Very well… Are you certain there is nothing you can do to help?"

"I can do nothing until our crisis is resolved."

"I see… In that case I will take up no more of your time. Go with the Great Maker, Laena."

"Until next time, Adinis," Laena replied, and the communication switched off.

"Well, Roger, it appears we can expect nothing from Tandor," Adinis said.

"They are after me," Roger said. "I'm certain that's why they have troops stationed in the Central Lands. They are patrolling for me."

"Quite likely. I am certain she is under an evil influence."

"Or she is the evil influence."

"That could be."

"And yet you tried talking to her anyways."

Adinis shrugged.

"Now I will try talking with the Premier of Hax," he said. "We have to try everything."

The Emperor manipulated his controls and soon reached the Haxian functionaries, but this time he was routed to their leader much more quickly.

Roger's eyes grew wide when the image of the Haxian Premier appeared on the screen. The man reminded him strongly of Doeren and his people. He had medium blue skin, blue hair, and the heroic physique which was common among northerners.

It's uncanny! If it weren't for his clothes I'd have thought for certain this guy was a full blooded northerner. So… this is what the Haxian upper class is like? Don't know how I feel about the ruling class being a different people from the regular citizens. But then, I guess they've been blending together for so long they probably have a shared cultural identity.

"Hello, Adinis," the Premier said. "What can I do for you?"

When he spoke his accent was more like Garek's than any full blooded northerner. Roger also noted that there was no formal greeting.

"Greetings, Amus, I hate to bother you like this, but I am in desperate need of a favor," Adinis said.

"What do you need?" Amus asked.

"Kaarum is moving against me, I need your help if the Empire is to survive."

"Yes, I have seen the reports… As always you are welcome to recruit as many of my people as you can afford to pay, and to do with them as you please once you have them."

"I fear that will not be enough, my friend. Could you not also give us formal help? You have the largest army in the world, short of the forces of Kaarum, but together we could beat them."

"Unfortunately I cannot give you that kind of help at this time. Have you been tracking the movements of Tandor?"

"I have."

"They are putting troops in the Central Lands, and are now poised to strike at us. If we get involved in the war with Kaarum and spread our forces then we may not be able to fend off their attack."

"But they have never attacked you before."

"They never attacked us because they knew they couldn't win, but if we send you all of our troops, or even half of them, then that situation could change. You know they have always competed with us, and they have never been our friend."

"At present they are occupied with a rebellion in Velta."

"That cannot last long."

"There must be something we can do for you in exchange for help. Maybe we can help you with the draenocks."

"The draenocks are just wild beasts that live in the far north, and the northerners have those things contained. The real threat is Tandor, and that crazy woman who is in charge of it. Have you ever seen her eyes?"

"I have not, except in pictures."

"Exactly, no one has. I think that she is an unnatural person."

"Amus, if you stand with us in our time of difficulty then we will stand with you in yours."

Amus paused to think for a few seconds.

"Your people have always been an ally of Tandor, would you really go against them?" Amus asked.

"The true ally is the one who stands with a friend in his time of difficulty," Adinis said.

"I agree, but your people have never involved themselves in the competition between Tandor and Hax, except for offering your services as mediator."

"Let me put it to you in a different way. If you do not help us then when we are overrun the Kaarumites will be on your door, and then you will face both Tandor and Kaarum. At that point you will no longer have the luxury of focusing your military might wherever you choose. Which is better? To divert troops to the Kaarumites now, defeat them, and then face Tandor with the Empire by your side, or to let the Empire fall and face both Tandor and Kaarum alone?"

"You present a strong case. Very well, Adinis, I can divert two legions to the Empire right now, but before I redirect any more troops I must discuss the issue with the noble houses."

"I thank you, my friend, but I may indeed need more troops later on."

"Honestly, I do not understand why you need any at all to deal with those backwards savages, but it's worth the troops if it gets you on our side against Tandor. It will be difficult to convince them to agree to send more troops at this point, but when the need arises do give me another call."

"I appreciate the efforts you are making on my behalf, Amus, go with the Great Maker."

"Go with the Great Maker, Adinis."

Adinis closed the channel and looked up to face Roger.

"It will not be enough," Adinis said.

"I didn't think so," Roger said.

"Suggestions?"

"We need to reach Doeren. We have to find a way around the Tandoran blockade."

"I do not think that will be possible. Tandoran sensors are at least as good as ours. Probably better, because of their space program they used to have. They will detect our vessels, even in stealth mode, and even if they did not then the energy dampening field around Velta would affect our ships as surely as it has affected theirs."

"Well what then?"

"Can your wife get in contact with her people in the Northern Wastes? If we had northerners on our side things would be much easier. We do have a handful of northern expats here, but not enough to win."

"I can ask her, but that's time she will have to take out of training the men."

"And there is no way we can get sokes…"

"Sokes!" Roger abruptly exclaimed.

"You have an idea?" Adinis asked.

"Yes. I don't know if it's a good one, or if it will even work, but I know a soke from the great tropical rainforests in the area south of Tandor. I can go try to negotiate with him and see if we can get any of his people to come here."

"He will help us?" Adinis asked.

"Maybe. Actually, I don't really know where he is, and I'm not sure he's even still alive, but it's worth a try."

"Take a stealth craft and go look for him. Offer him at least half of the Contested Area, with the possibility of additional land based on what we take from Kaarum."

"I will."

"Make it clear that he will be coordinating with us throughout the entire process."

"I will. When do you want me to leave?"

"Immediately. Take as many men as you need."

"Uh… Probably the fewer the better."

"Then take as many as you see fit, but do not go alone."

"No worries, I'll to my best. Well… my best may not be good enough, but I'll give a try."

"No man can be expected to do more than his best, and no reasonable monarch would require more of a man. Go with the Great Maker, Roger."

Garek—by KTVL

The Deep Place of Contemplation

ROGER SAT IN A CUSHIONY white chair, which conformed itself to the shape of his body, and watched the dark ocean shoot by beneath him. There was a ring going around the interior of the ship where he was sitting which appeared to be transparent, but in fact it was a ring shaped monitor that wrapped around the interior of the ship which was fed data by external sensors ringing the ship.

The ship was a medium sized stealth craft, which was actually capable of becoming transparent to the naked eye, or of giving the appearance of transparency, and the shape of the ship caused other means of detection to be reflected around it.

But supposedly it's still not good enough to get past the Tandoran military grade sensors!

For the first time since Roger left the village of Doeren he was heading back in a direction he already came from, but this time he had a medium sized military stealth craft, and a group of ten Imperial soldiers plus Garek. They would fly over the southern colonies and land near the edge of the forest where the southerners seldom dared tread.

The vessel would remain invisible while Roger went into the forest with Garek and one or two other guards. The rest would remain with the ship.

After convincing Garek to come, Roger took his leave of Aneme. She wanted to come but Roger told her that it was essential for her to remain behind and continue training the men. She agreed with his logic but was still not happy about the situation.

"The third best fighter in the Empire," Aneme said as they were preparing to leave.

"Who are the first two?" Garek asked.

"Myself and Roger, of course," Aneme replied.

"Of course," Garek agreed.

"And she means it in that order too," Roger added. "She always does tell the truth."

Roger felt it was important to bring Garek so that Garek would have hard proof of the sokes intention to cooperate, should they accept, and in the event that they did accept Garek would be there to coordinate and make plans.

There were only two problems with Roger's plan: The first problem was that he had no idea where Nirin would be, and the forest itself was larger than the Empire. The second problem Roger faced was that he had no way of knowing whether or not Nirin was still alive, but he suspected that he was.

By the time they landed it would be dark, especially given that the sun set in the east and they were heading west. It was the opposite of what Roger grew up with, but ultimately it was just one more alien thing which he came to accept as normal, just as he accepted the streams of light which occasionally flowed through the sky as normal now.

They flew at an altitude that was close to the edge of the atmosphere, and once they were over the forest they stopped and hovered in place at that height.

"Where would you like us to land, Commander General?" the pilot asked.

Roger came to stand next to the pilot.

"You know, I'm thinking that if he survived he would have reached the northern end of the forest first, and even if he's not still there then people would have seen him arrive," Roger said.

"People, sir?" the pilot asked.

"Yes people. Sokes are people too."

"Yes, sir, I apologize, sir."

If this is how it's going to be then we already have a problem…

As the pilot was about to begin his descent Roger ordered him to get out of the chair and took the controls.

"Sir, I don't think it's a good idea," the pilot began to object. "It's highly irregular, and you aren't—"

"Don't worry about it," Roger interrupted. "It's much safer than the things I used to fly on my home—"

Roger was about to say "homeworld" but stopped himself.

"My home… country," he said after a moment's hesitation.

"You mean Hax, sir?" the pilot asked.

The craft plunged rapidly as Roger took the controls, and for a moment everyone experienced a sensation of rapid plunge, as one might experience when an elevator first begins to descend.

"Ice of the north!" Garek grumbled. "Are you flying again… Mattis?"

"I am at that," Roger replied, noting the hesitation in Garek's voice to call him by his new alias name.

We can't have any slips like that in public.

Roger adjusted his descent and came in for a smooth landing near the edge of the forest.

"Not bad," Garek said.

"A flawless landing, sir," the pilot said.

"Alright, I have a sneaking suspicion that this guy is in this general area," Roger said. "So, Garek, you come, and you two guys also come."

Roger pointed at two of the guards.

"The rest of you stay here and guard the ship," he added.

As Roger and his company prepared to leave the ship, Roger reflected on how it would look to people who were standing outside, if there were any. It would as though a door of light opened in the air a little above the ground, given that the outer hull of the ship was invisible to the naked eye.

If something like this happened on Earth people would think they were seeing aliens.

The four men jumped from the opening in the side of the vessel and landed in the soft grass. Both of the moons were out so visibility was good. Roger paused to stop and look around as the door to the vessel slid shut behind them. To the north the land was mostly farms and grasslands, but there were abundant patches of forest, and off in the distance he could see the lights of a few small towns gleaming in the night.

Overhead the white moon hung, a little larger than Earth's moon in appearance, and the blue moon appeared to be about half that size. Due to the presence of the two moons each man was followed by two shadows angling off in different directions. It was a bright night, except for straight ahead where the largest forest Roger had ever seen loomed up like a fortress of darkness.

The trees were the tallest Roger had ever seen, which had also been true of the trees he saw in Velta, but these were a good deal more impressive than those.

"Just when you think you have seen the biggest tree of all… you find out that somewhere else there is an even bigger tree," Roger said.

"Are you getting philosophical on us?" Garek asked.

"This forest is like something straight out of a dream."

"More like something out of a nightmare. Don't tell me you also had a dream about this forest."

"Not this time, I just thought this would be a good place to start looking."

Roger looked around at the men who were with him, and then back to the forest.

"Well, let's get going then," Roger said.

He led the way and the men followed him into the forest. As soon as they reached the edge of the forest they began to have difficulty with the thick underbrush that grew around the bases of the tall trees. Fortunately, they were all dressed in Imperial armor, except for Garek who wore some Haxian light armor which looked like it had been borrowed from multiple sources.

The two guards that were with Roger took out their swords and began hacking the undergrowth out of their way.

"What are you doing?" Roger shouted. "Put your swords away before you make someone mad! If you're having a hard time then put your faceplates down and turn on your night vision."

The guards lowered their faceplates and activated their night vision. Roger was able to see well enough that he did not need his night vision. In fact Roger left his helmet back on the ship so using his night vision was not even an option.

Roger assumed that once they passed through the edge of the forest to the area beneath the colossal trees the undergrowth would grow thinner, as less light was able to reach the forest floor, but the further they went the more difficult it became to move forward. Roger could hear the sound of the guards struggling to push through behind him, and the sound of Garek cursing.

"Stop!" Roger shouted. "We are only here to talk!"

The leaves around Roger rustled as if a wind stirred them, and he felt himself being slowly forced back to the edge of the forest. With a sigh of exasperation Roger took out his sword, and for a second a shaft of white which had managed to pierce the forest canopy struck the blade and reflected off with a brilliant flash of light. Then he swung his sword and severed most of the plants which impeded his forward march, and his companions did the same.

But soon they found themselves entangled. Their feet were caught by vines, but as they hacked and slashed more came to take their place. Even so, they were able to hold their ground, until a heavy branch fell and struck down one of the guards. Roger stopped for one second to look back at the guard, and that was all it took. He was ensnared by vines and hoisted up into the air. As he watched from his high position the others were similarly ensnared.

But Roger did not give up. He pulled with all of his strength, and he felt the vines give a little. He was still holding his sword, and he was still able to turn his wrist. He managed to cut the vine on his right arm just enough to break it as he pulled with both arms. He swiftly cut the vines that held his feet and swung to a large tree using the vine that still wrapped around his left arm.

When he reached the tree he braced his feet against the enormous trunk and pierced his sword through the vine that wrapped around his left wrist and into the trunk. He clung to the sword with his right hand and took out his knife with his left. He was about 20 feet above the ground, which was too far to fall, but using his knife he was able to slide down the tree at a manageable pace, cutting through the bark and the trunk as he went.

When he reached the ground he went into a roll and came up to his feet holding both weapons. He continued slashing at the undergrowth as it closed around him, and after about two minutes of hacking and slashing he was free.

"Get out of here, Commander General!" the remaining guard shouted from about 40 feet in the air overhead. "Save yourself!"

Roger felt a finger touch his shoulder, and reacting on trained instinct he dealt the perpetrator a rotating kick to the chest as he turned around. His opponent tumbled across the ground and gasped.

"Give it up," said a smooth but menacing voice to his right.

Roger turned to see a tall soke standing off to the right.

"Will you fight the entire forest?" asked another voice, this time to his left.

It was another soke, and their eyes glinted green in the near dark of the forest, or gave off a slight glow of their own.

Roger remained in a combative stance and held his weapons toward each soke.

"We know you are a good fighter, but you are severely outnumbered," an incredibly deep voice rumbled. "There is no hope for you unless you turn back."

Roger was genuinely startled. The deep voice was like the groaning of an ancient tree formed into words. He looked around for the owner of that voice but could see no one other than the sokes who stood around him in silence.

"Who are you?" Roger demanded.

"That is our question to you," one of the nearby sokes said.

"Put away your weapons," rumbled the deep voice, and as it spoke some of the leaves rustled in the treetops far overhead.

"Alright," Roger said. "I'm putting my weapons away. Now release my friends."

"You are in no position to make demands," one of the sokes said.

"You will answer our questions first," the deep voice rumbled.

"Alright," Roger said as he sheathed his weapons.

"Why did you come here?" asked the deep voice.

"I came looking for a soke," Roger replied.

"Which soke?"

"A soke named Nirin, do you know him?"

"There are many sokes named Nirin. What do you want of this soke?"

"I need his help."

"With what?"

"I come on behalf of the Randaran Empire. The Empire is about to be attacked by the Kaarumites and it needs allies. As many as possible."

"And you are so desperate that you come to the sokes for help? This is unnatural. Humans have no dealings with sokes, and sokes have no dealings with humans. You are either a liar or a great fool. I think a liar is more likely."

"I'm not lying!"

"If you will not tell the truth then we can have no words. We are not a violent or hateful people. Killing and torture is repellant to us, so I cannot force the truth from you. I will show mercy. Take your people and go, but go with this truth; we will not allow your kind to wipe our kind from the face of the world. You have your lands, and we have ours. Leave us out of your events and doings, and we will not trouble you, but if you ever come back you will be killed."

"If you don't like killing then what about my man you hit with the branch? What about him?"

"He is not dead, only asleep. His metal skin protected him from the full strength of the blow, as we suspected it would."

"You suspected? And what if it didn't? Then you would have killed us, and only for coming to try to talk to you."

"Enough, I release your men. Take them and go."

Garek and the other guard were slowly lowered to the ground. Once they were free Roger ordered the guard to check on the other guard who the branch had fallen on earlier.

"He's fine!" the guard shouted. "He is waking up now."

"Let's get out of here, Mattis," Garek said. "These beings aren't going to help us."

"Listen!" Roger shouted. "I didn't come here to fight or cause trouble. We flew straight to you past all the humans in our invisible ship because we wanted to talk to Nirin."

"We have already given answer, human," said one of the sokes nearby.

"Listen," Roger said as he looked the soke directly in his glowing green eyes. "I am looking for a soke named Nirin."

"There are many Nirins, you picked a common soke name to confuse us with your story," the soke said.

"I'm looking for a Nirin who took a group of sokes up to Tandor and camped south of Ganthar," Roger said. "He was there to try to reclaim territory for the soke people. He was angry because both he and his wife were attacked by westerners. I met him in the forest south of Ganthar and we worked together for a while. We had a difference of opinion, but we reconciled, sort of, and then we tried to escape together because the Tandoran military was burning all of the forests around the city."

"Mold and detritus," one of the sokes muttered.

"Not entirely," said the soke who faced Roger. "I know of this one who he speaks of. Nirin was an angry man. The westerners violated his wife, and he killed them in his rage. He went to the place called Tandor with a small group, but there is no way that Nirin would ever call a westerner his friend."

"Look at my face," Roger said as he casually placed an arm against the large tree nearby and leaned in towards it. "Do I look like a westerner?"

"Humans all look similar," the soke said.

"Be serious," Roger said.

The soke turned his head slightly as he looked at Roger.

"He is not a westerner," the soke said flatly.

"This is a waste of time," said another soke. "They have been warned."

"But if I am a friend of Nirin, and you turn me away, then Nirin might be upset with you," Roger said.

"Nirin is not the authority here," the deep voice rumbled, and Roger felt vibrations run through his arm from the tree.

With a start he removed his arm from the trunk.

"What do you have to offer us that we should care to take you to Nirin?" the soke asked.

"I offer your people the chance to expand," Roger said. "You must be getting pretty crowded in here after being penned up all this time."

"If we want to expand we can do it without your help," the soke said. "You have seen the sort of land and people which lies around this forest."

"But you don't because you are scared of the humans just as they are scared of you," Roger said. "You're not afraid to defend your territory, but you're afraid that if you expand the humans will take away what little you still have. And you know, if they want to do that they aren't going to come in here with blades and armor like we did, they are going to fly over and drop devices that will burn your forest away."

"Brash and arrogant words!" the deep voice boomed.

"No, wait!" the soke in front of Roger said. "I want to hear more of what he has to say. I know this Nirin whom they seek. He came here some time ago and lies near the deep place of contemplation. I would like to take them there."

"I oppose," the deep voice said.

"But you are not in authority here either," the soke replied. "We are sokes. We have no men ruling over us, as do the first and second kindreds. We obey only the laws of the Great Maker."

"If they cause harm, then you will bear the blame," one of the other sokes said.

"How can they?" the first soke replied. "They are few and we are many. We can easily subdue them at any time, and they can take nothing from here without our leave."

"As you want it," the deep voice said. "But we will be watching. If they cause trouble they will not leave here alive…"

The deep voice grew deeper as it faded away. The other sokes took a few steps back until they were lost from sight in the underbrush. Only the humans and the soke who spoke on Roger's behalf remained.

"Let us go then," the soke said.

He began to walk deeper into the forest. Roger and his men followed, and they found that there were very few obstructions in their path. The sokes were no longer resisting them.

I wonder if the reason they even bothered to talk with us is because they expended too much energy trying to stop us at night? What would have happened if we'd have had this encounter during the day? Would they have just killed us?

"What is your name?" Roger asked after a while.

"What is yours?" the soke replied.

"What is in a name?" Roger said.

If he gave his Imperial name then Nirin would not recognize it, but if he gave his true name then both the soke and the Imperial guards who followed would know it. So he chose obfuscation instead.

"Is it the name that defines the man, or does the man define the name?" the soke asked.

"Who are you?" Roger asked in return.

"Now that is the question!" the soke said as he stopped walking and turned to face Roger. "I see you have knowledge of southern soke philosophy. You have indeed encountered our kind before. The question you ask is one which can only be answered with an interface, so that a true knowing can occur. If it were possible to interface with a human I would do so with you right now."

"Uh… right…"

The soke turned away from Roger and resumed his walk. Soon they heard the sound of water flowing, and when they came to within 20 feet of the river the soke turned and led them along next to it at that distance.

"There are dangerous things in the river that become active at night," the soke said. "They will ignore me because I don't have the scent of flesh and blood, but they might take interest in you. Perhaps you could defeat them with your blades, perhaps not."

As they followed the river it slowed and widened into a clear round lake, surrounded by rocky hills that seemed to form natural terraces as they approached the lake. At the other end of the lake were sheer cliffs, and a small gap which the river appeared to flow out through. The surface of the lake was so smooth that it reflected the night sky as a perfect mirror, and in many places around the lake there were incredibly tall reeds, some of which towered so far as 20 feet into the air.

"Behold, the deep place of contemplation," the soke said. "You will find Nirin here. He has been here for many weeks. He does not leave."

"Why?" Roger asked.

"He is troubled. Nirin did have a large following, but his mind is gone now."

"Well, maybe he just needs to see a friend. Lead on?"

"This is your part."

Roger shrugged and walked further on into the rim of lowlands that surrounded the lake. After a while he could hear someone talking. He held up his hand signing for everyone to be quiet and stop moving. Then he began walking again, following the voice to the source.

It was definitely the voice of Nirin.

"I failed, everything I have done is a failure," Nirin said. "It's all a failure!"

Roger passed through a thicket and spied Nirin up ahead pacing back and forth beneath an enormous tree.

"I tried, I tried… I did try, but none of it worked," Nirin continued. You know, you are a sad pitiful loser. Yes I know. I just wanted to bring her back all the way. No, you wanted to make them pay. I did make them pay! Yes, but then you wanted to go after them all, and you failed, just like you failed to protect your wife. Stupid bumbling idiot! You should have died in the fire…"

Roger took a few steps forward, deliberately breaking twigs and kicking rocks as he went in order to make noise, but Nirin did not respond.

"I wanted to die, but when the body fell away instinct took over," Nirin said. "What instinct? You were a coward afraid to die, just like you were afraid to live. I do want to die, but if I died I would go to the place of punishment. No eternal forest for me. Or maybe… maybe there's nothing at all after death? But there's no way I can be sure of that without dying. If only I was never born! Yes, that's the way it should have been."

"Nirin!" Roger shouted.

Nirin showed no indication that he was aware of any of them. He continued to pace and engage in his strange self-depreciating dialogue.

"I hate them all!" Nirin shouted. "But no, I really hate myself more than anything. It is all my fault, all of it."

"Nirin!" Roger shouted.

"Why do you cut yourself off from me?" Nirin screamed.

Suddenly Nirin turned and struck the tree that stood near him. He made a fist and struck the trunk so hard that Roger actually heard a sound like wood cracking.

"Curses of the dark realm!" he shouted as he shook his hand loose.

Some of the bark fell away from the tree trunk where he struck it.

Once more Nirin turned to face the tree and grasped it with his arms.

"Just please come back to me," Nirin said as he sunk to his knees. "I love you…"

His fingers remained embedded in the bark of the trunk as he slid to the ground, and he tore long deep gashes in the bark as he dropped.

"Well," Roger said as he turned to face the soke he came with. "Perhaps I can explain my proposition to you rather than Nirin?"

"Who is there?" Nirin suddenly demanded. "I said I didn't want to be disturbed! Leave me alone, all of you."

Roger approached Nirin and pulled him to his feet.

"Get a grip man!" Roger said.

"I… Roger?" Nirin asked.

The Mind of Nirin

"Yes it's me," Roger said. "What's the matter with you? Did you get brain damaged in the fire, or the soke equivalent of it?"

"Nothing is wrong with me, I just want to be alone," Nirin said.

"Well I came here to ask you for your help, but it looks like you won't be very useful in your current state."

"Bah!" Nirin said as he slapped Roger's hands from his shoulders and moved away.

Nirin took a few steps away from Roger, then paused as his eyes fell on the men who came with Roger.

"You brought them here Mevain!" he said as he pointed to the other soke.

"I wanted to hear what they had to say," Mevain said.

"What do you want, Roger?" Nirin asked.

"I'm going by Mattis now," Roger said.

The two guards gave one another a puzzled look but said nothing.

"You came here for a reason," Nirin said.

"I need your help with something," Roger replied.

"What is it?" Nirin asked as he approached the two Imperial guards who came with Roger.

"I have been made a citizen of the Randaran Empire, and I am a high advisor," Roger said. "I'm close to the Emperor."

"Humans and their titles…" Nirin muttered as he circled the guards.

"Whatever. The point is I am close to the Emperor, and he wants to form an alliance with sokes."

"An alliance with sokes? It's not done."

"Think about who I am."

"You mean 'what.'"

"Alright, what I am."

"It was your idea!" Nirin said as he turned and pointed at Roger.

"It was, but the Emperor wants me to make it happen," Roger said.

"How desperate your Emperor must be!" Nirin said with a laugh.

"If you'll just listen for a minute…"

"State your case and be done with it!"

Roger proceeded to explain to Nirin the pressure that the Emperor was under, and the danger presented by the Kaarumites.

"That sounds like a human problem to me," Nirin said. "If the Kaarumites are going to kill westerners then it is in my interest to let them."

One of the guards stiffened visibly upon hearing that statement.

"Oh," Nirin said as he took notice. "You don't like that, do you?"

Nirin approached the guard and stood close to him.

"What will you do then?" Nirin asked. "Will you strike me with your sword?"

The guard cast a troubled glance at Roger, but as soon as he turned away Nirin pushed him with one hand. The other hand seemed to be functioning at less than peak efficiency after striking the tree. It then occurred to Roger that the sound he heard which sounded like wood cracking was probably a result of the bones in Nirin's hand breaking rather than the tree.

The guard stumbled back a few steps and put his hand on his sword hilt.

"Yes, take it out," Nirin said.

"Nirin, stop," Mevain said.

"Nirin, stop," Nirin repeated in a mocking voice.

Then Nirin turned to face Roger and shouted, "How could you bring westerners here? You were my friend, you know how I feel about them!"

"So you won't help then?" Roger asked.

"NO!" Nirin shouted.

"Because you hate westerners."

"Yes!"

"All of them?"

"Yes!"

"For all time?"

"Yes!"

"Even the ones you don't know about?"

"Yes."

"How can you hate something or someone if you don't even know they exist?""Because I hate what they are."

"And what are they?"

"What kind of stupid dialogue is this? They are a race of humans who all have white skin and these kind of faces!"

He gestured toward one of the guards, both of which had opened their face plates when they started following Mevain.

"Is that why they deserve your hate?" Roger asked

"They raped my wife." Nirin replied.

"Did they all rape your wife? Think about it Nirin! You killed the men who raped your wife."

"I killed the men… who…" Nirin trailed off.

"Do they all deserve to die because some of them raped your wife?" Roger asked.

"They are a corrupt race."

"Yes, but everyone is corrupt, Nirin!"

"They're the worst."

"Is it possible that there is one decent person among them? Think about it. They are one of the most numerous races in the world."

"I don't know."

"Yes you do know. Even if all but one of them are completely bad, does that one good one deserve to die along with the bad?"

Nirin said nothing, but he seemed to be thinking it over.

"Does killing the bad somehow make up for killing the just along with them?" Roger asked.

"You are trying to cloud my mind," Nirin said.

"No, I'm trying to clear it. Think about Ganthar."

"I would rather not…"

"You need to think about it. Think about the horrible things you did there, and the things you tried to do. There were lots of men and women there who were just trying to live their lives, others who were struggling to get by. What if you had released your virus? What if it killed a man's wife? What if the man and his wife had no ill feelings toward the sokes or anyone else? If his wife died because of you should he go after all sokes for all time for revenge? Would any other sokes besides you deserve the blame?"

"Enough! I recognize that they are not all bad. I was wrong to try to release that virus on them. I said as much when I was in Ganthar. But that does not mean I want to help. I still have no love for those people."

"You have a lot of hate, but it seems that the real target of your hate is yourself."

"So you heard that?"

"Yes, you were talking rather loudly."

"And you chose to let me continue as you listened? Why did you not tell me you were there?"

"I announced myself a few times, but you just kept on going."

"So I see… I know what kind of person I am Roger. I don't need you to remind me."

"Listen, you can't change the past, but you can change the future. Now, your attempt to use the virus was stopped, so it's time to put that aside and focus on doing good with the rest of your life. I need you to use your powers of persuasion, and your leadership abilities to rally as many of your people as you can get. We have a world to save."

"I would help you Roger, if I could, but there is nothing left of me. I am completely spent and burnt out."

Roger shrugged and looked around at everyone who came with him. Mevain remained completely still, but his faintly glowing green eyes remained fixed on Roger. His expression was unreadable. Garek seemed like he was ready to go, and the guards looked as though they were anxious.

"What's up with the tree?" Roger asked as he pointed a thumb at the tree that Nirin had scratched.

Nirin sighed.

"My wife has gone into the tree, and she is dormant now," Nirin said. "For all intents and purposes she is a tree."

"What does that mean?" Roger asked.

"It means she's dumb, deaf, blind, senseless, unthinking, and unreachable. I have been trying to wake her up but it's no use. I know her mind is inside that tree somewhere, but it is so thoroughly inactive and shut off that I cannot get any thoughts or feelings when I try to interface with her."

Roger recalled what he knew about soke physiology, specifically their ability to form new bodies from large concentrations of vegetation. He also recalled that after being attacked Nirin's wife had difficulty emerging from a tree.

But... to go into another tree she would have to shed her physical body, which means...

"When did this happen Nirin?" Roger asked.

"When he was away in Tandor," Mevain said.

"And this fellow knew, but he did not think to tell me!" Nirin snarled as he pointed a finger at Mevain.

"I knew only that her body was found, and you were not here for me to tell," Mevain replied.

"So wait, you saw the body but you didn't think anything weird was up?" Roger asked.

"Weird was up?" Mevain asked. "I do not understand your meaning."

"You didn't suspect anything out of the ordinary was going on?" Roger restated.

"It is out of the ordinary for sokes to shed their bodies when they are not damaged, but there are some who do it for various reasons, and they are not condemned or investigated by the community," Mevain said. "Nirin himself has done it to create larger and more powerful physical forms. He is very much concerned with physical things."

Nirin grunted and raised a hand toward Mevain, and Mevain took a step back.

"Nirin, when and how did you find out your wife was stuck in that tree?" Roger asked. "Are you sure it's really her? You can't read her thoughts or emotions so how do you know?"

"I told her to wait for me in the deep place of contemplation. It is an ancient place of wisdom for the soke people of this land," Nirin said. "I said that if she grew tired of this place she should return to her family, and I would find her there, but she did not return to her family. I searched through this place and sensed a change in the normal flow of energy here. It was then I found her inside of this tree. I knew she was my wife because

I can recognize her energy form even as you would recognize the physical appearance of your wife."

"Alright, let's see if I have this straight," Roger said. "When Nirin was gone his wife shed her body and went into the tree. The body was noticed but no one thought anything about it because you are in a forest and there are lots of trees and plants around, so she was not in any danger. Am I right so far?"

"Essentially, but you forget that sokes are free to come and go as they please, and no soke impedes another or harms another," Mevain added.

"Under normal circumstances," Nirin said.

"I understand," Roger said. "So Nirin comes home and finds that his wife is not where she is supposed to be. He does some investigation and finds that his wife is stuck inside the tree, and nothing he does can wake her up."

"That is right," Nirin said.

"So does she even have a body in there?" Roger asked.

"I think she has some rudimentary organs, but probably just enough to connect her energy form to the tree so that she can be sustained by the energy it takes in from the sun," Nirin said. "Some sokes will do extended mergings with plants. I always thought it to be a strange practice. Only a few can do it, and it is usually only ascetics that even try. I think it would be terrible. I find it irritating enough to be stuck inside a plant and unable to move or speak during a normal regeneration process, and I regenerate faster than most. I have no idea why my wife has done this, but I cannot reach her, and I cannot be troubled with anything else while she is in this state."

"So if you had your wife back you would help?" Roger asked.

Nirin laughed.

"I never got my wife back after those fiends assaulted her," Nirin said,. "Her mind was always partway shut down and distant ever since that attack."

"You know, you are not the only one who had his lover assaulted," Garek said, speaking up for the first time. "At least yours is still alive."

"Roger, who is this man?" Nirin asked without even looking at Garek.

"He is another friend of mine," Roger said. "I can vouch for his character, better than I can vouch for yours actually."

Nirin snorted.

"You act like you're the only one who experienced loss and failure," Garek said. "What a poor sad baby you are, a weak child who is always a victim and has no control over his circumstances. If all you can do is give up and mope when you face problems then we are better off without you."

"Foolish bestial human!" Nirin shouted. "What could you know about the suffering of my wife, or the soke people? You know nothing of me!"

"Oh yes?" Garek said. "My lover was burned to death by the Kaarumites, and I could hear her death screams as I tried to break into the house to save her. The first woman I ever loved in the true sense, and she was tortured to death in a horrible way, by the Kaarumites, the same Kaarumites who are trying to spread and conquer the civilized world and do the same thing to many other couples. Maybe the only sort of life you value is your own, if you even value that, so you don't really care what happens to anyone else. If you are so bent on being useless, then be useless. Maybe you can also become a vegetable like your wife. But as for me, I would rather do my best to make sure that what happened to my lover never happens to anyone else."

"You dare..." Nirin said as he took a step toward Garek.

Nirin's eyes lit up with a bright orange light, brighter than anything he had ever seen on a soke before. The grass stirred as if blown by a sudden gust of wind.

"Roger, get this man out of here before I kill him," Nirin said.

Garek entered a combative stance and drew out his sword. The two guards also put their hands on the hilts of their swords and began to draw them.

"Go ahead and try," Garek said.

"Everyone calm down!" Roger said as he stepped between Nirin and Garek and held out his arms toward each. "No one is going to kill anyone, we're just talking. Put the weapons away, and everyone take a seat."

"Nirin is one of the most powerful sokes I have ever known, and he is the most powerful soke of this place," Mevain said.

Roger understood the implication behind Mevain's words, if Nirin wanted to kill Garek he could, and he may even be able to do it without his physical body. He would not be physically stronger than Garek, but he would enmesh him in plants or possibly even damage him with his raw energy form.

"I don't care," Roger said. "I'm the most powerful fighter in this place, and if anyone wants to start some violence they are going to have to deal with me first."

The guards slid their swords back into their hilts, and after a moment's hesitation Nirin lowered his hands and turned away from Roger and Garek.

"I cannot be provoked into joining your war," Nirin said.

Garek stood down and put his sword back into the hilt. Nirin walked a few paces back to the tree where his wife slept in her strange hibernation. He sat down on the ground with his back to the tree and his back seemed to sink in a little.

"I am tired," Nirin said. "I must rest for the remainder of the night."

"Well, either way, there is a woman here who needs some help," Roger said.

"What do you expect to accomplish?" Mevain asked.

"I don't know," Roger said. "Let's see."

Roger took a step toward the tree and held up his hand. A glowing pattern of white light appeared on the top and bottom of his hand. Roger placed his hand on the trunk of the tree and closed his eyes.

"So… you have been marked," Mevain said with a hint of awe in his voice. "That is not the work of Nirin, since he knows mainly to destroy and not to build."

"Shut your noise off, Mevain," Nirin said. "I appreciate your efforts, Roger, but if I cannot reach my wife you certainly cannot."

"You never told me her name, Nirin," Roger said.

"Sasha," Nirin replied. "But I call her something else in my mind."

"Sasha, I know you don't want to talk anyone," Roger said. "I know you have suffered greatly…"

Roger leaned into the tree and reached out with his mind.

"I know you want to leave this world, but there is one thing you have to know," Roger said.

When Roger first touched the tree he could sense nothing, so he intensified the power output going through his hand, and as he did so he could feel the energy drain out of his body. It was as if a tap had been opened, and the longer it stayed open the more tired he felt. After a few seconds he began to feel something, or thought he did. The tree was enormous.

He extended the field further and poured more energy into it. With the sudden outflow of energy he nearly blacked out. It was a struggle to stay awake and on his feet, but there was definitely another presence in the tree.

He could sense it there, it was smooth, and quiet. The experience was thoroughly abstract, but if Roger had to put it in human terms he could describe it as distinctly female though not precisely humanoid. It was more like a matrix of energy, and he could sense every layer of it that his field touched, so in a way the substructure was just as visible as the perimeter, and it was all very complex.

Too complex for Roger to understand at the moment, though he could potentially make sense out of it given a lifetime of study, but at the moment it was not necessary and he had other priorities. He sensed the mind buried deep within the matrix.

He got the sense that a wall which was partly psychological and partly structural was built to keep the mind from being touched. His first attempt to reach her did not work, so he intensified the power further and refined the beam. Still nothing happened.

It's almost like trying to wake someone up from a coma by talking to them, but there is no reason for this entity to be in a state of coma. But wait, sometimes people in comas can hear speech… My thought projections should be registered even if they aren't processed.

Roger decided that rather than trying to open her mind he would open his, and let her decide if she was interested in what he had to say. With one last burst of energy Roger tried to share his thoughts with her.

It worked. The mind opened a little, just a tiny crack, out of sheer curiosity. It was all the opening that Roger needed.

"I have to show you something," Roger transmitted over the link.

Though Roger was primarily focused on the matrix of energy and thought deep inside the bole of the tree, his normal human senses continued to register his environment, though his immediate awareness of the external environment was considerably dimmed.

Once he was finished with his transmission, or upload, he retreated from the soke matrix and gradually realigned his awareness toward the physical world, but as released his grip on the tree he slumped down. He was almost completely drained of energy and found it difficult to keep his eyes open.

The Imperial soldiers ran to his side and quickly turned him over onto his back.

"Commander General, are you alright, sir?" they asked.

Nirin walked by and cast a casual glance down at Roger, then he walked to the tree and put his hand on it.

"Well, it may have worked," Nirin said.

"I'm very tired," Roger said. "We will stay here for the night. Must sleep…"

"But, sir," one of the guards said. "We can't just—"

"Oh let him sleep," Nirin said. "If you want to be useful then you should set up a perimeter or do whatever it is you humans do in situations like this."

"There is no need," Mevain said. "Our people are all around us, and they will keep watch during the night."

"Even so, I want one of our men keeping watch overnight," Garek said.

"As you like," Mevain said.

"You keep the first watch," Garek said pointing at one of the guards. "After four hours you will switch with the other guard. I will also be awake for most of the night."

Mevain approached Roger where he lay and squatted down next to him.

"Let the restfulness of this place replenish you," he said as he laid a hand on Roger's chest and moved off.

Garek rolled his eyes and sat down with his back to a tree.

CHAPTER 10

Sasha

A s Roger drifted off to sleep his thoughts grew incoherent and reality faded. He fell into a deep and heavy sleep with no dreams, at least, no dreams in the traditional sense. On some level his mind still worked because he remembered Nirin's wife in the center of the tree, and he imagined that there was movement there.

Other than that he had no dreams, but the next day he woke up to a sound like wood creaking or groaning. Roger sat up and looked around. The sun was beginning to come up, but visibility was poor due to fog. One of the Imperial guards was fully awake, while Garek sat against a tree, partly awake as far as Roger could tell. The other guard was asleep, Nirin was asleep, and Mevain was nowhere to be seen.

"What was that sound?" Roger asked.

Garek sat fully upright and said, "What sound?"

Roger heard the sound again but saw no sign of movement. Roger stood up and continued to look around. Garek was now fully alert, and he roused the other guard who was sleeping. Then Roger saw it.

"There!" Roger said as he pointed at the large tree.

There was a fissure in the side of the tree that was not there the previous night. As Roger took a step towards it Garek placed a hand on his shoulder.

"Perhaps you had better let me go first," Garek said.

"Nonsense," Roger said as he shrugged off Garek's hand.

As Roger approached the tree they all heard a sound like wood groaning under pressure, and as they watched the aperture grew a little wider. There was a trail of sticky liquid running from the bottom of the aperture to the base of the tree, which gleamed in the morning light.

"Roger, I really think you should stay away from it," Garek said.

Roger stood next to the aperture and placed a hand on the trunk nearby. As he did so a loud gasp came from inside of the tree and a hand shot out. Garek and the guards immediately drew the swords but Roger held up a hand signaling them to stay back. The hand was pale, nearly white, but up close Roger could tell that it had a greenish tint to it.

The hand was definitely feminine, but it was covered with a layer of slime that glistened in the morning light, and trailed between each of the fingers. The hand groped around in the air outside while the being inside of the tree continued to gasp.

Roger took the hand and began to pull gently but firmly on it. As he did so more of an arm was revealed, and translucent slime combined with chunks of soft material oozed out of the aperture.

"I've got you," Roger said, "take it easy."

Garek and the guards did not know how to react, but they remained tensed and did not put their swords away. They were clearly disturbed by what they saw and the fact that Roger was touching the strange hand, but Roger had ordered them to stay back so there was nothing they could do unless something severe happened.

It was at that moment that Nirin woke up.

"What is going on?" he said as he looked up.

Then he saw Roger grasping the hand and pulling.

"She comes!" Nirin said.

Nirin ran to the tree and placed his hands inside the aperture. With one hand on each side he began to push. At first Roger thought that perhaps Nirin had gone mad, since Nirin was at best half as strong as he was, and Roger was not strong enough to affect the tree on any level with his bare hands, but as Nirin pushed the wood groaned and parted further. In the meantime Roger continued to pull on the hand.

When the aperture became wide enough a strange form stumbled out and grasped Roger for balance. The men who came with Roger were clearly on edge at this point. The being that stumbled out of the tree was like nothing that Roger had ever seen before. Her skin was so pale it was almost white, and there were deep lines in it which ran across her body without forming any sort of pattern that he could discern. Her skin was covered with a layer of slime, and her hair was entirely soaked with it. Her hair may have been a dark brown, but it appeared black due to the wetness, and much of it hung across her face. She did not look like a soke.

But Nirin did not seem to notice anything odd about her appearance. He embraced her and held her for some time. When he released her it was apparent that some of the slime had rubbed off on him. He pushed her hair back from her face and ran his fingers across her face to wipe away the slime. He had to stop a few times to fling it off his fingers.

The guards were clearly disturbed, and they let it show on their faces. One of them looked as if he were going to be sick. The fact that Sasha was naked seemed to be contributing to the awkwardness of the guards. When Roger saw how they were looking he snapped his fingers in their direction, and they immediately straightened up and lost their facial expressions. Then he motioned for them to turn around, which they did immediately.

"My wife! I missed you so much!" Nirin said. "Let us go wash."

He took his wife by the hand and began to lead her away.

Then Nirin looked back at Roger and said, "Wait here for us. I have to wash and clothe my wife but I will be back."

For a few seconds Roger watched them go, then realizing that he was staring he turned away. Although he saw Nirin's wife more as a curiosity than an object of lust, he still felt a sense of impropriety over staring at her. In the meantime Garek was still staring.

"I never saw a woman look like that before, not even a soke," Garek said.

"Don't stare, Garek," Roger said.

"Adimnor's blood, do you know how many naked women I have seen? This is nothing."

"Still, she's another man's wife and I don't want you to look. How would you feel if someone stared at your wife?"

Garek shrugged.

"I don't ever plan on having a wife," he said.

"In any case don't look," Roger said.

"They're gone now."

Roger turned to look behind him, and indeed they were gone.

"Why does she look that way Roger?" Garek asked. "It looks like she has no color, and what is wrong with her skin?"

"She emerged before she was fully formed," said a voice from behind.

All the men looked in the direction of the voice at once and spotted Mevain, with a group of five other sokes following him.

"How long have you been there?" Garek asked.

"I arrived as they were leaving," Mevain replied.

"Where did you go?"

"Home."

"Who are these others?" Garek asked gesturing to the sokes behind Mevain.

"They were here, but now we come to repair the tree," Mevain said.

"Repair the..." Garek trailed off as he turned his eyes back toward the tree from which Nirin's wife had emerged.

The huge gaping hole in the side was still there. As Roger and Garek watched the sokes took up positions around the tree and began to gesture. As they gestured Mevain placed his hands on each side of the rift and began to slowly push it shut.

Garek and the guards stared with open mouths as the sokes worked their native science on the tree. Roger was the only one who was unfazed by what he saw.

"So what about Nirin's wife Sasha?" Roger asked. "Will she get better?"

"Her body will return to its normal state with sunlight and nutrition, but I cannot say anything of her mind," Mevain replied.

"That's what I was asking about. She looked a little... different, when she came out of the tree."

"Her body will be well if she takes care of it. Sometimes sokes come out of a plant early because they are anxious, and it is not a serious thing. By the time a soke is developed enough to leave he, or she, is developed enough to survive. But there was some difficulty here because the tree was too great and too solid. Normally such trees are not used, but she never intended to reform, only to join, and to cease to walk in this world."

An hour later Nirin returned with his wife, leading her by the arm as they went. She was clothed in the traditional minimalist soke fashion, and she was clean and dry. Now that her hair was dry it was obvious that it was brown. Her skin had darkened to a creamy green color, but the random lines in her skin remained.

Sasha seemed to be fully alive, but something struck Roger as being a little off. It had to do with the way her eyes looked, and the way she interacted with her environment. Even when she looked directly at a thing it was as though she was looking past it.

When they arrived she did not even seem to notice the humans, except for Roger. She glanced at him and nodded once when their eyes met. Then Nirin released her hand and she wandered off to examine the tree where the other sokes were completing their repairs.

When she drew close to them some of them glanced at her with an unreadable expression, and did not take their eyes off of her while she was there, but she ignored them. She placed her hand on the side of the tree, then she walked away and began picking flowers.

"Roger," Nirin said. "I thank you for returning my wife to me. I had lost all hope before you came. What was it you said to her to get her to come out?"

"I didn't say anything," Roger said.

"Be serious."

"Really. All I did was share a thought with her, something I saw in a dream."

"What was it?"

"A vision of hope."

"Can you show me this vision?" Nirin said as he approached Roger and held up his hand. "It must have been powerful."

"I would be glad to," Roger said as he lifted his hand and grasped Nirin's hand.

Immediately the world changed as Roger's fingers closed on the back of Nirin's hand. He could sense Nirin, and he could see himself through Nirin's eyes.

"Show me the vision," Nirin said.

Roger showed him the vision. He had only to recall it in his own mind, and Nirin would see it too. When Nirin saw the vision he shrugged.

"That does not seem likely," he said.

"Your wife believes it," Roger said.

"Then I will let her have that belief, since it has served to bring her out of that forsaken tree. Regardless of the methodology, I am grateful to you for bringing back my wife, and I am at your disposal. Will you share the tactical situation with me over the interface?"

"As much as I can."

Roger closed his eyes and focused on the images of maps and video feeds regarding Kaarum and the Empire. He gave Nirin an understanding of the numbers involved, and the peril that western civilization was facing back in the Central Lands. A short time later Nirin released his hand and the link was severed.

"I understand now," Nirin said.

"How many people can you bring?" Roger asked.

"I do not know… I will bring as many as I can of course, but I cannot give you any estimate, and while I am willing to help you, I will need to offer my people some kind of incentive."

"The Emperor is prepared to offer you land."

"He will give us part of his Empire?"

"Maybe, but what we want is for your people to help us take some land, which you will be allowed to keep forever."

"So he needs us to take the land, and then he will 'let' us keep it? How can he give us land if we are the ones who take it? If we take it then the land is ours regardless of what he wishes to allow."

"It's not like that Nirin. We want to take back the contested area for civilization. The Empire cannot do it alone, and you cannot do it alone, but the Empire, your people, and the soldiers from Hax can do it if we all work together. It will be a team effort between three different groups, but once it's done then you and the Haxians will get the spoils, and if we are successful enough we will also take land from Kaarum, which means you would get even more."

"That sounds reasonable. But I would like to meet with this Emperor myself and hear what he has to say directly before I try to persuade my people. Once that is done I will organize my thoughts into a presentation and work to convince as many sokes as I can."

"When can you leave?"

"I can leave now. Mevain can care for my wife."

"I think your wife should come, it would be a good experience for her."

Nirin glanced at his wife, and Roger did as well. She was sitting on the ground holding a severed stem in her hand with a purple flower attached. She looked at the flower mournfully, then she placed the stem on the ground and held it steady. For a few seconds she looked as though she was concentrating, and as they watched leaves began to grow from the base of the stem. She released the plant and clenched her fists, watching the plant intently. The plant stayed in place and swayed gently in the breeze.

Sasha smiled and clapped her hands.

"That is very impressive, Sasha," Roger said.

Once more Sasha nodded at him, then looked back down at the stem she had caused to grow back into a whole plant.

"It's a child's trick," Nirin said quietly to Roger. "It is one of the first things a young soke learns, causing whole plants to grow from severed fragments."

"That is amazing!" one of the guards said as he stepped close to Sasha. "How is it done?"

Sasha acted as though she was noticing the Imperial guards for the first time. She bit her lip and leaned away from them as they stepped closer to her.

"It is well, Sasha, these men come from the other side of the world," Nirin said. "They will not hurt you."

Sasha went back to ignoring the guards and worked on planting more flowers.

"You see, Roger, she cannot go anywhere now," Nirin said. "Most of her mind is gone, and she is no longer an adventurer. She must be sheltered and protected, and kept far from danger and strange places."

"I disagree," Roger said. "She needs to be with you. Anyone can see that. I think new soil will be good for her, just like those severed flowers."

"I want to go," Sasha said.

She was looking up directly at Nirin, and her eyes seemed completely lucid for a change.

"She wants to go," Roger emphasized. "It would be good for both of you if she came."

"Perhaps you are right..," Nirin said. "Very well, she comes."

Sasha clapped her hands once and smiled. Then she rose up and skipped over to Nirin and took him by the hand.

"We will see the place that Roger showed me," she said as she looked upward and gestured toward the sky.

"Sasha," Nirin began. "I don't think that--"

Roger gave a loud intentional cough.

"I mean, yes, we will go to that place," Nirin said.

Sasha Emerges from the Tree
—by Roy Gilbertson

On the Way

ROGER AND HIS PEOPLE WERE escorted back to the edge of the forest by Mevain and a group of sokes. Nirin and Sasha were also with them. When they reached the edge of the forest, all but Nirin, Sasha, and Mevain turned back.

"I also wish to go with you," Mevain said. "I wish to see the ancient human land, and to travel up and down within it. I wish to know the state of the forests there."

"Alright, come on then," Roger said.

Then Roger looked out across the rolling plains with dark green grass and smaller forests, but he could not see any sign of his ship. It was still invisible, as per his orders.

"If only I could remember where we parked..," Roger said.

"What do you mean?" Nirin asked.

"Well, this is embarrassing, but I'm going to have to call my ship because I can't remember exactly where I left it."

"It is right ahead of you. Keep walking straight and you will bump into it in 50 paces."

"You can see it?"

"Of course I can. Sokes can see many frequencies of energy, and those we cannot see we can sense. Your ship is wrapped in an energy field that we can see, and to us is like a bright light on a dark night."

"Well that explains why there were sokes waiting for us as soon as we entered the forest. They must have seen us coming a mile away."

"More than that."

"Well then, let's get going."

The sokes were seated close to Roger, in the same section of the ship that displayed what was outside in a 360 degree circle. Once they were up in the air the circle that ran beneath and above them was activated so that they could see everything around the ship within sensor range. To Roger it felt like he was flying through the air in his seat, and it gave him an odd yet enjoyable sensation, but he was surprised when the sokes did not seem intrigued at all by it.

"What do you think about the imaging system Nirin?" Roger asked.

"What?" Nirin said. "Oh, you mean this…"

Nirin gestured at the visual display that encircled them.

"Yes," Roger replied.

"The image is not clear," Nirin said. "It is like looking through murky water at a fish below. Certain undesirable frequencies of energy are bleeding through excessively. If I could understand your control systems I could probably adjust for it, but for now I would prefer a… what do you call them?"

Roger shrugged.

"A transparent segment of the structure for seeing through," Nirin said.

"A window?" Roger asked.

"Window! Yes. Is there one which my wife can look out of? She would like to see the world pass beneath us."

"Yes, I can arrange that."

Sasha and Mevain were moved next to a window, but Nirin chose to remain with Roger and Garek.

"So, Garek is it?" Nirin said as he focused on Garek.

"That is my name," Garek said.

"You are not like Roger, or like these white men, these Imperials."

"No…"

"You were prepared to strike me down in the forest last night."

"Yes, and I would have thought nothing of it at the time, but now we have to put our differences aside and must work together. The cause is more important than the men."

"You misunderstand. I bear you no malice whatsoever. I understand why you were prepared to strike me, and I respect it. I was also prepared to strike at you."

Garek nodded.

"You talk about putting aside our differences, but it seems that there is very little difference between us," Nirin said. "I would not have even considered this if Roger had not opened my mind to the possibilities, but if I were a human I would be you, and you were a soke you would be me."

"Perhaps," Garek said.

"We are both men of serious intentions, and we are both men who are not afraid to kill," Nirin said.

"We are not looking to kill any more people than necessary," Roger said. "We are not in this to kill, we are trying to make a better world and save the civilization here."

"We all understand that," Nirin said. "But what I mean to say is that Garek is someone who I will be able to work with very well."

"Well, that's good, but let's just make sure we don't get carried away and do anything too crazy," Roger said.

"Let's also make sure that none of us are holding back from doing what needs to be done," Garek said.

"I would like to see the land that is to be given to my people," Nirin said. "Can you take us over it?"

"We are going to fly over part of it on the way back to the Empire," Roger said. "I'll let you know when we get there."

"I am also very much interested in seeing this enemy you spoke of in person," Nirin said. "I am anxious to see if they are as terrible as you have depicted them over the interface."

"They are much worse than that," Garek said. "Roger has seen very little of them. He has only seen a small fraction of their brutality."

"Interesting," Nirin replied.

"I have seen enough," Roger said.

It's like I'm using one type of crazy to fight another. I hope this works. So much responsibility... and this isn't even my world. Or is it?

To Roger it felt almost as though he had been in Avramis for a lifetime, and his memories of Earth were starting to seem more like a dream. He thought back to Earth, and the thought of a world with only one moon, not to mention one with lunar phases, now seemed alien and abnormal to him.

If I were to go back to Earth now, and look up into the sky, would I find it weird that there would be no patches or streaks of glowing light? Or when it rains there would be no rivers of light flowing through the sky in the wake of the storm? No light mingled with the rain? Would it seem unnatural, like something is missing?

But there were some things about this new universe that his mind was unwilling to accept, like the idea that the world was flat being one.

How can the world really be flat? How would a flat world even work? Where would the center of gravity be? How could it retain an atmosphere?

Roger shook his head. He knew his wife would never lie to him, but he could not accept that the world was flat without seeing the evidence with his own eyes, as much as he tried to convince himself that it was all true.

But right now I have other things to worry about than exploring the entire world.

Roger continued with his thoughts as Garek and Nirin discussed Kaarum. For the most part Roger did not listen, but at one point he thought he heard them comparing notes on whose lover was treated worse.

The next time he tuned in to their conversation, Garek was describing the various depredations of the Kaarumites, and methods used to combat them by Haxian and Imperial troops. Nirin sat listening intently, and at one point Garek struck his fist into his hand with a loud smack. Nirin nodded, and once more Roger turned away from them.

Roger's thoughts were completely interrupted by a message from the pilot that they were now over the contested area.

"Let's go and look out a window," Roger said.

Roger led Nirin into the pilot's cabin, where they were able to look out of a window directly ahead. The war-torn landscape of the contested area lay before them. Trees were sparse and scattered, and there were many charred spots on the ground of black rock, which was a result of the surface of the ground melting and solidifying after the heat of an earth scorcher.

"There are definitely no sokes here," Nirin said.

"Do you think your people can fix the land?" Roger asked.

"Of course we can, but keep in mind that we will repair it for ourselves, so that we may live there, we will not repair the land only to let it be taken by humans."

"Nirin, we have already discussed this. You are going to get half of the land for the rest of time, while the Haxians get the other half. We need your people to make the whole land livable, but the Haxians will protect you while you work. It's going to be a team effort, both before the battle and during it."

Nirin grunted.

"That's how it has to be, each participant has to get something out of this," Roger added.

"I understand, I just want to be certain that my people are not cheated," Nirin said.

"They won't be."

"What is that?" Nirin said pointing up ahead.

A trail of smoke could be seen rising into the air up ahead.

"Something is being burned," Roger said.

"Sir we have a distress call," the pilot said.

"Let me hear it," Roger said.

"This is Imperial Legion 359 under heavy attack by Kaarumites," a voice said over the ships communication system. "We are holding out in the city of Kenmar, request reinforcements!"

"I did not realize the Empire came this close to the shore," Nirin said.

"It doesn't," Garek said as he pushed his way into the cabin. "But the Empire likes to protect ungrateful people. They come out this far west to keep the Kaarumites from overrunning the rest of the western countries in the Central Lands, and those people return the favor with contempt and inaction."

"Contempt?" Nirin asked.

"Yes, most of them do absolutely nothing to help, while some of them actually blame the Empire for the conflict, accusing the Imperials of being warmongers," Garek said.

"And this is not true?" Nirin asked.

"Of course not, the Kaarumites attack because their religion tells them to make war on all unbelievers," Garek said. "The world would be a much better place without religion."

"I think you meant to say it would be better off without false religions," Roger said.

"That is essentially what I said."

"Well, I disagree. We need rules and moral standards that go beyond human laws. Besides, if you take away religions, then you still have race and species to fight over, and no reason not to."

"If it hadn't been for Kaarum, my girlfriend would not have been burned to death."

"I agree with you on Kaarum. It is evil trash, and lies. But would it have made you feel better if her family had killed her because you guys were a different race?"

"Yes," Nirin said. "Humans have treated sokes miserably because of our differences, and for no other reason."

"Alright, fine," Garek said. "I'll concede that my quarrel is mainly with Kaarum. Other than that… I guess I don't really care what people want to believe."

"There are no false doctrines among the sokes, just people who trust the Great Maker fully and others who prefer to take things into their own hands," Nirin said. "I am one of the latter, but since seeing Roger and the good he has worked I have moved toward the former. I believe it is possible he was put in our world for a reason."

"Sir, awaiting your orders," the pilot said.

"Let's go down," Roger said.

"We hardly have anyone here," Garek said. "There is nothing we can do for them."

"Every little bit helps," Roger said.

"The top priority should be to make sure Nirin makes it to the Empire," Garek said.

"But we can't just let these people die."

"Why not? People die all the time, and we can't save them. You have to think in terms of the greater strategy."

"That's awfully cold hearted."

"The mission has to take priority. If we go down there to fight, then Nirin and Mevain could be killed."

"That's actually the least of my concern, no offense, guys," Roger said.

"None taken," Nirin said.

"They can still make it back to the Empire and respawn in a forest there," Roger said.

"But what is served by throwing our lives away?" Garek asked. "How does it help?"

"I'm not trying to die," Roger said. "I'm just trying to help."

"We can still die, and it's more likely that we would just be killed along with the defenders than we would actually repel the invaders."

"So what is it you think that makes Kaarum so awful?"

"Everything about them."

"Including their disregard for life?"

"What do you mean?"

"They don't care about how many of their own people die as long as they win. It's the most disgusting thing about them, second only to the fact that they want to force their way of life on everyone else. You're already halfway to being like them."

"Have a care what you say to me."

"Am I wrong?"

"Right… wrong… You're tactically unsound. What do you expect to accomplish? Tell me."

"I don't know. But I have a feeling we should go down there. I've got faith."

"Faith in what? Your dreams?"

"No. This time I just have a feeling."

"That's really stupid. We're in a war for survival! You have to forget about feelings."

"Doing the right thing is more important than surviving at any cost."

"That attitude will be the end of you someday…"

"Wait," Nirin said. "The humans cannot see this ship, yes?"

"Not when the stealth grid is energized, no," Roger said.

"My wife can remain here with the pilot, while the rest of us step out to fight," Nirin said. "If anything happens to us the ship can go to the Empire without us, and I myself will go to the nearest forest to create a new body. I should like to see what the enemy is like for myself. If I have personal experience with them I can make a more powerful argument to my people."

"It's settled then," Roger said. "Pilot, relay their message on to the Empire, and tell the troops below that we will be landing in the northern part of their town."

"Well… there could be worse ways to die, and wetting my blade with Kaarumite blood is always a good thing," Garek said.

The ship landed near the northern edge of the city. It was a mid-sized city, with a few large buildings and small monuments. In the southern end of town many of the buildings were on fire, and there were bodies in the streets, both animal and human. Kaarumites and their animals could be seen swarming through the streets.

"Looks like the southern end of the city is already lost," Garek said. "Are you ready for a fight, Nirin?"

"I will do as much as I can to help, and yes, I am ready for a fight," Nirin replied.

"I don't see many plants down there," Garek said.

"There are not, I shall have to do my best to fight human style," Nirin said.

Garek picked up a one handed Imperial sword that was kept on the ship for emergency purposes gave it to Nirin.

"Do you know how to use this?" Garek asked.

Nirin turned the sword about and examined the blade.

"I know some of the basic rudiments of fighting due to my interfaces with Roger," Nirin said. "Some of his training bled through, but I sense it is only a fragment of what he knows."

"Alright, everyone out except for the pilot and Sasha," Roger said.

Roger took off his knife and tossed it to Mevain, who then turned it over and looked at it with a dubious expression. The door in the side of the ship opened with a hiss similar to that of a soda can being opened. The sounds of screams and distant explosions were heard immediately.

Before Nirin could step out Roger grabbed him by the arm.

"Listen, whenever other people are around who don't know my real name I expect you to call me either Mattis or Commander General," Roger said. "Do not use my real name unless we are around the Emperor, Garek, my wife, or her trainees. I'm very serious on that."

Nirin nodded, and Roger released his arm.

Once they were outside Roger was greeted by a tired looking soldier.

"What's the situation here?" Roger asked.

"They have taken the southern part of the city and are gradually moving northward," the soldier said. "We are outnumbered three to one, but more than that if you count their animals."

"What animals are they using?"

"Zangrons and gulogs."

"Continue."

"We have evacuated most of the citizens to the north, and we called the nearest western countries for evacuation and reinforcements but only the city state of Cernak has responded. They will be here in three hours with a handful of troops and shuttles to assist with the evacuation. The Kaarumites are moving north at an accelerated rate. At first we were able to hold them at bay by dodging in and out of buildings, but now they are demolishing the buildings and setting them on fire."

"Who is in command here?"

"I think I am. It has been over five hours since we heard from Commander Lukus."

"Do we have cold bombs?"

"None left."

"Are all the Kaarumites shielded?"

"Most are, I think, but as you know there are always a few Kaarumites that are not," the soldier said.

"If I may..," Nirin said.

Roger nodded.

"What variety of Kaarumites are they?" Nirin asked. "Are they the white or the brown?"

"They are—" the soldier paused when his eyes fell on Nirin. "Who… what, are you?"

There was a puzzled expression on his face.

"Answer him," Roger said.

"They are mostly southerners, I believe," the soldier said.

"Perfect," Nirin replied. "I am Nirin, a soke."

"Have sokes then returned to the Central Lands?" the soldier asked. "Have you come to fight with us?"

"We are returning, and yes, we have come to fight with you," Nirin said. "In fact, I believe I see what I need. Come, Mevain."

Nirin and Mevain approached a wall with a dark green leafy vine covering it. The vine had purple flowers, and large purple seed pods. Nirin and Mevain each picked a handful of the pods and returned to stand with Roger and Garek.

"Do you have a tactical map you can show us?" Roger asked.

"Yes, but it's not much of one," the soldier said.

"Show us what you have."

"This way."

The soldier led them into the foyer of a medium sized building which Roger took to be a hotel of sorts. There were a few other soldiers there, and a significant number of wounded. A holographic three-dimensional map was set up on the front desk. The parts of the city belonging to the Imperials were colored blue, and the portions controlled by the Kaarumites were colored red. There were a few blots of brighter red interspersed among the red area.

"Are these blots of brighter red where the Kaarumite troops are?" Roger asked.

"The map is not exactly precise," the soldier said. "The brighter blots are where we have seen intense concentrations of their troops, but they are all throughout the red areas of town."

"Alright, so some of the Kaarumites don't have shields, we can use that to our advantage."

"How?"

"There should be hunting implements here in town, projectile weapons with scopes."

"Yes…"

"Get a few men armed with those and station them in hard to reach places. Put them on the tops of buildings, or behind windows. They can zoom in with their scopes and pick off the men without the shield generating armbands."

"That would be taking some of the men out of the battle."

"Get some of the citizens to do it, as many as you can."

"It will be massively demoralizing to them," Garek added.

The soldier nodded to a lower ranking soldier nearby, and the man left immediately.

"What else?" the soldier asked.

"The key to fighting Kaarumites is to demoralize them," Garek said. "Usually they go into a mad suicidal rage, but sometimes they run in panic. We need to make them run in panic, and cut them down as they run."

"The brown ones are terrified of sokes," Nirin said. "Mevain and I could fill them with fear. We can use these."

Nirin held out the purple seed pods he had taken.

"What do you expect to do with those?" the soldier asked.

"Come, I will show you," Nirin said.

Nirin went outside and the others followed. He tore open one of the seed pods and placed one seed in the ground. He crouched down and held his hand out over the seed. As they watched a leafy shoot came up out of the ground and attached itself to his arm. The vine grew up around his arm as far up as the shoulder, and a few small runners began shooting across his chest before the growth stopped abruptly.

Nirin clenched his fist and the vine broke just beneath his hand. He then took the loose part and pressed it onto his arm, where it stayed fast.

"Incredible!" the soldier said. "I have never before seen such power! The Kaarumites will be hopelessly unmanned. With your people on our side there is no way we can lose."

An expression of smug satisfaction spread across Nirin's face.

"It will be good as long as the Kaarumites do not realize how vulnerable they are in close quarters combat," Roger said.

Nirin's expression suddenly became neutral.

"So what is the plan?" the soldier asked.

"Each soke will go with a platoon of men to the largest concentrations of enemy fighters," Roger said. "They will use the vines to ensnare the men and spread panic while your men attack."

"It would be better if the sokes were highly visible when the attack starts so that the southerners can see what they are doing," Garek said.

"Agreed," Nirin said. "We will put the fear of the Great Maker back into these cowards."

"I am going to go with Nirin to keep him safe, and Garek, I want you to go with Mevain," Roger said.

The plans were put into effect. As the Kaarumites marched through the streets some of them began to drop. Not many were killed, but a few men here and there would suddenly drop dead with no sign of an attacker nearby. It did not take the Kaarumites long to realize what was happening. They soon began to notice bloody holes in the bodies of the men, and they also noticed that the men who died did not have forcefield generators on.

"COWARDS!" one of the Kaarumites bellowed. "Come out and fight like men!"

He was unanswered, but that scenario repeated itself all over the city. It was not long before the men without shields began to fall back.

"Wow," Roger said. "Looks like about one out of ten of them doesn't have a forcefield."

Roger stood with Nirin at the edge of a large open park as the largest troop of Kaarumites was marching down a large street. They began to slow when they caught sight of Nirin, a yellow skinned humanoid figure with what appeared to be a dark leafy vine with purple flowers growing on his arm and across part of his chest.

"They've got to stop and think about it since they have never seen a man with yellow skin before, or with plants growing out of it," Roger said. "They aren't sure how to react."

"They'll be sure in a moment," Nirin said as he stretched out his hands and gestured.

Roger felt a tingle in his hand through the soke device, and at the same time vines began shooting out from the park and snaked their way toward the Kaarumites.

Some of the Kaarumites immediately turned to retreat and ended up stumbling into their fellows, while others held their ground, but none of them were willing to be the first to charge the strange figure in the park. It was not long before most of the Kaarumite troops could feel vines wrapping around their legs or running over their feet. They shouted and attempted to run, but the retreat was so spontaneous and disorganized that most of them simply collided with one another. In the meantime a squad of Imperial troops came out and began cutting them down.

"The Imperials are working with Alris!" one of the Kaarumites shouted. "Alris has returned!"

The number of Kaarumites was much larger than the squad of Imperials which ambushed them, but they were so overcome with fear that they could not even think about fighting. In a matter of minutes all but a handful of them were cut down. Those who survived ran southward through the city shouting about the return of Alris and calling for a retreat.

"Fools," Nirin said as he watched the battle from the hill.

"Yes," said Roger. "It was a pretty soft vine you used, easily broken, and actually a lot of them were breaking it as they panicked…"

"But they lacked the wits to realize what a fragile thing it was that assailed them. Now, if we were in a forest then I could have truly ensnared them."

"The next battle will be in a forest."

"I will take this news of their cowardice back to my people. Many will join us."

"Good. But we're not done yet. We need to finish cleaning out this city first, and you still have to meet with the Emperor."

"I can do this perhaps two more times, and then my energy will be spent and I must rest."

As Roger looked at Nirin his eyes rested on his right arm, which was not covered by the vine. A thin band encompassed his upper arm on the left, which looked simply like a thin band of fabric but which was actually a forcefield generator.

"Nirin, can you draw energy from that?" Roger said as he pointed at the shield generator.

"Possibly… But the energy frequency is quite different from anything I have ever used before, and if I draw too much from it at once I could damage my energy form. There is much power in this tiny band, and it is quite focused."

"But you were working on ways to interface human technology with soke technology."

"I will have my people work on the problem when they come."

"Good, because something like this will really make a difference during battle. If we could get your people to tap into Imperial power sources then you could make all your plants grow at night, and without limit."

"Perhaps. We will work on it."

The route was complete. Nirin and Roger routed one other large group of Kaarumites, while Mevain also routed two. Of course there were many Kaarumites spread throughout the city, but with the largest concentrations of their people gone the Kaarumites no longer had numbers in their favor, and the command to retreat quickly spread among them. The stragglers that remained were quickly and easily dealt with.

"This may have bought us some time, but they will certainly come back," Garek said. "We need to move swiftly while they are still overcome by fear."

"Agreed," Roger replied.

The governing council of the city thanked Roger and the sokes, as well as the Imperial commander.

"Without the protection of the Empire, and your timely arrival we would certainly have been wiped out," the governor said.

"Why thank them?" one of the councilors said. "Half of the city is wrecked. If it wasn't for them constantly stirring up the Kaarumites then they would leave us alone."

Nirin laughed.

"You idiot!" Garek said. "If it was not for the Empire you would have been worshipping Kaarum a long time ago. The Kaarumites started this fight, and they don't care whether or not you attack them first, they only care about turning everyone in the world into either Kaarumites or corpses."

Then Garek turned to the governor and said, "Governor, this man is a fool. You should remove him from your council."

"You see how they disrespect us?" the councilor said. "They are barbarians."

"You—" Garek began but was cut off.

"Garek, go get the ship ready for departure," Roger said.

Without a word Garek turned and went back to the ship.

"If your man is that well disciplined then why was he permitted to run his mouth so?" the councilor asked.

The pot calls the kettle black!

"Listen, regardless of what you think about Garek, he is essentially correct," Roger said. "The Kaarumite threat is a serious one. They have a religious text, which they firmly believe in, that tells them to go and take over the entire world. They will come regardless of what you do. You cannot bargain with them, because you are just outsiders going against their deeply held beliefs and sacred texts. Especially if you are not coming from a position of strength."

"Please," the governor said. "We are not here to argue. We just wanted to formally extend our thanks for saving our people from destruction. We hope that you will maintain a presence in our city?"

"We will."

"Then I thank you, and I apologize for the councilman. As you can see, we are not all of one mind. Our council is an elected body, so some of the councilmen represent different constituencies and political beliefs."

"Believe me, I understand. Go with the Great Maker, Governor."

"And you also Commander General."

CHAPTER 12

Sokes in Randar

"I T IS LIKE A GREAT mountain which has broken to pieces and scattered across the ground," Sasha said as she looked out the window when they flew over the city of Randar.

"Is that really how you see it?" Roger asked.

"I don't know. I never saw a city before I got in this flying machine with you. The last city was not as long as this one."

"It is quite sprawling… But look at it more closely and you will see the art and workmanship that went into making those buildings."

Sasha pressed her face to the glass and resumed her observation.

"Well, we might be too high up to see most of the details, but when we land you will see some really impressive construction and artwork," Roger said. "There are also some nice parks there which you can relax in."

"What are parks?" Sasha asked.

"Well… they are green spaces in the middle of a city. Spots of forests or gardens."

"Oh! I see green spaces. Do the humans grow them? Do people live there?"

"The humans do grow them, Sasha, but they don't usually live there, and they don't make them grow in the same way that sokes do."

"Yes, sokes do things that humans can't and humans do things that sokes can't."

"Would you like to visit some?"

"Very much!"

"I'll make sure it happens."

"But… I would be scared to go alone…"

"Well, don't you worry. I'll make sure you have bodyguards at all times, and I'll have my wife train you how to fight if you want."

"I want to meet your wife. She is so beautiful in your mind."

"You saw that?"

"I saw many things. When minds touch other things leak through. My husband saw your fighting, but I saw your feelings for your wife. Nirin used to feel like that for me…"

"I'm sure he still does."

"He feels much for me, but it hasn't been the same since…"

Roger placed a hand on her shoulder.

"Everything will be fine," Roger said. "Your husband has a lot of things on his mind right now, but he would do anything for you. I can tell you that much."

The ship landed in a secure area near the Imperial palace where a hovercraft was waiting for them. When the sokes stepped out of the ship they stood still and surveyed what they could see of the city, which was not much given that the compound they landed in was surrounded by walls.

"We need to keep moving," Roger said.

They got into the hovercraft and were taken to the Imperial palace. Out of the three sokes Sasha was the one who took the greatest interest in the surroundings. She ran her fingers along the relief carvings and felt the texture of any furniture she could get her hands on. Finally she settled in a large plush red chair with a bowl shaped seat.

"Tell the Emperor I'm here," Roger said to one of the guards.

"Right away, Commander General," the guard said as he saluted and walked away.

As they waited Aneme entered the room, followed by the Emperor's youngest son Demekus. She greeted Roger, then her eyes fell on Nirin.

"So, you have brought him," she said.

"I brought him, and his wife too," Roger said.

Immediately they heard the noise of something being dragged across the floor. Roger looked in the direction of the sound and saw Nirin's wife dragging her large chair next to an immense bay window, through which a good deal of sunlight flowed.

"Is that her?" Aneme asked.

"Yes," Roger said.

"What is she doing?"

"I don't know," Roger said. "Nirin, what's she doing?"

Nirin came to stand next to Roger as they watched Sasha drag the large chair. She looked at them once and smiled, then she settled into the enormous chair and curled up in the center.

"She is tired, and we were in the ship for some time without sunlight, so she is going to rest and absorb sunlight," Nirin said. "Are there any trusted guards you can have watch her? Is this place safe?"

"Of course it's safe, and yes, I can put some guards around her," Roger said

"Are there other female warriors like your wife?" Nirin asked.

"I don't know, are there?" Roger asked as he turned to Aneme.

"Not yet, but I would like to start training some women soon," Aneme said. "In the meantime Demekus can watch over her."

"I suppose that will have to do," Nirin said. "I just don't want my wife to be stressed. She is so delicate and fragile. If she woke up with a multitude of western men around her, it might…"

"I understand," Roger said. "Don't worry. Demekus is the Emperor's youngest son."

"He is also my best pupil," Aneme said. "But shouldn't we also introduce Nirin's wife to the Emperor?"

"As I said before, my wife is very fragile," Nirin said. "This whole experience has been very tiring and stressful for her. It would be better if we left her here to rest. She is not part of our tactical planning, nor does she have any understanding of those sorts of things. There is no reason for her to meet with the Emperor at this time."

"What if she wakes up before we return?" Aneme asked.

"Then keep her in the palace, or let her go out into the walled in area outside, but she must always be under guard and never alone," Nirin said.

"If that's how you want it," Roger said.

"Demekus, go," Aneme said with a nod in the direction of the sleeping soke woman.

Demekus nodded and went immediately to stand next to the chair in which the soke woman was sleeping.

A short time later the guard returned and announced that the Emperor was ready to see them. Roger, Aneme, Nirin, Mevain, and Garek were escorted to the Imperial office where they were all seated.

Roger made the introductions and the Emperor greeted the sokes in traditional soke fashion. Nirin nodded with approval.

"It is an honor and privilege to meet you," the Emperor said. "No one in this part of the world has seen a real soke in thousands of years. You may call me Adinis when we are alone."

"I thank you, Adinis, it was Roger who convinced us to come," Nirin said. "I do not believe anyone else could have done what he did. He is a friend of the soke people."

"I hope that in time my people and I can also become friends of the soke people."

"Perhaps you can…"

They spoke for hours, discussing the tactical situation of the Empire, what roles the sokes and Haxians would play, and how they would be rewarded for participation.

***

When Sasha opened her eyes they immediately locked onto Demekus, who had been watching her for some time. He had never seen a soke before and he found her curious. The way she was dressed would be considered lewd and inappropriate for the Empire, except in cases where a woman was swimming, but he determined that her intentions were pragmatic rather than vain.

They are photosynthetic, so it would make sense for them to expose more of their skin.

"Tavlon," she said shortly after her eyes were completely opened.

"Yes," Demekus said. "But only in part."

"I know. I see it in your eyes. The tavlons had eyes like a rainbow, lots of beautiful colors. Your eyes have a few colors but not all."

"How do you know about that?"

"I read about the tavlons when I was young. They were the most powerful people in the world, and they were good and wonderful people."

"Ha! I always suspected sokes had a written language."

"We do, how else is information saved?"

"The Watangas save it orally, passing it on down from generation to generation, but when that happens you get distortion, and you have no way of knowing what is distortion and what is truth."

"Yes, we are not like that."

"But most humans think your people are illiterate savages, like the Watangas. Your libraries and institutions are very cleverly hidden, which is what I suspected."

"They are intangible to all but sokes, without special help from sokes."

"Very clever, no wonder Mattis wanted you as allies."

"You call him Mattis?" Sasha said as she sat up in the chair. "His name is Roger."

"Yes, well, if you are in the know then you know we are supposed to use the alias names for Roger and his wife," Demekus said.

"But you are also 'in the know.'"

"I am, but there is no way you could have known that."

"A tavlon is a very important person."

"There are many people who are part tavlon in the Empire, and very few of them are privy to that information."

"But you are."

"Yes I am, but..."

Demekus studied the soke woman for a moment and a different thought occurred to him.

"Sometimes you just know things," he said.

"Yes," Sasha said with a smile.

"What's your name?"

"Sasha. What is yours?"

"Demekus."

"It is good."

"Would you like to go outside, Sasha?"

"Of course."

"But we are not allowed to leave the palace grounds."

"I know, but there is so much here it will take time to see it all."

"All the reason for us to not waste any time."

They went outside and began walking the grounds. The paths were composed of white and blue stone, which was imported from the far north. At first they followed the paths, but Sasha preferred to walk in the grass next to Demekus rather than on the path itself, and she was easily distracted. They passed pools with fish, small forests of different types of trees, and various fruit and flower bearing plants.

"Why so much open?" Sasha asked.

"What?" Demekus asked in return.

"It seems like much of this space is for grass, and not even flowers. Why?"

"Well, the open areas are used for different things, like assemblies, ceremonies, and sometimes games, but other than that I don't really know."

They passed a fountain which contained water spouts that shot up two to ten feet into the air. Without saying a word Sasha walked out into the water and began to probe the spouts. She stood in the spouts, put her hands in them, attempted to plug some with her hands, and even put her face into a few of the less forceful plumes of water.

"This is fascinating!" she said. "Your people manipulate water with such skill. So clever, making machines out of solid things and putting the water through them… We do similar things with energy. What do you call this thing?"

"It's a fountain," Demekus said.

"Fountain," she repeated. "I want one when my people make their new home in the Central Lands."

"I'll make sure you get one," Demekus said.

"Wonderful!"

"If you like this you should see some of the hanging gardens. There are gardens and fountains on so many levels, and there are waterfalls going all the way through. There are some huge fish in the bottom that come from all parts of the world, big fish the size of dogs, and you can even pet them."

"Can we go?"

"Not now, we have to stick to the grounds. If I take you out into the city it will be the end of my career probably."

"We will go later," Sasha said as she stepped out of the fountain.

She emerged from the fountain just as abruptly as she had entered. There was no announcement or hesitation, it seemed to Demekus that she just did whatever came to her mind. One minute she existed in one place, and the next she existed in another. Her actions struck him as both random and fluid.

"Do you want a towel or something to dry off with?" Demekus asked as he looked at her.

She was completely wet, but she did not seem to notice.

"What for?" she asked.

"Never mind," Demekus said.

Well… they do live outside all the time, so it's probably irrelevant to them whether they are wet or dry.

Sasha turned away from the path and began heading straight for a forest of exotic fruit bearing trees with purple and pink foliage.

"These are wala trees, exported from the far east," Demekus said. "They come from an area near the Kelvar Waste."

"I don't know anything about that place, and I have never seen trees like this before," Sasha said.

She walked into the forest and examined the trees. Demekus followed her as she walked. She stopped to examine individual trees, usually touching them, but sometimes only looking. Then at one point she put both of her hands on a medium sized tree and leaned into it. Demekus stood behind her and watched, speculating about what she was doing.

Her wet hair was pulled around to the front, so he was able to see most of her back. Her skin was green, and it had some faint lines in, like impressions left by strings that were wrapped too tightly.

What is that? I've never heard of sokes having marking like that, or seen it in any of the images of sokes.

The tree began to rustle, but there was no wind, and as Demekus watched new leaves began to grow and flowers opened up. The fruits which were on the tree began to grow larger.

"What are you doing?" Demekus asked, but the question quickly became irrelevant.

It was obvious that she was causing the tree to grow, and as he Demekus watched he noticed the bark changing and rippling beneath her hands. The trunk itself seemed to grow wider, and at the same time some of the mysterious lines on her back glowed with a golden light.

"Now this I have never seen," Demekus said.

The tree continued to grow, until it towered over all the others. Sasha then released the tree and the glowing effect on her back subsided.

She turned to face Demekus and said, "The tree could grow more."

"Apparently so…" Demekus replied.

"I am good at making things grow. Soon I will have all of my mind back, and I will be stronger than I ever was. The others have no idea yet."

"Then it is good you're on our side."

"I only want to help."

A question formed in Demekus' mind, but he did not feel comfortable enough with Sasha to ask her.

I don't know enough about Sasha or the soke culture to make certain I'm not violating one of their taboos. So it will have to wait…

They passed through the small forest, and as they neared the other side they began to hear voices, one of which was clearly the voice of Nirin.

"We can induce growth in many plants, your majesty," Nirin said. "But some plants are more receptive than others, they do not all grow at the same rate and they cannot all be made to. Of course each soke has different power levels and abilities, just as among you humans there are some who can run faster or jump higher than others. There is also a limit to how much we can make the plants grow, but all sokes can make them grow beyond what they would naturally."

As they neared the edge of the forest they could see a large number of people gathered out in the open. The Emperor Adinis Maxelis was there, along with Roger, Aneme, Garek, Nirin, Mevain, and a significant number of guards and observers. Nirin was demonstrating his powers of growth acceleration on different plants for the benefit of all the observers. Some of the men present could be seen recording.

I didn't know they were going to be here, but since I already heard part of their conversation they should know that we're here. It's wrong to spy on them.

"We must reveal ourselves," Demekus said, but Sasha was already on her way out.

As they neared the group Aneme noticed them, and nodded to Demekus signaling that it was acceptable for them to be there. He and Sasha took up places next to her and kept silent while Nirin carried on with his demonstrations.

"Of course in our own domain we have a much higher level of control over the plants, and we do not have to use so much of our own personal energy reserves to make them grow because we have all of our machinery in place," Nirin said. "We can redirect ambient energy, and during the day we have the energy of the sun to draw on but without our machinery it is quite draining for us."

"Which is where the Haxian mercenaries come in," Roger said. "They can provide cover for you while you set up your machinery."

"It will help," Nirin replied. "We can be much more effective with our machinery in place."

"You will have as many troops as we can supply, not just Haxians but also Imperial troops, and you will have air support as well," the Emperor said.

"We will create a bulwark against the savages," Garek said.

"Indeed," Roger said.

"But we cannot rely too much on any single tactic," Aneme said. "We use all of the resources available to us, and we must have multiple contingencies."

"My wife, the strategist," Roger said.

"What about aquatic plants?" the Emperor asked.

"All plants," Nirin said.

"What about fungi?" the Emperor asked.

"Although fungi have some of the same properties as plants, they are still not plants," Nirin said. "Fungi are heterotrophs, like animals and humans. They cannot utilize sunlight, and adding more energy only destroys the fungus. The closest we have ever come to controlling a fungus is lichen. As you know lichens are formed by a symbiotic relationship between a fungus and a photosynthetic partner, usually some type of algae. We can only exert direct control over the photosynthetic component, but with the proper care and fine manipulation the fungus can grow to accommodate the algae. There are few among us who are capable of such fine manipulation."

"Have there been attempts to control fungus?" the Emperor asked.

"Yes, but they rarely lasted for very long," Nirin said. "The great sage Ven Sendel spent his entire life trying to find a way to control and influence the growth of fungus. It is said that near the end of his life he claimed he was nearing a breakthrough, but there is no record of it. Our scientists maintain that it is impossible. Ven's grandson, Eldan Sendel, attempted to carry on

Ven's work and it literally drove himself insane trying to figure out how to control fungus. As a result there are those among us who consider it a dark art, and stories have been written about it."

"But why is it a dark art?" Roger asked. "When you say 'dark art' I think of something like sorcery, or necromancy."

"What is necromancy?" Nirin asked.

"It's a type of sorcery where people try to raise the dead, or do something unnatural with dead bodies," Roger replied.

"That is a good analogy," Nirin said. "Plants are the basis for all known food chains, except for some types of bacteria. Plants harness energy and create life. Fungi consume and destroy life, or the dead remains of things that were once living. They operate on a different principle from plants, so we have no way of controlling them, unless we decide to look beyond the bounds of the natural. There are many sokes who think it's evil to try to move beyond the bounds that the Great Maker set for us. But, if we were ever able to control fungi as we do plants, it would be very easy for us to destroy all other organisms. Just imagine; everything has some amount of fungus in it, or is vulnerable to some type of fungus.

"There's a rumor... I don't know if there is any truth in it... But we have this legend that Eldan Sendel actually succeeded in his research, and the cost of that success was his sanity. According to the same rumor, that is also why there why there are no records of his research. Whatever was found, and however he found it, was so horrific that it had to be destroyed."

"I see," the Roger said. "That does sound pretty bad."

"Did Eldan Sendel call on Gro-Sho-Var for the power to manipulate fungus?" Aneme asked.

"I don't know," Nirin replied. "That's one interpretation of the mythology."

"Maybe it's forbidden for a good reason," the Emperor said. "We'll not pursue the matter."

Once the demonstration was over the crowd began to disperse. But some of the observers surrounded Nirin and showered him with questions. As he answered their questions he looked over the shoulders and noticed his wife standing with Roger and Aneme. An anxious expression flitted across his face for a second before he returned his focus to the men who were questioning him.

"Your abilities are quite incredible," the Emperor said. "Your people will be a valuable ally."

"And I shall bring as many as I can," Nirin said. "What we must do now is prepare a demonstration which I can show to my people, so that we can convince as many as possible to join our cause."

"I agree, in fact I had my people recording so that we can create a demonstration for both the Haxians and your people."

"Very wise, but of course I will need to show different imagery to my people. They will not be as interested in seeing demonstrations of the natural abilities of sokes."

"My people will get you whatever you need. You need only tell me what abilities and technologies of my people you are most impressed with, and we can create a montage for your people to see."

As they spoke Sasha left Roger and Aneme and approached her husband. Demekus followed.

"Who is this?" the Emperor asked as she drew near.

"This is my wife, Sasha," Nirin said. "Sasha, this is Emperor Adinis Maxelis, keeper of western civilization in the Central Lands."

"My lady," the Emperor said.

"You have a nice place," Sasha said. "I especially enjoyed the water fountain."

One of Nirin's eyes narrowed slightly. Demekus noticed it but his father seemed not to.

"Which one?" the Emperor asked.

"The one back that way, on the other side of the wala trees," Sasha said as she pointed back in the direction she had come from.

"I'll see to it that your accommodations include a water fountain during your stay in Randar."

To Demekus' surprise, Sasha held out her hand with the palm facing toward the Emperor in the traditional Imperial greeting. The Emperor quickly reciprocated the gesture.

Roger nudged Nirin with his elbow. Nirin said nothing, but from the expression on his face it was clear that he had no idea what his wife was doing.

"If there is anything you need during your stay here, do not hesitate to come to me," the Emperor said.

"Thank you, I will," Sasha replied.

CHAPTER 13

Coming Together

Over the next few weeks things fell into place swiftly. Garek traveled back and forth between the Empire and Hax, along with some Imperial officials. Mercenaries began to sign up in the thousands, and in addition they also received the troops promised by the Premier of Hax.

Roger accompanied Nirin back to his homeland, where they worked together to recruit as many sokes as possible. Nirin and Roger gave speeches, and a presentation was disseminated throughout the soke energy network. At first the soke volunteers numbered in the hundreds, then after some time thousands volunteered, and from there the number of volunteers rapidly began to approach a million.

The sokes were ferried to back to the Central Lands in large cargo vessels equipped with stealth technology. At first they were deposited in key locations along the northern edge of the contested area, typically near the Empire, but Roger had a different plan.

"We have to do this in such a way that the Kaarumites don't see it coming," Roger said during a strategy session in the war room. "They already had some warning from Kenmar, that city we saved, but maybe they will write it off as a fluke."

The Emperor Adinis Maxelis, Nirin, Garek, and the other leaders and strategists were all present in the war room.

"What exactly are you proposing?" Adinis asked.

"This," Roger said as he tapped at a touch screen panel nearby.

The large three dimensional map of the contested area shimmered for a moment, and red triangles appeared in various places all across the map. As they looked at the projection closely they noticed that the red triangles appeared in areas that were greener than the surrounding area.

"I'm thinking we should start using the old tavlon ruins as bases for our troops," Roger said.

"We have always purposely avoided using those locations in our war with the Kaarumites," Adinis said. "That would be an unprecedented abuse of priceless historical sites."

"They might be the price you have to pay to keep your empire," Garek said.

"I'll admit, it's a gamble," Roger said. "But maybe the Kaarumites will still be too scared to approach those Tavlon sites until it's too late?"

"Maybe," Adinis said flatly. "Alright, what is it you have in mind?"

"The Kaarumites are so terrified of the ruins that they haven't gone anywhere near them for thousands of years, so there is already a healthy forest in place surrounding them," Roger said. "We can put sokes into those forests where they can have well-established forests to set up their energy matrices in, and from there they can expand outwards more easily. We can also refurbish the tavlon ruins and set up bases for our human soldiers inside. We can get a lot done right underneath the noses of the Kaarumites by using their own stupid religion against them. If we are sneaky enough then the entire area will be ours before they even know what is going on."

"A sound plan," Garek said.

"Are they really that stupid?" Nirin asked.

"They are," Garek replied.

"It is a sound strategy, as long as we can move the troops without being detected," the Emperor said.

"I believe we can, but we must set up a distraction for them," said one of the advisors present.

"They are likely to engage in a head on assault, as they have always done, so we should focus on conspicuously fortifying our southern border, as well as some of the key city states we are allied with," said another advisor.

"Then let us have it done," the Emperor replied.

"One more thing," Roger said. "I was thinking about something my grandfather told me, about not leaving your back unguarded. I would like to have sokes also placed inside the Empire, in this big forest reserve in the north."

"Sokes inside the Empire?" Nirin said. "How would that work?"

"They could be there as a semi-autonomous protectorate under Imperial command until all the wars are over," Roger said.

"All the wars?" Garek asked. "Are you thinking that something else is on the way?"

"I don't know what is on the way, but I want to make sure," Roger said. "Maybe if the sokes like it in the forest reserve they can stay there as Imperial citizens."

"Out of the question," Nirin said.

"The need exists," Roger said.

"I am not convinced of that," Nirin said.

"The sokes have a need for more land," Roger said. "We should make it a choice. Maybe we can get a new wave of immigrants who want new land but are not as eager to be part of the war?"

"Maybe… The sokes are a free people, we have no government or laws restricting movement, and anyone who wants to leave can. But I don't see why sokes, who know no government, would want to submit to human rule."

"It would be their choice, but the Empire would also have to agree to accept them" Roger said. "I'm against forcing one population on another without their consent, but if the Empire is fine with it…"

"We should be," Adinis said. "No one lives in that area, and there is no democracy or voting here, so there would be no reason for one group to be set against the other."

"Of course we won't force it on anyone," Roger said. "It has to be a choice all around. If the Empire and the sokes are both fine with the arrangement then we can go ahead with it. If not, then we won't. But I do think it's very important that we do this."

"That is reasonable," Nirin said.

During their time in Randar, Nirin and Sasha lived in one of the large hanging garden complexes, which was converted into the official soke embassy for the new soke nation which Nirin was to be in charge of after the war.

"I don't know how I feel about all this," Nirin said to Roger as they walked through the complex together.

"Feel about what?" Roger asked.

"This will be the first time in history that any soke people has ever been ruled by a government," Nirin said. "Unless you count the original kingship that the first soke man had over our people in ancient times. We are in new territory, and I can't help but wonder if we are doing a thing that is as wrong and unnatural as trying to control fungus."

"Well, if you're going to make that analogy, I guess I would say yes… But like those efforts to try controlling fungus, I'd say it's a moral gray area where we just don't know what will happen until it's tried."

"Still, every fiber of my being is uncomfortable with this proposition."

"That's good. No one should be comfortable with ruling over others."

"Is this really even necessary?"

"I don't know, but it will make things easier if we can just deal with you rather than every soke individually. I mean, we have to mobilize the sokes. Do you have another idea?"

"I don't."

Nirin came and went, sometimes going back to the Western Lands, sometimes going to the various outposts where his people were setting up energy grids in the Contested Area, and sometimes going with Garek to Hax in order to help him lure more mercenaries to the cause.

Sasha never left Randar. She primarily stayed in the soke embassy, or visited the parks and the Imperial grounds.

During that time of preparation they experienced some tentative attacks from the Kaarumites, which they repelled with the help of Haxian mercenaries. Roger wanted to keep the sokes a secret until the main confrontation occurred.

One of the costs of keeping the sokes a secret was that the constant engagements caused the Empire to run low on freeze bombs, and the production costs were beginning to weigh heavily on the economy. To alleviate matters, Nirin sent more sokes into the Empire to assist with food shortages, and sokes also agreed to settle in the northern forest reserve of the Empire.

Aneme finished training her men, and they each began to train their own trainers, which in turn began to train the soldiers. At the end of her last day she returned home, took off her shoes and gloves, and dropped down into a large soft reclining chair, where she leaned back with a sigh.

"Well, it's been a while since I've seen you," Roger said as he rose to greet her.

They had both been so busy that they did not always return home from work every night. Sometimes Roger slept in the war room, or overseas in the soke forest south of Tandor, or in one of the bases, while Aneme sometimes slept in her training facility.

"It is done Roger," Aneme said. "The men can take it from here…"

"How do you feel?" Roger asked as he knelt next to her chair and took her by the hand.

"Tired."

Roger moved around behind her and began massaging her neck and shoulders. He felt a slight bump on her neck when his fingers passed over the scar.

"What are your plans now?" Roger asked.

"I have none, other than being with you," Aneme said. "The men can carry on without me. I'll check up on them periodically, but going forward I'm going to spend most of my time with you now."

"Good to hear. I've missed you."

"How are all the plans?"

"Good, good… We have sokes in the Empire now."

"I know, I saw them. I hope it doesn't lead to problems later on."

"Same here."

"Differences can be problematic, but it may be that the sokes and Imperials are so different that they won't conflict because they don't overlap."

"We have repelled some rather heavy assaults, but I am told they are only the tip of the iceberg."

"You are saving the sokes for later," Aneme said as she leaned her head back and looked up at Roger.

"Yes," Roger replied.

"The Kaarumites are stupid but it's no secret that there are sokes walking around Randar."

"Yes, but they don't know what our game is, assuming they even believe the rumors. They don't know that the contested area is now riddled with our bases. We will unleash everything when they come for their final assault."

"Hmm…" Aneme said as she closed her eyes.

"Now that you have some time off, why don't we let the Imperial doctors check you out?" Roger said.

"What for?"

"To fix this," Roger said as he touched the right side of her neck near the scar.

Aneme flinched away from his touch immediately and pushed his hand away.

"I don't want them going into my head," Aneme said.

A chill ran down Roger's spine.

"Why do you say that?" he asked.

"Because that is what they will do, and I am not comfortable with it," Aneme said as she rose from the chair and began to walk toward the kitchen. "Please don't ask me to do that Roger."

"Aneme, why did you say you don't want them going into your head? I was talking about fixing the scar on your neck where that woman cut you. I didn't say anything about your head. Why would the doctors go inside your head?"

Aneme stopped walking and placed a hand on her neck.

"I said that?" she asked.

"Yes, and it's a little scary, I have to admit. Aneme, you've got draenock stuff inside if you. Don't you want it out?"

"I don't know…"

"That shouldn't even be a questionable thing. If you have to stop and think about it, or if you can't even think about it, then you're probably not thinking about it clearly enough to make a sound decision."

"I don't know. It makes my head hurt to even think about this."

"I'm afraid I have to insist on this."

"Well, if you insist…"

"Alright then."

As they walked through the Imperial grounds they passed Sasha as she was working on a patch of gourds. Much of the Imperial grounds had been converted into fruit and vegetable gardens to assist with the war effort. Everyone throughout the Empire was encouraged to do whatever they could to help. When Sasha saw them approach she stopped what she was doing and walked forward to meet them.

"Where are you two going?" Sasha asked.

"To see a doctor," Roger said.

"His idea," Aneme added.

"You should be glad," Sasha said as she began walking next to Aneme. "You have an injury the doctors can fix. There is nothing any doctor can do to help me."

"What?" Aneme asked.

"Yes," Roger agreed. "What she said."

"I will go with you," Sasha said.

Because of Roger and Aneme's high rank they were able to see a doctor immediately. Aneme stood in the center of a glowing circle while doughnut shaped metal apparatuses hovered up and down around her.

"It is a deep tissue scan," the doctor said. "We are going to map every cell in your body. In fact, we are going to construct a thorough image of your body down to the atomic level."

Aneme grunted but said nothing. She seemed more annoyed than frightened.

As if we are making a large fuss over a small thing…

"You have undergone examinations like this before, Aneme," Roger said.

"But they were conducted by my own people, and they found nothing each time," Aneme said.

"Imperial technology is considerably more advanced," the doctor said. "No offense."

"None taken, it's true," Aneme said. "But there is really nothing seriously wrong with me."

"'Nothing seriously wrong,'" Roger said. "In other words you know there's something wrong and you want to think it's not serious."

Once the examination was complete the light of the circle faded away and the machine receded up into the ceiling.

"If you will all excuse me, I must now examine this data," the doctor said. "The orderlies can escort you out."

He took a small crystalline square out of a panel and left the room.

"Are you sure it was a southern woman who cut you?" Roger asked.

"Tall woman, brown skin, long dark hair, dark eyes, sturdy build, sharp features," Aneme said. "She was unmistakably southern, but not Kaarumite. Why do you ask?"

"I'm just wondering if there is some connection between the draenocks and southerners."

"Who knows… I guess if I have the draenock touch there has to be. But as I said before, I have never been around real draenocks in my life."

"What if… Just what if draenocks do not always have to look like hideous monsters… The most dangerous trap is something that looks beautiful on the outside, and is all monster, poison, and death on the inside."

"Whatever she was, she had human intelligence. I don't think she was an animal."

The next day they returned to visit the doctor, and his analysis was complete. They sat in a room with soft cushiony chairs as the lights went off and a three dimensional holographic display of Aneme appeared in the center of the room.

"Well doctor, what's the verdict?" Roger asked.

The image enlarged to focus on Aneme's head and shoulders, and it became a translucent blue color, showing hints of musculature and skeleton beneath the skin. The scar on her neck was highlighted in red.

"As you know, this is the scar," the doctor said.

Suddenly a mesh of red lines shot outward from the scar in all directions beneath the skin, and from the larger red lines a mesh smaller lines shot out until the entire right side of her neck, head, and part of her shoulder appeared red.

"A fine network of unusual scar tissue runs beneath your skin as far down as your right shoulder, and as far up as your scalp on the right side," the doctor said. "As you can see it also runs beneath part of the right side of your face."

Aneme reached up and touched the side of her face. Roger placed his arm around her.

"But that is not all," the doctor said.

The image rotated so that it was facing forward, and the exterior of the image faded while the central nervous system lit up. A few of the red tendrils could be seen running into Aneme's brain, and some portions of her brain lit up with red light where the tendrils came into contact with her brain tissue.

"There are some slight irregularities in the brain as well," the doctor said.

"Aneme said that none of the northern doctors were able to detect anything beneath her skin," Roger said.

"Not surprising. Northern medical science is a good deal less advanced. If I had only given the data a cursory glance I would have missed it myself. It is a very fine and complex pattern of scarring. I believe it was left by a compound which was designed to linger in the system for some time, possibly years, and slowly work its way through the body, causing more damage as it goes."

"Well is any of it still there?"

"No."

"Is it a draenock injury?"

"That was going to be my question for you," the doctor said, giving a nod towards Aneme. "I have never seen an actual draenock injury before, but I have read papers on them."

"It was caused by a southern woman in Velta," Aneme said. "She cut my neck in a street fight and it became badly infected."

"Then it does not seem likely that it was a draenock wound, since the draenocks have not broken the northern vigil and I have never heard of a humanoid draenock, or a draenock capable of speech," the doctor said.

"Well was it a draenock type poison?" Roger asked.

"Without seeing the actual toxin itself I cannot make that determination with complete certainty, but based on what little I have read it looks like it could be," the doctor said. "When it comes to draenock wounds, the scope of the damage is always a good deal more extensive than the original wound, which acts as the entry point for the toxin. Unfortunately there is not a lot of data on draenock wounds in the Imperial database, and of the injuries that were recorded the manifestations varied too widely for us to determine what the pattern to them was, beyond scarring being extensive of course."

"How come there isn't more data on the subject?"

"Very few northerners come this far south, and my understanding is that the majority of draenock wounds which are not fatal are repaired. In the few cases where the wounds cannot be repaired by northern science the subjects are unwilling to accept help or to submit to an examination. Only data for a handful of cases exists, and in all but two of them the pattern of the scarring varies."

"Have you ever seen a southern poison cause damage like this?"

"No, but the southerners we interact with are mostly Kaarumites, or those non-Kaarumite southerners who colonized the land across the sea thousands of years ago. There are the southerners to the east who have closed themselves off from the world completely. Who knows what those people have become like over the years?"

"Can you repair Aneme's damage?"

"Yes, she will be in perfect condition once we are done."

"What is involved in the treatment?"

"Laser surgery and nano-reconstruction. Every abnormal cell will be removed and replaced with a healthy cell. She will need to spend about two days in a regenerator."

"Are you alright with that?" Roger asked his wife.

"I don't know," Aneme said. "I won't lie and say that I'm comfortable with it, but…"

"Yes?" Roger asked.

"Doctor, can you have the image show my full nervous system in blue along with the scar tissue in red?"

"Certainly," the doctor said.

The image changed to show Aneme's full central and secondary nervous systems in blue, which clashed brilliantly with the lacing red of the scar tissue.

"I'm no doctor, but to me the red looks almost like another nervous system," Aneme said. "Could it be competing with my nervous system?"

"The resemblance is superficial, the bulk of your scar tissue does not consist of nerve cells," the doctor said. "However… it is certainly interfering with your natural nervous system, and might even be affecting your thought processes."

Aneme continued to stare at the diagram but said nothing. Roger and the doctor continued to stare at her, awaiting her response

"The northerners have similar procedures to the operation I suggested," the doctor said after some time. "But the techniques and equipment are a good deal less advanced. That is the main difference."

"I guess there's no other way," Aneme said. "Take it out."

CHAPTER 14

The Calm Before the Storm

ROGER KEPT BUSY WHILE ANEME was in surgery. He was only allowed into the chamber where she was being kept once during the entire process. She was in the center of the room contained in a large pod. The sides were of metal and the front and back appeared to be made of some sort of transparent material. The wall was covered with monitors, and each had an image of some part of her body at varying levels of magnification, or contained readouts of some sort. The pod itself was attached to a metal arm that came up from the floor.

From across the room Roger could tell that there were many devices inside the pod itself, and that his wife appeared to be suspended in some sort of gel.

Roger approached the pod hesitantly. He paused as he made his way toward it, contemplating whether or not he could bear to see his wife undergoing surgery. When he finally looked inside he was horrified by what he saw. He called immediately for the doctor, who informed him that everything would be fully reconstructed and guaranteed that his wife would be whole when the process was over.

"I understand that in your world when a body part is removed it cannot be replaced, but every civilized people in our world has the ability to biologically reconstruct missing parts," the doctor said. "We had to remove a good deal of damaged tissue from your wife but she will be whole again once we are finished, and completely natural. There will be no synthetic parts."

"Yes, but… I wasn't expecting all that," Roger said.

"I did warn you that it would be disturbing."

"I know, I know… But please doctor, she is very important to me. If anything happens to her I don't… Maybe I should have just let it be. She was fine the way she was."

"You did the right thing, and she made the decision herself. Go home and keep busy. I will call you when she is released."

When Aneme was released from the hospital Roger was there waiting for her. She appeared to be healthy and whole, as if nothing had ever happened to her.

"Roger!" she said as she hugged him. "It's unbelievable, I feel so different now. I had forgotten what it was like before."

"You look great," Roger said.

"Yes, the scar and all its effects are gone now. I feel so different, so much better. I feel like… like I have walked a long distance with a heavy pack on my back, and now it's gone, suddenly. I feel stronger and lighter, watch."

Aneme jumped where she stood and flipped over in the air, coming back down on her feet and facing Roger.

"There was always this tense feeling in my head that I had gotten used to over the years, but now it's gone," she said. "I can also think more clearly, and my reflexes are a lot better. I should have gone to see a western doctor a long time ago. I suffered for so many years for no reason. I punished myself needlessly, but now I am whole again. Why did I punish myself for so long?"

"I don't know, but now that you are thinking more clearly, tell me again about that southern woman who cut you," Roger said.

"Ah yes, that woman. I remember it clearly, the knife sinking into my neck, and that thing entering my body. I could feel it tugging on my mind almost immediately. I had to struggle to stay myself. There was something unnatural about that woman, as if everything that makes a person good had been boiled away, and the thickly concentrated evil that remains was packed into one person. Undiluted. She didn't spare me out of mercy, she spared me out of spite. I would not be surprised if I saw her again someday."

Roger mulled it over for a few seconds, then hugged his wife and kissed her.

"Well, we can deal with that later, if it happens," he said. "For now, I'm glad to have you back and completely whole. Just when I think I'm getting used to this world something amazing happens and I get surprised and dumbfounded all over again. Anyways, let's get home. We have lots of work to do."

Roger and Aneme spent a good deal of time in the war room with the Emperor, Nirin, Garek, and the Imperial war ministers. The Kaarumites continued to attack periodically, but every attack was repelled.

"They are probing us," the Emperor said.

"Agreed, the forces they are throwing at us are only a small fraction of what they have available to them," one of the advisors said. "They are looking for weak points to focus their attacks on."

But the men Aneme trained were doing their job. They trained other men to assist them, and they began taking entire regiments off duty for basic training in the northern arts, which they learned quickly by making heavy use of the learning drink. Once basic training was complete was complete they were put on leave to recuperate from the learning drink, and then sent back to the front.

It was not long before all the men were trained in basic Northern Arts, and once that was done they began to cycle troops off the front for advanced training. But once all the men were trained in basic they repelled the Kaarumite attacks with a good deal more ease. Instead of continuing their attacks the Kaarumites pulled back, and there was silence on the front.

"I can't believe they have stopped," Roger said.

"No, they are planning something," Garek replied.

"We need to rapidly complete the advanced training and make all of our final preparations for the onslaught," Aneme said.

"I agree," Adinis said. "Do whatever needs to be done."

"Your Majesty," Nirin began. "I believe it would be in our best interest for my people to also be armed and trained."

"It would be wasteful to throw your people into direct combat," Garek said. "They will be much more helpful to us in support positions, making the plants and forest grow to provide cover for us and traps for our enemies, and they can also supply fresh food to the troops."

"Yes I know, and I am not suggesting that we throw my people on the front lines, but they should be able to help if they come into close quarters with an enemy," Nirin said.

"Even so, we don't have the time to teach them, because the learning drink does not work on sokes and the Kaarumites will attack soon," Garek said.

"We can transfer knowledge through the interface," Nirin said.

"Wait," Roger said. "I thought that it was mostly only images and feelings that could be transferred, not knowledge and techniques."

"That often true, but there is always a bleed over of some knowledge and techniques during long interfaces," Nirin said. "You and your wife have the ability to interface with sokes. You could connect with me and imagine yourself going through all the steps and moves. From my perspective it would be like I was practicing the moves myself, or whoever you interface with. If we learn the most fundamental basics then we can flesh it out into a full fighting art on our own. We just need a few people to learn and then we can create a database and write programs to teach other sokes. We should also be given weapons so that we can easily kill any Kaarumites we encounter in the forest."

Garek looked like he was about to argue but Roger held up his hand.

"I think it's a good idea," Roger said. "We need everyone to be as prepared as possible."

"What do you have in mind Roger?" the Emperor asked.

"The sokes should each be armed with a sword or dagger," Roger said. "I would say they have more than paid for it with the food they have grown for us."

"Agreed," the Emperor replied. "What about training?"

"Northerners spend most of their childhood learning basic combat training," Aneme said. "But, Roger and I do have the ability to interface with sokes because of our implants. We can interface with a few who have powerful enough minds to acquire knowledge and they can use whatever method they want to disseminate it."

"I will find someone with those capabilities," Nirin said.

"Your wife will do," Aneme said.

"My wife does not—"

"She does."

Aneme and Nirin locked eyes and stared at one another for a few seconds. Then Nirin nodded his head in agreement and looked away.

Immediately after the meeting Aneme went to the hanging garden which had been converted into the soke embassy and met with Sasha, while the Emperor requisitioned swords and daggers for the sokes. Over the next few weeks the weapons were distributed, and Sasha and Nirin set to work creating a rudimentary basic combat training program for the sokes.

One night the Emperor came to meet with Roger and Aneme in their quarters and share dinner with them. He said his wife was away in the agrarian provinces further north giving speeches at women's charity events designed to spur domestic production while many of the men were away at war.

"This war is a severe drain on our economy, even though the enemy is silent for now," Adinis said.

"But has that not always been the case?" Aneme asked. "Your people have been at constant war with the Kaarumites as my people have been with the draenocks, and before that you were a bulwark against invasions from the east."

"Well, as you know our Empire is much older than the cult of Kaarum," Adinis said. "Before the Chaos War we were not in a constant state of defense against the forces of evil. We had attacks from time to time, but we were large enough and our economy was strong enough to repel them when they came. Unfortunately, our ancestors were lulled into a false sense of security by silence, and in that silence our enemies regrouped and built up such a force that they could overwhelm us with one strong fatal blow. They nearly did. Were it not for the intervention of your people there would be no Empire today."

"But that was all a long time ago, and the Empire has survived," Roger said.

"It survived but never fully recovered," Adinis said. "Our enemies have waged almost constant war on us and whittled us down in size. The respites between attacks have grown shorter and shorter. Now again they are silent and building up. We have done our best to prepare, and we have many warriors from Hax, but if we could again have northerners come to our aid…"

"Impossible," Aneme said as she shook her head.

"Will you at least try?" Adinis asked.

"They will probably be enraged to find that your people have been taught the Northern Arts," Aneme said. "They will not help, best case scenario."

"Perhaps we could offer them help against the draenocks once our enemy is defeated?"

"What sort of help?"

"A thorough scouring of the Northern Wastes to root them all out, and medical assistance with repairing all the individuals who have the draenock touch."

"The most I can do is return to my native den in the Northern Wastes and present a case," Aneme said. "But once they have learned that I taught your people the northern arts they will consider me a traitor and, at best, they will not listen to anything I have to say. My father might help us, but you said that there was no way we could get past the Tandoran blockade and the forcefield that surrounds the Velta."

"I've got an idea," Roger began. "Maybe the way to go about this is to talk to some of the northerners who are already living inside of the Empire? They can go back to their dens and bargain for help."

"I really do not think we can count on help from northerners, but Roger's plan stands a better chance of success," Aneme said. "If you want, I could help you draft a bargain to offer those people."

"Something troubles me..," Adinis said.

"What?" Roger asked.

"Northerners have been leaving the Empire," Adinis said. "There were never very many here, but over the last two weeks about 2000 have emigrated out."

"Any idea why?" Roger asked

"They probably realized that the troops were being trained in the northern arts, and they no longer feel safe here," Aneme said. "They will also be greatly concerned over who revealed their secrets to outsider. You see, even though you have northerners in the Empire they still see themselves as a separate people. The northern people have a bunker mentality, and many of them see the entire world as either a threat or a potential threat."

"You don't think it has anything to do with the impending Kaarumite attack?" Adinis asked.

"No way," Aneme said.

"We don't need them," Roger said.

"If the Great Maker is with us then no one can stand against us," Aneme said.

"And yet we still do our best to prepare," Adinis said.

"We are commanded to do every good thing we set to do to the best of our ability," Aneme said. "We have done our best, and we will keep doing our best. I am willing to help you draft an agreement to present to the northerners living in the Empire if you want to enlist the aid of their native dens."

The Emperor was silent for over a minute, and he looked down as he chewed his food slowly.

"Yes," he said as he looked up again. "Even if they do not come during this war, I believe we will need it for a later time."

"I'll do it," Aneme said.

"Adinis," Roger said. "There are some things that have been bothering me, and now that things have gotten calm before the big storm, I have had some time to think."

"What troubles you?" Adinis asked.

"Well, when we first arrived in Randar some men tried to kill you. Did you ever figure out what that was all about?"

"Yes we did actually… The men resisted all attempts at interrogation. They said only that they were Imperial citizens, and that they did not care for the way things were being run. Of course we knew this was a lie due to our truth machines, but they volunteered no information. We could tell only that they were not Kaarimutes, and that they were westerners. During the investigations we found that only one of the men was a natural born Imperial citizen. The others were all immigrants. We also found that they were all members of the Brotherhood."

"How did you figure that out?"

"As you know we have machines that can map every cell in the body without being physically invasive, and we scanned each man. One of our doctors noted that there was a subtle pattern of scar tissue which all of the men shared on the interior side of their lower lips. He elected to examine the men, and he found a small triangle etched into each man's lower lip on the inside of his mouth, so that if the man should roll out his bottom lip it would appear as an upside down triangle."

"The symbol of Gro-Sho-Var," Aneme said.

"And the symbol of the Brotherhood as well," Adinis replied. "After finding the symbol the men were asked very specifically if they were members of the Brotherhood. Since they all either chose to remain silent or lied by saying no, we knew that they were."

"Why does the Brotherhood want to kill you?" Roger asked.

"They have many of the world's leaders hanging on their strings, but the Empire has continually refused their presence," Adinis said. "They approached me for membership three years ago, and when I refused they said that I was foolish, and that without them I would not be able to avert 'certain catastrophes'. I took it as a threat and ordered them to never appear before me again."

"Why did you even meet with them in the first place?"

"It was not by choice. They tried to arrange a meeting with me on many occasions, but I refused each and every time. They finally caught up to me when I was on tour in a small western country to the northwest of here. It was a group of men at a nearby table who were there before I arrived."

"So they did try to kill you eventually? The scum!"

"Yes… Although I really think that their threat implied more than an assassination attempt."

"What else?"

"I don't know yet."

"Whatever happened to the assassins?" Aneme asked.

"They were executed publicly," Adinis replied. "You two must have been so busy that you missed news. I would have preferred to execute them privately, but they attempted to assassinate the emperor publicly, so they had to be executed publicly according to our law."

"Makes sense," Roger said.

"Was there anything else on your mind Roger?" Adinis asked.

"That crystal I found in the Plaza of Two Moons… Did you ever figure out what was on it?"

"Not yet, but my best men are working on it. You will be there when we view its contents for the first time."

"Thanks. It's very important to me."

CHAPTER 15

The Horde

ROGER STOOD IN A HIGH place. Whether he was on top of a tall building, or a hill, or just somewhere in the air was impossible to tell, but what he could be certain of was the view. There were men, thousands, or perhaps millions, spreading out as far as the eye could see, covering the grassy plains like ants on a piece of food that was left on the ground.

As he looked closer he could see that there were many beasts among them, and a few brutal looking women here and there tending the beasts. The Kaarumite horde was on the move.

Suddenly Roger surged forward, or at least the view changed in such a way as to give the impression of that. The Kaarumites and the occasional broken weathered husk of a war decimated tree shot beneath him with increasing speed. The numbers of Kaarumites were definitely in the millions, perhaps more.

The speed at which they went by increased until the landscape below became nothing more than a grayish blur. Finally it began to slow, and an enormous man loomed up ahead. The man was easily twice Roger's height, and as Roger approached he leaned his head back and roared. The sound that came out was anything but human. It was more like the roar of a giant beast, or a herd of beasts.

Roger knew immediately that he was looking at none other than Atuskus-Var, the alleged son of Kaarum. When he finished his roar he looked down at Roger and smiled. Although his appearance was humanoid, the intelligence that looked at him from behind those eyes was definitely not human. Roger had a somewhat similar experience the first time he spoke with sokes, but the feeling of otherness is where the similarity ended. The impression he got Atuskus-Var was that he was neither soke nor human, and there was a malevolent hunger to him.

Atuskus-Var opened his mouth as if he were going to speak, and then everything blurred and Roger found himself lurching into an upright position on his bed. Aneme was on the other side of the room already dressed.

"What?" she asked.

"They are coming," Roger said.

"Yes, I also just received word from the Emperor. He wants us in the war room."

Roger got dressed quickly, and together they went to the war room, where they found Garek, Nirin, the Emperor, and the usual collection of Imperial strategists. There were multiple maps projected up into the air at varying levels of magnification. The Empire had many drones hovering far above the world, which the backward Kaarumites lacked the technology to reach, so they were afforded with a full view of the approaching armies and plenty of advanced warning.

"They are coming," said the Emperor.

"They have crossed the line into the contested area, all along the line, and by their movements we are projecting that they are going to hit all along the northern defense line so that they can overrun the western city states and hit us from both sides," an advisor said. "They are holding nothing back this time."

"Ships!" Roger said. "What about ships?"

"We are prepared to dispatch the majority of our air vessels," the advisor replied. "They will decimate whatever air forces the Kaarumites have and they will bomb the approaching army with freeze bombs. The Kaarumites are marching close together, so we have given our aircraft a wide dispersal pattern. It is estimated that we can reduce their numbers by 30 to 40 percent."

"No, I mean what about sea vessels? Much of the Empire is bordered by the northern coast of the Sea of Randar."

"They have none because we have allowed them to have none, except for a few small fishing boats. They are technologically moribund. The most sophisticated piece of technology they still remember how to build is the personal forcefield generator. When it comes to vehicles all they have been able to do is conduct sloppy maintenance on vehicles which are already thousands of years old, or build simplistic ground vehicles which generally operate with wheels."

"What do you mean you have 'allowed them to have none'?"

"The Kaarumites have on two separate occasions attempted to build large sea vessels for transportation purposes. In both incidences we attacked by sea and decimated their construction sites. They had made it no further than large steel ribs for the hull. Building is not an area they excel in."

"I want to fly in the bombing raid."

"With respect Commander General," the advisor began. "I don't think that would--"

"Granted," the Emperor interrupted. "I want you to take charge of the mission, in fact. You will be my eyes and ears. I will make the necessary call, but you had best make haste. Report to South Randar Airbase."

Roger nodded. He kissed his wife and ran out of the War Room.

South Randar Airbase was a large complex a few miles south of the city proper, but still within the suburban area which was informally considered a part of Randar. It was one of many, and in fact it was one of the smaller Imperial airbases.

When Roger arrived he was saluted.

"Commander General," the leading officer said.

"You know why I'm here?" Roger asked.

"Yes sir. We have received orders from the Emperor that you are to be given an aircraft and put in charge of the squad that is soon to be deployed from this airbase."

"That's right."

"And you have also been given discretionary powers over the entire fleet."

"Well... That's... good?"

I wasn't expecting that! The whole fleet?

Roger boarded a sleek white aircraft, which was similar in size to the airplanes he flew back home, but considerably more advanced and responsive. Since being in the Empire he had done some flying, but this would be his first combat situation. The first time he flew an Imperial air fighter he found it difficult, but once he understood the layout of the controls and got a feel for how the vehicle responded he found it to be a good deal easier than the USAF fighter planes he was trained on originally.

He strapped himself in, and when the rest of the squad signaled that they were ready he took off, rising straight up into the air, and then shooting forward at a rapid pace. It was not long before they cut diagonally across the Sea of Randar and were soon over the war ravaged Contested Area.

Most of the land was a dull yellowish or greenish color, with a few darker spots of forest, and a significant number of black marks from earth scorchers going off.

"Wonderful place," Roger muttered.

"What's that sir?" a voice said over the receiver.

Oh man! I forgot that this thing was on perpetual broadcast. I better watch what I say since everyone in the fleet is listening.

"Nothing," Roger said. "I'm just reflecting on how wonderful this place is."

Laughter came back through the transmission. As much as Roger liked and respected the northerners, he found the Imperials much easier to get along with. The northerners seldom understood sarcasm, and when they did understand they usually found it irritating.

Now that I think about it… they don't joke very much about anything. Though I've seen that they can have attitudes and do insult people sometimes.

Up ahead he saw a sort of blackness spreading across the ground, like an ant mound which had been stirred up.

"Kaarumites!" Roger shouted.

There were a few vehicles here and there among the swarm of enemy soldiers. They were bulky and sloppy looking things that ran on the ground with wheels or caterpillar treads. Most of the Kaarumites were on foot, but many were mounted.

"What a bunch of barbarians!" Roger exclaimed. "Are they really going to walk the entire way?"

"They have too many people to transport, and they have never been good at mass producing vehicles," one of the men said.

"At that rate it will take them weeks to reach us."

"But they will reach us all the same."

"Let's just do what we came to do. It's unbelievable that they would put so many men and animals out in the open like that knowing what our freeze bombs can do."

Roger gave the order for the others to follow him, and he sped out over the Kaarumites dropping freeze bombs as he went. The others in his squad did the same.

The bombs did nothing. They hit the ground like nuts falling from a tree.

"What is this?" Roger asked. "Is it possible that all of the bombs are bad?"

"It doesn't seem likely sir, and yet, here they have done nothing," one of the other pilots said.

"I'm calling the other squads…"

Roger called the other squad leaders and found that the same thing had occurred all along the enemy lines. The bombs were dropped but they did absolutely nothing.

"They have found a way to counter our technology!" Roger said. "The Emperor must be told."

"Impossible!" a voice said over the transmitter.

"Is it more likely that all our bombs are defective?" Roger asked.

"No, but… Kaarumites don't invent things."

Maybe we've got more on our hands than just Kaarumites to deal with?

Roger called Randar and informed the Emperor of what was happening.

"Order everyone to pull back for now," the Emperor said. "We must come up with a new strategy."

Thousands of Imperial aircraft pulled back, all across the length of the Contested Area, and returned to their respective bases.

"I don't understand what happened," Roger said as he entered the war room.

"Obviously they have found some way to nullify our bombs," one of the advisors said.

"How is it possible?" the Emperor asked.

"It's not!" Garek said. "They have obviously received external help. The question is, who helped them?"

"I thought that the Empire did not share the freeze bomb technology with anyone?" Roger said.

"We did not, at least, not knowingly," the Emperor said. "We cannot discount the possibility of espionage."

"The Kaarumites are not clever enough to infiltrate," Garek said. "Nor are they clever enough to understand such technology."

"But don't they build personal forcefield generators?" Roger asked.

"They do, but that technology is nearly as old as the world itself," an advisor said. "They have not created or invented any new technology since Kaarum became the dominant faith in the south. Throughout their entire existence they have continued to build and repair technology which is thousands of years old. If they have anything new it is typically because they took it or someone sold it to them."

"So the question remains, who would help the Kaarumites and why?" Garek said.

"Perhaps we should attack them now," Nirin said. "My people are ready to move against them."

"The plan was to let them get further into the contested area before we start the attack," the Emperor said.

"That was before we knew the Kaarumites were immune to the freeze bombs," Garek said.

"Agreed, they had a surprise for us, but we also have a surprise for them," Nirin said.

"Vaila," the Emperor said as he turned to Aneme. "You have trained the men who trained our army. Do you think they can compensate for the higher numbers of enemy soldiers they will have to face due to our bombs not working?"

"I wish I could tell you for certain, Sir," Aneme said. "But all I can promise you is that they will do their best."

"We need a miracle," one of the advisors said.

"We cannot count on something like that," Garek said.

"We need more men," another advisor said.

"We have gotten all we can get," Garek said. "What we need to do now is kill as many of those filthy savages as we can so that even if they win they won't be a threat to anyone else for some time. Perhaps Hax will finish where we left off."

"They will not come into this Empire," Roger said.

"How can you be sure?" Garek asked.

"What?" Roger said, "Sorry, I was starting to drift off a little. I've been awake for a long time. I was just thinking out loud."

"Do you have any suggestions, Mattis?" the Emperor asked.

"Well one thing is we need to keep track of those Kaarumites," Roger said. "We have stealth craft. Let's send them out for constant surveillance. Let's see if we can get some actual answers about what these people are doing. Let's also try to slow them down a little. We should have the sokes make the forest grow up ahead of them so they don't have a clear path. But let's not let them see the forest growing just yet. We should also start expanding the forests behind them."

"That sounds prudent," one of the advisors said.

"Yes, we should have them completely enclosed," the Emperor said.

"I agree with that," Nirin said. "The only thing I would add is that we must catch this man Atuskus-Var. Perhaps once he is killed they will lose their confidence."

"But when do we strike?" Garek asked. "We must whittle down their numbers before they go running amok in a mad panic."

"For certain small groups and individuals wandering alone should be picked off," Nirin said.

"Most certainly," Garek agreed. "But when do we decide to launch the primary attack?"

"I think we should wait until we have them completely surrounded, and then we should hit them as hard as we can," Roger said. "But not so hard that we can't sustain the attack."

"The plan is sound," the Emperor said. "Let it be executed at once."

"I would like to oversee the matter personally," Nirin said.

"Very well. You can depart from South Randar Airbase whenever you are ready. Will your wife also be going?"

"No!" Nirin said. "No... She must stay here in Randar where it is completely safe."

"As you wish," the Emperor replied.

CHAPTER 16

The Temple

THE EMPEROR DECIDED TO LET Roger, Aneme, and Garek have the seventh day off, which was a worship day for all followers of the True Belief. The Emperor also elected not to go to the War Room on that day, but all of them were to remain on call in case any emergencies arose. But the sokes were taking no rest. They were hard at work gradually surrounding the Kaarumites with forest.

It was decided that once the Kaarumites were surrounded, the bulk of the Imperial army and the Haxian soldiers, mercenary and otherwise, who were not stationed in the old Tavlon cities would attack from the front. Once the attack was underway the sokes and Haxian soldiers hiding in and around the old tavlon cities would emerge and attack from the rear and sides.

The Kaarumites advanced slowly but surely. The attack was imminent but still over a week away. In the meantime Roger and Aneme attended a religious service with the Emperor.

The service they attended was not in the Temple of Randar. The Emperor liked to attend services at different sanctuaries each week. On this particular worship day they were joined by Garek, for the first time.

Roger wondered if it might not have something to do with the topic of the sermon. Once it became known that the entire Kaarumite army was advancing the war became the main topic of most sermons across the Empire. When Garek found out Kaarum and the war had become the primary topics of the sermons he expressed his approval to Roger.

"The most important thing the religious leaders can do here is get people psychologically prepared for the war," Garek said.

"You mean… prepared for death?" Roger asked.

"No. Prepared for war, ready to fight and kill for their homeland. Even if their religion forbids them from personally hating their enemies, if they hate the ideology that moves their enemies then that's just as good. There should be hate and fear."

"Garek… I don't think that hate and fear is the point."

"It's also good that they are refuting Kaarum, that savage religion of death. Kaarum should be attacked from all angles. Finally the holy men will earn their keep."

But there is something going on with Garek. Inside of the war room he's his usual rough and ready self, but outside of the war room he has gotten more philosophical and pensive.

Throughout the service Garek was passive almost to the point of seeming inert, and Roger got the impression that something was weighing heavily on his mind.

When the service was over Roger and Aneme were about to return to the palace to have lunch with the Emperor, when the Emperor invited Garek to join them. Garek simply nodded his head. Throughout the meal Garek said very little. He seemed to be deep in thought.

"Are you alright man?" Roger asked.

"I don't care for all this waiting around," Garek replied. "I would like to go to the war front and coordinate with Nirin and my people directly."

"We will all go there soon," the Emperor said.

"Really?" Garek said. "You also?"

"Indeed," Adinis replied. "The leader of Kaarum goes with his people to war. We also will go. We will take the great floating city of Leonus, built by my great ancestor Emperor Castilon before the waning of the Empire. It was the largest mobile symbol of Imperial civilization ever built, and one of the oldest symbols of Imperial power."

"Adinis!" the Emperor's wife shouted. "Husband… How can you..?"

"How can I risk myself on the front?" Adinis asked. "Or do you mean to ask; how can I risk one of the oldest and most valuable Imperial monuments?"

"Both!"

"This is an all or nothing battle, my wife. This time both sides are committing everything. At the end of this battle one side will be permanently destroyed, never to rise again. If we lose the battle then there will be no more Empire, and they will destroy all of our valuable artifacts and monuments anyway."

"But if we boarded the floating city with certain experts and scholars we could float elsewhere in the world and we could carry on the spirit of our civilization," Lanicia said.

"Where in the world could we go?" Adinis asked. "The whole of the world is claimed by one entity or another. No, my love, we must throw everything we have into this war."

Garek nodded with approval.

"The floating city will not fall easily," Adinis said. "It has been refitted with new power systems and the latest forcefield technology. It has multiple layers of shielding and redundant power sources. It will be used as a mobile base of operations, a platform for our air vessels to refuel, and a field hospital for wounded soldiers."

"I think the idea is splendid, your majesty," Garek said. "I cannot wait to be a part of it."

"And so you shall, my friend," Adinis said. "Haxians, Imperials, and sokes will fight together for freedom and civilization everywhere."

Garek momentarily rose and saluted the emperor.

OK, now that's just awkward. There is such a thing as a little too much enthusiasm. Especially for Garek, this is way out of character.

"There can be no cause, no war in the history of man more noble than this," Garek said as he took his seat.

Awkward!

"It's a clash of civilizations," Roger said, keeping his eyes on Garek

"It is a clash of civilization verses savagery," Garek said as he clenched his fists.

After the meal Garek took his leave, and a few hours later Roger and Aneme also left.

Once their food settled Roger and Aneme sparred for a while, then Roger decided that he wanted to go out.

"I want to see the Temple of Randar to the Great Maker," Roger said. "I keep hearing how awesome it is but I have yet to see it in person."

"It is too late for us to attend a service there," Aneme said.

"Yes but that's a good thing, because that means there won't be many people there, and we should be able to go in and look around."

"Assuming they will let us."

"Of course they will. We are high ranking Commander Generals. The only guy higher than us is the Emperor."

"Alright."

They drove in the hovercraft as far as they could, but they were not able to park near the Temple. They had to park elsewhere and walk the rest of the way. The Temple was in one of the densest parts of the city, with massive buildings crowded close together, leaving no room for a large assemblage of people except for perhaps in the streets. The buildings were ancient, and had elaborately carved facades.

After seeing nothing but stone and pavement for some time they suddenly came upon a large green space surrounded by a smooth white wall.

"The Temple Grounds," Aneme said.

Two elaborately dressed guards wearing what appeared to be some sort of ceremonial garb stood outside the wall, and on either side of the open gate. Roger and Aneme passed them without a word.

The interior of the Temple Grounds was similar to the Imperial grounds, but more pragmatic. Near the path it was like a city park, with grass on the ground, and large ancient trees growing next to the path on either side. But further off in the distance were orchards, farms, and even some livestock. There were also small buildings within the complex but those were a good distance from the path.

"Originally the Temple Grounds produced its own food for the priests," Aneme said. "Of course many donations were brought for their sustenance, and for the offerings, but the early Emperors wanted the priests to be self-sufficient in case there were any problems with the national food supply."

"Makes sense," Roger said.

"I guess today it is more of an affectation. The priests have plenty of food, and animal sacrifice is no longer a requirement."

They passed few people on the path as they made their way to the Temple. None of them looked particularly priestly to Roger. They all looked like regular Imperial citizens, although there was an unusually high presence of northerners and southerners thrown into the mix.

"This is the most northerners I've seen in one place since we came here," Roger said. "Is something going on that I don't know about?"

"You know the majority of my people are very religious," Anme said. "Many northerners make it their life's goal to go to the Temple of the Great Maker in Randar at least once. Most never get the chance to go."

"I'm surprised you didn't go sooner after we got here."

"We have been so busy, and Adinis has not yet gone there for a service. At least, not since we have been here."

"Yeah… I'm sure he's gone before. The guy likes to church hop. It's probably only a matter of time before he goes there again."

"Church hop?"

"Sorry, I used an English word again without thinking. 'Church' is what we call the buildings that you call 'sanctuaries,' and 'temples.'"

"And the hopping?"

"Because he goes from place to place, like a frog hopping around."

Fortunately there was a word for 'frog,' in that alien language, at least, there was a word assigned to a creature which was reasonably frog-like.

The Temple loomed up in front of them. It was at least five stories tall. The exterior was a smooth bright white material. Aneme said it was stone, but Roger could not see the outline of any individual stone blocks, or any sort of patterns, texture, or blemishing on the walls. It was pure, bright, and solid. In the partly cloudy evening light the Temple almost appeared to be giving off light of its own.

"I kind of expected it to at least be a little faded," Roger said.

"This place is meticulously cleaned and maintained," Aneme said. "There was also some tavlon engineering that went into this design."

They stood on a large porch carved of the same material as the temple itself, with large smooth round columns joining with the patio roof overhead. On top of the patio roof was a balcony which Aneme told Roger the priests would use to address large crowds in the courtyard.

Directly ahead of them were the doors to the temple itself. The doors were made out of a blood red semi-translucent glossy material. There was some abstract imagery carved into the doors consisting of strange creatures which appeared to be chimeras containing both humanoid and bestial elements. There were also strange devices that looked as though they could have either been mechanical or biological. Roger leaned in to study the strange carvings further.

"Do those things have eyes on them?" Roger asked.

Aneme nodded and placed her hand on the doors. Roger did the same. It felt smooth and hard to the touch, like the crystal walls of the cave he visited with Aneme back when they were still living in Velta, before any of the trouble had started for them.

"Did you read the story of the changing of the doors?" Aneme asked.

"Yes, but I don't remember all the details," Roger said.

"The doors were originally composed of northern crystal imported here from the Northern Wastes at great cost."

"Now I remember. Yes, the doors were blue, then a prophet turned them red, or something."

"Yes. When the prophet Theomon came he touched the doors of the Temple, and they turned red. He said that the Temple was now open to everyone, for any and all time."

"A deeply moving and powerful story sister," said a voice from behind.

Roger and Aneme turned to face the newcomer, who appeared to be a full blooded northern male, even though he was dressed in Imperial fashion.

"My apologies, I did not mean to disturb you, but I also came to visit the Temple, and I could not help but overhear your conversation," the man said.

"It's alright," Roger said.

"As a northerner I find this particular miracle to be especially powerful, and personal," the man said.

"I think we all do," Aneme said.

"Ah, so then you can relate," the northern man said. "You also must have some northern ancestry."

Aneme said nothing. The man walked past them and placed his hands on the doors.

"I find the dispensations and the changing of the covenants especially fascinating," he said. "They are my favorite topics of study when it comes to theological matters."

He paused for a moment as he ran his fingers over some ridges which were apparently intended to represent rays of light.

"When I was very young I once created a chart of the various dispensations, for comparison purposes," the northern man said. "All the youngsters in my community did it during the early days of their education. It was one of the first assignments following the mastery of writing…"

The northern man turned away from the doors to face Aneme and said "Perhaps you have done something similar?"

"Perhaps," Aneme replied.

"My apologies," the northern man said. "My name is Anos… Anos Mart, and you are Commander Generals… Mattis and Vaila Maxelis I believe? Is that correct? I have seen you with the Emperor on several occasions."

"Are you following the Emperor?" Roger asked.

"What?" Anos asked. "No! Nothing like that, sir. You see, there are two sanctuary services I like to attend, and the Emperor appeared at both of them. I saw the two of you with him. I tend to sit near the back of each service. Perhaps you did not see me?"

"How long have you been living in the Empire, Anos?" Roger asked.

"I have been here for twenty years. I was badly wounded by a draenock. The vile creature bit my leg off, and I was poisoned with the draenock touch so that the good surgeons were not able to reconstruct a new one for me. The only choice left to me was to move to an advanced western country where they could cure the touch and repair the damage. A one legged warrior is not much good against the draenocks."

"What made you choose the Empire?" Roger asked.

"Of all western nations the Imperials are most like us northerners in temperament and values," Anos said. "But if you have been living here for some time you probably are probably already aware of this."

"Perhaps," Aneme said.

"Perhaps?" Anos questioned.

"An argument could be made for Hax as well," Aneme replied.

"The Haxians have more of our blood, but less in common with us in terms of character," Anos said.

"Well, I suppose you would be in a position to know."

"Indeed yes. Well… I must be going. Perhaps we shall meet again?"

"Perhaps," Aneme said.

Aneme took Roger by the hand and held him in place as they watched Anos leave them.

"Well that was interesting," Roger said.

Aneme shook her head and gave Roger's hand a squeeze. She pointed toward a western man dressed almost entirely in red, with an unusual pattern to his clothes that Roger had never seen the like of before.

"One of the priestly class," Aneme said. "The style of their clothing has not changed since the time of Randar."

Aneme tugged on Roger's hand and led him to the priest.

"Excuse me, minister, I don't mean to impose but, if it is not too much trouble, could you admit my husband and me to one of the prayer rooms?" Aneme asked.

The priest looked them up and down, and when his eyes fell on their rank insignia he seemed to sigh a little.

"Of course, sister," the priest said. "Follow me if you will."

The priest led them through a small door on the side, which was used as a service entry. The floors of the hallway were paved with blue northern crystal, and overlaid with elaborate rugs from time to time. The walls were white, and carved with mostly floral patterns. Sometimes there were images of abstract creatures like what Roger saw on the main doors of the Temple.

At one point the priest instructed them to remove their shoes before proceeding further, and they were required to step through what resembled a small indoor spring. The surface of the shallow pool frothed with some kind of foam. Roger could feel his feet tingle as he stepped through the warm sudsy water.

They passed next to a large open area with a variety of what appeared to be large ceremonial structures. Then they entered another hallway, and were shown to a room which was only about six by six feet in diameter, but there was a low bench which reminded Roger of kneeling benches which existed in churches back on Earth.

For lack of anything better to do Roger knelt down, while Aneme remained standing until the door was shut and the priest was gone.

"Terrible," she said.

"What is going on?" Roger asked.

Aneme seated herself on the kneeling bench next to Roger, but due to its closeness to the ground her knees came up nearly to her chin.

"What?" Roger asked.

"We can talk safely here," Aneme said. "The prayer rooms are sound proof, and there is no surveillance equipment in the Temple."

"What is the problem?"

"That man knows what we are, or at least what I am."

"What man? The priest? Or that northern guy?"

"The northerner of course! Anos Mart."

"But how? You didn't tell him anything."

"He suspected, and he interrogated me. I can recognize a northern interrogation when I see one. I have conducted interrogations before, so I know the northern style, and that is how a northerner interrogates another northerner."

"When would a northerner interrogate another northerner? Under what circumstances?"

"When a northerner is suspected of being a traitor."

"Oh come on."

"No, I knew this could happen. When you teach an entire non-northern nation the Northern Arts it is bound to attract attention, and there were already northerners here. After seeing us with the Emperor someone was going to suspect the truth. Now that man knows for certain that I am a northerner. You he is not sure about. He will report back to his fellows and they will decide what action to take against us."

"How can you infer all that? I would think the first guess ought to be that we are Haxians."

"He was fairly certain that I had northern ancestry, but what confirmed it for him was the question about charting the dispensations. All northern children from the central northern dens are required to do that as part of their early childhood education."

"Alright… What can we do?"

"We should go to the front and join the war effort, with Nirin and Garek."

"Well, Adinis said we were all going to go there anyways. We are going in his floating city thing."

"We need to go sooner. We should go tonight. We can stay in one of the ruined tavlon cities with the Haxians and sokes around us."

"And then what?"

"After the war we can move on and establish new identities elsewhere."

"No. I refuse to keep running for the rest of my life, and I refuse to be scared of your people. We haven't done anything wrong!"

"We have betrayed one of the most guarded secrets of the northern people. Technically I am a traitor."

"Nonsense, and anyways it's been done before with the Haxians. Their version of the northern arts got old and outdated. So will the Imperial version."

"None of that matters."

"Well if you want to go to the front early we can, but I'm not bailing on the Empire. When did you want to leave for the front?"

"Tonight."

"No way. If we do that then we will definitely look like people with something to hide. Why don't we just go back home and sleep on it?"

"Alright…"

They returned home, and there were no incidents on the way. The guards saluted them as they passed. When they went to bed Roger fell into a deep and heavy sleep.

CHAPTER 17

Questions

"WHEN DO WE TAKE OFF?" Roger asked as he stood next to the Emperor looking at the massive structure.

"Tonight," the Emperor Adinis Maxelis replied.

"It won't take the Kaarumites long to notice that they're surrounded, and my guess is that they already know something weird is up."

"But we shall hit them with everything we have."

The floating city of Leonus was not actually floating at the moment. It rested on top of a large steel framework in a military base north of Randar. Many large tubular structures protruded from the base of the city, and dim blue and green lights occasionally pulsated from them for short intervals before winking off. Roger was unable to tell what the foundation of the floating city was made of, whether it was metal, stone, or some composite material, but it looked incredibly heavy.

On top of the foundation was an impressive metropolitan looking city, with tightly packed buildings with smooth rounded edges.

When the city was new the buildings must have gleamed like gold and silver in the sunlight.

Roger knew that Leonus was constructed over 10,000 years ago with the help of tavlons, and that as old as it was it was still looked a good deal more advanced than anything he had ever seen on Earth before he left. He also knew that as heavy as the city might be, there were elements or devices built into the foundation which kept it partially afloat at all times, or at least lessened the effects of gravity so that the steel framework could hold up the massive city.

"Where is your wife?" the Emperor asked.

"She is visiting with some of the men she trained to instruct the army," Roger replied. "She has been trying to keep them around lately."

"Why?"

"Well… they did their training, so she is using them for something else. I think she is a little nervous."

"About the war?"

"Not the war, something else."

"Do you want to talk about it?"

"She thinks that her people are going to come after us."

"Is that a possibility? It would be very bad for both our peoples if that happened."

"I don't think it will happen. Northerners may be upset over what happened but they are still northerners. Highly religious, traditional, and honest people. They could never turn on the Empire."

"Very well. Go and fetch your wife. You two should be aboard prior to take off. I have assigned you quarters near mine."

"Alright, I'll go and get her."

Roger left the Emperor and returned to his personal hovercraft. It would only take him about ten minutes to return to Randar at the speeds the hovercraft was capable of.

As he sped down the road he saw very few vehicles, and from the vantage point of a speeding vehicle the countryside appeared very much like Earth. He passed by farms and forests, and saw herds of animals, and small white buildings which he took for houses.

But of course if I was going slow enough to actually look at things they wouldn't look exactly like Earth.

Finally the tall buildings of Randar loomed up ahead. Randar was actually ringed about with suburbs, not as expansive as one might find around North American cities, but still enough to provide a small buffer between the large metro area and the countryside. But at the point where Roger entered Randar the farmland went directly up against the urban area.

It was not long after Roger passed into the city when he came across a road block. A police officer dressed in white was waiving at him frantically to slow down.

"Now what?" Roger mumbled.

The road was completely blocked, and there were no turn offs that he could spot. He stopped the vehicle and rolled down his window as the police officer approached.

"What's going on?" Roger asked.

"The road is blocked up ahead," the officer said.

"I need to get into the city. How do I get around this?"

"I should say getting into the city is the least of your problems right now," the police officer said as he lifted a gleaming white sphere about the size of a golf ball and hurled it at Roger through the open window.

"What?" Roger shouted as he narrowly dodged the object.

The object hissed and began to release some sort of fog while the police officer outside took a few steps back. Roger fumbled the door open and rolled out of his car. He quickly came to his feet and took out his sword. The police officer did the same.

"What do you mean by it?" Roger demanded, "Who are you?"

"Stop and think about it, traitor, anyone can color their skin," the police officer said.

Roger looked into the man's face more closely, and noticed that he did not have the characteristic features of the western race, which in Earth terms would be described as Mongoloid. His facial structure was consistent with that of the blue skinned northern race, which in Earth terms would be described as Nordic.

Roger felt an immediate surge of adrenaline.

The northerners had come for me! They pieced everything together like Aneme said they would, and now they were going to hold me accountable for betraying their secrets!

"I don't have any quarrel with you," Roger said.

"That's not how I see it," the man replied as he approached.

The man entered a combative posture and began to circle around Roger. Since he had no way of knowing that Roger was not a northerner, he would come at him with all the force and training at his disposal.

First he's going to circle, then he will launch exploratory attacks, and after that the real combat is going to happen in a swift exchange of moves…

Roger had never fought a full blooded northerner who was fully sober, other than his early attack on Doeren before any of his training had begun. But in that situation Doeren was not trying to really kill or even incapacitate him.

"You can come with me voluntarily, or you can come after receiving some damage, but either way you will come," the man said.

"I don't think so," Roger said.

Roger was going to shout for help but the man struck like lightening. He moved so fast that Roger almost could not see his movements.

Almost!

Roger dodged and blocked. The man withdrew and struck again, still with a probing attack. The man was clearly trained in the advanced school of speed, but he was still three times as strong as Roger. Roger could feel the superior strength in the force of the blows he deflected. As he struggled to dodge and deflect the exploratory blows, it occurred to Roger that the actual battle would be similar to a woman fighting a man, which was not necessarily impossible, but it meant that the odds were in favor of Roger's opponent.

Roger heard steps from behind. There were at least three other people approaching, and by the sound of their footfalls he determined that they definitely men, and probably northerners rather than Imperial soldiers coming to his aid.

There was only one thing I can do here…

Roger charged his opponent and quickly tried to shift so that all of his enemies would be on the same side.

His opponent dodged his blow and slipped to the side.

Success!

All of his enemies were on the same side, and beyond the northerner disguised as a police man Roger could see three hooded and gloved figures dressed entirely in white coming towards him. They were powerfully built, and beneath their hoods he could see blue skin. They were each carrying metal tubes in their hands which were each about a foot long at first, but they suddenly expanded to become full length bow staffs as the enemies approached. From that Roger could infer that they at least intended to take him alive, for whatever that was worth.

The newcomers quickly ran into place. Two fell in on either side of the fake policeman and fanned out a bit, while the third took a running jump and flipped over Roger's head to land somewhere behind him.

In a split second Roger decided that it was time for some acrobatics of his own. He would leap through the gap on his right and make a run for it, but as soon as his feet left the ground a hard metal tube struck him across the shins and he fell face first onto the ground. He felt something strike him at the base of the neck and then everything went black.

He heard a dull ringing in the black emptiness for what felt like a few seconds, and when he woke up he was strapped into a chair with metal bands, and shirtless. There was something hard going around his neck which prohibited movement of his head, and a throbbing pain ran through his lower legs, which upon further reflection he found it was actually an amalgam of both dull and sharp pains.

His legs felt warm with pain where they struck him, and he suspected that both bones and skin were broken, or at least fractured. He also guessed that the skin was damaged, but it was impossible to tell if he was actually bleeding without looking down. His neck and head were throbbing.

Aside from the area directly around the chair where he sat, the room was dimly lit. There were at least about five or six people in the room, all northerners, and there appeared to be some medical equipment present.

"Well, look who is awake," said a soothing female voice.

"Why have you taken me?" Roger asked. "Don't you know who I am?"

"We will ask the questions here," said a rough male voice.

Good cop bad cop?

"The problem is, we don't know who you are, but we intend to find out," said the female voice.

"Whoever he is, he's unusually fragile," said another male voice.

"Don't make excuses for your lack of control," said another man.

A northern woman came into the light dragging a metal chair behind her. She deposited the chair so that it's back was facing toward Roger, and then she sat in the chair backwards and leaned toward him against the backrest. Her demeanor was entirely relaxed and casual. She was a darker blue than Roger had ever seen before on any northerner, almost a sea blue, but without any element of gray to it. Her hair and eyes were the same color.

A man stepped into the light next to her and stood there with his arms crossed. He was massive, with upper arms that were at least as big around as Roger's head. Roger speculated that this man might be strong enough to lift a small car by himself given the difference in strength between northerners and normal humans.

"You are concerned about your neck," the woman said. "Two of your vertebra were cracked by the blow. You were nearly killed. The device around your neck is repairing the damage."

"Why bother?" Roger asked. "Don't you plan on killing me anyways?"

"Why would we do that?" the woman asked.

Roger opened his mouth but before he could say anything the woman held up her hand.

"Wait," she said. "Connect him before we go any further."

Another northern man began placing small round white circles on Roger's chest and face at varying points. Then he stepped back and handed the two interrogators each a small black panel, on which glowing displays appeared.

"Now tell me, stranger, is there any reason why we should kill you?" the woman asked.

"No," Roger said.

"Confused readings," said the man.

"Yes, I see that," the woman replied. "It means that he is either an extremely practiced liar or he is uncertain."

"He might also be conflicted," the man said.

"What is your name?" the woman asked.

"Mattis Maxelis," Roger said.

"Same readings," the man said.

"What is your other name?" the woman asked.

Roger said nothing.

"Perhaps his wife will be more forthcoming," the man said.

"What have you done with my wife?" Roger demanded.

"We are asking the questions here," the man said.

"You are making a very serious mistake," Roger said. "They are going to come looking for me."

"We are not in Randar anymore, and we will be well outside of the Empire before they start looking," the man said.

"I don't think so," Roger said. "I'm supposed to be on the floating city when it leaves, and it leaves in three or four hours."

"He is telling the truth," the woman said.

"It doesn't matter," the man said. "He is not going anywhere until we want him to."

"What is your other name?" the woman reiterated. "Was 'Mattis' the name you were given at birth?"

The man snarled and took out a blue knife. With one swift motion he rammed the knife down through the metal armrest between two of Roger's fingers, and the knife handle pressed down against his fingers keeping them immobilized. Roger was startled.

The woman held a hand out toward the man indicating restraint.

Definitely the good cop bad cop routine!

"Did you, or did you not teach the Northern Arts to outsiders?" the woman asked.

Aneme did most of the work, but Roger occasionally stopped in to assist. He said nothing.

"It is a yes or no question," the woman said. "If you can truthfully answer no then we will release you. Can you truthfully answer no?"

Again Roger was silent, his heart beat faster.

"Which zone are you from, and what is the name of your current den?" the woman asked. "What is the name of your native den if it differs from your current?"

Roger said nothing.

"If you do not give us the name of your native den then we will take you back to our den to dispense justice upon you," the man said.

"We can determine your zone through a genetic sampling, in spite of your best efforts to conceal the matter," the woman said.

"Ah!" the man said as he looked down at his panel. "He really does not want us to determine that."

"Take the sample," the woman said.

Another northerner came and took a blood sample from Roger. He carried the sample to a console in the corner and inserted the tube into a round hole.

"The genetic markers will tell us exactly which families and clans you belong to," the man said.

A minute went by and the medic said nothing. The interrogators alternated between staring at Roger and staring at their panels. About five minutes went by and the medic was still silent.

"Well?" the man interrogator finally asked. "Why are you silent?"

"I was double and triple checking the results, sir," the medic said. "He doesn't have any of the traditional northern family markers."

"He's not a northerner?"

"That's the confusing part. The general pattern of his DNA is like ours, but without any of the tribal markers. He could be from some unknown clan, except that… This is so weird!"

"What?"

"There's no enhancements. Granted, we can't tell where the parts of our genome that our ancestors edited end and the natural DNA begins, but there's none of that in this man. He's like some sort of weak parody of a northerner. No wonder he shattered so easily!"

"Perhaps there is something wrong with your machine?"

"No sir, I ran a sample of my own blood through it and it came up perfectly normal."

"So what does it mean? Where is he from?"

"I don't know sir, but I am running a more comprehensive scan on his DNA, full mapping. It will be about ten minutes before I can say anything definitively."

Great…

"Listen," Roger said. "If you let me go then I will make sure the Empire lets you go free."

"We do not fear the Empire," the man said. "We are returning to the north and you are coming with us. If we cannot determine where you are from then you will stand trial for treason, on the grounds that you deliberately trained outsiders in the northern arts."

"But if I'm not from your country then you have no legal grounds for prosecuting me," Roger said.

"That is your opinion," the man replied.

"It would be much easier to return you to your native place, if you could tell us where that is," the woman said.

"Northerners have taught outsiders the northern arts before," Roger said.

"You are talking about Hax of course, and that came about through a mixing of blood following conquest, not an open betrayal," the woman said.

"Don't debate with him," the man said. "Let him save his arguments for the trial."

"Seems like I am already on trial," Roger said.

"When you are on trial it will not 'seem,' it will be as real as the cold and the dark of the Northern Wastes," the man said.

Roger elected to remain silent until they spoke to him again. Inside his head he prayed for the safety of his wife. He hoped that she was able to make it to the war front before the northerners went after her.

Well, they won't take her as easily as they took me. She at least had the original trainees were with her, including Demekus, when I left her in Randar.

"The results are compiled," the medic said, interrupting the silence.

CHAPTER 18

Results

"**W**ELL?" THE FEMALE INTERROGATOR PROMPTED.

"He is not a northerner, at least, not in the sense that we are," the medic said.

"How is this 'detailed' analysis any more enlightening than your original opinion?" the male interrogator asked.

"Well, I have been able to determine that he is not a westerner nor southerner, nor a person of mixed race."

"Then what is he?"

"I we are looking at another derivative of the original northern strain, pre-modification. That would put his point of origin somewhere outside of our range of geographic awareness. He has to be from some uncharted or fringe territory. But I don't know where that would be."

"But what's uncharted? Every part of the world is claimed by some known people."

The brows of both of Roger's interrogators furrowed simultaneously. Then suddenly a light seemed to appear in the woman's eyes.

"Are you from the Eastern Lands?" she asked. "Yes, or no."

Roger did not answer. He did not want to give them any information, out of the fear that they might eventually guess that he was from another world.

Once the toothpaste is out of the tube it can't be put back in.

"Are you some kind of Kaarumite?" the man asked.

Roger laughed.

They have no clue! But that is interesting that they brought up the Eastern Lands. Is it possible that there could be people more like me over there?

"He is not," the woman said.

"He is using medications to artificially disguise his skin," the medic interjected. "I can run his DNA through the computer and extrapolate what his natural coloration looks like."

"Do it," the male interrogator said.

"It's done," the medic said a few minutes later.

Roger's interrogators left him for a minute to go examine a display on one of the medical screens near where the medic was working.

"Unbelievable," the female inquisitor said.

"Is it some kind of mistake?" the male inquisitor asked.

"No mistake," the medic said. "This is his true pigmentation. No wonder he prefers to hide it."

"It's almost like what the Watangas have," the woman said.

"But it is still different," the medic said. "Under normal circumstances this fellow would have a reddish undertone. No one in the known world has pigmentation like that."

"What are you?" the woman said as she turned to Roger.

"Someone who is very dangerous for you to keep prisoner," Roger said.

"Is he some kind of artificial life form?" the woman asked. "Something grown in a lab?"

"I don't think so," the medic replied. "The only thing to do is take him back to our den and let our scientists and inquisitors analyze him thoroughly. Once he's there, we can do a base pair by base pair comparison with DNA from all the different human races that we have on file and determine which group he has the most in common with in terms of over-all percentage. That will give us some idea where he is from since we don't have the time or the equipment to make any solid determinations here."

"But we do," said the male inquisitor.

The man walked back to where Roger was seated and pulled the knife up out of the arm rest. Roger flexed the fingers that had been held in place by the handle of the knife. They had begun to grow numb from the circulation being cut off.

The male interrogator turned the woman's chair around and sat in it facing Roger.

"I am going to ask you yes or no questions, and you will answer me or you will experience physical consequences," the interrogator said.

"What are you doing?" the woman asked.

"Getting some answers," the man replied.

The man held down the ends of Rogers fingers with one hand, and with his other he held the knife about two inches above Roger's first finger.

"Are you from the Eastern lands?" the man asked.

Roger said nothing, but his heart began to beat rapidly. He knew that if he had been captured by Kaarumites they would most certainly have used some sort of physical torture on him by now, assuming they did not kill him right away.

But northerners were supposed to be different! They don't use torture, except on extremely rare occasions when they sometimes punish a psychotic criminal by doing to him or her what they did to someone else!

But those types of executions were rare, and Roger had never heard of Northerners using torture as a form of interrogation. They had their truth machines. The northerners were pragmatic, but not cruel. According to everything he had seen, heard, and read, they tended to be highly religious and lived by a code of not doing to others what they would not want others to do to them.

"I will ask you one more time," the man said. "Are you from the Eastern Lands?"

Again Roger did not answer.

Suddenly the knife dropped. It dropped so gently that Roger did not feel its touch at first. He saw, rather than felt, it dig deep into the skin of his finger. The first thing he felt was the warm blood trickling down the outside of his finger. A few seconds later he felt a slight irritation.

His inquisitor gripped the blade loosely with two fingers.

"I stopped it before it could go very deep," the inquisitor said. "This time I only cut your skin, but if I let this blade slip any lower it will cut through your muscles and become lodged in the bone. If you persist in being obstinate after that I will cut your finger off. As you know, northern blades are the sharpest in the world. You won't feel the pain right away but you will definitely feel it later. We can always regenerate missing body parts for you but there are many things I can cut off before it becomes necessary to do that."

Roger remained silent and tried to keep a straight face. He had been told that all the civilized peoples of this alien world had the technology to fully repair any missing or damaged body part, but he was not eager to test those claims on himself.

"I ask you again, are you from the Eastern Lands?" the inquisitor repeated.

Roger said nothing.

"Very well," the man said.

The blade sank lower, and Roger could feel a grotesque warm sensation in his finger. It was an odd sensation that he had never felt before. He felt a thrill of fear and horror run through him.

This guy is serious!

"Malak, stop it," the woman said.

"Sir, what are you doing?" the medic demanded.

"I'm getting answers from this fool," the male inquisitor, apparently named Malak, said.

"This is not our way," the woman said.

"If it bothers you then get out," Malak said. "All of you get out! I will get the answers."

Roger's head was swimming. He felt like he was going to vomit. He thought that perhaps he should just tell them everything. Things could certainly not get any worse for him.

But then there are worse people who I could be captured by even if I do get out of this… The less people who know my true nature the better.

"We have drugs that can make him talk," the woman said. "Let's just get him up north."

"If you let me go, I will forgive everything," Roger said. "I will tell the Emperor to let you go. Why don't you help us in the war?"

"I'm cutting it off," Malak said.

"Malak, you are out of order," the woman said. "I am relieving you of duty."

"You can't relieve me of duty," Malak said. "We aren't an official northern regiment, we're refugees, so we don't have to follow any regulations. Just step outside and I will finish this quickly."

"No, if we return to our people we are under the code of conduct again," the woman said.

"We need to find out who all of his accomplices are before we return," Malak said. "We have to bring them all in. Our people will understand."

"But I don't, sir," the medic said. "I'm afraid I cannot allow this either. The professionals can get anything from him without the use of torture and mutilation."

Malak scowled at them both, then he pulled the knife up out of Roger's finger, much to Roger's relief. Unfortunately the relief was short lived as Malak put the knife down on Roger's wrist.

"The stakes are higher this time, stranger," Malak said as he rested the knife on Roger's wrist.

What happened next occurred so fast that Roger never quite understood it. The woman put her hand on Malak's arm and a flurry of motion followed. Somehow the medic also became involved and when everything settled Malak was dead on the floor with a slit throat and some other wounds.

The woman had a deep cut on the side of her face and two smaller cuts on her upper arms. She stood over Malak holding a knife of her own. The medic's nose had been crushed and was bleeding. It was all over in under a minute.

"Record that we have performed a field execution on Malak Santary, following an escalation of violence, after being ordered to stand down following erratic behavior," the woman said. "Specifically, unwarranted physical mutilation of a prisoner."

"Agreed," the medic said as he wiped at the blood on his face.

During the fight all of the other northerners had paused in their duties, but after the woman spoke they returned to what they were doing.

"Thank you for saving me," Roger said.

"You are not saved," the woman said. "Since you refuse to give us answers here we will take you to our native den, and turn you over to our inquisitors and medics, who will extract any and all pertinent information. There is still a chance that our elders will determine that an execution is in order, or yours, assuming we are able to derive your point of origin."

"You still think I'm a northerner?" Roger asked.

"I do not know what you are because you have told us nothing but you will soon enough."

"Where are we?"

"That is none of your concern."

"But it should be of concern to you. If we are still in the Empire they will be looking for me, and since you have a facility here then I think we still are. So where in the Empire are we?"

"That is not information you need to know."

"Oh come on. Maybe if you give me something I will give you something."

"You will give us everything we want to know anyways, as soon as you are transported to our facilities back home. In the meantime, we will bandage your wounds," the woman said. "Medic!"

The medic carefully applied a healing salve to Roger's finger and wrist, and bandaged the wounds.

The woman ordered the men to remove the body of Malak.

"Listen," Roger said. "Come fight with us. We need any and every soldier we can get. Aren't you concerned about the Kaarumites overrunning the Empire?"

"There are things in this world much worse than the Kaarumites," the medic said as he finished with Roger's wounds.

"Listen, the floating city is probably about to take off," Roger said. "They will be looking for me even now. I don't know where I am or how you brought me here, but if you let me go then I will arrange to let you go. If you help us in the war then I will arrange to have the Empire help you with the draenocks.".

"You can do that?" the medic asked.

"Yes," Roger said.

"He's just talking," the woman said.

"No, look at your panel. He's telling the truth."

The woman looked down at her panel and reiterated the question.

"Yes!" Roger replied. "You can speak with the Emperor yourself. I understand that you were just trying to protect your people, and I know that you saved me from this crazy guy. If you let me up I will personally take you to the Emperor and put in a good word. If you help us then we will help you. Yes the Imperials know the Northern Arts, but that just puts them in a better position to help you. If you are in charge now then it's up to you. Make the right choice. Make the smart choice. You can save your own people."

"I am not authorized to speak for my den," the woman replied. "We have been away for over ten years now, and out of contact."

"But aren't you in charge of this group now that Malak is dead?"

"This 'group' is not a formal thing with an established leader. We're really just concerned northerners who decided to take matters into our own hands. We don't even all originate from the same den."

"But you can still speak for us to your den, and maybe the other guys can talk to their dens."

"You will have to give me full disclosure before I can report back to my people."

"If you are trustworthy then I will tell you everything."

"My people will want full tech upgrades at the very least."

"I can get that for you," Roger said.

The woman fell silent and her eyes narrowed.

"What do we do?" the medic asked. "He is being completely truthful. He did give away the Northern Arts, but we do need technological and logistical help. We are thousands of years behind westerners technologically."

"I know… I know…" the woman said.

"What is your name?" Roger asked.

"Marla," she replied.

"Where are we right now, Marla?" Roger asked.

"In the northern forest reserve, still in the Empire," she replied.

"They are going to come for you soon. There are sokes in this forest. If any of them spotted you then Imperial troops will be coming here soon."

"How can there be sokes here?" Marla asked. "There are no sokes in the Central Lands."

"There are now."

"How can you be sure? And why would they work with humans of any sort?"

"Because, I brokered the alliance, and the Empire brought them here. We have an alliance with the sokes and the Haxians. We are going to divide up the Contested Area between them, and maybe even part of Kaarum, but in order to do that we have to win. We think we can win but it's going to be hard, and it's going to be close. A lot of men are going to die. Please, we need all the help we can get."

Marla hesitated. She looked down and her eyes moved back and forth rapidly.

"What are we going to do?" one of the other northerners asked.

"You have to let me up before they get here," Roger said. "If they come here and find me captive like this then it's going to look real bad."

Marla quickly released Roger, and as he got up he felt a series of sharp pains in his legs that caused him to wince.

"You guys also broke my shins, didn't you," Roger said. "I can tell that they aren't fully repaired."

"I apologize for that," Marla said. "We didn't know you weren't a northerner until we ran the genetic analysis."

"Yes… I'm a bit more squishy than a real northerner would be."

"I take it you won't tell us what you really are?"

"No. Not right now anyway."

A northern woman came running in and announced that Imperial soldiers were approaching from all sides.

"I will go outside to meet them," Roger said. "Give me your forcefield generator, and quick."

Marla quickly removed an armband and placed it on Roger's arm.

"I'll go out alone and let you know when it's safe to follow," Roger said.

Roger was escorted into an adjacent room with a latched metal door at the other end. Marla undid the latches and turned a wheel in the center, and the door opened and sunk inward. The door slid off to the side and Roger stepped out into the forest.

He took a few steps and looked back. A dull gray hovercraft sat on the ground behind him, which was about the same size as the average mobile home back on Earth. Marla nodded at him from inside the door. A sleek white aircraft came to hover over the roof of the dull gray vehicle. A few other white aircraft hovered away at some distance, and Roger could make out armored Imperial troops approaching. There were many of them. He waved as he saw them, and they came.

He saw Aneme among the troops, and when she saw him she came running. She hugged him for some time and then released him. Roger would have kissed her forehead but he was unable to bend his neck. A scowl spread across her face.

"What happened?" she said as she glared at his injuries.

"Northerners," Roger said.
"Did you escape?" Aneme asked.
"They let me go."
"Just now?"
"Yes."
"Are they in there?" Aneme asked pointing towards the gray vehicle.
"Yes," Roger answered.
"They will be held accountable."
Aneme drew her sword and motioned toward the vehicle.
"Wait!" Roger shouted. "Wait, it's not that simple."

CHAPTER 19

Embassy

ROGER DID HIS BEST TO explain exactly what happened. Aneme settled down as he explained and returned to her usual calm demeanor, but Roger could sense that she was still simmering on the inside.

"Just think about it pragmatically, we need to have all the help we can get," Roger said. "We have been looking for a way to get northerners on our side for a long time."

"Very well, let the brave people come out so that I can meet them," Aneme said.

Was that sarcasm?

"Marla come out," Roger said.

Marla came out and stood next to Roger. Immediately she recognized Aneme as a northerner and offered her the formal northern greeting. Aneme hesitated, then she placed her hand on the other woman's shoulder and allowed her to do the same.

"Well now, that's good," Roger said.

"It was a field execution?" Aneme said.

"Yes, the commander was out of control," Marla said. "We gave him sufficient warning."

"Who authorized your mission?" Aneme asked.

"No one, we took matters into our own hands as patriotic northerners, but we were planning on returning both of you to your respective dens for trial."

"No one authorized your mission, and yet you still dared to lay hands on an Imperial Commander-General? The highest rank possible short of being the Emperor?"

"Yes. I apologize for the damage to your husband, but being a northerner—"

"I understand why you did it."

"Then you bear no grudge?"

"I didn't say that either. Our religion forbids grudges, but this isn't the Northern Wastes. You do understand that when people lay hands on Imperial officers in the way you did they are typically executed?"

"Yes, and I won't ask you for any favors. If we're guilty by Imperial law, then it is what it is. We brought it on ourselves."

"You followed the unwritten laws of our people, but they conflicted with the written laws of the Empire. I understand why you chose to do what you did, and though I don't at all care for how you laid hands on my husband, I do thank you for protecting him from your commander."

"You shouldn't thank me. Everything I did was in accordance with our ways, from beginning to end. My commander was in the wrong. I'm just glad we were able to resolve this without more fighting."

"So am I. It's not good for the family to spill its own blood."

"I promised her an audience with the Emperor, and dismissal of any charges against her and her people," Roger said.

"I'm sure that will be no problem," Aneme said.

The rest of the northerners came out of the gray hovercraft, and everyone was taken to the floating city of Leonus. Roger was placed inside of a medical regeneration pod, where he was put into a deep sleep.

He awoke later to find Aneme standing outside of the pod waiting for him, along with Marla and the northern medic, whose name was Venn. Both of them appeared to be fully healed, and were dressed in casual Imperial attire.

"How long was I out for?" Roger asked.

"Ten hours," Aneme replied. "There were some complications in your neck."

"Still amazing."

"The Emperor is ready to meet with us."

"Let's go right away."

The interior of the floating city of Leonus was no less impressive than the Imperial Palace. The walls were covered with relief carvings, which were either in gold, stone, or in some places enormous jewels. The floors were made of some glossy black material that may have been stone. Even though the exterior of the city was weathered with time, the inside appeared new and fresh with gleaming brilliance wherever one looked.

The technology that went into the making of Leonus was more advanced than anything Roger had seen back on Earth, with the exception of the craft he had arrived in, but the structure itself was older than the Great Pyramid of Egypt.

I can almost feel the antiquity of this place!

Roger could also tell that the style, materials used, and much of the technology was old by current Imperial norms. He hoped that the amazing antique structure was not simply being sent to its destruction.

What a shame it would be if that happened!

The faces of all three of the northerners remained expressionless. If they were impressed by anything they saw there was no way of knowing. Aneme had already briefed the Emperor on what transpired, and what it was Roger wanted to do while Roger and the wounded northerners were being healed.

When they arrived in the office of the Emperor, Marla and Venn saluted.

"I thank you for the show of respect," the Emperor said. "Please be seated."

Everyone sat down in front of the Emperor's desk.

"You do understand that under normal circumstances what you did would be considered as an act of terrorism, and treason since you and all of those with you were nationalized as Imperial citizens some time ago," Adinis said.

"We understand," Marla said.

"I have chosen to drop all charges because Mattis asked me to," the Emperor said. "But nothing like that must ever happen again."

Marla and Venn nodded.

"I am sorry to begin our conversation on such a sour note but some things have to be stated openly for the sake of formality," Adinis said.

"And to establish where all parties stand, no doubt," Venn said.

"Precisely," Adinis said. "But now that it has been stated we can move on to more agreeable matters."

"If you will pardon me, sir," Marla said. "But just for further clarification; is our pardon contingent upon an alliance? Because I cannot make decisions for my people."

"No," Adinis replied. "Your pardon is because of Mattis. You are free to walk out of this office right now if you wish and no action will be taken against you."

"Oh."

"So you wanted to discuss an alliance?"

"I am interested. But first we must have full disclosure, because there are many things that I do not understand. We must know some of your secrets before we can reveal ours. You already have the Northern Arts, but to know the location of our den is another matter."

"What do you want to know?"

"To start off with, do you intend any harm against the northern people? OR the other free peoples of the Central Lands?"

"We do not."

"Would you be willing to repeat that into a truth machine?"

"You are impertinent!" Aneme interjected forcefully.

"Please forgive my associate," Venn said. "We northerners are a cautious people, distrusting of outsiders, and we are not as polished as natural born Imperial citizens. Our society is a simple one, and our ways are direct."

"I understand," Adinis replied. "I would submit to a truth machine. I can have the necessary equipment brought here if you wish."

"I would like that, as well as a record of our conversation, including the readings," Marla said. "For the sake of fairness Venn and I will also be connected."

"I will have some brought immediately," the Emperor said.

"If you please sir, we would like to use our own equipment," Marla said. "Our people will be more accepting of the results that way."

"Whatever it takes," Adinis said.

"Go and get it," Marla said to Venn.

Venn left and returned some time later carrying a locked metal chest. He opened it up and began removing the equipment. The medical scanners and sensors were connected to everyone present, and the equipment was switched on. Once the equipment was activated Marla repeated her questions to the Emperor and recorded the results.

"And now, for the benefit of my people, what exactly is your tactical situation, what are you willing to offer my people, and what is the story behind Mattis and Vaila?" Marla asked. "We already know that Mattis is not a true northerner. What is he and where is he from?"

"Mattis, are you willing to disclose?" Adinis asked.

"Do you think it's a good idea?" Roger asked.

"It might be necessary to secure their cooperation. Whether it's good or not... that's not a judgment I can make for you."

"Who is going to hear all of this, Marla?" Roger asked.

"Just the elders of my den," Marla replied.

"Well... you can't make an omelet without breaking a few eggs..."

"Make a what?"

"Don't worry about that. My actual name is Roger Strauss."

"I have never heard such a name before. Where are you from?"

"Another universe."

"A what?"

"A separate reality, where the laws of physics and the structure of the universe are different. Listen..."

Roger briefly described the structure of the solar system, and explained how he arrived in their universe as best he could. He recounted the training he received from the northerners in Velta, and summarized the events that followed as best he could without giving away any more sensitive information than necessary.

"An incredible story," Marla said.

"But he is not lying, and that would explain why we could not match his DNA with anything known," Venn said.

"Yes I know, and I don't think anyone here is lying either, but it just seems too incredible to be true," Marla said. "But... there are prophecies about a man from another world. I had no idea what those prophecies meant, until now. Well... I had an idea, but I thought the man of another world would be a holy and flawless man from the heavens."

"That doesn't sound like me," Roger said.

"We are prepared to offer you land and technology in exchange for help," Adinis said.

"How much land and technology?" Marla asked.

"That depends on how many people you can bring," Adinis said.

"They disclosed their secrets, it is only fair that we share ours," Venn said as he turned to face Marla.

Marla nodded.

"We come from Kenna Den," Venn said. "Which is one of the largest dens in the south-central region of the Northern Wastes. Kenna Den is probably the most powerful den in its zone, according to the estimates. Our people patrol regularly an area that is about the same size as a third of the Empire, but our people assist other dens all across the mid-section of the Northern Wastes.

"Our den is large, but it is incredibly overcrowded, with the average family just sharing a one room apartment. That is why many of our people have emigrated south over the last 200 years. We tried to establish two new dens in recent years, but it is difficult to do that without being discovered by the draenocks. We succeeded in establishing a smaller den to the west of Kenna, but the one we tried to dig toward the east was discovered by draenocks during the building process and destroyed.

"We have more people than ever before permanently living in temporary shelters on the surface, due to overcrowding, and that is very dangerous. We would like to coordinate with all the other dens so that we can permanently reclaim the surface, but the most we are able to do is collaborate here and there for specific strikes."

"Don't northerners trust other northerners?" Roger asked.

"Usually, but the majority of northerners do not even like to disclose the location of their home den to other northerners for fear that they may be captured and forced to reveal it," Venn said. "We are what our enemies have forced us to become."

"With the full force of the Empire behind us we could do serious damage to the draenocks, and if the other dens see how effective the alliance is they may want to join," Marla said.

"We are willing to relocate as many people to the south as are willing to go, but in the meantime we would like as many fighters as possible to secure the land necessary," Adinis said. "Also, we are in desperate need of new technology," Venn said. "Our medical technology and computers are thousands of years out of date. We have been patching them up as best we could, but it has gotten to the point where many of our people have even forgotten how to maintain the existing technology. There are less than 100 of us who understand how the medical technology is put together, and fewer still who know how to manufacture new parts."

"That is pretty terrible," Roger said.

"The continuous emigration has resulted in a brain drain," Venn replied.

"I am willing to send technical experts and materials as a show of good faith prior to the arrival of any troops from your den," Adinis said.

"Most kind," Marla said.

"Do you have any additional materials we can take back to show our people?" Venn asked. "Perhaps some presentations showing what you and your allies are doing, and what kind of power and technology you have? Maybe even a live soke to talk to our people?"

"I can give you the footage you want," Adinis said. "As for a live soke, I don't think that any of the third kindred would fare well up in your frigid climate, but I will ask Roger to find one who is willing to go with you if you can guarantee his safety."

"We will guarantee it with our lives," Marla said.

"Very well," Adinis said. "Roger, see to it."

"I'll see what I can do," Roger said. "But they need to know what it is they are getting into up there with the cold and all."

"When can you be ready to go?" Adinis asked.

"When we have the footage and the soke," Venn said.

"Come to me when you are ready, and I will have my people transport you and your belongings as far north as you wish to go," Adinis said. "They will wait at a designated point for your return."

"I understand," Marla said. "We will do our best to convince them."

The Emperor delayed the launch of the floating city of Leonus for another day, in order to see to it that the northerners had everything they needed before they took off. All of the northerners who had captured Roger boarded a medium sized air transport which sat on one of the circular air pads of the city.

Roger was able to find a soke who was willing to go with them. It was a 20 year old male soke with bright green skin, and his primary motivation for going was because he thought the "place of the blue ones" would be interesting as an abstract sight to see.

"After this, I should also like to see a coral reef," the young soke said.

"You do understand that this is for a mission, right?" Roger asked.

"Of course, and if there is a mission to a coral reef later on I also volunteer for that."

"Alright, but be careful. It's going to be frigid cold up there, and the nearest suitable plants will be a good ways off in case you have to respawn. You won't be able to do much photosynthesis up there, and you need to make sure you wear whatever clothes the northerners tell you to wear."

"I understand."

Roger wondered if he had not sent the soke off to a slow death, or at least the death of his current body.

Even if something happens, the energy form should be able to migrate far enough south to generate a new body in a forest some place.

Roger, Adinis, and Aneme watched the air vessel shoot off into the northern horizon at incredible speeds.

"Now we launch," the Emperor said. "We have delayed for long enough."

"And if the northerners agree to the terms and come back?" Roger asked.

"We will be called, and you or your wife will return to Randar to coordinate directly with them," Adinis said.

Roger & Aneme in Leonus
—by Ivor Kovac

CHAPTER 20

Air Battle

ROGER STOOD WITH HIS ARMS folded behind his back. The wall in front of him was nothing but a series of windows, and the setting sun filled the room with yellow-orange light. He watched as they passed over the contested area.

Aneme entered the room from behind and put her hand on his shoulder.

"What are you looking at, my husband?" she asked.

"Forests… and forests, and forests…" Roger said. "The land looks so different from when we were here last."

"And it will be even more different when this is all over."

"I cannot see that far ahead."

"Of course you can," Aneme said as she leaned her head against his shoulder.

Roger placed a hand on her head for a minute, then he ran his fingers through her long black hair, which she now often wore loose and free except during training or combat.

I guess it means she's feeling more confident and relaxed.

She was still completely black and white except for her eyes and lips. Roger wondered if after the battle they could revert to their true colors and names. He wondered if, after the successful defeat of the Kaarumites, the Empire and its alliance would be strong enough to resist Tandor.

But even if they are… can I justify putting them into the position of defending me from Tandor just so that I can look like my normal self again? Tandor's not just going to stop.

He felt certain that at some point in time Aneme would return to her normal pigmentation. He had two dreams about her back on Earth. The first one had already come true in the cave of blue northern crystal. The second happened in a place he had not seen yet, and she was entirely blue, as she was when he first saw her, but her hair was longer.

"That didn't happen yet," Roger muttered.

"What?" Aneme asked.

"But it wasn't like any place I saw in the Empire…"

"What is it Roger? What place?"

"Sorry, I was just trying to make sense out of some old dreams."

"Do you want to talk about them?"

"Do you miss having blue skin and hair?"

"I never really thought about it. Things are what they are. I am glad my injury is finally gone and that I can be with you during this world changing time."

"I still don't understand how you had the draenock touch without having been touched by a draenock."

"Let's not worry about that right now. Why don't you get some rest while you can? We are going to be in the battle zone soon enough, and there will be very little peace then."

"Alright… I am feeling tired."

Aneme took him by the hand and led him back to their quarters. As soon as he hit the bed he was asleep. He felt a slight sensation of falling.

He awoke later to the sound of a siren blaring. Immediately he rose up and went into the tactical center where he found the Emperor, his advisors, and Aneme already waiting for him.

"What's going on?" Roger asked.

"We are over the battle zone," the Emperor said.

Roger looked at a holographic display of the ground beneath them, and the formerly green fields had become black with enemy units.

"Put them on," the Emperor said.

A holographic projection of Garek appeared next to the table in the center of the room, and another one of Nirin appeared close by. A few more showing various generals, some of which Roger did not know, also appeared.

"The attack has started," Nirin said.

"Confirmed," said Garek.

"Confirmed," said another general, and then another.

"There is confusion in the forward Kaarumite ranks," the Emperor said.

"That is our doing," Nirin said. "The stupid Kaarumites attempted to march on into the forest ahead of them, so we began ensnaring them and attacking them as best we could with the foliage. We have killed hundreds of them already with the help of the Haxians."

"My pleasure," Garek said.

"Some of them have panicked and run backwards while their fellows behind them continue to press on," Nirin said. "There is some killing of Kaarumites by Kaarumites as those in retreat encounter the bulk of their ranks, who do not yet know what is going on."

"Savages," one of the generals said.

"If possible we need to get some of their equipment, specifically one of those things they are using to nullify the freeze bombs," Roger said.

"I will see if I can get one for you," Garek said.

"Garek, don't take any unnecessary risks," Roger said. "Just do it if it's convenient."

"Any excuse to kill these savages is a convenience. By the way, are you coming down Roger?"

"Yes, as soon as it's possible for me. Do we have any idea where those devices are?"

Garek shrugged, and Nirin shook his head, the other generals did not know either, but there were many vehicles dispersed throughout the Kaarumite army, most of which ran on wheels or caterpillar treads.

"It may be these," said one of the advisors present.

He tapped the visual display in the center of the table until it zoomed in over a boxy looking metal device with a series of antenna on it.

"I have noted that they are distributed equidistantly throughout the Kaarumite ranks," the advisor said.

"Find one near the edge of their ranks, preferably close to Garek or Nirin, and I will go down and get it," Roger said.

"I think I can do just tha—"

The advisor was cut off by another alarm.

"Now what?" Roger asked.

"I don't know, but we are getting mass readings in the air," an officer said. "Coming up from the south."

"Show me," the Emperor said.

A large screen behind the Emperor lit up to show the southern horizon. Off in the distance they could see a swarm of specks in the air, like a flock of black birds.

"Enlarge," Roger said.

The image zoomed in to show a fleet of dull gray colored airships. Some were immensely large, while most were medium sized, but there was also a significant number of small one-man fighters.

"Where did they get all those ships?" one of the officers asked.

"They have been saving them for such an occasion as this," the Emperor said. "They are sending everything they have against us this time."

"That does look like a lot of ships," Aneme said.

"It looks like a swarm of locusts," Roger said.

"A what?" someone asked.

"But what good are they?" Aneme asked. "Their ships are thousands of years old, and we still have more than they do."

"Yes," Adinis said. "But even an old ship can be deadly if armed with modern weapons and shields."

"Do you think they are?" Aneme asked.

"Why not?" an advisor said. "Someone gave them the technology to nullify our ice weapons."

"I want all combat vessels currently in Leonus deployed, as well as any that are sitting idle back in the Empire," Adinis said.

"Wait!" Roger said. "Do we really want to deploy all of the ships in the Empire?"

"Perhaps not," the Emperor said. "Officer, modify the orders. I want to leave behind a skeleton contingent of airships."

"Yes, sir," an officer said as he picked up a headset and prepared to make a call.

"Once all the combat fliers are deployed from Leonus, I want our type one and type two shields up, nothing will get in or out," the Emperor said.

"I want to go," Roger said.

"Go," Adinis replied. "You are in command of the Leonus fleet. Stay in constant contact with us while you fight."

"Sir!" Roger said as he saluted and ran out.

Roger boarded an Imperial fighter craft which was about the same size as the military airplanes he used to fly back on Earth, but it handled a good deal more smoothly and responded far more quickly.

He took off vertically and sped off with a flock of other gleaming white aircraft. Once they were outside of the regular forcefield for Leonus they received a signal from the Emperor that he was raising the type one forcefield.

The type two forcefield was standard for all military vehicles and personnel, as well as many military installations. It was the sort of forcefield that would block fast moving objects and high level energy bursts, but allow for air and slower objects to pass through. The type one forcefield would admit nothing, not even air. It was therefore seldom used except in large facilities which could recycle their own air, or it was used to shield part of an area.

As the Imperial aircraft approached the ancient Kaarumite vessels they let loose with a volley of freeze missiles. The missiles struck against their forcefields and crumpled, or bounced off harmlessly.

"Hold your fire!" Roger shouted to the entire fleet. "Hold all firing of freeze missiles!"

"Mattis!" the voice of the Emperor shouted over the communicator. "What is happening?"

"Our freeze weapons are ineffective against their airships as well," Roger said. "Whatever they have to protect themselves on the ground must also be in the air!"

"Try your other weapons."

"Will do, sir."

The other type of weapons the aircraft were equipped with were earth scorchers, which were designed to release incredible amounts of heat, sufficient to melt dirt and stone, along with a concussive wave of energy.

Roger waited until the Imperial craft were flying among the Kaarumite vehicles before he gave the order to fire. He knew that the Kaarumite vessels would all be equipped with forcefields, probably all type two, which meant that a single shot would not destroy any of them. He focused on a large lumbering Kaarumite ship, which was so dark it almost appeared black, and he sent a message to his squad to target what he targeted.

Roger flew so close to the vehicle that he could make out the large clumsy looking rivets on the patchy and rusted exterior, then he let loose with his weapons. Two of the missiles made it out before the whole world seemed to be swallowed up in an orange light, obscuring Roger's view of everything momentarily.

His vehicle lurched sharply, as if struck, and the next thing he knew he was about a mile above the fleet, from which point the clouds looked like tiny puffs of cotton. The blast had deflected him into the upper atmosphere.

As he looked down he saw another series of bright flashes which quickly erupted into tremendous spheres of orange light before disappearing. His squad was targeting the same ship that he did.

When the explosions stopped Roger dropped back down to the battle. The ship was still flying, and it was undamaged, other than some black char marks on the top. Apparently the forcefield around it had been skin tight.

So we aren't going to be able to fly in close detonate a weapon on the ship itself.

A more conspicuous effect of the explosions was that the enemy fleet was now more spread out and scattered, which Roger guessed was probably a result of the concussive waves of energy striking against their shields. Further down Roger could see that the forest was burning in many places, but fortunately it all seemed to be in the tops of the trees.

"We need to find a way to get around their shielding," Roger said. "If we were any closer to the ground we might have hurt some of our own people with those explosions."

The Kaarumite fleet slowly regrouped and continued on north toward where the battle was taking place on the ground.

"Mattis," the Emperor said. "I want you to run close quarters reconnaissance and see if you notice anything unusual or out of place."

"Understood sir," Roger said.

Roger and his fellow pilots wove in and out among the Kaarumite air vessels. The enemy ignored the Imperial aircraft completely and pressed on toward the battlefield. Off to his left Roger noticed an Imperial fighter collide with a one man Kaarumite fighter. The two objects bounced off of one another in a way that reminded Roger of pool balls.

They both tumbled through the air, but it took the Kaarumite fighter a bit more time to stabilize and stop rolling. The shields kept both craft from being damaged, but the Kaarumite craft seemed to lack the high quality concussive dampening field that existed inside of Imperial craft in case of collision.

But the Kaarumite aircraft did stabilize, and as soon as it did the pilot quickly sped back into formation. Something about the movement of the Kaarumite air fighter struck Roger as frantic on some level. Then an idea occurred to Roger.

Roger turned the nose of his aircraft toward the zenith and shot upward at a 90 degree angle from the ground. The sky grew a little darker ahead of him before he slowed down and leveled off. When he looked down the enemy aircraft were a series of tiny specks, but some specks were larger than others.

"Computer, take a still image of the enemy craft beneath and display image on secondary monitor," Roger said.

One of the monitors beneath the viewport lit up with an image of the enemy fleet and the landscape below.

"Highlight the carrier sized vehicles in red," Roger said.

The carrier sized air craft were vehicles that were over two hundred feet in length. Some of them were literally as large as Earth type marine aircraft carriers. A series of red specks appeared on the screen. They were spaced equidistantly and formed a grid of sorts.

"Now highlight all the other enemy aircraft in blue," Roger said.

A good deal more blue specks appeared, and they were all clustered within a certain radius of the red specks.

"Send this image to the Emperor and the strategists in Leonus," Roger said.

"Is this what I think it is Mattis?" the Emperor asked a few seconds later.

"Yes," Roger replied. "They are clustering around the big ships. I am going to fly in close and see if there are any unusual devices on the outsides of those ships. I will put my cameras on live feed and transmit what I see directly to you."

Roger knew that the Kaarumite ships would seem entirely alien to him, and that he probably would not be able to tell what was beyond the ordinary with any of the ships, but if there was anything added to the outside then someone in the strategy room might be able to point it out.

Roger wove in and out of the Kaarumite vessels, and took recordings of their tops and bottoms. He ordered the rest of the Imperial airships to do the same.

"Mattis, we are not seeing anything unusual on the outside of the Kaarumite ships," the Emperor said. "We want you and your squad to fly up and take some sensor readings. Scan for any sort of energy field or radiation. Do a full spectrum scan if necessary. Transmit the data to us as you receive it."

Roger complied.

A short time later the Kaarumite fleet was hovering over the Kaarumite forces below. Originally the Kaarumite forces stretched across half of the Contested Area, but they were forced to compress their lines in order to avoid the abandoned tavlon cities. They seemed unwilling to break up their lines, and as a result their lines now stretched for miles upon miles toward the south.

"Hey, war room!" Roger said after about 15 minutes of silence. "You guys have anything yet?"

"Nothing yet," the Emperor responded.

"So basically we can't hurt them and they can't hurt us, but we have already wasted some missiles," Roger said.

The Kaarumite air fleet continued on and ignored the Imperial vessels. When they came within firing range of Leonus they ignored that as well.

What are these guys doing?

But before they reached Leonus the enemy fleet abruptly split into three groups. One went to the forward end of the Kaarumite troops where they struggled against the forest and the hidden Imperial and Haxian forces, and the others went to the east and west sides. They then proceeded to blast the ground with earth scorchers.

Large spheres of bright orange and yellow light appeared and swallowed up large portions of the forest. When the light subsided all that remained was a blackened crater, and sometimes parts of the ground even glowed for a few minutes.

"Can we blast their troops?" Roger asked.

"In addition to their personal forcefields they seem to have large type two forcefield generators covering their ranks," said one of the advisors.

"Come back for now, Mattis," the Emperor said. "We will leave half of our fleet on continuous patrol."

"Alright, I'm coming in," Roger said.

Roger Watches the Sun Set in Leonus
—by Ivor Kovac

CHAPTER 21

Sabotage

A PORTION OF THE TYPE ONE forcefield around Leonus was lowered long enough for Roger and some of the other Imperial aircraft to fly in. As soon as Roger landed and deactivated his craft he made a straight run for the strategy room. He found that Garek, Nirin, and many other generals were present as holographic projections. Nirin was already talking when Roger arrived.

"It's unacceptable," Nirin said. "Many of my people have had their bodies destroyed in these attacks. You should have equipped all of us with personal forcefield generators."

"There have also been some casualties on my side, even with personal forcefield generators," Garek said.

"I would like everyone to send me casualty reports as soon as possible," the Emperor said. "And I want to have personal forcefield generators assigned to any sokes who are going without."

"That is not possible," one of the advisors said. "We barely have enough to go around as it is. We have to prioritize."

"So!" Nirin said. "You automatically assign a lower status to my people. I knew it all along! The white ones really are all the same!"

"Nirin!" Roger shouted as he came to stand next to the Emperor. "Stop!"

"I have ordered all of my people to pull back from the front lines," Nirin said.

"Good," Roger said. "Everyone should do that for now. It looks like they are carving a perimeter."

"We underestimated the intelligence of our enemy," said an advisor.

"No, the enemy is stupid," Garek said.

"How can you say that?" the advisor replied. "Look at what they have done. They are one step ahead of us!"

"I can say it because they are. Kaarumites are the most stupid, violent, backward people on the face of this world."

"But you're wrong, and now we are going to reap the results of our wrong doings," the advisor said.

"What wrong doings?" Garek said.

"Yes, I would also like to know what you mean, councilman," the Emperor said.

"We always treated the Kaarumites like they were stupid, and now it turns out that we have been underestimating them this entire time," the advisor said. "They have new technology which we do not understand."

The Emperor nodded in agreement.

"Who is this idiot?" Garek asked.

"I'm not wrong!" the advisor said. "I have been working with you for the last two weeks and you still don't know my name?"

"If I knew who you were I would not have asked," Garek said.

"Mendarius!" the advisor replied.

"Well, Mendarius, you are wrong," Garek said. "The Kaarumites have never invented a single thing, except for some torture devices and tattoos. All of their technology is thousands of years old, and when they suddenly show up with a new piece of technology the first thing you think is that they invented it? Get serious man! Someone helped them. Once we slaughter these morons we can find out who did it and kill that person if necessary, but first we have to find a way to counter their technology so that we can prevent them from bombing us."

"We are stalemated for now," Roger said.

"I think I might have something," a technical advisor said.

"What do you have?" the Emperor asked.

"I have been running the data retrieved from those scans through our computers, and I have gone over it three times," the technical advisor said. "There are energy fields radiating from the insides of the larger ships, and from the unusual devices we saw on the ground among the Kaarumites earlier. It is a strange energy field which we have never seen the like of before."

"My people were able to sense those fields on the ground, but we had a harder time locating the source," Nirin said.

"You should have said something," the advisor said.

"You should have said something!" Nirin echoed back. "You know my people can sense energy fields."

"Enough!" Roger said. "What can we learn from this?"

"The smaller ships are all clustered within the fields generated by the larger ships," the advisor said. "If we take out the larger ships we can obliterate their antiquated air fleet, and we can resume an all-out ground attack on them."

"The bombings have stopped," Nirin said.

"Confirmed," an advisor said.

"What is happening now?" the Emperor asked.

"The enemy fleet is regrouping to hover over the ground troops, and the ground troops seem to be on hold for the time being," the advisor said. "Maybe they are going to make camp?"

"I've got it!" Roger said as he snapped his fingers.

"Got what?" Nirin asked.

"I have an idea!" Roger replied. "But I need northerners to make it work, or at least northern swords."

"We do not have either available to us at the moment," Mendarius said.

"Wait," the Emperor said. "What is your idea?"

"We land men on all the big ships," Roger said. "We have them cut through the exterior and drop an earth scorcher bomb on the inside, just beneath the forcefield. Then we bail, and the big ship blows up. We should be able to land on the ships if we move slowly, because they only have type two forcefields. Then, we need a northern weapon, which should be able to cut through the metal plating, and we need a northerner because a regular human might not be strong enough to do it."

"We have no northerners or any of their weapons," an advisor said.

"We do have some northern weapons stored in one of the treasure rooms here," the Emperor said. "But most of them are over 1000 years old. When it comes to cutting they are no more efficient than current Imperial weapons. However… they are more durable."

"Anyways even if they are 1000 years old the Kaarumite ships are older, and they won't be expecting such an attack," Roger said.

"Mattis," Garek said. "I do have some men who are close to full blooded northerners. I can send you 20 men right now who are large and powerful, and at least twice as strong as a normal human man of their size and build. How many do you need?"

"I would like to have at least 200, which would put four on each of the large ships," Roger said.

"That will take some time," Garek said.

"Time is something we don't have," Aneme said.

"But they are still for the time being," Mendarius said.

"Garek, have those 20 men ready," Adinis said. "We will use Imperial soldiers for the rest of the Kaarumite ships."

"I'll go and take care of that right now," Roger said.

"Be careful," Aneme said as Roger left the room.

Roger gathered together the men he wanted and armored up with them. The armor they put on had the standard anti-gravity equipment built in, which would slow down their fall should any of them fall from the aircraft.

Roger decided to put five men on each enemy ship instead of four, which would be in addition to the pilots of the small troop transports, who would remain inside of the ships. All of the men were equipped with the old northern weapons, which would be able to cut through the hulls of the Kaarumite ships.

When the Haxians arrived Roger looked them over. They did appear to be very much like northerners, but both their equipment and mannerisms were Haxian. Roger also equipped them with the old northern weapons and broke them up into teams. He created one team that was all Haxian, and the others he broke up so that no more than one Haxian was on each team that had a Haxian. Since there was a total of 50 teams and only 20 Haxians most had to go without, but he did include a Haxian in his own team.

"The solid Haxian team is to be a rapid strike team," Roger said. "If they get theirs done first I want them to go and assist whoever is struggling the most. In fact, when any team gets done I want them to go and assist another. We need to be as quick as we can be. Once we take down those big ships then we all pull out and let the air fleet hit the remaining Kaarumite ships with their freeze missiles. Once they realize what we are doing things are bound to get ugly. They may let loose with their earth scorcher missiles. If you have to bail or you get knocked over the side then make for the nearest tavlon city once you hit ground. Everyone got it?"

"Understood," they said.

The men loaded into small troop transports and shot off into the air. Roger fidgeted as he stood behind the pilot and watched the enemy and Imperial air craft go shooting by. He would rather be flying the ship himself but he felt it was more important that he personally direct the mission.

The large Haxian stood close by. The man was about three inches taller than Roger and he had a powerful build. He could sense the man's eyes staring at him.

"Yes?" Roger said as he turned to face the Haxian.

The man did look like a full blooded northerner, but Roger knew that he would have at least some western admixture given that his family had lived among them for thousands of years, and the original northern ruling class had never been dogmatic about racial separation. If he were a true northerner he would be at least three times stronger than Roger, or perhaps more given his greater size. But at the very least he would be over twice as strong as Roger, and probably a vicious fighter.

"Sorry," he said. "I was just trying to figure out what part of Hax you were from. It's good to see that some of our people have gotten to such high positions in the Empire."

"I'm not a Haxian," Roger said.

"Really? What are you then?"

"Don't worry about that right now."

"Alright."

"Where are you from, soldier?"

"The province of Melnar. It's in northern Hax, kind of toward the center."

"What's your name?"

"Varis."

"Well, Varis, for the sake of the mission I hope you have the strength of the northerners running in you."

"I have some of it. My muscles are at least twice as strong as what a westerner has got."

"Prepare for landing," the pilot said.

The ship landed on the back of a large gray Kaarumite ship.

Roger put his helmet on and the rest of the men followed his example.

"Don't forget to magnetize your boots," Roger said.

One of the men held two small gray metal spheres, which were the earth scorcher warheads. One of them would be sufficient to completely melt the interior of the ship to molten metal, but the man brought two for good measure.

Fortunately the ships were not moving so there was very little wind. Their feet clanged across the hull of the Kaarumite ship as they walked. There was rust in many places, and the surface appeared to have been patched and re-patched in many places. In fact, close by them the corner of a panel appeared to be sticking up.

"Perfect, we'll start with that," Roger said. "Varis, see if you can pull that thing up."

Varis was able to fit his fingers under the corner of the panel that was lifted up. He pulled and strained with all his might. It came up another inch but stopped. Roger could hear Varis groaning behind his helmet.

"Let's get these rivets cut, and quickly," Roger said.

Two of the men quickly worked their swords under the panel, careful to avoid Varis' fingers, and began to saw through the rivets that were still in place. In the meantime Roger got behind the panel with Varis and helped him pull. The remaining soldier stood watch and held onto the explosives.

As the men cut through the rivets the panel began to come up more.

"What can you see down there?" Roger asked.

Suddenly there was a loud boom like thunder, and a bright flash of orange light. Roger looked up to see the skeleton of a tremendous Kaarumite airship fading away to glowing orange embers as it fell toward the ground.

"What's in there?" Roger reiterated.

"Scaffolding," one of the soldiers said.

"Throw the bombs in and let's get out of here," Roger said.

The soldier holding the bombs depressed a portion of the exterior and turned the top on each one.

"One minute!" he said.

"Get back to the ship, quickly!" Roger said.

They quickly ran to the transport and took off. As the Kaarumite ship fell away behind them there was a flash of orange light and their ship was struck by a shockwave of energy. They were knocked off course for a few seconds but the pilot quickly rectified the error. A short time later ten other Kaarumite ships blew up.

"Get us to another ship," Roger said.

As they made their way to the next Kaarumite ship another one blew up, but now the Kaarumite fleet was on the move. They surged northward beyond their troops on the ground and well past the floating city of Leonus.

When Roger stepped out onto the next Kaarumite ship the wind beat against him with heavy force. He had to crouch down to make it to the area where the Imperial soldiers were at work trying to cut through a panel.

But as he approached the Imperial soldiers a small one-man Kaarumite fighter swept in and collided with the men. There was a flash of light as forcefield struck against forcefield, and the men were hurled up off the surface of the vessel and into the air. Some of the men were immediately knocked over the side, while others came back down onto the hull but because of the winds and the motion of the vehicle they also tumbled over the side.

"Mattis to Leonus!" Roger shouted. "Mattis to Leonus!"

"Leonus here, what do you need?" the voice of Aneme replied.

"Have our aircraft run interference!" Roger said. "Our men are getting knocked over the side!"

"Understood," she replied. "Be careful out there."

"I'll try," Roger replied.

Roger made his way to the place where the men had been working. They were cutting through a large metal panel which seemed fairly thin. Roger and his team began cutting and after a few seconds a large hole was created.

"They were cutting a larger hole than necessary," Roger said.

Beneath the hole was what appeared to be a ventilation duct.

Roger ordered his men to throw in two bombs and again they took off. A short time later the ship blew up behind them, and then another exploded, and another.

They landed on another ship where the men were struggling with a thicker panel. Some of the men assigned to that ship had also been knocked off. Roger and his men quickly helped them create an opening. Then they threw their bombs in and took off.

As the numbers of large Kaarumite mother ships dwindled the Kaarumites became more frantic, and the fighting more intense. On one ship Kaarumite warriors came out onto the back of the ship to fight with Roger and his men. Many Kaarumites were killed and knocked over the side, but a few Imperial soldiers were also knocked over the side as well.

One of the Kaarumite ships pitched to the side and sent half of the Imperial soldiers over the side, but due to the anti-gravity components in their armor they were able to descend slowly and safely into the forest below.

As they moved on to the remaining ships the numbers of soldiers grew as everyone was focusing on what was left. On some of the ships all of the Imperial soldiers had been knocked off relatively early, and in some cases the second group to land was also knocked off. In an act of desperation some of the Kaarumite fighters let loose with earth scorcher missiles. Men were blown far into the air and the fleet was pushed apart.

Roger and his team, along with twenty other men, were about to take off when a Kaarumite fighter swept in and fired a missile. Roger barely had time to shield his eyes before the brilliant flash of orange light blocked out everything. He was sent hurtling through the air, and when he opened his eyes he was far away from the ship and falling.

Fortunately the anti-grav units in his armor activated, so his fall was about what it would be if he were back on Earth skydiving with a parachute. As he watched the sky above him erupted with spheres of orange light.

Roger felt a sudden acceleration in his downward motion. He looked down and noticed that the glowing lines on his armor had gone out. Then suddenly the glow resumed and his fall was arrested. It felt somewhat like a downward moving elevator stopping. But as he looked down at his armor once more, he noticed that the lighted parts of his armor were flickering and pulsating.

As he descended he experienced sudden bursts of downward motion with greater frequency.

Well, if I'm meant to die then I'm going to die one way or another…

He was nearly at the treetops when the anti-gravity elements shut off completely. Branches broke against his armor as he fell through the forest canopy. He tried to grab onto the branches on his way but it was no use. He struck the ground and lost consciousness.

Storm in the Sky

ROGER AWOKE TO FIND STRONG hands grasping each of his appendages. He was being carried someplace. He kept his eyes shut and remained limp. When the opportunity came he turned over with all of his strength and broke the grips of each of his captors. As he rose up from the ground he drew his sword and entered a combative stance.

"Hold!" said one of the men nearby.

Roger looked around and noticed that they were all Imperial soldiers. He relaxed but did not put his sword away.

"What's going on?" Roger asked.

"You fell out of the sky, sir," one of the soldiers said. "We were taking you to the nearest tavlon city for medical care."

"I don't think so," Roger said. "I have to get back up to Leonus."

"In that?" the soldier said as he pointed up toward the sky.

Roger heard a loud boom, and as he looked up he saw the sky was full of orange flashes, and that it was beginning to grow overcast. There were flakes falling down from the sky. Some of them were warm and ashy, while others were cold and icy. Suddenly a strong gust of unusually cold wind blew and took his breath away.

"A storm is brewing up there," the soldier said. "It looks like the heat generating weapons and the cold weapons are wreaking havoc with the atmosphere."

"Well… storms do happen when a warm air mass meets a cold air mass, and here we've got a bunch of warm and cold going off together," Roger said.

Suddenly Roger felt dizzy and stumbled. The environment seemed to be in motion around him.

"You hit your head sir," the soldier said. "We need to get you back to the tavlon city where we have medical facilities set up. We need to go before the Kaarumites move into this area. The storm has them acting more crazy than usual."

Roger nodded to signal his agreement, and they began their walk toward their nearest base. He walked with the soldiers for as long as he could, but Roger often stumbled as he went. When they met up with a larger group of soldiers Roger was placed onto a stretcher and carried the rest of the way.

"We have been picking up others that fell from the sky, but you are the first Commander General we found," an officer said. "Are you a member of the royal family?"

Roger was both unwilling and unable to respond. Everything around him was becoming hazy, and he was only dimly aware of being taken into a stone tunnel.

He woke up later to find himself on a bed. His helmet and armor had been removed. He sat up to look around, and determined from the architecture and surroundings that he was in a tavlon city.

The walls and ceiling were made entirely of stone, with badly chipped and shattered relief carvings on the walls. Parts of the ceiling glowed dimly with a faint blue light like that which filters through the clouds on a stormy day. All around the room were stands with bright white lights on them, and fresh looking medical equipment with glowing displays. The Imperial technology stood out against the ancient tavlon ruins.

Roger shook his head swiftly in an attempt to shake off the grogginess. An attractive female westerner came to him immediately and attempted to push him back down onto the bed.

"That won't be necessary, I think I'm good," Roger said.

"Let him up," said an Imperial medic.

"How long was I out?" Roger asked.

"Just two hours since they brought you in," the medic said. "Commander General…"

"Mattis Maxelis."

"Right, sir."

"What happened to me?"

"You had a concussion and some internal bleeding. It looks like your anti-gravity devices timed out."

"They did. Listen, I need to call Leonus."

"I will show you to a communications station."

As Roger followed the medic through the dimly lit stone hallways they passed both Imperial and Haxian soldiers, as well as a few sokes here and there.

"How is the battle on the ground?"

"Everyone has pulled back and is awaiting orders."

"Summarize."

"When we first engaged the Kaarumites they were terrified. They ran back against their own ranks to get away from the sokes, and were killed by their own people. The battle was going well until the Kaarumite air fleet arrived and started burning the forest. Now we have all withdrawn to a safe distance. Those who could have retreated to the old tavlon fortresses, which the Kaarumites are afraid to approach, for now…"

"It's amazing that after all these millennia the halls are still lighted. Tavlons really knew how to build things to last."

"Yes, they have been outlasted by their creations."

"I don't understand that."

"Perhaps when we are gone the sokes will go among the ruins of our civilization and wonder where we went, and marvel that our buildings have outlasted us."

"Well that's awfully morbid."

"It makes sense, the first born often dies first, and the youngest child outlives his seniors."

"Mattis!" said a familiar voice.

Roger turned to see Garek enter the main corridor from an adjacent room.

"Garek!" Roger said. "It's good to see a familiar face."

"Did you get blown off of the aircraft?" Garek asked.

"I sure did."

"What about my men?"

"I have no idea. I'm sorry, my friend. I landed all by myself and hit my head a few times on the way down I think."

"Well… they were good men, and they knew what they were getting into."

"The communications station is this way, sir," the medic interjected and gestured to a room.

"Thank you, medic," Roger said. "I'll let you get back to your duties."

The medic nodded and walked off.

"You had better call them quick, your wife is heavily worried about you," Garek said. "I think she wants to send out search teams."

"Which is not something we have the time or manpower for," Roger said. "Come with me, Garek. We will check in together."

Roger entered the room and activated the communication station. He reached an operator in Leonus and was soon routed to the Emperor himself.

"Mattis!" the Emperor said. "We were all very concerned. What is your status?"

"I am fully functional and good to go," Roger said. "What's going on in the skies?"

"The large Kaarumite vessels have been destroyed," the Emperor replied. "Many of the smaller Kaarumite vessels are using their earth scorchers to clear a path through the forest, but they are being picked off now that the large ones that were generating the energy field are out of the way."

"Mattis, please come back to Leonus, you have done enough out there," Aneme said.

"Wait, there is something I want to try with Garek first," Roger said.

"What is that?"

"I want to try to get one of those devices that they have generating the energy field on the ground. We need to understand how that technology works, and where it came from."

"There are other people who can do that."

"Yes, and they are going to help me do it."

"Then wait for me, I will also come help."

"No, I want you to stay on Leonus."

"And what if you get attacked by another Kaarumite woman? What are you going to do?"

"Garek and Nirin will have my back. Anyways, there is something else I want you to do."

"What is that?"

"I'll let you know when it comes up. Have a medium sized transport ready to land near my signal."

"But—"

"Understood," Adinis replied, cutting off Aneme before she could protest further.

"End communication," Roger said.

The communication device switched off.

"Now what?" Garek asked.

"Now we call Nirin," Roger said.

"Alright."

"So call him."

Garek laid his hand on the panel and said, "Route to Field Commander Nirin."

After a minute of silence the voice of Nirin came over the device, but there was no visual component to it.

"What is it?" Nirin asked.

"Nirin, it's Mattis," Roger said.

"What do you need?"

"How far are you away from the place where Garek is stationed?"

"Not very far."

"Can you come and meet me there?"

"When do you want me there?"

"Right now if possible."

"I will take me ten minutes to get there. Is it something you can't tell me over the communication lines?"

"Yes, come as quick as you can."

"Alright."

Once the communication was closed Roger armored up and told Garek to select a group of 200 men.

"Suicide!" Garek complained.

"No, it's going to be a surgical strike," Roger said. "We will be in and out."

"It will be a drop compared to a pond."

"So how many would you bring?"

"At least 90% of the base here."

"And what do you do when they launch earth scorchers at us?"

"Our shields will protect us."

"From the initial blast, but then the men still get vaulted up into the air, and who knows where they will come down or into what sort of conditions they will land?"

"Well… if we are going to do it then we need to have surprise, shock, and speed on our side."

"That is why I called Nirin."

"I am here," the voice of Nirin said from the doorway.

Roger and Garek turned to see Nirin as he took a step into the armor room.

"Nirin," Roger began. "I need a huge crazy burst of plant growth."

"Not from the front I hope," Nirin said. "The ground is still smoldering from the earth scorchers, and they are laying down more of those wretched bombs even as we speak."

"No not from the front… from the side."

"What is it you have in mind?"

"I want to snatch a piece of their equipment, one of the field generators that they are using to block the Imperial freeze bombs. I want to shock and alarm the Kaarumites so that we can get in, take it, and get out before they have time to react."

"Show me where the piece of machinery is in relation to their army."

Roger led Nirin to the makeshift strategic center set up in the old abandoned tavlon city and showed him a three dimensional holographic map.

"Here," Roger said pointing toward an area near the edge of a large clump of Kaarumite warriors.

"I think about 50 of my people should be sufficient to cover your entry and withdrawal, but come, follow me and I will show you another idea I had," Nirin said. "This idea occurred to me after the men of this base began painting their armor green for camouflage purposes."

Roger and Garek followed Nirin back out of the tavlon city and into the forest. The sky was overcast, and the wind blew randomly in varying directions with strong gusts, sometimes carrying droplets of rain.

"I think it might rain," Roger said.

"No doubt," Garek added.

"If it rains then that will greatly assist my people," Nirin said.

Nirin reached down and picked up a net of leafy vines woven together. He lifted it up and tossed it over Roger. Then he pulled it down over Roger's head and helped Roger pull his arms through the sides. After that Niring picked up another one and put it on Garek.

"I had my people begin making these things once we pulled back from the front," Nirin said. "My theory is that if all the men wear these things then not only will it contribute to the camouflage effect, but it may also give the Kaarumites the impression that you have been infected with some sort of plant essence by the sokes. It will play on their ancient fears of Alris and his people."

"Brilliant!" Roger said. "Garek, go and get the men out here, we will have them put on these things before we go to battle."

"Many of my people are standing by with more," Nirin said.

Nirin snapped his fingers and other sokes began appearing. They stepped out from behind trees, or rose up from bushes or from tall patches of grass.

"Go get the men, Garek," Roger reiterated.

Garek nodded and ran off back into the tavlon city, and a short time later the men began to line up outside. As the men lined up the sokes outfitted each man with a net of his own. Once everyone was equipped they began their march for the enemy lines.

When they neared the edge of the forest they could see the Kaarumite troops milling about, eager for a chance to spill some blood and clearly frustrated at having to wait. Suddenly it began to rain intensely, and a great deal of cursing rose up from the Kaarumite ranks. Chunks of ice were mixed in with the rain. Some of the faster moving chunks of ice bounced off of an invisible barrier high above the troops, and then resumed their fall to the ground.

When Roger gave the signal riotous growths of vines shot speedily across the ground toward the unwary Kaarumites. The growth of vines was followed by a growth of trees and shrubs. When the Kaarumites saw it they screamed and began to fall back upon their own ranks, abandoning whatever vehicles or animals they had nearby.

When Roger and his men charged forward the enemy broke into a mad stampede in the other direction. There were shouts of "soke kind!" accompanied by a variety of curses and calls to Kaarum for mercy. Any animals which did not retreat with their Kaarumite masters were killed. Kaarumites who did not run quick enough were also cut down. To Roger it was somewhat like watching a crater form in slow motion, with the retreat of the Kaarumites being analogous to the retreat of soil away from the center of the impact.

A few Kaarumites fell down as they attempted to retreat. Some of those who fell were pierced through the back or decapitated by Haxian soldiers, but others the sokes fell upon and quickly bound with vines as they screamed and cried out to their fellows for assistance. Roger had never before seen such unbridled fear. A few of the captured Kaarumites attempted to kill themselves with their own weapons but they were quickly disarmed by the sokes and Imperial soldiers.

As the Kaarumites continued to retreat Roger spotted one of the strange box like devices he was looking for. The device was mounted on a wheeled frame which could be either connected to a vehicle or harnessed to an animal.

"Now!" Roger shouted into his field communicator. "Bring the ship now!"

The foliage continued to grow rapidly beyond the device for another 50 feet as the soldiers took up positions around the strange object. In the meantime a sleek white aircraft descended from the clouds and shot in Roger's direction. Roger waved his arms until the craft took notice and came to land behind him.

The new plants continued to grow until Roger and the soldiers were surrounded by a forest of mid-sized trees and abundant ferns and shrubs.

When the ship landed the bay door in the back of the craft opened and two Imperial soldiers stepped out.

"Grab that thing and load it quickly!" Roger said as he pointed toward the device.

A group of men sheathed their swords and surrounded the device on all sides. They picked it up and carried it into the Imperial shuttlecraft and backed away.

"Go!" Roger shouted. "Take off!"

The door on the back of the transport ship slid shut and the craft swiftly rose up into the air. Roger watched as it darted off toward Leonus and disappeared into the cloud layer.

"Retreat back to base!" Roger said.

Nirin snapped his fingers and the sokes picked up the bound Kaarumites and began to run with them.

"Why not just kill them now?" Garek asked.

"Because I have a better use for them," Nirin said.

"Nirin, leave them!" Roger said. "The Kaarumites are going to blast this part of the forest any minute now! We don't have time for this!"

"Trust me, it is well worth the effort," Nirin replied. "You and your men can run on ahead if you wish. I have a plan for these ones."

"Nirin, I need you in one piece, not regenerating off in a tree someplace," Roger said.

"If it's that important I'll have my men carry the Kaarumites," Garek said. "They can run faster with such burdens than your people. No offense."

"None taken," Nirin said.

"Mattis?" Garek asked.

"Trust me, Mattis, I know what I am doing," Nirin said.

"And my men are prepared to take the risk," Garek said.

All this time the entire party had been moving at the pace of the sokes who carried the large screaming southerners.

"Alright!" Roger said. "Alright, but it had better be worth it."

Nirin clapped and the sokes dropped their burdens. Garek gave an order and his men picked up the Kaarumites in their stead. There were twenty Kaarumites taken hostage altogether.

"I want everyone to head back to base as fast as possible now, we need to clear this area!" Roger ordered.

The Imperial soldiers and unburdened Haxians shot ahead, with the sokes and the Haxians who carried the Kaarumite hostages trailing increasingly further behind.

"Don't take them all the way to the base," Roger whispered to Nirin.

"I know," Nirin said. "Don't worry."

"I'll keep pace with you," Roger said.

"No, you run on ahead, your wife will worry," Nirin said.

"I'll keep pace with him," Garek said. "You go on ahead, Mattis. I mean it."

Roger nodded and broke into a sprint. Ten minutes later he heard a loud boom far behind in the direction from which he came and a gust of warm air struck him in the back with such force that it caused him to stumble for a second.

I hope they all made it!

CHAPTER 23

Green Skin

ROGER STOPPED RUNNING TO LOOK behind him. He saw no one but he did hear multiple aircraft shooting overhead. He could not see clearly through the forest canopy to make out whether they were Imperial or Kaarumite, but judging by the sound he guessed it might be a mixture of both. He turned away and resumed his run, and eventually he began to catch up to some of the men who were not quite as fast as he.

When he passed them they began to run faster in order to keep up, but the idea of outrunning any of his men back to base sat ill with Roger. He slowed down to match them, and when he no longer heard the aircraft he slowed his pace further.

"I… think…" Roger gasped. "I think… we can… slow down, men…"

Roger dropped to a moderate jogging pace and the men matched his pace, much to their relief. They did not stop until they passed the perimeter of guards, both human and soke. Roger slowed to a walking pace and stopped just short of the opening to the old tavlon city.

"You men go on ahead," Roger said. "Get some well earned rest. I am going to wait for the rest to arrive."

"Thank you, sir," the soldiers said as they continued on to the fortress.

Roger removed his helmet and sat down with his back against a tree. He faced away from the tavlon city toward the direction from which he came.

"Guard!" he shouted after he caught his breath.

"Sir!" an Imperial soldier said as he stood before Roger and saluted.

"Did the others all make it back?"

"Everyone in front of you has returned."

"Well that's brilliant. Who all was in front of me?"

"All of the Imperial soldiers made it back, and so did most of the Haxian mercenaries. None of the sokes have come back yet."

"Alright, take off for the day, soldier. My guess is it's near the end of your shift anyways."

"It is. Thank you, sir."

"The sokes are back," said a voice next to Roger.

Roger jumped at the sudden closeness of the voice, and turned to face the speaker to find that it was a soke.

These guys are the only beings on this alien world who get this close without me hearing them coming. I swear, they must slide through plants like a snake through the water...

"How many?" Roger asked.

"Not all," the soke replied. "Only ten."

"Have one of them report to me right now so that I can find out what happened," Roger said.

Without saying a word the soke walked off, and returned a minute later accompanied by another soke.

"Report," Roger said. "Did everyone make it?"

"Everyone made it," the soke replied.

"So where is everyone then?"

"Nirin and Garek kept most of them back. They are doing something with the prisoners."

"What are they doing?"

"I do not know what Nirin has planned for them."

"Then take me to them."

"Follow," the soke said as he turned his back on Roger and began to walk away.

Roger followed the soke, and after a while he could hear the cries of men who were either frightened or in pain. Roger quickly ran to the source of the sound, and he found Nirin, Garek, and the rest of the sokes and Haxians who had lagged behind lashing the Kaarumite prisoners to trees. Thick vines wrapped around their arms, legs, and torsos until they were held fast.

"Kaarum!" a particularly large Kaarumite shouted. "Father of Light! Save me!"

"Shut up!" Garek said.

"Kaarum help me!" he shouted again.

Garek punched the man in the rib cage with such force that it sounded like the beat of a drum. The man coughed, and then resumed his shouting.

"Please, Kaarum, do not forsake me!" the Kaarumite shouted.

"Fool! Cry out to your stupid make-believe god! He can't save you because he's not real."

Some of the Haxian soldiers chuckled. Garek struck him another blow, but this time from a different angle. The sokes seemed to be passive and distant, which was typical of the 3rd kindred until one got to know them on an individual basis.

"Kaarum failed to stop that one," Garek said. "But maybe if you scream louder he will stop the next one? Let's give it a try."

"Garek!" Roger shouted.

Garek halted with his fist cocked back and looked in the direction of Roger's voice.

"Ah, Mattis," he said. "Just in time for some sport!"

"Garek! I'm telling you to—"

"Please, Kaarum, I have killed so many in your name!" the Kaarumite bellowed. "Free me, and I will double that number! Please master!"

The words caught in Roger's throat. Instead of stopping Garek he watched as Garek struck him again and again. Roger could not bring himself to feel sorry for that man. Finally it was Nirin who stopped him.

"Enough!" Nirin said. "I want them alive."

"They can be hurt and still be alive," Garek retorted.

"No torture," Roger said.

"Why not?" Garek demanded. "Do you think they're all innocent? Just regular soldiers? They would do so much worse to us if the situation were reversed! These people make belts and straps out of human skins!"

"I said no, Garek. That's all I have to say."

Garek stepped away from the Kaarumite and walked to stand within inches of Roger's face.

"You heard what that man said," Garek said in a quiet voice. "He has killed 'so many' for his Adimnor forsaken religion. Do you remember what they did to your wife?"

"I remember, and I also remember we killed all the ones involved in that," Roger said.

"Other men have wives besides you! How many of those people he killed do you think he killed quickly? Or on the battlefield? We all know what a Kaarumite is. They deserve to die."

"Maybe so, and by the time this war is over many of them will be dead, probably most of them, but I still said no torture. We don't make our rules based on what they do. When we die we all have to give an accounting for what we did. What are you going to do if you're standing in front of the Great Maker and he asks you why you tortured a man to death, and all you have to say is that it's because you think he might have done something similar to someone else?"

"I don't believe in your god concept any more than I believe in theirs. If by some odd chance whatever intelligence designed this world happens to be looking on, then I suspect he would be thanking me for cleaning it up for him."

"Well, Garek, if you can't be convinced then you'll just have to follow my orders without being convinced. For now, I want you to get your men and go back to the tavlon city. We are done for the day."

"Actually, I'm still using the Haxians," Nirin interjected. "I need some of them to stay on to help us guard the Kaarumites."

"Take as many as you need and dismiss the rest," Roger said.

Garek began to walk off but Roger grasped him firmly by the upper arm and pulled him back.

"I didn't excuse you yet," he said.

Garek looked him in the eyes but said nothing. His eyes narrowed, which reminded Roger somewhat of Aneme, but in Aneme's case it indicated that she was thinking. There was nothing in Garek's eyes but seething rage, but despite the difference in attitude, it still caused Roger to reflect upon the fact that Garek had some northern ancestry.

Garek's eyes were less narrow than those of the average westerner, and there was the faint yet unmistakable powder blue complexion to his skin. Many Haxians had northern ancestry, but the way it manifested seemed to vary. One man might have predominantly northern features and a northern physique, but chalk white skin, while another man might have medium blue skin and more western features. Then there were those like Garek who were more of an even combination.

"When I make my decision then the argument is over," Roger said. "Do not contradict me or attempt to scold me in front of any of the men. I don't care whether they are Imperials, Haxians, or sokes, you got it?"

Garek nodded, but jerked his arm free with excessive force.

"Now go back to the tavlon city and wait for me," Roger said.

Garek walked away, and the majority of the Haxian soldiers followed him. Only five remained with Nirin.

"Now what is it you want with these Kaarumites, Nirin?" Roger asked.

"Psychological warfare," Nirin said.

"No torture."

"None whatsoever. In fact, I can promise that neither my people, nor the Haxians under my supervision will harm them."

"Alright, so what do you have in mind?"

"Look at them," Nirin said as he gestured toward the restrained Kaarumites. "They are terrified."

The Kaarumites did indeed appear to be terrified. Some of them had passed out, while others quivered and mumbled, and some wept like women in a state of grief.

"You have to be careful, Nirin," Roger said. "If you keep them restrained like that too long they will eventually realize that nothing sinister is going to happen to them and will lose their fear of sokes. We had a Kaarumite girl with us when we were on the run through this area in the first place, and she was as terrified as those men when we made her go inside of a tavlon city, but when she realized that nothing was going to happen she lost her fear. Of course, she also lost her religion, but we don't know if all Kaarumites will act that way. If they lose their fear without losing their religion then we are up a creek without a paddle."

"I intend to keep that fear alive," Nirin said.

"Again, what are you going to do?"

"They are scared that we are going to change them, so I plan on changing them."

"Whatever happened to not harming them?"

"I will not permanently harm them. Of course, I don't have the knowledge or genius to recreate Alris' work on Landira, but I do have some cunning chemists. As you know, many sokes know how to mix up potions that can temporarily change the color of a person's skin…"

"Yes…"

"Well, I had my people create a potion that will turn the human skin a bright green color, but not right away. It will become green with exposure to sunlight. It will happen quickly, and the effect will last for at least half a year, but no permanent changes will be made to their bodies. I intend to make them drink the potion, and once they begin to change colors I will release them. If they return to their people they will spread fear and panic, and they will demoralize the enemy."

"How will that work?"

"It will be somewhat like a temporary tattoo rather than causing their bodies to produce green pigment, as the color changing potions humans ingest do."

"If they return to their people they will be killed."

"Perhaps, or perhaps their people will run from them in fear, and the fearful stories will be spread."

"Still seems like a gray area to me."

"If Garek were here he would no doubt tell you that—"

"That the Kaarumites would subject us to far worse things if they captured us."

"Yes, and—"

"And that they are anything but innocent victims."

"So you understand then."

"And I would say the same thing to you that I did to Garek."

"You know the Empire does not take Kaarumite prisoners. You must either kill these men or release them. If we simply release them as they are now they will rejoin the ranks of our enemies, and we will still have to kill them. Or, you can kill them now and send them to their eternal destination. Or, you can follow my plan, and we can release them in such a way that it will provide us with an increased tactical advantage. The Haxians have suggested that we pierce them over wooden spikes and leave them out to die slowly, but I think that my way is both more effective and benign."

Roger stood still and thought about it. He looked on at the writhing Kaarumites who were still conscious.

"Alright, get it done," Roger said.

"Do you wish to supervise?" Nirin asked.

"No, I'll leave it all to you. Just don't let the Haxians do anything crazy while I'm gone."

"You have my word. My people have already gone to fetch the potion. We will have them ingest it shortly, and then tomorrow they can be on their way."

"You!" shouted a loud voice.

Roger looked in the direction of the Kaarumites and saw that one of them was also looking in his direction.

"Yes, you!" the man repeated.

"What do you want?" Roger asked.

"You are unchanged by them?"

"Yes."

"For the love of Kaarum you must free me!"

"I don't think so."

"For Kaarum's sake, have mercy on a fellow man!" the Kaarumite shouted. "We can get out of here together, before they change us!"

"He is clearly delirious," Nirin said.

"I don't care at all for Kaarum, and I already know all about how you people view your 'fellow man,'" Roger said. "But save your strength, you are going to be let free soon enough," Roger said.

"Blaspheming heretic! I'll rip your stomach out through your throat, and then I will hunt down and ravish every female member of your family! I will—"

The man stopped short and cowered as a soke approached him.

The soke climbed up the lattice-work of thick vines in which the Kaarumite was enmeshed. Some of the vines moved beneath his touch and the leaves rustled as if a slight wind stirred them.

"Kaarum have mercy… Kaarum have mercy…" the Kaarumite muttered over and over again.

The soke was carrying a crude clay pitcher with a rough handle. When he reached the level of the Kaarumite's face he held the pitcher suspended over his mouth and said "drink."

The Kaarumite closed his lips tightly and turned his head away. The vines rustled and hissed, and the Kaarumite's head was turned to face upwards and held firmly in place. With his other hand the soke pinched the Kaarumite's nostrils shut, and a short time later his mouth opened. The soke began to pour a clear liquid into his mouth that looked just like water. The Kaarumite gagged and choked.

Once he subsided the soke said, "Drink, or it will go badly for you."

The Kaarumite drank.

"I think the smarter ones among them will not return to their people," Nirin said. "Or at the very least they will wait until the effects have dissipated before returning."

"Agreed," Roger said. "I think it is going to take something drastic to shock these people out of their culture. This may be just the thing to help that process along."

"Although I cannot claim to understand these people, I believe that it will definitely take more than this, but this is a start."

"Well, we can talk about it later. I need to get back to the base. Feel free to join me once you're done here. I'll see if I can get the cooks to prepare us some roasted meat."

"I may do just that."

Nightfall

THE SUN WAS SETTING AS Roger returned to the old tavlon city. The sky overhead was a dark purple color, while off in the eastern horizon a bright yellow-orange glow still prevailed. The immense tavlon city cast a long shadow over the forest as Roger approached.

However, this tavlon city was not as well preserved as the one which Roger, Aneme, and Garek had taken refuge in when they were wandering through the contested area before. This ancient city was more weathered along the exterior, and it had several large holes blown in it at various points.

Roger was told that they were ancient scars from a war between the Empire and Hax that happened over 6000 years ago. The tavlon cities, already abandoned at the time, were simply caught in the cross fire. When the Haxians came into the region they gutted what was left of the tavlon cities for new technology.

From what Roger was told, he was able to infer that the Haxians of that day were very much like the Axis Powers of Earth during the Second World War, not only in their mannerisms and goals, but also in the way they viewed and treated outsiders. It was only after they were crushed by the northerners that the ground work was laid for the modern nation of Hax, which supposedly bore very little resemblance to the original Hax.

As Roger paused to survey the damage he could not help but wonder how much trouble this world might have been spared if the once powerful

Haxians of that day had directed all of their might against the Kaarumites rather than the Empire.

"Well, the Haxians of today are helping at least," Roger said as he resumed his walk.

As he passed into the tavlon city he was greeted with salutes by Imperial soldiers and respectful nods from Haxian mercenaries. He found Garek waiting for him near the armory.

"Come on," Roger said. "We need to report to the Emperor."

Garek followed as Roger returned to the communication station.

"Your Majesty," Roger said once communication was established. "Did you receive the device?"

"We did, Mattis," the Emperor replied. "I cannot thank you and your men enough. Gather their names and I will have all of them issued a commendation, sokes included."

"I'll do it."

"Our scientists are looking over the machine right now, including some sokes that we brought in, they have a keen understanding of energy fields as you may know. But so far the most we have been able to figure out is how to turn it on and off, and to adjust the radius of the field."

"Well I'm sure that if those barbarians can figure out how to use it then our people can as well."

"Did you sustain any casualties?"

"None."

"The Great Maker was with you."

"Any orders, Sir?"

"Hold position for now, and get some rest if you can. The remainder of the Kaarumite fleet has headed north toward the Empire. They are blasting a wide path through the forests, and they are hitting the ground so hard in some places that the surface is becoming molten and solidifying into rock. We want to take out the remainder of their air fleet before we have any of our men expose themselves on the ground."

"A sound plan, Sir."

"Under the circumstances I am going to have to ask you to spend the night where you are. The battle is too fierce in the air for safe passage, and your wife agrees."

"Understood."

"We also do not wish to reveal the location of any of our bases of operation by sending aircraft at this point."

"I understand. I just wish there was some way I could be part of the battle."

"You have done enough for now. Get some well-earned rest. We will speak again tomorrow."

"Wait, has there been any word from the Empire? What about the northerners that were going to try to help us?"

"No word, other than the standard check in. Everything is well on the home front, but we have not heard from any of the northerners."

"Well, I guess it will take some time. I imagine they will be very difficult to convince."

"Keep it in your prayers. Do you wish to speak with your wife?"

"Of course."

"Husband," Aneme said as she appeared on the screen.

"How are you doing up there, babe?" Roger asked.

"I am doing well, other than worrying about you, but I trust that you know what you are doing. Are your dreams still guiding you?"

"Not at present, but I also haven't been able to get any good and proper sleep lately."

"Something will come up."

"Is it very dangerous up there?"

"Leonus is well protected. Some Kaarumite ships have crashed into the type two forcefield, and we have also been shot with a few missiles, but nothing can get through. I am probably in the safest place there is to be right now. I just feel bad for Demekus. He wanted to come to the battle so much but was left behind."

"Well, we probably should not talk about that over the communications network."

"I understand."

When the conversation was ended Roger motioned for Garek to follow him and they headed for one of the dining areas.

"What is Nirin doing with the prisoners?" Garek asked.

Roger quickly explained Nirin's plan, and Garek was pleased.

"Pure genius," Garek said. "I would very much like to go and assist him."

"Not tonight," Roger said.

Roger and Garek picked up their food, which contained large chunks of dark brown meat that resembled some sort of pot roast.

"I wonder what it is?" Roger asked.

Garek sniffed at his plate and said, "Roast sonolar I should think."

"Seriously?" Roger asked. "One of those big blue dinosaur things?"

"I don't know what 'dinosaur' means, but if you are talking about one of those tremendous reptiles with the long tail and long neck that the Kaarumites sometimes use in battle, then yes. A small troop of Kaarumites was ambushed and killed yesterday, sonolar included, and the cooks thought it would be a good source of meat."

"Interesting. In that case I will try the sonolar."

The sonolar was served along with some blue and purple vegetables which Roger had come to be familiar with some time ago.

Garek was about to sit down at a private table reserved for officers when Roger stopped him.

"No," Roger said, "I want to eat somewhere with a view. Let's eat on the balcony."

"What balcony?" Garek asked.

"Hey," Roger said as he waved one of the cooks in his direction. "If Nirin comes here looking for us tell him we have gone to the balcony."

"Balcony, sir?" the cook asked.

"There is a big hole that starts in the third level and runs up for three floors in what used to be tavlon living quarters. I call it the balcony because it's open to the air and has a nice wide view. It's on the southwest side. That's where I'm going to be."

"Understood, sir," the cook replied.

"Let's go, Garek," Roger said.

"Why?" Garek said.

"For the view," Roger said. "Come."

Garek followed, and it took them nearly ten minutes to get there. They went up three flights of stairs and passed on into a dimly lit corridor. The guards saluted as they passed.

"I didn't expect to have to go up three flights of stairs before getting to sit down and eat," Garek groused.

"There's more to eating than just eating," Roger said. "It's also about relaxing."

"What foolishness. Do you think I'm a teenage girl that must 'feel' everything?"

"You know what, Garek, sometimes you have too much attitude."

"Maybe, but I am what my life has made me."

"Or your life is what you have made it."

"Perhaps a bit of both."

They passed through a narrow doorway and were greeted by open air and a panoramic view of the forest. Since the tavlon city was built on higher ground they could see across much of the forest, and off in the distance they could still see flashes of light as Imperial and Kaarumite forces fought in the air. Through the holes in the cloud cover they could see bright stars gleaming in the night sky.

Roger seated himself on the floor and bid Garek to do the same thing. Once Garek was seated he immediately fell upon his food. Roger took one cautious bite of his sonolar meat, and found, very much to his surprise, that it was quite good. He began to devour it quickly.

"Garek," Roger said after his hunger had been partly sated. "I want to make sure that what happened today never happens again."

"What do you mean?" Garek asked.

"You have been in the army before, and you have been on a police force. You understand why discipline is important. I don't mind if you have suggestions to offer, and I don't mind if you even respectfully point out problems with some plan that I have, but once I have made a decision on the battlefield then that has to be the end of the discussion. There cannot be any attitude, it's bad for discipline and morale."

"I know, and I'm sorry, but the Kaarumites just drive me absolutely mad."

"Well, please make sure that it doesn't happen again. If I have to take disciplinary action against you then that is also not going to be good for morale."

"It won't happen again."

"Good. Now tell me, why is it you hate the Kaarumites so much?"

"Does there need to be any one reason?"

"When we were trying to convince Nirin to join us, you said something to him about the Kaarumites killing a woman you loved."

"Yes."

"Tell me about her."

"She was the first woman I ever loved, and I have never loved another like that since then. The love I had for that woman was at least as true and intense as the love you and Aneme have for each other."

"And the Kaarumites burned her to death?"

"Not just any Kaarumites, her family. You see, I was in love with a Kaarumite woman, but she was less religious than most Kaarumites. We were going to go away from there together... Maybe go back to Hax, or settle in Tandor or the southern continent beneath Tandor..."

Garek rose up and began to pace.

"How did you meet?" Roger asked.

"I was posted there," Garek said. "I was part of a group of Haxian mercenaries working for the Empire, and we were occupying a town that had been retaken from the Kaarumites. If I had only gotten there quicker I could have stopped them!"

Garek turned to face Roger.

"I didn't need to wait until my post was up!" Garek shouted. "I could have taken her and left at any time. No one would have done anything with me. Those savages killed their own daughter! I heard her screaming through the door, and I couldn't get in until it was all over, but I made them suffer before I killed them. I want to make them all suffer and die. And why not? That is all they do to other people wherever they meet them in the world, and whenever they have large enough numbers to overpower them."

"What was her name?" Roger asked.

"What?"

"The name of the woman."

"Mareesha... I will never forget her..."

"What if, in your haste to kill all of the Kaarumites, you kill another man's Mareesha?"

"Unlikely."

"But it's a possibility that cannot be logically eliminated."

Garek said nothing.

"I definitely agree that their insane death cult needs to be destroyed, but I don't think we need to kill every last one of them to achieve that," Roger said.

"If we win this battle Kaarum is going to be a land populated by widows and children," Garek said. "Maybe we should press on and invade their worship cities? We can destroy them and desecrate their temples. We may as well take our momentum to its natural conclusion."

"I will discuss it with the Emperor when the time comes, assuming that we win."

"I hope we do win," Garek said as he re-seated himself on the ground and began to finish off what was left of his food.

"Slightly different subject," Roger said. "Have you thought about settling down and getting married after the war is all over?"

"I am not the type of man to settle down easily, but I do have a strong idea of what I would like."

"Do you have someone in mind?"

"There you are!" said a voice at the door.

It was Nirin, and in addition to a plate of food he was carrying a large clay jug which hung on a twine rope that was draped over one shoulder. In his other hand he held three glasses which clearly belonged to the galley.

"It took me so long to find this place, even with asking the guards for instructions," Nirin said. "These tavlon cities are dreadfully confusing, and none too comfortable on the feet."

"You want me to get you a cushion?" Roger asked.

"If you can manage without one then I can."

"Well come on in and take a seat. The view is awesome from here. What is it you have in that jug?"

"It's a soke drink," Nirin said. "It helps muscle tissue regenerate after an extended struggle. Of course, I imagine it is a good deal more effective on sokes than it is on humans."

"Is it safe for humans?" Garek asked.

"Of course it is," Nirin replied.

"Well, have a seat, friend," Roger said. "The sonolar is especially delicious."

Nirin seated himself on the floor next to Roger and Garek and poured a creamy yellow liquid into the glasses for each of them. Garek immediately drank his down while Roger hesitated and sniffed at the strange liquid. It did not smell bad, or particularly good, just alien. He carefully took a sip, and found that the flavor was to his liking.

"Good stuff, Nirin," Roger said. "I hope it doesn't cause any weird side effects."

"It will not," Nirin said.

"Well then," Roger said. "Garek was just about to tell us about his ideal woman."

"That should prove interesting," Nirin said.

"Go ahead, Garek," Roger said.

"Alright…" Garek said. "How do I explain?"

"How about from the beginning," Roger said.

Nirin laughed.

"Very well," Garek said. "You might say that the woman I want is all women, and no woman."

"That doesn't make much sense," Roger said.

"Well, I know you are happy with Aneme, and Nirin is also happy with his wife, but I'm sure when you were single there were many women you found attractive, even if the majority of women did not appeal to you," Garek said. "Even after you married Aneme, you are still able to recognize an attractive woman when you see one."

"Go on," Roger said.

"Well, not all the women you find attractive are the same, there might be two women who you consider equally attractive in all areas even though they look different from each other. What does it mean when one woman has blue eyes that you find highly attractive, and another woman has brown eyes that you find just as attractive?"

"It means I'm a little flexible."

"Yes and no."

"You're making less sense now."

"Hear me out… Suppose you meet a woman with blue eyes and straight black hair. You like that a lot, but then later you meet a woman with wavy brown hair and green eyes, and you find that you are equally attracted to both? What does it mean?"

"It means that I'm flexible, and capable of appreciating lots of things. Or it means that more than one variety is attractive."

"No."

"Alright then, tell me what it means."

Hopefully I'm not going to be sorry for asking about this…

"You think it means that you're being flexible or broad-minded, but two things that are different cannot be equal, ever," Garek said.

"Then?"

"There is an underlying essence that makes a woman attractive. It runs through all women, but not in equal quantities, and manifests in a variety of ways, which is why we can find more than one woman attractive. It does not matter whether the woman has brown eyes or green eyes, but how much of the essence of womanhood went into the making of that woman."

"What?"

"Now, imagine if you could distill that essence into one vessel and fill it to the brim. You would have the woman who is all women, in every meaningful way. You would have the ultimate woman, who could satisfy any desire or preference. Hair color, skin color, eye color, and to a certain extent facial features are all just secondary or ancillary manifestations of this essence. You would not even notice them on such a woman. All that you would know is that you're adrift on a sea of desire, but unlike the ocean, it's water you can drink! In such a situation man can never go thirsty, but if he's taken out of it and put into a dry place then he will feel thirst more strongly than ever before, and he'll do nothing but long for the return to that place."

"Huh…"

"Such a woman is the perfect being to satisfy a man like me, who finds it difficult to settle down with one woman out of a desire to experience every type of woman. The westerners, the southerners, the Haxians, and the northerners are all only partly filled with the essence, and not in the same way. The woman I want is she who is filled fully to the brim."

"Alright."

"Do you understand now?" Garek asked.

"Not really," Roger said. "What about you Nirin?"

"I must confess, such a pre-occupation with physical appearance is alien to me," Nirin said.

"Really?" Roger said. "Please explain?"

"Although we sokes certainly appreciate physical beauty, it is not the primary motivating factor during the match making process," Nirin said. "The primary factor is psychological compatibility. I appreciate that my wife is physically beautiful, but I also find all other soke women beautiful. I find my wife more beautiful mainly because she is my wife. We sokes are beings of dual forms, we have our energy form and our physical form. The energy form is rather abstract, and difficult to describe to outsiders. It is also something that is sensed rather than physically seen. The physical form is primarily viewed as a tool or vehicle."

"How does that work?" Garek asked. "I mean, if you find all the women attractive then doesn't that mean you have no beauty concept?"

"We do have beauty concepts," Nirin replied. "For example, we think the green grass of a valley beautiful, and the leaves on trees as well. Although each blade of grass and each leaf is different, how do you say that one is beautiful and another ugly if they are both healthy and strong?"

"But we are talking about women," Garek said.

"Sokes are different from humans," Nirin said. "As you may have noticed, the physical differences between us are simply not as great as those that exist between humans. There is no deformity among us, and the aging process does not change the appearance of the physical form. If a soke is unsatisfied with his or her coloration it can be changed, but most of us do not care to change it. Those of us who are more powerful can change their shape to appear as anyone. But, the small differences that exist naturally between us are viewed positively rather than negatively."

"Well, I never really have seen an ugly soke before," Roger said.

"So do you think we human males are foolish to care so much looks?" Garek asked.

"Not necessarily," Nirin replied. "I understand that you are permanently locked into one body until you die. I am certain that on some level you are driven by instinct, and that, given the diverse range of looks you have, preferences will vary. But to be honest I have no idea what it is like to be human, and I never found human women particularly attractive or appealing. There are some soke men here and there who maintain that they are intrigued by human women, even though they would never approach one, and they sometimes talk in detail about the physical appearances of the women, but I do not know whether they genuinely think that way or if they are mimicking a behavior that they saw in others."

"Well, here's to women," Roger said as he lifted his glass of yellow liquid. "Whether they be blue, white, or green. We still need them."

Garek and Nirin said nothing. Garek raised an eyebrow while Nirin poured more of the liquid into Roger's cup, assuming incorrectly that Roger wished for a refill.

"Guys," Roger said. "You're supposed to lift your glasses and touch them to mine."

"Why?" Garek asked.

"It's an Earth custom, to show that you agree," Roger said.

"Oh," Garek said.

They both lifted their glasses and touched them to Roger's.

"We agree, Roger," Nirin said.

"Now what?" Garek asked.

"Now we drink the stuff down," Roger said.

They drank.

"A peculiar custom this is," Nirin said after he emptied his glass. "Perhaps I will introduce it among my people. It has been so long since any new customs were introduced."

"Do your people have glasses?" Garek asked.

"We occasionally drink from clay vessels," Nirin said.

Emissary

Once Roger finished socializing he was escorted further into the tavlon city to a section that had been established as crew quarters. He was given an apartment to himself. It was an ancient set of rooms which must once have belonged to a tavlon family, and consisted of two rooms and a bathroom.

I wonder how many people lived here back in the day?

The doors were long gone, and so was any carpet or furnishings. The walls were surprisingly intact however, particularly when compared with the rest of the city. There did not appear to be any damage done to his chamber.

He walked around and examined the relief carvings, but most of what he found was carvings of animals, landscapes, and floral patterns. Eventually he came across some humanoid figures carved into a portion of the wall, but they were of such a small size that he was unable to tell whether they were intended to be human, soke, or tavlon. He guessed that they were supposed to be tavlon, but given their size and the lack of color he could not eliminate the possibility that they might not also be sokes or humans.

Finally Roger lay down on the cot they had placed in the room for him and immediately fell asleep.

As he slept he dreamt that he was moving along the corridors of the floating city of Leonus. There was some kind of disturbance going on there. People seemed frantic and concerned. Then everything changed and he was moving down a different set of corridors. He saw a man working vigorously at a set of controls, and he felt the distinct impression that he was up to no good.

Roger awoke with a start, and for a second he imagined that the figures on the wall were moving. He quickly hurled himself out of bed and activated his soke implant, flooding the room with light.

Everything was normal. He checked the time and found that only a little more than an hour had passed. He stepped out into the hallway and ordered one of the guards to bring him a portable communication device and route it through to Leonus.

When the guard returned with the device he called Leonus and demanded to speak with his wife.

"Is everything alright up there?" Roger asked.

"Yes," Aneme replied. "But nothing has changed. Please try to get some rest. I was just going to bed myself when you called."

"Alright, but be on the lookout. I had a dream that something bad happened."

"What happened?"

"I don't know. I didn't finish the dream. Maybe it was nothing. I'm going to go back to sleep. You be careful up there, love. Call me if there are any problems."

"I will."

Roger tried to go back to sleep after he hung up with his wife, but he found it difficult. Finally he called a soldier and asked him to bring him something to help him sleep. The guard returned with some sort of drink, which Roger swallowed rapidly, and immediately Roger felt tired.

He returned to the cot and fell into a deep sleep.

***

Aneme went to sleep shortly after her final discussion with Roger. She began to wake as the sun rose, but was sped to full awareness by a call at her personal communication station.

"Commander General Vaila," the voice said over the communicator.

"Yes," Aneme replied.

"You are needed in the war room, madam."

"I'm coming at once."

Since Aneme had slept with her clothes on all she had to do was put on her sword and shoes in order to prepare. The sword she kept secured in its sheath and hidden under her pillow. There was no risk of danger because she was so disciplined that even in her sleep she remained still and in control of herself.

Soldiers saluted her as she walked down the hall toward her destination.

"What is the situation?" she asked when she entered the war room.

"Have a look," the Emperor said as he pointed at a glowing monitor.

"What are they doing?"

"Just hovering there. They wanted to come in but I refused them. They keep repeating the same message over and over again."

Aneme puzzled over the image.

"Is this a live feed?" she asked.

"It is," the Emperor replied.

An ugly looking medium sized vessel filled the viewscreen. It hovered just outside of the type one forcefield that enclosed Leonus. Occasionally it drifted from side to side and had to be straightened out by a burst of energy.

"What is their message?" Aneme said.

The Emperor pressed a button on the console and a forceful masculine voice began to speak, "I repeat… We require face to face negotiation. We want to end this war, but we will settle for nothing else."

"A trick?" Aneme questioned.

"I assume so, which is why I denied their request," the Emperor said. "Once they are inside of our forcefields all they have to do is detonate one bomb and that is the end of Leonus. As far as Kaarumites are concerned they will be richly rewarded in the next life for killing unbelievers."

"We don't have internal forcefields to cordon off portions of this city?"

"No, Leonus is an old design. When my ancestor built it he thought that it made more sense to pour all the energy into the external forcefields to keep enemies from entering. He saw redundant internal forcefields as a pointless waste of power."

"They must believe they are losing to try something so desperate. They surely cannot have many airships left. Why wasn't this one blown out of the air?"

"The remainder of the air fight has moved off to the north, and yes, they have very few ships left. This one came in from the south, and it is unarmed. We detected no earth scorchers aboard but we only would have been able to detect active warheads. They could have the component parts for something aboard and quickly work to assemble it while we negotiate."

"I am curious to hear what they say, even if it is all lies. We might still learn something that they don't want us to learn. Is there any way we can safely let them in?"

"I am open to suggestions," the Emperor said.

"I think we should hear what they have to say," said the advisor Mendarius. "We can always let them land and seize their ship quicker than they can assemble an active warhead."

"Not necessarily," Aneme said.

"We should blow them out of the sky," another advisor said.

"Well that is terribly uncivilized," Mendarius said. "They are here under a truce."

"We agreed to no truce," the other advisor said.

"Warn them off," another advisor said.

"But what if they really want to negotiate?" Mendarius asked. "We would be missing out on an excellent opportunity to end this war before it gets any worse."

"Kaarumites do not negotiate," the other advisor said.

"They do not negotiate from a position of strength," Mendarius corrected.

"Everyone knows that under normal circumstances Kaarumites do not negotiate," Aneme said. "Even when they are vastly outnumbered they prefer death over surrender or compromise. The closest I have ever heard of any Kaarumites coming to a negotiation was when they were vastly outnumbered by Imperial forces, and ordered to leave an area and not return upon pain of death."

"There was one occasion during the reign of my great, great, grandfather when a group of Kaarumites agreed to a prisoner exchange," Adinis said.

"That is new information to me," Aneme said.

"So then... we will waste this opportunity?" Mendarius asked.

"I do think we should hear what they have to say, and I would like to be present and part of the process," Aneme said.

"Which brings us back to the issue of how it can be done," the Emperor said.

"Is there a way we can isolate the landing pad?" Aneme asked.

"There might be," an advisor said. "As you mentioned before, sir, we have no internal infrastructure to generate a local forcefield. But, we might be able to rig up some mobile emitters to set up a type two forcefield around the pad where they are stationed. That would allow them to move out of the area but it would still contain any explosion."

"Check on that and see if it can be done," the Emperor said.

"We also need to secure their ship to the landing pad so that they don't attempt to fly it to another part of the city and blow themselves up," Aneme said. "Can you shoot them with some grappling hooks and tethers before they come in?"

"Can we?" the Emperor repeated to his team of advisors.

"We will get right on it sir," an advisor said.

Half an hour later the technical advisors stated definitively that all of Aneme's precautions would be possible, but that it would take at least five hours to set up with everyone working as fast and hard as they could.

"Then we have no time to waste," the Emperor said. "Begin at once."

"Yes sir," the advisors replied.

"Send an announcement to that ship that we will allow them to negotiate, but that they must submit to having their ship tethered and searched upon arrival," the Emperor said. "Any weapons they have will be confiscated."

After the announcement was sent a deep masculine voice replied, "We accept your terms."

The technicians and soldiers worked quickly to make everything ready for the landing of the Kaarumite vessel, and once it was they opened a hole in the type one forcefield and ordered the vessel to halt until all of the tethers were attached.

Aneme and the Emperor watched via a monitor in the conference room as metal cables shot up and wrapped around parts of the ship and latched themselves magnetically to the hull. They pulled the ship slowly inward, and as it neared the landing pad it was secured by two metal grappler arms and lowered down onto the pad.

Fifty soldiers rushed out onto the landing pad and surrounded the vessel, while others waited just inside of the building.

A door on the side of the dingy gray vehicle fell open and swung down onto the ground with a loud slam. Two white Kaarumite soldiers stepped out and stood to the side. They were mostly bald except for a circular spot of hair growing out of the top center of their heads, which was allowed to grow long. They wore no clothing but some tattered red pants fastened about with three belts of some sort of hide, and shoes made of a similar material. Their bodies were covered in black tattoos consisting of stylized animals and various Kaarumite words and symbols. Their ears were notched and pierced. One of the men also had an eyebrow pierced, while the other had his cheeks pierced.

"So barbaric!" one of the advisors said. "Why do we even let these disgusting animals onto our ship? It's against all our laws and sensibilities."

The men were on the tall side for members of the white race, and powerfully built, yet they were also rather narrow around the waist so that the tops of their pelvic bones stuck out slightly.

They were swiftly made to stand with their hands against the craft and patted down by the guards. One of the men looked directly at the camera and smiled. He flicked out his tongue, which was split down the middle so that it looked forked.

For the first time it occurred to Aneme that the majority of her people might be misguided in their unwillingness to help the other races fight against the Kaarumites.

The draenocks are bad, but this was something that may very well be a greater evil. What was the use in holding back the draenocks if the rest of the world becomes populated with such people?

Next a large bald southern Kaarumite stepped out of the vehicle. He stood more than a head taller than the white Kaarumites, but he wore similar clothing and was similarly tattooed, except that his torso was dominated by a large black skull design. This man was completely bald, and he had a piercing running through the area just beneath his lower lip.

He was also searched immediately upon stepping out. He tried to resist at first but the Imperial soldiers forced him up against the side of the vessel and two of them held him in place while another patted him down.

A group of Imperial soldiers then boarded the vessel and forced out two more Kaarumites, which were then searched. One of the remaining Kaarumites was of the large southern variety, but there was something different about the third one. At first Aneme thought he might have been a white Kaarumite, or Randargan, but upon prolonged examination she realized that he actually had pale blue skin.

Like many Kaarumite males he had long hair, no beard, and the obligatory sun tattoo on his forehead, but he wore a shirt, and his clothing was mostly black.

"Strange," she said quietly.

"What?" the Emperor asked.

"Look at that one," Aneme said pointing at the unusual Kaarumite.

"The one wearing mostly black?" the Emperor asked.

"Yes… He must be of Haxian descent."

"It is possible, but I have never seen a Haxian convert to Kaarum before."

"Let's see what we can find out."

After being searched the Kaarumites were led inside, and flanked by Imperial guards on all sides. As they proceeded down the walkway all but two of the Kaarumites smiled. The two who did not were the large bald southern Kaarumite and the light blue one.

"What are they smiling about?" one of the advisors present asked.

"They think that we are afraid of them," Aneme said.

The Emperor sent a message to the guards instructing them to find out which of the Kaarumites was the ambassador and to have him brought into the conference room. The rest were to be detained, and kept away from their ship.

The large bald southern Kaarumite with the skull tattoo on his chest was singled out, but he motioned for the pale blue one to follow. The blue one took a step forward but the guards blocked him.

The large bald one proceeded to argue with the guards, insisting that his aid should be allowed to follow, and that if he were detained there would be no further negotiations.

"I think we should let that other one come as well," Aneme said.

The Emperor contacted the guards and ordered them to allow the other man through as well. A short time later the doors to the conference room opened and the Kaarumites stepped in flanked by guards.

The large bald Kaarumite glowered as he entered the room. His eyes were yellow, and the area around each eye was either tattooed or painted black, as were his lips. He was quite an imposing figure, who towered at least a head taller than everyone else present in the room.

"Which one of you is the Emperor?" he said with a deep masculine voice.

"You will introduce yourself first," said one of the Imperial guards.

"I am Ambassador Vorgok Garomaros," the large Kaarumite said. "This is my aid Feren."

"I am Emperor Adinis Maxelis," the Emperor said as he stood up. "I greet you in the name of the Great Maker."

The large southerner made a disdainful choking noise upon hearing "Great Maker."

"Do be seated," the Emperor said motioning toward some empty chairs at the end of the table.

The large brown Kaarumite sat down while his aid remained standing. Vorgok looked around at everyone who was seated, and when his eyes fell on Aneme he scowled disdainfully.

"I see you suffer your women to be seated in your places of council," Vorgok said. "I am surprised you would allow me to see such weakness."

"You will speak with respect when you refer to Commander General Vaila Maxelis," the Imperial officer said.

"Am I supposed to be impressed by such titles?" Vorgok said. "Titles can be made up and given to anyone, but that does not make that person anyone of importance. What value could a woman bring here? Every intelligent man knows that a woman cannot make sound decisions. They are as weak in mind as they are in body. In Kaarum we do not ask our women what they think, we tell them what we want them to think, and if they disagree we beat or kill them. A woman is nearly as witless as the animals, which is why they relate to them better."

"Enough," the Emperor said. "Did you come here to parley with us or to discuss your philosophies?"

"I came to parley, but I was surprised by the presence of a witless woman," Vorgok said. "I cannot expect much from men who care what a woman thinks. You should remove her from this place."

"Listen, you utter savage," one of the guards began. "When it comes to wits, strength, or battle prowess the Lady Vaila is your better in each area. If you would care to test it…"

The guard who spoke was one of the original men Aneme had trained, and she knew full well that she could outmatch the barbaric southerner in a physical confrontation, but she could not shake the feeling that there was a hidden purpose behind his presence there, and that he may be trying to throw up some sort of smoke screen.

The Emperor held up his hand, "I said enough, either you are here to negotiate or not. Now say what you came here to say or I will have the guards take you out."

"Yes you and your guards…" Vorgok began. "I did not know the high and mighty civilized Imperials treated ambassadors with such disdain. You acted as if we were common criminals."

"It is unusual for the Kaarumites to establish embassies or parley," Adinis replied.

"Yes, but we are now living in different times. This time we have what it takes to destroy your precious Empire completely."

"Then why negotiate with us?"

"It is not out of sympathy for you or your people. We simply wish to keep the resources and the machinery of the Empire intact. All throughout history we have operated by obliterating native cultures and civilizations. Atuskus-Var, may truth light his way, has declared that we can advance more as a civilization by allowing some of the heretics to work for us. I came to negotiate with you."

"Very well, ambassador, but you must realize that we do not wish to surrender to you, nor do we see a need for it. We have obliterated your air fleet, and your army on the ground is surrounded."

"Yes, we know that you have entered an alliance with the wood demons. Very dangerous. Under normal circumstances we would have returned to our own land immediately, but these are not normal circumstances. We are led by Atuskus-Var, the son of Kaarum. We see his power and wisdom with our own eyes every day. Atuskus-Var is stronger than the strongest champions of the northern witch people. He could unwrap your strongest warships with his bare hands, as you would unwrap a piece of meat.

"The wood demons cannot touch him with their sorcery. He comes to the battlefield even as we speak. You cannot win this conflict. The power of Kaarum shines down on us from above, the son of Kaarum comes to join the battle on the ground, and the spirit of Kaarum burns in all of us. Your forces will melt before us, and your Empire will be ravaged to the ground unless you surrender. You Imperials think us stupid, but we have a great surprise in store for you. You think us cornered and trapped below, but we have only begun to fight. The force you see on the ground is only the vanguard."

"Impossible!" one of the advisors said. "We have been watching your people from—"

The Emperor raised a hand to cut him off.

"What are your terms?" the Emperor asked.

"Your majesty!" the advisor exclaimed. "Surely you don't mean to—"

"I want to hear what he says," the Emperor replied.

"A wise choice, your majesty," said councilman Mendarius.

Aneme focused her attention on Mendarius.

"My terms, 'your majesty' are as follows," Vorgok said. "You will surrender to us completely and escort us back to your Empire. Once there, you will assist us in disarming your people. We will appoint one of your sons to succeed you, and you yourself shall retire to a luxurious estate in a place of your choosing. Your son will be the lead civil administrator for your people. All production and trade in your Empire will be overseen by Kaarumites. Anyone who wishes to convert to Kaarum shall be treated as equals and allowed to serve in the Kaarumite army. Anyone who does not shall be allowed to keep his religion, but he will pay taxes to Kaarum. We will allow you to keep your religious buildings and services, but you will not engage in any public displays of religion outside of your homes or religious structures. I have a list of terms which outlines the relationship between Kaarumites and heretics following your surrender."

Vorgok removed a scroll from a pouch he wore around his waist and slid it across the table toward the Emperor. Adinis picked up the scroll and untied the string around it. The brown paper unrolled and trailed across the floor. The Emperor frowned as he read from the scroll.

"This is unacceptable," the Emperor said.

"Which part do you object to?" Vorgok asked.

"Everything I have read so far."

"What have you read?"

The Emperor looked up and studied the man's face, but Vorgok appeared to be completely serious.

"Well, 'A Kaarumite man shall be permitted to take wives of any of the heretics he chooses, but no heretic shall approach a Kaarumite woman for marriage or relations. Any heretics seeking to build, amend, or repair a non-Kaarumite religious structure must first get permission from the Kaarumite magistrates that will be appointed to administer law enforcement in each of the provinces. Heretics may not purchase land from Kaarumites. Heretics may not bear weapons over six inches long. Heretics may not bar the way of Kaarumites when they are walking, riding, or driving. When a Kaarumite is walking heretics must step aside…'"

The Emperor placed the scroll back on the table and pushed it away with his fingertips.

"This is an insult," the Emperor said. "You surely cannot expect me to take this document seriously."

"I find it to be highly reasonable and generous," Vorgok said. "Traditionally we would take whatever we want from you by force and force all of your people to choose between conversion or death."

"I would like to offer a counter proposal."

"Say on."

"We split the Contested Area between us with a nice even line down the middle. We keep the northern half, and you keep the southern half. Neither of us will cross into the other side, and we will cease all hostilities. If you like we will formally recognize Atuskus-Var as king of all Kaarum."

"He is already king of all Kaarum, and we already have these things you offer. We make you an offer out of the generosity of our hearts, to spare your people and your culture, are you so foolish as to reject it?"

"We will not surrender."

"You will surrender now or you will surrender later, I come to offer you—"

Vorgok halted as a new officer arrived and began whispering in Aneme's ear.

"If you will excuse me," Aneme said as she rose.

The Kaarumite Ambassador Disembarks
—by Roy Gilbertson

CHAPTER 26

Treachery

R{OGER AWOKE WITH A START.} He remembered the entire dream, and he felt a sense of urgency. He rushed out of his apartment and ran to the nearest communication station. He immediately made a call to Leonus.

"I want to talk to Commander-General Vaila," he said to the soldier on the other end.

"She is in a meeting sir," the officer said.

"What sort of meeting?"

"Negotiations with Kaarumites."

"Is that some sort of joke?"

"No sir, the Emperor is also there."

"Forget about it, go and get my wife. It's an emergency."

"Understood sir."

A few minutes later Aneme greeted him over the communication channel.

"Are you by yourself?" Roger asked.

"I can be," Aneme replied.

"I need you to get to a control room, it's in your building but three levels down from you. Something bad is about to happen, I think. Also send down a ship to pick me up."

"We cannot send a ship to pick you up, you know what the Emperor said."

"Send it off to the north. I'll have my people watch for it. But first get to that control room."

"Alright."

***

Aneme took out her earpiece and handed it back to a guard. Then she motioned for two other guards to follow her. She got into an elevator and dropped three floors. She knew which control room Roger was talking about but she did not know what exactly to expect when she got there.

When she reached the doors she found that they would not automatically open for her, which made some sense because the Kaarumites were aboard. She entered her passcode and the doors slid open only part way.

"What is this?" she mumbled.

She took out her sword, which was one of the old northern swords that had been stored in Leonus and ordered the guards to do the same.

"Open this door!" she shouted.

"I can't, the door seems to be jammed," said a voice from within.

"Jammed with what? How?"

"I don't know," the voice said, sounding somewhat frantic.

"Then I will unjam it."

"No wait, just give me a few minutes and I can get it open!"

Aneme took out her sword and slashed a huge chunk out of the door. Although the sword was nearly 1000 years old, it was designed for cutting through the monstrous draenocks of the north who contained a good deal of metal in their bodies. The door to that particular room was considerably older and softer than that. Once enough of a hole was cut Aneme kicked it in.

She burst into the room using a clearing move with two swords, designed to hit any opponents that might be waiting by the walls, but instead she saw only one man feverishly at work on the console.

"Halt!" she ordered.

The man kept hitting the keys, and in fact seemed to be in a hurry to finish whatever he was doing.

Aneme bounded across the room and grabbed him by the back of his collar. With a single burst of effort she flung him away from the console and half way across the room. The man attempted to run but the guards restrained him. There was a look of wild fear in his eyes.

"What were you doing there?" she asked.

The man simply shook his head.

"Very well," Aneme said. "Tie him up, and get a physician in here quickly with drugs and interrogation equipment."

"You can't do this to me!" the technician said. "I'm an Imperial citizen and I have rights!"

"If you answer my questions then I will not have to use the drugs."

One of the guards made the necessary calls using the intercom system.

"Well alright, ask me your questions now and I will answer truthfully," the technician said.

"And get another technician in here too," Aneme said. "I want someone here to undo whatever he did."

Then Aneme turned to the technician and said, "You have lied to me from the beginning. There is no point in asking you questions without a lie detector."

"The door really was jammed!" the technician exclaimed.

"Because you jammed it."

"Baseless accusations!"

"If so then that will be verified once the lie detector arrives."

The technician was tied to a chair, and when the medic arrived with the equipment he was quickly hooked up to a lie detector.

"What did you do?" Aneme asked.

The man said nothing.

"Who do you work for?" Aneme asked.

The man said nothing.

"How many more of you are there on board?"

Again, the man said nothing.

"Inject him," Aneme said.

"You can't do this!" he protested.

"I'm doing it," she stated flatly.

In the meantime another technician arrived and began examining the computer console where the traitor was at work.

"What did he do there?" Aneme asked.

"I'm not certain, but it looks like he was doing something with the shield grid," the new technician said.

"Find out what it was."

In the meantime Aneme put in a call for the Emperor, who stepped out of the room to take her call.

***

When he heard about the traitor the Emperor called a recess to the negotiations and had the Kaarumites escorted to quarters, where guards would remain close by, and access to restricted areas would be limited to only those with high level clearance.

Once the Kaarumites were gone the advisors began to question the Emperor.

"What's going on?" one of them asked.

"We caught a saboteur," the Emperor replied.

"What sort of saboteur, what was he doing?" the advisor Mendarius asked.

"I do not know all of the particulars, but Vaila is conducting the interrogation," Adinis said. "If the man knows anything then she will get it out of him."

"This is a dark and accursed day!" Mendarius said.

"No my friend, the Great Maker truly has his eye on us," the Emperor said. "It is better that the saboteur was caught, because now we can find everyone he was working with, assuming he was not working alone."

"Well in that case… You leave me with no choice."

Mendarius wrapped an arm around the Emperor's neck and pulled him in close. Immediately swords were unsheathed all around the room, and both guards and advisors took a step forward.

"Stop!" Mendarius shouted. "Stop or he dies instantly, and don't you struggle either, Emperor."

Mendarius held the back of his hand near the Emperor's head, and a small needle could be seen protruding from a ring on one of his fingers.

"This is laced with a fast acting toxin, all I have to do is touch him once and he is dead faster than any of you can do anything about it!" Mendarius said.

"If you kill me you will never make it out of here alive," the Emperor said calmly.

"No, and I do want to make it out of here alive, but if I can't do that then I am going to kill you before I do," Mendarius replied.

"What do you want?" one of the advisors asked.

"Give him nothing," the Emperor said.

"If I get nothing then you die," Mendarius said. "I just want a ship," Mendarius said. "Give me a ship and clear a launch pad. Once I'm on the ship the Emperor is free to go. It's an even exchange, one life for another. I know the Emperor does not really want to die. He has a wife and family to get back to. I don't really want to die either. No one needs to die if everyone cooperates."

"Orders?" a nearby officer asked.

"If anything happens to me then I want Commander General Mattis Maxelis in charge until the war is over," Adinis said.

"I want my ship now!" Mendarius shouted.

"Make a ship ready for him," Adinis said.

"Sir?" the officer asked.

"Make a ship ready for him," the Emperor repeated calmly.

"No tricks, or the Emperor dies!" Mendarius said.

One of the officers went to a communication station and ordered a ship to be made ready for departure and left unguarded.

"The ship is ready for you on launch pad six," the officer said.

"Let's move," Mendarius said as he gave the Emperor a push. "Nobody follow me."

***

Once the Emperor was gone Aneme called the command center.

"Where is the Emperor?" she asked.

"The Emperor has been taken hostage," an officer replied.

"What? How? By who?"

The officer quickly explained the situation.

"We aren't going to let him get away are we?" Aneme asked.

"We cannot let him take the Emperor off of Leonus, but we are willing to let him go for the time being," the officer replied.

"Unacceptable."

"But, my lady…"

"Since when does the Empire give into terrorists? Be prepared to act immediately when I call you back."

***

Mendarius continued to push the Emperor down the hall. His mind was continually at work on the problem of how to get out of his predicament. The Emperor Adinis Maxelis was not worried about himself, but about his wife and children, and the Empire.

I am too deeply involved in the war effort to stop now!

But the needle was right next to his neck. He thought about making a run for it but Mendarius' arm was there to slow him down long enough to poke him with the needle. He thought about trying to fight but unless he was able to put Mendarius out with one swift blow then he would be just as dead as if he tried to run. He regretted not taking the time to learn from Aneme or some of her trainees.

Foolish of me. If I survive this, then I should learn the Northern Arts. Better to know them and not need them, then need them and not know them.

"Why are you doing this?" the Emperor asked.

"Because I want to live," Mendarius replied.

"That is not what I meant. Why betray us in the first place, Mendarius? There is no reason for it."

"Why not?"

"You are not a Kaarumite, so why help them?"

"I don't care about the Kaarumites any more than I care about you."

"Are you working with the Brotherhood then?"

"No… and as you know they have been kept out of the Empire for some time, although I will never understand why you have such a particular hatred for them. It seems so random."

"Who are you working for then, and what did they offer you?"

"I'm not telling you who they are, and all they had to do was offer me lots of money, more money than even you take from the treasury. With enough money a man can be comfortable anywhere. It's nothing personal."

"Who wants me killed and why?"

"I'm not telling, and when you capture the others they will not be able to tell you anything useful either."

"So there are others then, besides you and the technician?"

"Of course there are. The oldest empire in the world is going to have a long list of enemies. I don't know whether or not the world will be better without the Empire, but I don't really care. I only care about myself, and I have already been paid well for what I have done so far."

As the rounded a corner they saw Aneme standing at the other end of the hallway with two guards.

"Ha! I knew someone would try to stop me," Mendarius said. "Don't forget I can kill him any second."

Mendarius pressed the ring dangerously close to the Emperor's neck.

"I did not order this," the Emperor said.

"I don't care, if they don't get out of my way you are just as dead," Mendarius said. Then he turned to Aneme and shouted, "I want you out of my way! One move and he's dead!"

"You are almost to the ship," Aneme said. "Let him go now."

"Do you think I'm stupid? He's coming with me until I reach the ship."

Mendarius held onto the Emperor tightly as he approached Aneme. He came within ten feet of her before he reached the door leading to the launch pad. The door was large, round, and gold colored with a built in locking mechanism. Aneme's eyes narrowed as Mendarius stood waiting for the door to unlatch.

"If you kill him I can't promise you a clean death," Aneme said.

"Oh I'm so frightened, ice picking whore," Mendarius said.

Aneme clenched her fists and one of the guards favored her with a curious glance.

"Oh yes, I know what you are, cave wench, and I know that some of the other advisors knew but they were all under orders to keep it a secret," Mendarius said. "They didn't tell me because I joined the team later. I'm sure that Vaila Maxelis is not even your real name, and I certainly intend to sell this information to my employers once I meet up with them. Now open this door!"

Aneme walked toward the wall right next to the door and entered her code. The door unlatched and slid away to the side.

"Now lower the type one forcefield," Mendarius said.

Aneme glanced toward the Emperor and made eye contact.

"Do it," he said.

Aneme placed a call to the operating center and ordered the type one forcefield to be lowered. A few seconds later a strong wind gusted by, and from then on the wind continued to blow but with less force.

"Now let him go," Aneme said.

"I don't think so, he's coming all the way to the ship with me, and I want you and your guards to step out as well," Mendarius said.

Mendarius stepped outside a few paces, and was followed by Aneme and the guards. The ship sat on top of the roof of another building, which was connected with the building they just stepped out of by 100 feet of causeway.

"Shut the door," Mendarius said.

Once the door was shut he ordered Aneme and the guards to remove their communicators and throw them over the side of the causeway.

"You have everything you need," Aneme said.

"I think I might take the Emperor with me, just for added insurance," Mendarius said.

"I cannot allow that."

"Then I will kill him here."

"If you take him then he will certainly be killed, and you will have gotten away."

"But if I leave him then how do I know you did not sabotage the ship? What assurance do I have that the type one forcefield will not be raised as soon as I try to leave?"

"That is a risk you will have to take, but if you try to take the Emperor I will kill you."

"Very well," Mendarius said. "Then I want you to disable your men with this knife."

Mendarius took out a knife of bluish metal with a one sided five inch long blade and held it out to Aneme with his other hand.

"It's an old northern blade from the stores here, you can stab them in the knees so that they cannot follow," Mendarius said.

What sort of mind casually conceives of such evil? And how did such a man get into my trusted council?

"You will do no such thing, Vaila," the Emperor said.

"Do it!" Mendarius shouted.

"I will not," Aneme said.

"Back up then, all the way against the wall!" Mendarius said.

The guards took two steps back but Aneme hesitated.

***

Aneme locked eyes with Mendarius, preparing to strike, and secure in the knowledge that she could hit him with the speed of a striking snake. There were over 100 ways she could take him down, and under current conditions most of them would be fatal.

I have no problem if that's what has to be done.

Suddenly Mendarius did something Aneme did not anticipate. With a quick stroke he slashed the Emperor in the back with the knife and pushed him into her. Then he took off running down the causeway as fast as he could.

Warm liquid spilled onto Aneme's hands as she caught the Emperor. It happened in a second. The Emperor's back was slit open from an area two inches below the rib cage to the collarbone. Skin, muscle, and bone were neatly severed, and the internal organs beneath were visible.

"Attend to him!" Aneme shouted to the guards as they rushed to her side and carefully took the Emperor into their arms.

Aneme raced after the retreating figure of Mendarius. As he ran he turned his head to look behind, and when he saw Aneme charging after him he began to run faster. But Aneme ran as fast as she could, and the space between them diminished rapidly.

Mendarius was nearly at the ship when Aneme pushed him from behind. The force of her momentum sent Mendarius tumbling across the deck. Somehow he managed fumble his way back up to his feet.

His eyes gleamed with delight when he saw that Aneme had not drawn out her sword. He still managed to hold onto his northern knife, but before he could make another move Aneme struck. With one hand she grabbed the wrist of the hand that held the knife, and with her other hand she struck him behind the elbow, catching his arm in a vice and breaking it instantly.

Mendarius screamed in pain, but it was only for a split second because next he was struck in the head. Aneme struck him a few more times before she realized that Mendarius was no longer conscious. The blows were less than precise, and were dealt with all the force she could muster.

When his limp form fell to the ground she nudged him with her foot, then dug her fingers into his clothes and lifted him up. Mendarius' head lolled back, and it quickly became apparent that there was no life in his body.

"Oh well," Aneme said.

She allowed herself to inhale and let out a slow breath, then she ran back to the place where the Emperor had been wounded. The Emperor was lying face down on the ground, and one of the guards was holding his back shut as best he could.

"He is still alive," the guard said as she approached.

"Have you called for help?" Aneme asked.

"Copius went to get help. What of the traitor?"

"I killed him."

"I hope it wasn't too quick!"

"He got what he deserved."

But I actually didn't mean to kill him, as much as I wanted to... We needed him for interrogation, and know we'll have to find out whatever it was he knew the hard way. The fact is I lost control. I haven't been that angry since the incident with that southern woman who cut me and gave me the touch.

Minutes seemed like hours to Aneme as she watched the Emperor struggle to hang onto life. His already troubled breathing grew increasingly more ragged. Eventually help did arrive, and the Emperor was carefully loaded into a mobile medical pod and whisked away to the nearest surgical center.

Aneme ordered the guards to remove the body of the traitor and quickly caught up with the medics as they made their way down the hall.

"What is the prognosis?" she asked.

"Not good," one of the medics said.

"Do you think he will survive?"

"I don't know, madam."

"I will leave you to it then."

Aneme returned to the command center and ordered one of the officers to send a shuttle for Roger immediately.

"But, Commander General," one of the officers replied. "The Emperor said—"

"I know what he said, but my husband is supposed to be in charge while the Emperor is down, so he needs to be here," Aneme said.

The officer nodded and gave the appropriate orders.

Roger in Charge

ROGER WAS NOTIFIED OF WHAT had happened before the shuttle arrived.

To think that guy was with us as a trusted advisor the whole time! None of us had him figured out!

When Roger returned to Leonus he found Aneme waiting for him.

"Will the Emperor survive?" Roger asked.

"I don't know," Aneme replied. "They said that the situation was bad, but I have yet to receive the medical report."

"I can't believe I'm in charge now..."

"Did you see that the Emperor would be hurt in your dreams?"

"No... I just saw people running around frantically, and I saw the man in the control room as you found him."

"What should we do?"

"I want to find out who the other traitors are before we do anything else."

"I will take you to the traitor we have in the control room."

When Roger and Aneme reached the control room they found that the drugs the traitor was given had taken effect. The man slumped in his chair, as much as was possible given that he was tied up, and his head swung slowly from side to side.

"Wake up you!" Roger said.

The man looked up slowly but seemed to have difficulty focusing on Roger.

"What is your name?" Roger asked.

"Valis Maxelis," the man replied.

"Maxelis? Are you actually related to the Emperor?"

"We have distant common ancestry."

"Disgusting!" Roger shouted. "Shame on you! You filthy—"

Aneme cleared her throat.

"What did you do on that console, Valis Maxelis?" Roger demanded.

Valis said nothing. His eyes rolled and drifted around the room randomly.

"Allow me, husband," Aneme said.

"Do it," Roger said.

"Did you sabotage any of our systems?" Aneme asked.

"I… tried," Valis said.

"Confirmed," said the other technician. "He was about to initiate a timed overload in the type one forcefield generators."

"Is that forcefield up now?" Roger asked.

"It is," the technician replied.

"Did you do anything else?" Aneme asked.

"No," Valis replied.

"Are there other saboteurs aboard?" Aneme asked.

"Yes."

"Are they soldiers?"

"No."

"Support staff?"

"Yes… and one advisor."

"Was the advisor Mendarius?"

"Yes."

"How many saboteurs are aboard?"

The technician's eyes lost focus and began to wander. Aneme stepped close and forced him to look her in the eyes.

"How many saboteurs are aboard?" Aneme asked.

"I…"

"You will be executed for treason if you do not cooperate," Aneme said.

"There are three others."

"Tell me their names."

Valis slowly mumbled three names, and Aneme ordered the guards to go and immediately apprehend those men.

"Are you working for the Kaarumites?" Aneme asked.

"No," the traitor said.

"Are you working for the Brotherhood?" Aneme asked.

"I don't know," Valis replied.

"Why are you doing this?" Roger asked.

"I hate the Empire," Valis replied.

"Why?" Roger asked.

"Just hate it. Hate the way of life… Hate the politics and religion… Want to see it destroyed… Don't care who does it."

"Do you know what any of the Kaarumite plans are?"

"No…"

Roger turned to Aneme and said, "When you are finished here have this man locked up and join me in the command center. I want all the traitors locked up separately and interrogated."

Aneme nodded.

When Roger returned to the command center the officers saluted, and the advisors asked him what was to be done next.

"Have we heard from the northerners yet?" Roger asked.

"Do you mean the ones that you negotiated with?" one of the advisors asked.

"Yes," Roger replied.

"Not a word. In fact we have not heard anything from Randar since the last standard check in."

"When was that?"

"Nearly a day ago."

"Let's check in with Randar right now."

The advisor nodded and they made a call to Randar.

"No response," the technician replied.

"Why not?" Roger asked.

"Unknown, but there is no indication that the signal was even received," the technician said.

"Check the communication systems for sabotage."

The technician nodded and set to work on his console. As he worked, other technicians and engineers flooded into the control room until it had nearly twice the amount of people that it did before.

"Well what about it?" Roger asked.

"We have not found anything yet, sir," one of the technicians said. "According to diagnostics there is nothing technically wrong. We are therefore checking the hardware manually to make certain we didn't miss anything."

"Maybe we are going about this the wrong way. There might be something going on externally that is blocking our communications."

"There is nothing coming from the Kaarumites other than those energy fields that stop our freeze weapons from going off."

"No, no... Not the Kaarumites... The traitor said that they were working for someone else."

"Sir?"

"Suppose that you were a third party that wanted the Kaarumites to win, and you wanted to find a way to cut us off from communicating with our home base. How would you go about it?"

"Well... I suppose I could do it by setting up a zone of interference."

"Where would you set it up and what equipment would you use?"

"I could use ground stations, or I could use air and space vehicles."

"Alright, I want you scanning for any energy fields that might cause interference, and I want men out in air and space vehicles looking for any devices that could be used."

"I'll get on it right away sir."

"Now someone take me to the Kaarumite 'ambassador,'" Roger said to all present.

"Ambassador Vorgok Garomaros is in his quarters, sir, under guard," an officer said. "Would you like me to take you there or have them brought to a conference room?"

"Take me to them, and follow me with a few guards."

Roger was led down a few floors to an elaborate hallway with dark red carpet and inlaid gold relief carvings on the walls. There were evenly spaced doors going down the entire length of the hall on one side. Some of the doors had guards stationed outside of them.

"Those are the rooms where the Kaarumites are being kept," the officer said.

They stopped at one of the guarded doors and the officer ordered the guards to open the door. They keyed in a set of commands and the door sunk into the wall and slid to the side.

Roger and his escort of soldiers entered a large apartment suite with one wall consisting entirely of windows, which afforded a panoramic view of the city. A large bald Kaarumite sat in a round bowl-like chair, and swiveled it to face them as they entered the room.

"Well?" he said.

"Well what?" Roger asked.

"Have you decided to surrender?"

"No, I have come to dictate terms."

"Oh really? And why does your Emperor not come to dictate these terms himself?"

"Listen, 'ambassador,' there was an assassination attempt on the Emperor, and he has placed me in command for the time being."

"How pitiful."

"I want to see your people hiking south in the next hour. I am going to send them a message. If they don't leave then we are going to beat them back."

"They will not obey your orders."

"Then you will follow my message with one of your own."

"I will not."

"I thought you might say that. Bring the other one in here…"

One of Vorgok's eyes narrowed as he scrutinized Roger. A short time later the light blue skinned Kaarumite was escorted into the room.

"What is your name and function?" Roger asked the pale blue man.

"I am Feren Saben, an aide to the ambassador," the blue man answered.

"Do you know why I brought you here?" Roger asked.

"I do not."

"I brought you here because I believe that you are the smartest one in your group. Of course, it may be that you seem smarter because you don't talk as much, but we will find out for certain soon enough."

"Humor," Feren replied flatly.

"Not humor," Roger said. "Call it a loss of patience, if you want."

"I'm listening," Feren replied.

"You do not take orders from him, Haxian!" the ambassador shouted.

"Haxian!" Roger said. "That's what I thought. You are a convert?"

"Yes," Feren replied.

"Listen, Feren, I am going to order the Kaarumites to go back south and never return," Roger said. "I want you to back me up. Will they know who you are?"

"Some of them might, but it will not matter," Feren replied. "They will do as they were told."

"That makes me sad," Roger said. "Many Kaarumites are going to die if you don't cooperate."

"Stop talking to him!" Vorgok boomed in the loudest voice yet. "Feren, don't listen!"

"You be quiet or I will have you gagged," Roger said.

"How dare you!" Vorgok shouted. "I am an ambassador!"

"Shut it," Roger said as he quickly held his hand up in front of the Kaarumite ambassador. "Now, Feren, what do you mean it will not matter? You don't have the authority to speak for Kaarum?"

"I have some authority, but I cannot go against the ambassador, and I cannot command the men below," Feren said. "But even if I could, it would make no difference. Atuskus-Var is on his way. If you do not surrender before he arrives then you will be defeated. You see, I was not forced to convert to the Truth of Kaarum. I converted when I saw the power and majesty of Atuskus-Var. He is the son of a god, and I fear him more than I fear anything you might do to me, so under the circumstances I refuse to cooperate."

"Ha!" the ambassador laughed.

"Very well," Roger said. "Tell him to come in now..."

"Who will you bring in now?" Vorgok asked. "Will you also try to convince my guards? They can barely read, and they have no authority."

"Not exactly," Roger said.

The door slid open again and a yellow-green soke stepped through the doors. A leafy vine grew over one side of his body.

"Gentlemen, this is Vinis, he is a soke, as you may have guessed," Roger said. "Come closer Vinis."

As the soke stepped toward Roger and the ambassador, the enormous Kaarumite fell backwards out of his chair and attempted to scramble away.

"Hold him," Roger said.

"You can't do this to me, you disgusting heretic!" the ambassador shouted as he squirmed away. "No!"

Two guards gripped him by the arms, but it took a third to completely restrain Vorgok's in his mad struggle to escape.

"Kaarum will smite the hands from your arms, and those of those of your children and children's children for this outrage!" Vorgok shouted.

But as it became impossible for him to struggle the ambassador resorted to chanting "Kaarum annan… Karum annan…"

"Before you consider rejecting my terms, ambassador, I want you to look closely into the face of your enemy," Roger said.

The soke stepped closer to the Kaarumite ambassador, who was on his knees as the guards held him in place. The Kaarumites eyes grew larger as the soke leaned in. The soke's irises were a pale yellow color, which was so light that it almost looked as if he only had pupils.

As the soke leaned in the vines growing on his body rustled slightly, as if blown by a gentle wind, but there was no actual wind in the room. The Kaarumite jerked backwards away from the soke with surprising force, but the guards held him in place.

"Is something wrong, ambassador?" Roger asked. "Maybe you are ready to change your mind about leaving?"

As the ambassador watched, tiny string sized runners began to migrate out from the vine across the soke's skin, and the vine began to expand to cover more of the soke's body. When a new leaf budded and opened up rapidly on the soke's neck the Kaarumite ambassador's eyes rolled back and his body went limp.

"Put him over on the bed for now," Roger said. "Let Vinis help carry him there."

"You can't," Feren said.

"Can't what?" Roger asked.

Feren waved his hand dismissively and said nothing.

"You are not afraid of the sokes?" Roger asked.

"I am not," Feren replied.

"You don't buy into everything that Kaarum teaches."

"It is the teaching of Kaarum that the forest demons, which you call the sokes, exist to try the hearts of the unfaithful, and to deny humanity access to parts of the world that Kaarum does not wish for us to possess."

"Then you must believe that Kaarum does not want you to have the Empire," Roger said.

"No. Kaarum has ordained that we would take the Empire, and he has given us his son, Atuskus-Var to make certain that it happens. You see, the sokes draw the life of their bodies directly from the power of Kaarum. We Kaarumites draw the life of our spirits from the same source. It is true that the majority of Kaarumites are terrified of the sokes, especially the brown skinned southerners, but this time Atuskus-Var is with us, and the sokes can have no power over the son of Kaarum. He is above humanity, and above the people of the forest. The power of Kaarum is with him. I see that you shake your head at my words, but once you see Atuskus-Var you will know that he is not human."

"I have seen footage of him, and he's quite large but that doesn't mean that he is a son of Kaarum or that Kaarum is even real."

"All you need do is look up into the sky to see Kaarum."

"Listen, that is a really backwards and superstitious world view. Just because the sun is there and it's bright does not make it a deity or even any other sort of sentient being. It's not scientific or—"

"Rational," Feren said completing Roger's sentence. "Yes, I also once thought like you. I used to think the Kaarumites were nothing more than backwards, ignorant, barbarians, whose only advantage was in numbers. You see, most of the world does not know this, but there are actually heretics that exist in Kaarum. They are few and far between, and they live in constant fear, but they exist there because the Kaarumites need foreign scientists and skilled workers to maintain some of the more complex technology.

"They are slaves, kept in pens and concentration camps, or in towns with walls around them. If they are allowed to wander loose they must wear a badge that marks them as approved heretics. If they say anything negative against Kaarum publicly they are simply killed, or tortured slowly to death.

"I was born of Haxian parents who were kidnapped by Kaarumites 100 years ago. My parents were deists, and so was I. I grew up in Kaarum, only knowing Kaarum, and hating it. I prided myself on my rationality, and hated my captors. I always thought their beliefs backwards, and their religion foolish, but when Atuskus-Var came to my town I saw that he was more than man. Not only is he of an immense size, but he is also of immense and inhuman strength."

"But so are the northerners," Roger replied.

"The northerners are strong but they do not compare with Atuskus-Var," Feren said. "Atuskus-Var grinds stones to powder with his bare hands, as you might crumble a ball of wet sand. He folds metal with his bare hands as if it were paper. When he came to my town he lifted a sonolar with his bare hands. When he speaks you can hear his words in your mind. He is more than man, he does things that no man can do. Therefore, as irrational as I may have found the arguments for Kaarum, the practices of it, and the idea of the sun being a sentient being, I was faced with incontrovertible evidence for it."

"So basically you saw something that you couldn't understand, so you accepted the first explanation that was posed to you for it."

"The only explanation."

"Well then tell me what you think of this," Roger said as he held up his hand.

Roger caused a swirl white light to appear on his palm, and it grew brighter until it was painful to look at. As he concentrated his thoughts on the soke implant, the light changed in color, going from red, to green, to blue, to purple. Then after a few seconds Roger closed his hand it disappeared almost instantly.

"Is that something you can explain?" Roger asked.

"No," Feren replied.

"Have you ever seen such a thing before?"

"I have not. What is it?"

"What if I told you I was a son of Kaarum?"

"It would make no sense, because then I would have to accept that the sons of Kaarum are in opposition to one another."

"So basically, we both have an ability which you don't understand, and yet you conclude that one of us is a son of Kaarum while the other is not. Do you suppose it is possible that neither of us are sons of Kaarum, and that there might be another explanation for our abilities?"

"You are trying to trick me…"

"No tricks. What you just saw me do is something I can do anywhere. Listen, you are a reasonable man. You used to recognize that the arguments for Kaarum are messed up."

"I used to believe that."

"You have also seen what sort of society the Kaarumites have built. You told me that they needed foreign scientists to keep their technology running."

"They do use foreign scientists to maintain some of the more complex machinery so that they can do other things."

"No, your words were that they needed foreign scientists."

Feren said nothing.

"Because you know that with that backwards ideology of theirs they can't achieve anything," Roger said.

"They have to devote all of their attention to spreading the Truth of Kaarum," Feren said. "It is the conflict with the rest of the world that drags them down. Once the entire world is Kaarumite then Kaarumite civilization will flourish."

"Oh come on! They haven't done any flourishing in the part of the world they already had for thousands of years. They aren't being dragged down by unbelievers. They have their own land and it's still not enough for them, so they go and make war with unbelievers. Don't you think that if their society was guided by the will of the higher power it would be more advanced? Why is it the least advanced place in your world?"

"Technically the Kelvar Waste is less advanced, but I do take your point. Very well, I am listening. Why do you suppose Atuskus-Var is so powerful?"

"I don't know, but there are a few possibilities. He could be genetically engineered, like the northerners…"

"He is more powerful than they, and the Kaarumites have no such technology."

"Perhaps other parties were involved covertly."

"What sort of parties?"

"Who gave the Kaarumites the technology to block the Imperial weapons?"

"Perhaps some of the foreign scientists that were captured."

"Does that seem likely to you?"

"No…"

"Another possibility is that he is not from this world. Or perhaps his father is not."

"What do you mean by that? Earlier you said 'your world' when you were talking about how primitive Kaarum was. Do you know something of other worlds?"

"My point is that there are other possible explanations for Atuskus-Var being the way he is. You know how violent, backwards, and ignorant the Kaarumites are, so there is no reason for you to accept their explanation of things."

"The logic of your position is sound. I am willing to reconsider my position, although I will not be completely convinced one way or another until I see the outcome of the battle."

"One more thing. Why is this man called 'Atuskus-Var'? Is it a coincidence that he has 'Var' at the end of his name, like Gro-Sho-Var?"

"I don't know what the significance of his name is, but I believe he was named by the high priests of Kaarum."

"Alright, I am going to separate you from your fellows because I want you to see what is going on, but you will be under guard at all times."

"I would very much like to witness the battle. I will cause no trouble."

"Very good," Roger said. "The guards will escort you to the command center."

Kaarumite Flight

As Feren was escorted out of the room the Kaarumite ambassador began to stir. He cautiously rolled over and came to an upright position.

"Well?" Roger said. "Have we had a good nap?"

"You dare speak to me in such a disdainful fashion?" the ambassador said.

"Well… you did pass out from… fear."

"Kaarum will tear the soul from your body and torment you for 10,000 years in the fires of his wrath!"

"Oh yes, I'm really scared now. You tried to kill my Emperor."

"I did nothing of the sort."

"Your allies then."

"I did not come here to listen to your baseless accusations, little man. I came here to offer you an alternative to death."

"Liar."

"Have a care, fool!"

"You want to know how I know you're lying? Because our communications are jammed. You are setting some kind of trap for us, and I'm going to find out what it is."

"Brave words. You do not have the power to oppose us."

"You're forgetting I still have the sokes," Roger said. "Vinis, tell Nirin that I want him to release all of the prisoners now."

The Kaarumites head jerked sharply in the direction of the soke. It was as if he had forgotten that the soke was there, and was suddenly filled with fright at the reminder of his presence.

"Now let's drive that rabble back to Kaarum, patch me through to the external loudspeakers, I want to tell the Kaarumites something," Roger said.

Two minutes later a portable communicator was placed in Roger's hand.

"This device is tied in with the speakers, when you turn it on they will be able to hear you," the officer said.

Roger depressed a button on the side and began to speak, "Now hear this, now hear this… People of Kaarum, as you may have discovered by now, there are sokes in this forest fighting against you alongside our warriors. We are releasing the prisoners that were taken by the sokes. You may find them to be somewhat… different looking. I want you to leave the contested area and never come this far north again. I give you one hour to leave, and if you are not gone by then we are going to push you out with all the force at our disposal, sokes included."

"What have they done to our men?" the ambassador asked.

"Activate that monitor," Roger said as he pointed to a flat black area on the wall.

One of the officers nodded and manipulated a set of controls nearby.

"Show him," Roger said.

The monitor lit up to show a scene somewhere on the ground in the forest. Terrified screams and wails of despair broke the silence, sounding very much as Roger imagined the hopeless cries of lost souls freshly arrived in Hell, souls which have suddenly realized where they are and that their greatest fear is to be lived out for eternity.

The camera moved to the right, and soon the sources of the screams became visible. A green skinned Kaarumite could be seen running across the view, while another knelt on the ground screaming as he looked at his hands. Two sokes were visible, as was a Haxian soldier. The Haxian bent with laughter as a group of large green Kaarumites went running by in fear. Then Roger saw a tall Kaarumite woman with green skin stagger by and collapse. The Haxian laughed even harder.

That was a sight which truly disturbed Roger, but he kept his composure for the sake of the Kaarumite ambassador and the men present.

So... Nirin decided to treat the women as roughly as the men, or is that because of the Haxian influence?

Roger did not believe that Nirin violated his orders to avoid the use of torture and permanent physical harm, but the shock of what happened was clearly too much for the Kaarumite woman to handle. Roger had given Nirin permission to color all the captured Kaarumites green, but it did not cross his mind that any of the women would be captured.

Still, they inserted themselves into this warzone and aren't innocent by any means. That woman has probably killed more men than the average Kaarumite soldier through the use of her animals. Even if we showed them mercy, if the situation were reversed they wouldn't show us any.

"Merciful Kaarum!" the ambassador exclaimed. "Kaarum annan, Kaarum annan..."

"More of your people will share their fate if you do not leave this place and never return," Roger said.

The ambassador turned away from the monitor and regained his composure.

"You have brought to life one of our oldest and greatest fears," Vorgok said. "I believe now that if it were not for the son of Kaarum we would all perish, or be converted to those... things. But Atuskus-Var is greater than man, greater than the forest demons. He will burn them all away when he comes."

"Right," Roger said. Then turning to the soldiers he said, "Keep this monitor on, but have it show a view of the fighting from the air. I want him to be able to watch what happens if they don't leave. Keep him under guard, and if he changes his mind about surrender then bring him to me."

Roger left the Kaarumite ambassador and returned to the command center. Once there he watched the Kaarumites below. There was movement on the ground, but the army did not appear to be in retreat, simply stirred up. After 20 minutes had passed some of the Kaarumites could be seen running back to Kaarum, but their numbers were small, and many of them were attacked by their fellows as they attempted to retreat.

"I thought that would have psyched them out for sure, but it looks like they hate us more than they fear the sokes," Roger said.

"What exactly have the sokes done to them?" Feren asked.

"The sokes made them drink a potion which turned their skins green. The change is not permanent, but it will last for half a year or so."

"So you have not recreated the process that Alris used on Landira?"

"Not by a long shot… But as far as they know we have, unless they have gotten wise to us."

"Unlikely. It is as you said, they hate you more than they fear the sokes, but those of them with more fear than hate are running."

"And what about you?"

"I have neither fear nor hate. I am a prisoner, who has been granted the privilege of being an observer as well."

"Hmm…"

"But for what it is worth, I would like to believe that you are right. I just need to see some incontrovertible proof."

When the hour was up the majority of Kaarumites were still there. Less than two percent of them had fled.

"Kaarumites, your hour is up!" Roger said over the loudspeakers mounted at various places on the floating city. "You will now be driven out!"

"Orders?" asked one of the advisors.

"Begin the attack," Roger said.

The necessary orders were given, and the attack started. The first thing that happened was that vines shot out across the charred ground that surrounded the Kaarumites. They could be seen writhing, and hacking at vines that grew rapidly and ensnared them.

Since the ground was melted and reformed into solid stones the sokes had to spread their influence across those charred areas before they could begin to forest the area in which the Kaarumites waited. But it was not long before forest began to swallow up whole sections of the Kaarumite army.

Some attempted to flee into the burnt areas but those too began to grow into a full-fledged forest as the roots of trees grew in around the perimeter and began to break up the stone. A short time later moss and grass crept in, followed by vines and saplings. There was no portion of the battlefield immune from the influence of the sokes, it just took some more time and effort to absorb the charred areas.

The battle raged for an hour as Roger watched. He knew that beneath the forested areas the Kaarumites would be assailed by Imperial and Haxian soldiers in addition to the sokes and their plants.

After the second hour passed Aneme came to stand with Roger and watch the battle.

"What did you learn from the traitors?" he asked.

"None of them are Kaarumites or members of the Brotherhood, but we did get the names and locations of the people that they are working for," Aneme said. "They all knew who the other traitors on board were, and most of them were put here to sabotage the shields and propulsion. We managed to stop that, but Mendarius was put in power to provide false intelligence, and to get the Emperor killed."

"False intelligence?"

"Yes… Supposedly the numbers of Kaarumites that are attacking are much greater than all the estimates. What are we going to do?"

"You mean, he altered the data?"

"That's what they told me."

"That's what I sensed in my dream… Kaarumite soldiers spreading all across the contested area, like a sea of people…"

Roger fell silent and remained so for nearly five minutes, until an officer called his attention to one of the viewscreens.

"Sir!" he said. "The Kaarumite forces are in retreat! They are going back south!"

Roger looked back at the screen, much of what had been the open battlefield was now covered with forest, but a steady stream of Kaarumites could be seen retreating south. However, the majority of them were fighting just as hard as ever.

"Something is not adding up." Roger said.

"What's wrong?" Aneme asked.

"Why would the traitors wait until after the air battle to take down our shields, and risk exposing themselves in the process?"

"The traitors were instructed to wait until after the air battle to lower the shields, but none of them had any idea why."

"But that makes no kind of sense… Unless, they have something else waiting to hit us with…"

Roger walked away from the viewscreens and began to pace.

"Man!" he said out loud, in English, without thinking.

"What, sir?" one of the advisors asked.

"Has anyone figured out how to get around that device the Kaarumites have?" Roger asked. "The one that blocks our freeze bombs?"

"Not yet, sir, but the scientists tell me that they are close to understanding how it works," one of the advisors said.

"Tell them I want a way around it before nightfall," Roger said.

"Nightfall, sir?"

"You heard me."

"Understood, sir."

"And what about those technicians I sent to find the interference? Any word from them yet?"

"Not yet, sir."

"Have them also go over the satellite data."

"The what sir?"

Once more, Roger had used another English word without thinking. There was no word in the native language for "satellite," but he was so focused on the situation that he was more annoyed with the men for not understanding him than he was with himself for lapsing into English.

"The machines that are suspended in space, the spy machines that receive telemetry and watch the Kaarumites," Roger said.

"Of course sir," the advisor said.

"Mattis," Aneme whispered. "We should go talk privately."

"What?" Roger asked. "Why?"

"It's important, and it will be quick."

"Alright."

Aneme led Roger back to the conference room where they had met with the Kaarumite ambassador and sealed the doors behind them. They were completely alone.

"You are slipping up and using words in your native language," Aneme said.

"Am I?" Roger asked.

"Yes. You need to be careful."

"I guess I did. Well… It's not like they have any idea that it's English. They probably just think it's some other dialect, or that I'm babbling."

"That's still a problem. If it looks like you are cracking up under the stress then people are going to question you and take you less seriously, which means they'll be slower to respond at crucial points. Or… they may suspect that you are not what you appear to be."

"But what do we appear to be? Even with the white skin we don't look like real westerners."

"They probably take us for Haxians, but if you keep using English words then they will know you aren't a Haxian, and they might start wondering where in the world you do come from, or questioning whether you really are even from this world."

"How can they think I'm an alien? That ought to be like… the last thing anyone guesses."

"Your bone structure is fully northern, but your muscles far weaker than they ought to be for someone who is as structurally northern as you are."

"Thanks for the vote of confidence."

"I'm not saying that to be mean. The fact is, people with your characteristics don't exist in this world, and wouldn't exist at all if you hadn't come here by accident. You have to be careful. Keep using English words, and, at best, they may start thinking that you are losing your mind. You are the leader now, you have to lead. Everyone is looking to you, myself included."

"Alright, I understand."

"Good."

"Shall we go back out then?"

Aneme sighed and slumped a little, then ran her hands through her hair.

"Stressed?" Roger asked.

"Why do you ask?"

"Never saw you slouch, ever."

"I suppose. I never expected to be in command of so many people before, especially not foreigners. But I'll be alright."

"When this is all over, we will find a place to call home, and we will build a life together," Roger said as he took Aneme by the hand.

"Wherever you are is home for me," Aneme replied. "But I'll be glad when we can rest."

"And of course now is not the time to rest."

"It's not…"

Aneme opened the door and they stepped out into the command center, still holding hands. The advisors and officers noticed the two of them holding hands but tactfully ignored it.

Roger glanced at Aneme to see if she was concerned with how they might appear to the advisors, but her facial expression was unreadable. As he studied her face, the thought occurred to him that he was not entirely comfortable with his wife being in the battle zone, even though he was there himself.

"Vaila," Roger said. "Can you go back to Randar and find out what is going on? I want you to see if you can get those northerners to come. I want to send you with some battle data to show them, assuming that it's even possible to make contact with the northerners."

"If you want me to go, I can," Aneme replied.

"I really want to know what is going on back in Randar, and why they haven't sent any ships to check on us even though they haven't heard from us in a while."

"I'll do it."

Roger downloaded a summary of the battle as well as the battle statistics onto a portable data storage device which looked like a small transparent green square of glass, but was in fact a device with more storage space than the most powerful computer back on Earth.

Roger tucked the device into one of Aneme's pockets, and as she turned to go he kissed the side of her head. To his surprise she turned around and hugged him in front of the men, then she turned to go. Roger watched her leave, and when he was gone he activated a monitor to track her progress for as long as he could.

Unlike Roger, Aneme did not know how to fly and had no experience with flying machines of any sort. She boarded a small swift craft which was piloted by an Imperial soldier. Once they were aboard and the ship was sealed, the hangar door opened and they sped out across the city of Leonus.

As the shuttle neared the perimeter of the city, Roger opened a hole in the type one forcefield to allow them out. Three of the standard one-man fighter craft accompanied them through in order to serve as escorts.

Roger watched on a viewscreen as the speedy aircraft swiftly vanished from sight into the northern horizon. Then he turned his attention back to the battle.

Even though many of the Kaarumites were fleeing, it seemed that the majority of surviving Kaarumites were still fighting on. Roger stood over the large table in the center of the room which projected a three dimensional holographic display of the ground below up from its surface.

As Roger stooped over the table he saw the forest grow in one place and quickly swallow up a group of Kaarumites. In another place a sonolar lay dying with its legs cut off. He felt a swell of pity for the majestic sauropod. The creature had no idea why it was fighting or what it was fighting for. It was only goaded on by cruel masters to pain and death. Though the animal was an unwilling participant, allowing it to live would mean the death of more Imperial soldiers.

But how much is anything done in, or by Kaarum, done willingly? Are any of them really willing participants?

Roger was able to slide the display around on the table by moving his fingers within the projection, and he could zoom in on any area by double tapping. He moved the display to focus on an area where the forest was glowing and zoomed in. The ground was littered with dead and dying Kaarumites and the red furred feline zangrons. There were Kaarumite women among the dead.

Roger shook his head and moved the display. In another area he saw many more Kaarumite dead, but there were some dead Imperial soldiers among them. He moved the area again and a Haxian soldier slit the throat of a large Kaarumite that was trapped beneath the heavy branch of a tree.

"You are troubled by all of this," said a smooth voice.

Roger looked up and saw Feren looking at him from across the table. He had forgotten about the black clad Haxian Kaarumite. In some ways the man reminded Roger of himself and Aneme. His features were almost entirely northern, but his skin color and smaller build gave him away as something else.

"What did you say?" Roger asked.

"You seem to be emotionally affected by what you are seeing below," Feren said. "You find it disturbing."

"Of course I do, what sane man wouldn't?"

"I should think it was normal for commanders to become hardened to battle."

"Maybe…"

"Unless perhaps they have seen very little of actual war. But if so then…
how does one become a commander?"

"I think, that the day a commander becomes detached from the
suffering of his people, or hardened to death in general, then he's no longer
fit for command."

"That is not the Kaarumite philosophy. In Kaarum, those who are
troubled by death or killing are not seen as fit to lead. People exist only to
serve Kaarum, and a heretic's life is worth even less. Women have more
children and send them off to battle as soon as they come of age, and
while they are gone the women still have more. Parents seldom even form
relationships with their children, other than instructing them in the Truth
of Kaarum. Sometimes parents will kill their own children if they behave
in a displeasing fashion, or if they are too independent minded. The most
education the majority of Kaarumites have is the ability to learn how to
read, and that is only if they are educated at all. Many are not."

"That's horrible."

"But it has made Kaarum strong."

"It has made Kaarum stupid, and it only reinforces my theory that we
need to end this war with the conquest of Kaarum. I think we may press
on to the Kaarumite holy cities and destroy them. That should thoroughly
refute the false garbage death cult of Kaarum."

Feren shrugged.

"As you will," he said. "I for one do not care for the Kaarumite lifestyle
and standard of living, but I recognize the pragmatism of their philosophy."

"It's pure evil and it needs to be destroyed," Roger said.

"You do realize that, assuming you win this battle, if you press on to
the holy cities of Kaarum you will be attacked by every man, woman, and
child until you have completed your task?"

"Maybe not if we have sokes with us."

"They attack you even now, in spite of your sokes."

"Alright, but not all of them are attacking."

"Most are attacking. Atuskus-Var gives them strength."

"Someone patch me through to Nirin," Roger said.

A minute later the face of Nirin appeared on one of the monitors that
surrounded the display table.

"Nirin," Roger said. "How goes the battle?"

"It goes well, my friend, but both humans and sokes alike are expending a good deal of energy. As you know the sun is going to set in a few hours. If we do not gain a clear victory before that then the sokes will be able to do very little to help during the night."

"Alright, I want you to change tactics a little here. I want you to focus less energy on making plants grow, and instead make yourselves more visible to the enemy. Get up on the front lines and charge with the humans, but make it obvious what you are."

"Many of us will have our bodies destroyed."

"Or, they will be terrified of seeing you and run away."

"Yes… that might work. I have noticed these people have a tendency to kill their own warriors when they try to retreat back through the lines. It seems like they're afraid of contagion."

"Just give it a try. Try it with a few of your people at first, and if the strategy works then switch to having all of your people do that."

"Understood."

"Interesting," Feren said once the monitor switched off.

"How so?" Roger asked.

"Now you will test their faith, and we will learn whether they fear Atuskus-Var more, or the sokes."

I'm not sure what to make of this guy. He's as cavalier about killing as a normal Kaarumite, but he's way too ready to renounce his faith. Have I taken in a spy? But if he's a spy, then who's spy is he? Is he working for the Kaarumites, or is it for someone else?

Roger considered having Aneme interrogate Feren when she came back.

"Is there anything you're not telling me?" Roger asked.

"Such as?" Feren replied.

"Such as what the enemy has planned and where they are going?"

"They plan to crush the Empire, you can see them below, and I have already told you that more are on the way."

Roger felt a surge of frustration.

What is the deal with this guy? Either this guy is holding back, or the Kaarumites make no complex strategies. I can't believe he just doesn't know anything.

"I should think your first priority would be to break through the interference," Feren said.

"It is a high priority," Roger replied. "That's why I have my technicians working on it, and why I have sent my wife to Randar to check on things personally."

Another hour passed, and finally the Kaarumites began to retreat in large numbers. At first, many Kaarumites were killed by their fellows as they attempted to retreat, but soon the bulk of them began to withdraw as a group.

"They run," Feren said reflectively. "Will you give chase?"

"I have to think about that," Roger said.

"They run to Atuskus-Var."

"Atuskus-Var again…"

"You will have to deal with him in order to end this."

"Fine then, let's have the fleet run reconnaissance in the south," Roger said as he turned to one of the generals. "I want them to spread out over the contested area and head in a general southerly direction. Have them do their best to keep tabs on the retreating Kaarumites. Let's find out where they are going, and what else might be coming, if anything."

"But sir, the interference is going to cut them off from communication," one of the technicians said.

"I know, I know," Roger said. "But the airships are fast. They can go and come quickly. I don't want any unpleasant surprises."

"As you wish, sir."

CHAPTER 29

Unpleasant Surprise

NEME SAT IN THE BACK of the aircraft and watched the land shoot by as they sped along. For a brief moment she felt frustrated as she considered the possibility that Roger sent her away to keep her safe, but she quickly dismissed that notion.

If Roger sends me away it's for the purpose he stated, and because he feels I'm the best one for the job. He was probably guided by one of his dreams, which means it's absolutely crucial for me to reach Randar.

As they neared the border of the Randaran Empire the pilot attempted to send another call to Randar. The first two times he attempted to call Randar he received no response, but this time his call was answered.

"We are under massive Kaarumite attack!" said a frantic voice when the pilot asked for permission to land. "We have been trying to call the Emperor for hours. The Kaarumites have come down from the north, and they have stolen aircraft from some of the western city states. We need more air support!"

"Is the command headquarters compromised?" Aneme asked.

"Last news we heard was that it is in lockdown," the voice replied.

"What about the Imperial Palace?"

"Under heavy attack!"

"Understood," Aneme replied. "Signing off."

"Why did you do that?" asked the pilot.

"Because we don't know who that person is," Aneme replied. "He might be a Kaarumite agent responding to our call. Take us over the Imperial Palace, if everything looks clear then drop me off and get back to my husband. Tell him what the situation is here, and ask him to send some of the air fleet back right away."

"Understood."

"And I want the escort fighters that came with us to stay in Randar and help fight off any air attacks that might be in progress."

"I will convey your orders."

As they flew into Randar they noticed that a massive storm was brewing to the north, and that large plumes of smoke were rising from many places in the city. Some very ancient buildings had been demolished, and there were bodies in the streets.

"This is terrible, how did they get around us?" the pilot asked.

"I don't think they did, at least, not recently," Aneme replied.

"What do you mean, Commander General?"

"Haven't many of the western states been taking in Kaarumite immigrants for years?"

"They have. Everyone knows that Kaarum is an awful place, full of war, violence, and poverty. Supposedly those people just went north for work to get away from it or find work in a safe place. They went around our blockade, of course, going on ships, mainly."

"'Supposedly.' Why even suppose such a thing when Kaarum is concerned?"

"I don't know. It's pretty obvious that the reason Kaarum is awful is because it's full of Kaarumites. That's why we don't allow them into the Empire unless they renounce their religion first. There is something wrong with the thought processes of other western peoples, or maybe it's their governments. The official rhetoric from their governments was that that those Kaarumite people would be just like westerners once they settle in, but you know they still wear their traditional clothes and tattoos. As an Imperial it is very frustrating, we do our best to keep the world safe, and those of our race who don't have the misfortune of having to live next to the Kaarumites decide to let the enemy in around behind us."

"Yes."

"You think it's all the Kaarumite immigrants and their descendants? A lot of those people were born in western nations and have lived there for years. Do you really think they would still care to attack?"

"I don't think that makes any difference and I doubt you do either."

"Those barbarians were probably just biding their time then…"

The pilot flew over the palace grounds, and found that the Kaarumites had breached the walls in a few places, but Aneme was unable to tell if they had gone through because most of the grounds had become an incredibly dense forest.

"Just put me on the roof and be off," Aneme said. "Your top priority needs to be to get word of what has happened here to my husband."

"Acknowledged," the pilot said.

He hovered down within seven feet of the roof and opened the door on the side of the vehicle. Aneme jumped out and landed in a roll, but swiftly returned to her feet. She waved at the pilot and he took off immediately. She ran to the edge of the roof and looked out into a dense forest of tall trees, with creeping vines growing everywhere.

She could hear distant screams and shouts coming through the forest.

This is obviously the work of sokes, which means that the Imperial heir is probably still alive and being protected by them.

Since she had landed on a part of the palace that was only one story tall she was easily able to drop from the roof and land on a walkway of white stone that ran near the edge of the palace. The drop put no stress on her superior northern physiology. She landed in a crouch and took off running immediately.

On one side of the walkway was the palace, and on the other was the incredible forest which had not been there before. It was not long before Aneme arrived at a doorway. She found it guarded by two nervous looking Imperial soldiers.

"Halt!" the shouted as they brandished their weapons toward her. "Who goes there?" These guards were armed with long bladed pikes.

"Commander General Vaila," Aneme said. "I need to speak to whoever is in charge at once."

"Commander General!" one of the guards said. "Have you brought reinforcements? What of the battle?"

"The fighting was still going on when I left. Now please, I'm in a hurry. Tell me who is in charge and where I can find him?"

"That would be prince Aderos. He's still in the palace. We can admit you."

Prince Aderos was the oldest son of the Emperor, and he was to inherit the throne after Adinis. Aneme was relieved to hear that he was still alive.

"I thank you," she said as they opened the doors.

Once inside she was quickly escorted to a room deep in the center of the palace and below ground where the heir was being kept. He stood slumping over a three dimensional display of Randar, with his hands resting on the table. When Aneme's presence was announced he quickly became alert.

"Commander General!" Aderos said. "We have been trying to call you for hours. Is there any word of my father?"

"I would like to talk with you alone," Aneme said.

"Do we have time for that?"

"It is absolutely essential."

"Very well…"

Aneme waited until they were alone and all the doors were shut before she spoke.

"Your father is in serious condition, he may not survive," Aneme said.

"What?" Aderos shouted. "What happened?"

"Councilor Mendarius was a traitor, he tried to kill your father."

"Where is he now?"

"In the plain of eternal desolation, I should think."

"You killed him?"

"Yes. But we found other traitors as well. We must be very careful."

"I understand… Take me to my father."

"Impossible."

"Why? With my father gone or incapacitated I am in charge."

"Have you looked at what is going on outside recently? We aren't going anywhere until we deal with the Kaarumites here."

"Yes, but—"

"I also have to keep you safe and alive since you are the Imperial heir."

"Of course… You're quite right. But I wish I could do something. Who is in charge of the battle now?"

"My husband is in charge, and he sent me here to re-establish communications. Now help is on the way, but we need to do something about all of these Kaarumites in the meantime."

"So Roger is in charge…"

"By your father's orders, yes."

"You said help is on the way? How so?"

"I sent my pilot back and told him to take word to Roger of what was happening here. Most of the Kaarumite army was still there when I left, but their airships have been decimated. So he should be able to spare some of the fleet to come back to the Empire."

"Yes, that's good. My father left very few ships here."

"But we cannot sit around and wait on those ships. We need to do what we can about these Kaarumites. Where are they coming from?"

"They are coming from the north in a constant stream. Those idiot nations we have been working to protect for thousands of years have been taking in Kaarumite immigrants for the last few hundred, and now all of those people are coming against us and the other westerners are surprised by it. My father and I warned them so many times, saying that they should all follow our example and deny entry to all Kaarumites. But they just called us bigots and insisted that the Kaarumites had only come for economic opportunities or to escape violence, and that they were assimilating."

"How could they say that?"

"Well, it's true that Kaarumite countries are violent, and most of the job opportunities for them are either fighting or farming. The only way the average Kaarumite can move up socially is by raiding his neighbors and taking their loot, or by immigrating to a new place where things are just handed to them. Before they started moving north, a lot of the western states set up these programs of government aid for the poor. Which meant that people who were unemployed could receive money from the government as long as they were unemployed. Those policies made those countries desirable places to live for the unambitious and unmotivated people of all races and cultures. Kaarumites flocked to those countries in large numbers, and once there they received money in exchange for not working. As they bred and had more children the governments of those countries increased their tax funded stipend."

"I never heard of that before."

"That is why they think the economic opportunities attracted Kaarumites, and indeed in other countries some of them did actually get jobs, all of which are unskilled manual labor, but jobs nonetheless. Still, they always retained their tattoos and traditional clothing, and they bully the native people, especially as their numbers grow. Some of them did eventually become successful and abandon their religion, removing their tattoos and dressing like westerners. But for every Kaarumite that assimilates there are about 100 who don't."

"That is very sad and disgraceful. It's a shame that others must suffer for their foolishness."

"Yes."

"So they are coming toward us from the north and the westerners from those other countries are doing nothing to stop them?"

"I don't know, there has been some fighting and killing along the way, but there are also westerners who have joined in on their attack."

"Converts?"

"Not converts, just young people who want to have nice things but are too lazy to work for them. The looting culture of Kaarum appeals to them, and some of them genuinely hate western civilization and want to see it destroyed. I don't understand their psychology too much, but essentially they are losers who blame their surroundings for their failure in life and so they want to change it through violence. The Empire is the prime symbol of western civilization, and everyone knows it's full of wealth and antiquity. A tempting target for any barbarians to loot."

"Disgusting! But what exactly is the tactical situation here?"

"It has been some time since I saw a full tactical overview, but the last thing I heard was that they are streaming in from three different places on the northern border, and most of them are coming to Randar once inside. At first they were coming in at seven different points, but the sokes in the forest reserve stopped many of them and cut off their entry routes. The sokes are working to expand the forest as much as they can without destroying roads, houses, and farms, but the Kaarumites continue to pour in, and they have stolen airships from the western countries that hosted them. Of course the majority of the stolen vehicles are not technologically on par with ours, but there are so many more of them, and they are decimating the countryside and parts of the cities with their earth scorchers."

"Have you heard anything from the northerners we were trying to secure aid from?"

"Nothing, but I have been cut off from the underground command center. I should have been there to begin with, but now I can't get there at all. I have failed the Empire."

"Well… the soke forest will keep the Kaarumites from coming in here, but they may still hit the palace with earth scorchers. It's not safe for you to be here. We need to evacuate you to a stronger building, or to the underground command center."

"I am open to ideas."

"Where is your brother Demekus? I know he was left behind in Randar."

"Last I heard was that he was protecting the Temple with a group of elite soldiers while they worked to raise the forcefields."

"The Temple is protected by forcefields?"

"Of course, it's the most important structure in Randar. It has type one and type two forcefields, and multiple layers of them with independent power sources. But they were having some sort of malfunction."

"There is something suspicious going on here…"

"What do you want to do?"

"I want you to put on some regular soldier armor. Then we will go with a group of soldiers and will make for the Temple. Once we secure the Temple we will get your brother and move on to the underground command center."

"I don't know very much about fighting. I think I would only slow you down."

"I doesn't matter. It's my duty to protect you. Just stay close to me and try to stay out of trouble."

"I should have learned, like Demekus…"

"You still can. Once this is all over I will teach you."

"If we survive."

"We will survive."

"You and Roger seem quite capable."

Aneme scrutinized Aderos. There was something about his comment and his tone of voice which struck her as being out of balance, at the very least.

"All Roger and I want to do is save the Empire, not rule it," Aneme said. "The Empire needs the Maxelis family. Roger and I have nothing but admiration and respect for your father. If he does not make it then everything falls to you, and you have a lot to live up to. My husband would say, 'you have big shoes to fill.'"

Aderos looked down at his feet for a second, then shook his head and turned away from Aneme.

"Of course you're right," Aderos said. "I'm sorry."

"That's alright," Aneme said. "Now please hurry and suit up, this palace is an easy target for the Kaarumite airships if they decide to fly over."

Aneme escorted Aderos to an armory and the guards helped him suit up with the solid white armor of a common Imperial soldier. Once he was dressed Aneme selected four soldiers and they ran through the palace toward the primary vehicle bay. Though he knew nothing about fighting, Aderos was physically fit, so he had no difficulty matching paces with them.

Aneme selected a fast and durable vehicle which was capable of holding about ten people comfortably. She ordered everyone to get aboard and seated herself in the driver's seat.

"Have you ever driven one of these things before?" Aderos asked.

"I have driven ground vehicles before, but not this particular model," Aneme said.

"But the northern ground vehicles are not nearly so responsive with handling."

"Don't worry about it."

She started up the vehicle and drove it slowly up to one of the large metal bay doors. Once the door opened she sped out and shot down the driveway, but soon had to fire the breaking thrusters in the front of the vehicle as the path was obstructed by massive trees. They had grown right up through the pavement, which now existed as broken up rubble about the bases of the mighty trees.

The vehicle slowed but did not stop in time to miss the trees entirely. Aneme swerved but the side of the vehicle still struck against the mighty trunks. Everyone inside the vehicle lurched to the side uncomfortably. Aneme slowly backed the vehicle away.

"Heavenly messengers defend us!" Aderos said.

"Relax," Aneme said. "We just need to find a different way out. Worst case scenario we have to go on foot."

Aneme backed away further, and as she did so a green skinned soke woman stepped out from the forest. Aneme recognized her right away. She hit the necessary button to make the window next to her go down.

"Sasha!" Aneme said. "Can you help us get out of here?"

"My friend Aneme!" Sasha said.

"Call me Vaila when other people are around please," Aneme said.

"I heard you crash. All the paths are blocked. I did it on purpose to keep the Kaarumites from getting in."

"You mean you made all of this grow by yourself?"

"There were two others helping me, but I did most of it. I have changed, and no one understands how much yet."

"We have to get out of here."

"Why?"

"I have Aderos with me, I have to get him to the command center, but first we need to get to the Temple."

"I will go with you."

"Negative. You need to go hide yourself. Nirin would be so upset if anything happened to you."

"All places are the same in this place as long as the dark worshippers are here."

"Well then come with us and I will try to get you back to Nirin."

Sasha turned to face the trees in their path and swung her arm in a slicing motion. Aneme heard the sound of wood cracking and splintering, which was in turn followed by the sound of wood groaning and creaking. As Aneme and the passengers watched many of the trees in front of them began to topple over, broken off close to the ground.

"Such power!" Aderos said.

Sasha looked back toward the vehicle and smiled. Then raised both her arms and held them out in front of her toward the forest. The indented lines running throughout her skin began to glow with a golden light, and suddenly the sound of wood breaking could be heard again, but this time it resulted in a narrow elongated path through the forest all the way to a clear space near the end of the palace grounds.

Sasha lowered her hands and the glow subsided. Then she walked to the vehicle and knocked on one of the doors. Aneme opened the door and Sasha stepped on board and sat down next to the soldiers. Aneme noticed that the thin lines on Sasha's body were no longer random. The overall design seemed to be symmetrical, although what structure or image they were supposed to represent escaped her.

"Now you should be able to hover over the fallen trees and get out," Sasha said.

"Let's give it a try," Aneme said.

"How did you do that?" Aderos said.

"Sokes have some control over plants, we manipulate energy and have a natural affinity for the growing things," Sasha replied.

"I know, but… I have never seen such power before. Even for a soke that has to be a lot of power."

"How would you know?" Sasha asked.

"I guess I don't. But still…"

"It is," Sasha said. "I have a new configuration which very few sokes have ever achieved."

"Listen, Sasha," Aneme interrupted. "I want you to stay close to me. If anything happened to you Nirin would blame me, and, not to sound insensitive, but we really need this alliance."

"I understand," Sasha said. "You can worry about me the least of all. I come to help you, and I will stay in Randar to save it."

As they sped down the road they passed bodies from time to time, most of them were Kaarumite, but there were a few Imperial citizens who had been killed as well.

"Animals!" Aderos said forcefully. "Blasphemers and swine!"

Aderos let out a guttural howl and leaned forward, gripping the sides of his head with armored hands.

"What's wrong?" Aneme asked.

"So many of my people have been killed, and I can't even defend them!" Aderos said. "Or avenge them! I didn't take it seriously when you started offering training classes… It should have been me that died, not my people."

"This is all my fault!"

"It's not."

"If I could trade places with them I would."

"You're a good leader, but keep it together. Now isn't the time to let your emotions run away with you. We've got to keep our heads clear."

As they traveled through the city they passed some Imperial soldiers fighting with Kaarumites, and a few foreign westerners from further north attempting to loot shops and homes. As they rounded a corner and came to a straight road with no exits for a while, the way was blocked by Kaarumites. From the rear end camera footage Aneme could see that the Kaarumites were also closing off the road behind them.

Trouble at the Temple

"Now what?" Aderos asked.

"Hang on," Aneme said.

She hit the accelerator and the vehicle shot forward toward the enormous leering Kaarumites. Some of them dove to the ground while others tried to run, but many of them collided with the vehicle. Those without personal forcefield generators were immediately killed, but those who had them bounced off the vehicle and landed elsewhere.

The vehicle was also equipped with a type two forcefield, so when it moved as fast as it was now moving anything it hit was deflected away, but the force of the blow still slowed their forward momentum.

The Kaarumites were enraged by the vehicular attack, and further up ahead more of them poured into the road. Aneme sped on and hit more of them but the vehicle slowed a bit and lurched as it plowed through the enormous Kaarumites.

"They are an insane lot," Aderos said.

"I always knew they were fanatics, but I never understood exactly how much before coming here," Aneme said. "They are at least as evil as the draenocks…"

For a few seconds there were no more Kaarumites, but then the street ahead filled with them. As their numbers swelled they came running toward the vehicle. Aneme accelerated to full speed and plowed into them, but this time there were too many, and the vehicle soon became mired in a thick crowd.

They began to bang and hack at the vehicle. Aneme deployed the landing struts and disengaged the hover mode in order to stabilize the vehicle.

"I'm getting out," Aneme said.

Aderos grabbed her by the arm as she began to edge toward the door.

"You can't!" he said.

"I have no choice, I have to keep you safe," she said as she pulled free. "Now you and Sasha stay inside while the men and I clear the streets."

Aneme pushed the door open with enough force to knock over the Kaarumites who stood outside. With one hand she locked and slammed it behind her, and with the other she drew her sword. The Kaarumites smiled evilly and made cat calls when they saw her. She knew exactly what it was they would do to her given the opportunity, but she was determined not to give it to them.

The first wave of Kaarumties who charged her were swiftly cut in two, then she launched herself onto the front of the vehicle with a backflip. The Kaarumites groped for her and surged toward the vehicle, but every single one of them was either killed or wounded. One of them climbed onto the back of the vehicle and attempted to jump down at her, but she turned and dealt him a roundhouse kick as he descended through the air, which deflected him off to the side of the vehicle where he landed among his fellows.

The Imperial soldiers opened the doors in the back of the vehicle, charged out, and closed the doors after themselves. Their support eased some of the burden, though the untrained Kaarumites were hardly a challenge to Aneme, and their large unprotected bodies were easily devoured by the northern steel of her blade.

There was now fighting all around the vehicle, and the bodies of slain Kaarumites began to pile up. As the battle intensified Aneme felt the need to acquire a second sword since there was no opportunity or need for grappling.

As a Kaarumite attempted to attack her from behind she turned on him rapidly, and as she dodged to the side of his blow she grabbed the back of his sword hand from the outside, and cut off his arm at the elbow with her sword. Then she gripped the additional sword with her other hand as the severed arm dropped away. She turned away from him and cut open two other Kaarumites who charged her, and at the same time she kicked the man who she took the sword from so that he fell back among his fellows and bowled some of them over.

The Kaarumite sword was far inferior to her northern blade, but given the fact that most of the Kaarumites had no armor and that she had superior strength it was still more than adequate as a secondary weapon, and it allowed her to maintain greater distance between herself and her attackers.

Aneme was charged by three Kaarumies from different directions. With one swift motion she slashed the man in front of her, and dealt a backward kick to the flat end of the sword that the man behind her was carrying. The sword was sent flying through the air with such speed that it stuck in the neck of the third man. Then she swiftly rotated and finished the man she had disarmed.

It was all over in a little under five minutes, and all of the Kaarumites who had attacked them were dead. Aneme and the soldiers got back inside the vehicle and started it up. Although the vehicle had been dented, and in some places punctured by the Kaarumites, it still worked.

Aneme sped through the city as fast as she was able, and ran down any Kaarumites who attempted to bar their way, but this time they did not encounter any crowds large enough to stop them, until they reached the Temple.

The gates to the Temple grounds appeared to have been blasted open, and bits of twisted burning metal could be seen around the damaged portions of the wall. A wild crowd of Kaarumites was pressing against the aperture where a group of Imperial soldiers fought staunchly to defend the temple. Although there were already many dead Kaarumites on the ground, and more were joining them each second, the invading barbarians continually threw themselves at the Imperial soldiers with reckless abandon.

Aneme sped toward the crowd of Kaarumites and sharply turned the vehicle sideways at the last minute in order to hit as many of them as possible with the broad side of the craft. Many Kaarumites were knocked over and to the side. They shouted with anger and surprise, but before they could recover Aneme and her group of soldiers leapt out of the car and began cutting them down.

The soldiers inside the Temple walls were emboldened by their sudden arrival and the ferocity of the attack, so they charged out with renewed energy and drove the Kaarumites back. Once all the Kaarumites were either gone or dead a soldier wearing the blue and white armor of an officer stepped up and saluted Aneme.

"Commander-General!" he said. "It's good to see you. I take it you received our distress calls? Is more help on the way?"

"Hello Demekus, it's good to see you," Aneme replied as she recognized his voice. "No, I'm afraid we never received any distress calls. We lost all contact with the Empire, and I was sent to find out how things are here."

"Things are terrible here, but so many more of them are dying than us. I think we can still win this if they stop soon."

"Any idea about how many more of the enemy there are?"

"None, but it would have been a lot worse without the sokes protecting so much of our northern border."

"I sent my pilot back to the fleet to request help, but there are many Kaarumites out in the contested area, so it might take them some time to reach us."

"Well, now that you are here things are already getting better. You are the greatest warrior I have ever known, and all the men here think so too."

"Thank you. What is the situation here?"

"They had a problem initializing the forcefields. We have been defending this place all day. There are guards all throughout the Temple grounds and around the perimeter. Some of them got inside the grounds but none of them made it to the Temple itself. About an hour ago they ran a vehicle into the gates. The vehicle exploded but our personal forcefields protected us. I can't say the same for the gates though."

"Yes…"

"The men are tired, but we have to defend the gates for about half an hour more before the forcefields can be raised."

"Then we will help you until then. In the meantime I have your brother here. I want someone to escort him inside of the Temple."

Aneme opened the door of the vehicle and motioned for Aderos to get out.

"No wait," Aderos said. "If my brother can fight then so can I."

"We cannot risk letting both of you die," Aneme said.

"We have other brothers," Aderos said.

"No Aderos, the Commander General is right," Demekus said. "You should go into the lower levels of the Temple and stay hidden."

"I will not hide while the Temple is in danger," Aderos said. "I am the heir to the throne."

"My point exactly," Aneme said.

"Which means that I must set a positive example for the people," Aderos continued. "I will defend the Temple. If the Great Maker wants me to inherit the throne I will survive."

"I understand," Aneme said. "But I hope you will understand if I don't want to put you on gate duty."

"Where do you want to put me?" Aderos asked.

"Just be prepared to back us up in the second line of defense," Aneme said. "You and Sasha can stay together and watch each other's backs."

"But—"

"There are many skilled soldiers who are also working the secondary line of defense."

"Very well," Aderos replied.

"Everyone get to your positions!" Demekus said.

"I want someone to bring my vehicle inside the grounds before the Kaarumites return," Aneme said.

Demekus stopped one of the men and Aneme handed him the key card for her hovercraft. The soldier walked out into the street and opened the door to the vehicle, but even as he started the vehicle Aneme heard another sound.

A speeding aircraft shot overhead and looped back around once it had flown over the Temple. It began to head directly for the Temple when an Imperial aircraft cut across its path so that the two collided at a sharp angle. There was a brief flare of light as their forcefields struck against one another, and then the foreign craft was deflected down toward the ground where it skipped like a stone across a lake before it came to be lodged in some trees.

The engines still glowed with life but the craft did not move.

The pilot must be unconscious, or dazed from the crash.

Aneme ran to the craft with her old northern sword drawn, and when she reached the cockpit she rammed her sword through the metal and pried open the cockpit. The craft was of some sort of western design, but Aneme was not skilled or knowledgeable enough to tell exactly where it was from. The pilot, however, was clearly a Kaarumite.

As Aneme looked down the pilot began to stir. He snarled and attempted to slash her with a knife, but she quickly ran him through and pulled the body out of the aircraft.

"Now we have another ship," Aneme said. "Even if it's unarmed we can still use it to carry messages through the interference."

"He tried to ram the Temple!" one of the soldiers said with apparent shock in his voice.

"Which only underscores the need for us to have the shields up," Aneme said.

"Go and check the progress of the technicians, and tell them what just happened here," Demekus said to the soldier.

Aneme heard a sound like distant thunder and looked off in the direction from which it came. To the north of the city she could see flashes of red light reflecting down from the thick cloud cover. In some places there was a perpetual red or orange glow, which could either mean that something was burning on the ground or there had been so many flashes of red light beneath the clouds that the light had begun to condense in the cloud layer, in keeping with the nature of light in her universe.

Roger had told her that in his universe light had no physical substance, and could not condense into a liquid, but Aneme had a hard time imagining a universe structured like that.

"For a long time the airship fights were moving off to the north, but now they are coming back," Demekus said.

"That's not all that's coming back," Aneme said as she pointed toward the gap in the wall where the gates once stood.

A new band of Kaarumites was approaching the gates. Aneme and Demekus made their way back to the gate, but even as they did grappling hooks were thrown over the walls and pulled tight. Kaarumites began to scale the walls in different places around the Temple grounds and jump down. As soon as they righted themselves they all ran for the Temple.

The fighting was so intense at the gates that it took Aneme and Demekus some time to notice what was happening.

"Fall back and spread yourselves out evenly!" Aneme shouted. "Don't let any of them reach the Temple!"

A charging Kaarumite suddenly disappeared in a flash of red light, and Imperial guards were sent flying in all directions. Once the flash subsided there was a hundred foot circular charred spot on the ground where once there were trees and grass. The guards bounced across the ground like stones skipping across a lake until they lost enough speed for the forcefields to allow them contact with the ground, at which time they tumbled for a few feet before coming to rest. Some of the soldiers did not get back up after tumbling.

"Kill them quickly!" Aneme shouted.

The fighting grew more intense as more Kaarumites poured in.

Where are they coming from?

Aneme felt herself beginning to tire. Her arms and legs were burning, and she was breathing as rapidly as she possibly could. For the second time in her life she felt that her northern training and superior physiology would not be enough. The first time was when the strange southern woman cut her neck. But this time might very well be the end, because these were Kaarumites, and they would have no mercy.

They are mad with their bloodlust, and eager to destroy or desecrate the Temple.

Someone next to her was breathing raggedly and loudly. Out of the corner of her eye she saw that it was Aderos, the crown prince. For a split second she thought to order him back, but she was unable to speak or take her attention away from the numerous enemies before her. Suddenly she felt an odd sensation near her feet, somewhat like static electricity. But she could not afford to look down.

She was growing tired, and some of the men near her had already dropped to the ground. She began to slow. A tall Kaarumite stood manipulating a device on his belt, just out of arm's reach. Aneme would not be able to reach him in time to prevent the explosion. But it never came.

A vine shot up from the ground and wrapped itself around his neck like a whip. As the Kaarumite looked up the vine suddenly went taut and he was jerked forward in such a way that he fell directly onto Aneme's sword.

Aneme and the Kaarumite were both equally surprised. The grass around the Kaarumites suddenly grew to be waist deep, and vines snaked up out of the grass and ensnared them. Some of the Kaarumites ignored it and managed to pull free, while others swung around wildly with their weapons. The brief distraction allowed Aneme and the Imperial soldiers to catch their breath and finish off the Kaarumites nearest them.

Aneme looked around quickly and saw that Sasha was nearby gesturing with her hands, the lines on her body were glowing with an intense golden light. Aneme had never seen her glow so brightly before, and for a few seconds she took her mind off the battle.

"Look out!" Sasha shouted at her.

Aneme dodged back just in time to avoid a wide clumsy blow from an enormous Kaarumite, but she lost her footing and fell. A second later the Kaarumite was lifted from the ground and swept through the air. It was as if an invisible hand had picked him up and tossed him away. He landed awkwardly about 30 feet away and attempted unsuccessfully to get up. Even from a distance Aneme could tell that something was broken.

Off to her left Aneme heard a choking sound. She turned to see a large Kaarumite standing rigidly and gasping for air. There were two indents forming on his neck, as if thumb sized invisible bands were constricting there. Aneme quickly regained her composure. She took out her sword and sliced his head off.

"Are you doing that, Sasha?" Aneme asked without turning to look at the soke woman.

She thought it would be best to keep her eyes on the battle.

"Yes," Sasha replied.

The Kaarumites began to panic, and shouts of "soke!" could be heard all throughout the Temple grounds. Aneme killed the Kaarumites who were near her and quickly looked all around the compound. The plants everywhere had gone wild with growth and movement. The Kaarumites who remained alive were stumbling over themselves trying to get away.

It was not long before they were all either dead or in retreat. As the last Kaarumites made their way toward the open gate, trails of ground swells approached them from many different directions, as did rapidly growing vines along the surface. In some places where the ground swelled thick roots broke the surface.

She is using the tree roots!

"Sasha be careful!" Aneme said. "Don't use up all your energy!"

Roots came up from the ground and began to form crude woody spikes which partially blocked the door, but they did not grow fast enough to stop the Kaarumites. In their mad dash for freedom the Kaarumites jumped over the roots. Sasha gave it one last push so that they grew more rapidly but it only served to snag the last Kaarumite by the foot as he jumped over. He crashed onto his face on the sidewalk beyond the Temple grounds but quickly rolled to his feet and took off running.

Aneme relaxed and turned to face Sasha, who was also panting now. The light coming from her body slowly faded away until it was out.

"That was incredible," Aneme said.

"Yes," Demekus said. "Everyone will remember this day. I am certain the fear of you will run through their entire community. By the way, how did you do that?"

"I..." Sasha began, but was still panting heavily.

"Take your time," Aneme said.

Suddenly Sasha raised both her hands and a bright light flashed. Aneme quickly threw her arm over her eyes and looked away. She heard the sound of a crash followed by a deafening explosion, and then nothing but the sound of flames crackling.

She uncovered her eyes and blinked a few times. In front of her the air seemed to shimmer, and beyond that much of the ground had been blasted bare of vegetation. The border between the grass and the freshly charred ground was a slowly curving line. On the other side of the line burning bits of debris and twisted metal were strewn across the ground.

Aneme reached out her hand and felt a solid surface in front of her where the air shimmered, and received a slight electric jolt.

A forcefield!

At first she thought that perhaps the Temple forcefields had activated just in time, but neither a type one nor type two forcefield would cause the air to shimmer in that fashion.

Aneme looked back at Sasha once more. She was holding her hands high. The lines on her skin were glowing brightly, and so were her eyes. Suddenly the light went out and she collapsed. Demekus caught her as she fell.

"Sasha!" he said.

Aneme rushed to her side and helped Demekus lower her gently to the ground.

"She's not breathing!" Demekus exclaimed.

"She has no pulse either," Aneme said as she felt the soke woman's arm and neck.

Aneme felt something wet strike against her hand. A drop of red light had landed there. It was like glowing blood. As Aneme looked up more drops began to fall. The storm was over the city now, but suddenly the drops of liquid light began to strike an invisible barrier higher up and trickle down the sides.

The Temple forcefields have switched on, but just a minute too late for Sasha!

CHAPTER 31

The True Attack

"CAN YOU HEAR ME SASHA?" Aneme said. "It's no use..."

"Sasha!" Roger said as he awoke with a start.

Roger had fallen asleep in his chair. It was a large red cushiony chair set up in his office near the command center on Leonus. His office was mostly dark, lit only by a few small glowing panels, and outside the window night had fallen, and there was an intense storm going on.

"What will I tell Nirin?" Roger mumbled.

Better to tell him nothing until I see it with my own eyes...

"Sir?" said a voice at the door.

Roger looked up to see an officer standing in his doorway. The officer was briefly lit up by a flash of lightening.

"What is it?" Roger asked.

"I thought I heard you shout," the officer said. "I wanted to make sure that all was well with you."

"Sorry, bad dream," Roger said.

"Yes sir. I will leave you to your rest."

"Wait! Give me a status update."

"The Kaarumite survivors were still making a mad dash for the south, but in one way the forest has worked against us because they were lost to our sight once they entered there. As you know we had the sokes close up the area behind them. The storm is massive, and it is covering most of the contested area and some of the areas beyond. Visibility is poor."

"Have the air fleet come back for now. Has there been any word from the Empire?"

"None yet."

"Progress on the jamming field?"

"The technicians believe they have found the devices responsible. They are a series of Imperial relays above the atmosphere, but the technicians have not determined how to shut them off yet."

"Destroy them."

"Yes, sir."

"What about the progress on the machines that were preventing our ice bombs from going off?"

"The scientists are still working on a way to counter the effect. They say they are closer now than the last time you asked."

"Well have them work quicker. I have a feeling that we are about to need that technology."

"Understood, sir. And, sir, about those devices that have been stopping our warheads..."

"Yes?"

"They are definitely not Kaarumite. Some of the technicians think the technology might be Tandoran."

"Those rotten people!"

"Or at least, they found Tandoran components inside the devices."

"Hm..."

"I will let you know if there are any further developments, sir."

"Thanks."

The officer left, and again Roger was alone. Occasionally the room was bathed in white light as lightning struck outside. Sometimes the lightning actually struck against Leonus' shields creating what seemed like an even brighter flash as the energy was diffused across a larger area.

"What does it all mean?" Roger said as he thought about the image he saw of Sasha apparently dying.

Of course when a soke body died that did not necessarily mean that the soke was dead, as the energy form could generate a new body elsewhere using certain types of vegetation. In this case Sasha had incurred no physical trauma, but she had spent a good deal of energy defending the Temple, and she used her energy in a way that Roger had never thought was possible, even for a soke.

Roger witnessed the battle at the Temple, but nothing that happened prior to that. He considered going back to sleep to see if he could find out what happened next, but he was too restless now. He also realized that what he saw could either have already happened, or it might be something that was preventable.

Roger got up, left his office, and returned to the command center.

"I want to send a fourth of the fleet back to Randar immediately," Roger said.

"We are unable to communicate with most of the fleet," an officer said. "The interference is—"

"I ordered for those space devices to be destroyed."

"We are attempting to override their command protocols."

"I told you to just blow them up!"

"They have erected type one forcefields."

"So shoot the forcefields until they max out. No forcefield is invincible. Throw everything we have at them until they break."

"But sir, with the fleet gone that could take a long time, perhaps a day, maybe two," a technician objected.

"Then you had better get started right away," Roger said.

"Understood sir," the officer replied.

Roger paced around the command center for a minute. He was feeling tense and frustrated, and he needed to vent his nervous energy. Some of the officers and technicians looked at him nervously, probably taking his high-strung behavior as a sign of displeasure.

He walked to the three dimensional display of the ground below projected across the surface of the table in the middle of the room. He could see nothing but the signs of wind and rain disturbing the vegetation below. Massive lights shone down from Leonus, providing some illumination to the forest in the dark of the night.

The lighting served the dual purpose of illuminating any potential enemies and providing some energy to the sokes below, who were partly photosynthetic.

Roger looked away and paced some more, then stopped and declared, "I know what I need!"

"Sir?" one of the officers asked.

"I need to talk to that Kaarumite ambassador," Roger said.

"Do you mean Feren? The Haxian convert?"

"No... Not him. The other one... Vorgok."

"Do you wish to have him summoned here?"

"No! I will go to him. You and you, come with me."

Roger pointed at two soldiers as he made his statement, then walked out the door.

The soldiers followed him down the silent hallways without saying a word. Roger had gotten used to having guards go everywhere with him, so he asked them along without thinking. But when he thought about it he decided that it was probably for the best given what happened to the Emperor. There was always the chance that there were more traitors around.

Even though it's not easy for traitors to infiltrate the Imperial army.

The guards were armed and clad in the white armor of soldiers without officer rank, the same armor which had been modified following Aneme's specifications. Roger, on the other hand, was dressed only in the white and blue clothing of a high ranking officer out of armor. When he was in battle he wore the blue and white armor of an Imperial officer.

Technically there was no uniform requirement for any rank above general, and Commander-Generals could wear whatever they wanted, but they often wore uniforms of regular generals with an extra insignia included. Roger chose to follow that custom. On the other hand, Aneme preferred to wear black, which was usually a custom made light armor. She had only worn the Imperial style armor when she was training the men, and it had to be custom made just for her because there were no female soldiers in the Empire.

Aneme...

When they reached the room where Vorgok was being kept the guards posted outside of the door saluted. Roger ordered the men to wait outside the door.

"Sir?" one of the guards asked.

"It's alright," Roger said. "I know what I'm doing."

The guards nodded and opened the door. Roger stepped inside and it slid shut behind him. The Kaarumite ambassador's room was dark, but like his office it was occasionally lit brightly by a flash of lightening outside.

Roger could see the form of the enormous Kaarumite and the bed he slept on silhouetted against the transparent section of the wall. Roger scowled and fumbled with the panel on the wall that controlled the lighting.

Roger squinted as the abrupt brightness of the lights pained his eyes, but he quickly adjusted. The Kaarumite still did not stir.

"Wake up!" Roger shouted.

The Kaarumite did not react.

Roger walked to the side of the bed and kicked the mattress several times, jolting the massive Kaarumite each time.

"I said wake up, you!" Roger shouted, this time more loudly.

The Kaarumite stirred and sat up slowly, straightening into an upright position with his eyes still closed. His back became completely rigid, and he turned his face up and lifted his arms out and up.

"Praise be to Kaarum, the beneficent, and the most kind," he said. "His mercies are eternal, and his wrath of even greater duration."

Then he opened his eyes and looked around the room puzzled.

"It is dark out," Vorgok said. "It is not yet day. Why have awoken me? It is most rude to awake one of the noble houses before daybreak."

"What was that little thing you just did?" Roger asked, suddenly feeling curious in spite of himself.

"It was the morning devotion, a sacred and holy ritual which all Kaarumite men must keep when Kaarum greets them at the start of the day. It is no little thing, and it is not a thing to be mocked or taken lightly."

"The women don't keep it?"

"It is not for women. Women exist at our pleasure, just as we exist at the pleasure of Kaarum. We thank him for suffering our existence, as our women thank us with a different ritual."

"Sounds wonderful," Roger said sarcastically.

"When you woke me I thought it was morning," Vorgok said. "It is forbidden to wake a man of the noble houses before dawn unless his life is in danger, and, although my eyes may deceive me, I see no danger here."

"Your taboos mean nothing to me."

"Impertinence! Why have you awoken me? Have you come to surrender?"

"You call me impertinent? Seriously? Have you listened to yourself talk lately?"

"So! You have come here only to heap disrespect upon me. How civilized. I thought the so-called civilized races of man treated ambassadors with a certain amount of respect and… immunity."

Vorgok put his feet on the floor and walked away from the bed.

"True ambassadors, yes," Roger said.

"So you have come to mock and disrespect me, and you have left your guards outside!" Vorgok said.

The Kaarumite turned to face Roger, and walked until he stood between Roger and the door. He sneered at Roger as he stretched his arms and cocked his head from one side to another.

"And you are unarmed as well!" Vorgok said. "You are either very brave or very foolish!"

"Or I'm neither and I just know I can take you," Roger said.

"Very well, what have you come to say?"

"Why are you here?"

"To negotiate your surrender, I should have thought that would be obvious. Yet in spite of our good and benevolent intentions you wantonly attacked my people, and unleashed the forest demons to work atrocities on their bodies!"

"Oh stop! I'm tired of being lied to."

"You dare?"

"Just stop the act. The fact is I saw your people invading Randar, and I want you to explain yourself!"

Roger was telling the truth, in one way he did see the Kaarumites in Randar. But he did not see it with his eyes, and the possibility existed that his dream may have been just that. In addition, he had no way of knowing whether what he saw had already happened or if it was yet to happen, or if it were a possibility that he could avert.

That's why I have to speak with the Kaarumite alone, to shed some light on that dream.

The Kaarumite laughed.

"So…. You have broken through the interference," Vorgok said.

"What do you mean by it?" Roger asked.

"By what? The invasion of the Empire or my presence here to negotiate with you?""Both."

"Well, we were never serious about negotiating with you. Kaarumites do not negotiate with heretics. Everything that happened was part of a well laid plan that was hundreds of years in the making. We sent people to live among the foolish westerners further north, and to grow in numbers. We took advantage of their misplaced empathy and foolishness. The smart western nations kept us out, but the stupid ones let us in, and thus we infiltrated western society. The attack you drove off yesterday was just an attempt to get all of your forces, or as many as possible, to leave the Empire. The negotiations were a ruse to get you to stall for time as our forces invaded your Empire from the rear."

"But I anticipated you, and put sokes along a big chunk of the northern border."

"And yet many of our people still made it to Randar."

There was no way Vorgok could know that. He must be trying to probe me for information.

"A steady stream of them will flow into Randar, which will add up to nearly the same numbers that you fought off yesterday," Vorgok said. "But the true attack is yet to come. You thought Kaarum had been emptied against you, but that is because the traitors in your midst fed you false information. The full might of Kaarum is yet to come, and you are worn down and tired, and your homeland is under attack. They will fill the 'contested area' from top to bottom, and they will conquer you. Then truth and peace will reign throughout all the world."

"Truth!" Roger repeated with disgust. "You are nothing but a liar, and all I see from your people are lies and murder."

"It is acceptable to lie to heretics and to our women when it suits our purposes, and it is not murder to slay a heretic. Truth and peace are the territory of those who believe and worship Kaarum."

Which means this guy could be lying to me right now…

"I can see the anger in your eyes, you wish to kill me," Vorgok said.

"I won't kill you," Roger said.

"Why not?"

"I have something more appropriate in mind."

"Torture then? I thought Imperials didn't torture? But it matters not. I am prepared for torture. Torture for Kaarum means a greater reward in the next life."

"No torture. I just want information."

"I will give you none, other than what I have already disclosed."

"Then I will hand you over to the sokes."

Suddenly Vorgok's eyes grew larger. Roger should have taken that as a warning but instead he turned his back on the enormous Kaarumite and headed toward the door. His keen senses heard something whoosh through the air, and Roger was able to dodge just in time, but another blow came a split second later. Roger dodged the second blow but his feet slipped a little. He stumbled around the Kaarumite while striking a powerful blow to the back of the larger man's arm.

Fortunately the Kaarumite also stumbled, and Roger was able to quickly subdue him with a hold.

"I have diplomatic immunity!" the Kaarumite snarled.

"You would if you were a real ambassador, but by your own admission you're not," Roger said. "You're only a diversion."

"No, no! I am a real ambassador! I'm here to negotiate! We can still negotiate!"

Vorgok attempted to squirm free but Roger compensated by shifting the pressure on his hold.

"But we already established that you are a liar," Roger said. "You are going to stay with the sokes until I'm convinced that you are ready to cooperate."

"No please!" the Kaarumite shouted. "Kaarum anan… Kaarum anan…"

Roger twisted the Kaarumite's right arm as he removed his hand from the left arm in order to reach for the control panel on the wall. In spite of his best efforts the Kaarumite groaned with pain.

"Guards!" Roger said as the soldiers entered the room. "Take this guy and send him to Nirin."

"No wait!" Vorgok shouted. "I'll cooperate! What is it you want to know?"

"I don't believe you are sincere."

"I'll cooperate!" the Kaarumite shouted as the guards began to drag him away.

He thrashed around wildly so that one of the guards had to hit him again.

"For the love of mercy don't do this!" the Kaarumite shouted.

"Wait!" Roger said just as one of the guards was preparing to knock the struggling barbarian out.

Roger stepped out in the hall and stood in front of the Kaarumite. He looked the large southerner in the eyes and saw genuine fear there, a fear which clearly bordered on madness.

This guy really is desperate!

"I'll tell you what," Roger said. "We have devices that can tell when a man is lying…"

The Kaarumite scowled partly for a second, which was what Roger expected. He did not like the idea of being hooked up to a lie detector. Even now the man was determined to be as unhelpful as possible.

"I'm going to hook you up to one of those devices," Roger said. "But I warn you, if you lie even once on anything, no matter how small, or fail to answer any question that I ask, then I am turning you over to the sokes and you won't leave the Contested Area without having green skin. Am I clear?"

The Kaarumite clenched his jaw and looked down. He was clearly unhappy with his options, and he seemed to be trying to decide which of the two was worse.

"Either you agree or you don't," Roger said. "If you don't then I will have them take you to the sokes right now and I will tell them that they can do whatever they want with you, short of killing you. But, if you help us then I will release you after this battle, regardless of which way it goes."

"I will cooperate," the Kaarumite said.

Incredible! Their fear of the sokes really goes beyond anything rational, or does it? Was there something more to the story that Layla and Oran didn't tell me? I wonder… Or maybe Oran and Layla didn't know everything? If there was a different group of sokes in the world that played by a different set of rules then people from Oran and Layla's group might not be privy to some information.

"Alright, let's do this," Roger said. "Prepare a room for interrogation, there are some things I would like answers to right away."

The Kaarumite "ambassador" was taken to a small room where a medical table with restraints and lie detecting equipment was set up. The Kaarumite was placed roughly on the table and strapped down. He tried to resist when he saw the table so the guards had to use force.

"That's not earning you any brownie points," Roger said.

"Any what?" Vorgok replied.

"I'll be asking the questions here!"

The lie detecting equipment was connected to the Kaarumite, and a medic was tasked with monitoring the readings. It reminded Roger of what happened to him when he was newly arrived in the alien world, and being interrogated by Aneme's father.

"Do you know the names of any traitors in our midst?" Roger asked.

"I only knew of Mendarius by name," Vorgok said.

"Are there more traitors in the Empire?"

"I do not know, you have already caught more than I knew of."

Roger looked over at the medic and he nodded, indicating that the Kaarumite was telling the truth.

"Who are the Kaarumites working with?" Roger asked.

"I am not privy to that information," Vorgok said. "All I know is that we have received technological help from some foreigners."

Again the medic nodded.

"What is coming at us from the south?" Roger asked.

"Atuskus-Var himself comes with most of the men of Kaarum, as well as the trained beasts and the women who oversee and direct them," Vorgok said. "Half of Kaarum comes… It is the greatest military muster in the history of the Central Lands. At least half a billion come against you, but it is hard to keep track of numbers for certain. It could be more than that."

The numbers Vorgok was talking about added up to more than twice that of the army of the People's Republic of China back on Earth, and that was the modest estimate that Vorgok gave. Roger felt his heart sink, but he had to ask one more question.

"What else is coming?" he asked.

"Airships," Vorgok replied.

"How many?"

There are 100 carrier sized ships, perhaps 1000 or so medium sized, and I don't know how many fighters," Vorgok said. "We have been long in preparation for this battle."

Roger scowled and asked the medic if Vorgok was lying. The medic shook his head.

"Where did you get all that from?" Roger asked. "I thought you people couldn't build new ships?"

"For thousands of years we built no new ships," Vorgok said. "These were constructed with the help of outsiders."

"What outsiders? Who else is involved?"

"I do not know. I swear by Kaarum and his abundant generosity!"

"Could it be Tandor?"

"I have no idea."

"Yes or no?"

"I suppose it is possible. Historically they have hated us, but they have changed recently, and their last chancellor who was killed by northerners had a Kaarumite father. Now I hear that his wife is in charge, making Tandor the joke of the world for having a woman leader."

"Alright, that will be all for now," Roger said. "Lock him up and watch him. Make sure he doesn't try to kill himself."

"You are not an Imperial!" Vorgok said as Roger turned his back to leave.

Roger felt a chill run down his spine.

"You may have them fooled but not me!" the Kaarumite shouted.

Onslaught

"GET HIM OUT OF HERE and lock him up!" Roger said.

"You know your commander is an outsider yes?" Vorgok said as the Imperial soldiers released his bonds and laid hands on him to take him out of the room.

"If I were you I wouldn't push my luck," Roger said. "You know I could hand you over to the sokes at any time."

The Kaarumite scowled and said nothing. In the meantime Roger wondered if the Kaarumite really knew something about him or if he was just running his mouth. He remembered when they were hiking through the contested area with Sarvana before she abandoned her belief in Kaarum. She used to run her mouth about all sorts of things, some of them quite random, but the purpose was to rattle her captors on some level.

Roger decided that he would spend some time interrogating the Kaarumite alone, but that would have to wait. At the moment he had more pressing matters to take care of.

When he got back to the command center he was told that Aneme's pilot had returned, and that he was asking to speak with "Commander-General Mattis."

Roger ordered the man brought to the command center and spoke with him in front of all the advisors and tacticians. The pilot informed them of the situation in Randar and asked for ships to be sent there, and to be able to return there himself.

"I have already ordered a fourth of the fleet to go to Randar, but I guess it's taking a while for the orders to disseminate because of this interference," Roger said. "I don't know that we can spare any more than that. We have very few aircraft or flying vehicles of any sort here, and those we do have are presently engaged in trying to destroy the objects causing the interference. I need you to fly south and take orders to the fleet directly," Roger said.

"Sir!" one of the tactical advisors exclaimed. "One of the automated space devices has been demolished."

"Excellent," Roger said.

"Wait… I'm getting more readings here… The rest are down. We should be able to communicate now."

"Now that's what I call progress, call the fleet."

"Sir we have incoming calls from the fleet," a communications officer said.

"Let me hear what they are saying," Roger said.

The communications officer put one of the transmissions on speaker.

"We are under heavy attack!" a frantic voice said over the speakers. "An air fleet has come up from the south. We request backup. Leonus come in!"

"Let me talk to him," Roger said.

"Go ahead sir," the communications officer said.

"This is Commander-General Mattis," Roger said. "What is your situation?"

"Sir! Great Maker be praised! We didn't know what happened to you. We are under massive attack by an unknown fleet which has come up from the south. The markings on the ships are Kaarumite, but the design is different from anything I have seen before. They appear to be new ships. How can the Kaarumites have new ships sir?"

"We are still working on that. What are they doing?"

"The large ships have initiated a massive burning on the ground below with earth scorchers. They are cutting a wide swath through the forest, bigger than ever before, but are still avoiding the tavlon cities apparently. The fighters are attacking us. They are using their earth scorchers and ramming us. Some of them even have targeted energy beams which are hitting us badly. A few of our fighters have been destroyed. I believe our numbers are roughly equal."

"Freeze warheads are ineffective still?"

"Yes sir."

"I am going to have to give you some orders you won't like."

"We are at the ready sir."

"I need some of the fleet to go back to Randar."

"Is Randar under attack?"

"It is."

"Understood sir."

Roger redirected a portion of the air fleet to return to the Empire to deal with the airborne attackers there. He gambled on the supposition that since the Empire was under attack by stolen western ships they would not have the special protective fields against the freeze bombs, and as a result the ships would soon be able to return to the battle.

Maps of the contested area were displayed on many monitors around the command center and at various magnifications. Roger kept his eye on a real time map that depicted Imperial aircraft as blue dots and Kaarumite aircraft as red dots. It was like looking at a tremendous cloud of dueling gnats. Roger watched a flock of blue dots attempt to break away, but they were followed by equal numbers of red dots.

"Bloody Adimnor!" Roger exclaimed, then quickly added, "Pardon my French."

"Sir?" one of the advisors asked.

"Never mind, order them back. Order them to initiate a holding action as much as possible. We have to contain the Kaarumites."

"Yes sir."

"I guess Randar is on its own…"

Roger watched as the red and blue dots that broke away returned to the larger cloud, which was also gradually making its way north.

"Sending our airships north will only compound the problem in Randar," Roger said. "What's the good if they just bring more enemy ships with them?"

"It's unbelievable that the Kaarumites would have such numbers and strategy at their disposal," one of the advisors said.

"But it's happening and we have to deal with it," Roger said. "Get that other guy in here, that guy Feren, the Haxian Kaarumite."

A few minutes later Feren was brought into the command center and Roger explained to him everything that had transpired.

"I told you that the numbers were not in your favor," Feren said. "None of this surprises me, even though I didn't know the exact details."

"Did you know that they would attack the Empire from behind?" Roger asked.

"No, but I did not discount the possibility either."

"Did you know that your friend Vorgok was not a real ambassador and that you were sent here as a distraction?"

"I was never specifically told so but I suspected as much. They sent me to present a more civilized face to the negotiations, sincere or otherwise."

"Do you know anything that could help us now?"

"I know very little. Obviously they did not wish to supply us with information which might be valuable to you, in the event that we were tortured or interrogated with drugs. You must believe me when I say that I have no idea what they are planning next, beyond an all-out frontal assault."

"That's not very helpful."

"Atuskus-Var is coming, and he is like nothing you have ever seen before. He is not human."

"We'll see about that. Someone patch me through to Randar, I want a live status update."

"Sir, I have been monitoring communications from Randar since we broke the interference," the communications officer said. "There are many requests for reinforcements, and… the Temple was attacked."

"Put me through to the command center in Randar," Roger said.

"Yes sir," the officer replied.

A minute later one of the monitors lit up to show the command center beneath the surface of Randar where Roger had spent so much time planning and devising strategies with the Emperor and the advisors.

"Commander-General Mattis!" the officer on the screen said.

"Hello Raynold," Roger said. "What is the situation there in Randar? Do you have any word from my wife? Where is the Imperial heir?"

"Sir, the situation is terrible here. Kaarumites are everywhere, and there is a constant stream of them flowing in from the north. But, it could have been much worse were it not for the sokes inhabiting the northern forest reserve. On the ground the Kaarumites are suffering disproportionate casualties but we still have losses. There is still fighting all over the city, and in some of the smaller cities further north, but if we could cut off the flow of Kaarumites then we could probably end the ground fighting. The greatest problem is the airships. They have decimated the countryside. So many farms have been lost. Many of our cities have suffered damage, including Randar. The Kaarumites have stolen many airships from other western nations, and most of the fleet is with you. Is there any way you can send some of the fleet back to stop them?"

"Negative. The fleet is engaged in battle with a massive Kaarumite air fleet."

"Seriously? How is that possible?"

"I don't understand it either, but there is nothing I can do."

"That's terrible, what are we supposed to do?"

"What about my wife and the Imperial heir?"

"Oh, I'm sorry, the last I heard your wife was with the Imperial heir at the Temple. They managed to protect it from destruction and will eventually try to make their way here. I don't know where they are at the moment. I am trying to coordinate everything across the Empire, and there is a new distress call every minute. The airwaves are a complete jumble, but we are doing our best. To be honest I would rather be out in the streets of Randar fighting."

"I understand. But you can't be. Have you heard anything from the northerners?"

"Nothing yet."

"Keep me apprised."

"Understood sir."

When the communication switched off Roger struck his fist down onto the display table in the center of the room. It was not a terribly hard blow, just a small outburst of frustration that released a small noise. If any of the tacticians and officers present noticed they remained tactfully aloof.

"What will you do?" Feren asked.

Roger turned his back on Feren and returned to his office. It was night outside, and even though the storm had begun to abate the cloud cover was still complete. There were no stars or moons to be seen. Roger's eyes narrowed as he looked out across the spires of Leonus to the western horizon. The horizon seemed a good deal further off than the horizon would be on Earth.

For the most part both the ground and the cloud cover appeared black, except for a few spots of white light which looked like snapshots of lightning flashes beneath the clouds, frozen in time. Then Roger looked off to the south.

The southern horizon was aglow with a red light. At first it was just a thin red line off in the distance, but it gradually grew. After a few minutes the red glow extended, doubling in size, and Roger could make out distinct flashes of light amid the redness. Rivulets of red light began to edge their way through the clouds, preceding the glowing redness.

Roger pressed a button on his desk and summoned three of his tacticians.

"Is that what I think it is?" Roger asked.

"They are burning the forest," one of the tacticians said. "According to our pilots and the feed from our space equipment they are also decimating random parts of the forest, in addition to the path they are clearing."

"Can it be they are trying to hit sokes?"

"Maybe, but it seems fairly random."

"No, they are trying to drain the energy of the sokes by forcing them to repair the forest…"

"They will be here in a few minutes," another tactician said.

Roger watched as the horizon grew brighter, and more of the clouds and land beneath were bathed in a red light. It was like watching a sunrise but with no sun. As the battle drew closer they could hear the rumbling of explosions, like distant thunder. Whole sections of forest disappeared in flashes of red light, leaving scorched earth, with a few lines of glowing red among the charred black.

Suddenly there was a loud boom and a blinding flash of red light. Roger instinctively covered his eyes and turned away from the window. More flashes and booms occurred, and the last one sent a tremor through the city.

"Filter!" Roger shouted.

The windows in Roger's office darkened so that the flashes of red light were no longer unbearably bright. He could see fighters of both sides darting about beyond the forcefields of Leonus. They looked like clouds of insects at the distance his office was from the edge of the city.

From time to time the city's shields were lit up by an explosion of energy, but most of the explosions now occurred between the fighters. The battle had come to Leonus.

"Well gentlemen, this is going to be the battle that makes or breaks us," Roger said. "Let's get back to the command center."

As the men stepped out of the room one of them put his arm in front of Roger before he could pass through the door.

"I would like to have a word with you," the tactician said.

"Alright," Roger said. "But make it quick."

"I don't understand why you are letting that Kaarumite walk around in our command center."

"The Kaarumite? Oh… you mean Feren."

"It is a tremendous breach of security."

"Well, if we lose then it won't matter, and if we win then it won't matter because we will disable Kaarum forever before we let him go."

"That does not address the issue of a security breach. Why do you want to have him there?"

"I want an observer. We are making history here, and someone should be there to testify. Maybe he will write a book someday. But, if he is a spy then I want to give him a chance to reveal himself and the people he is reporting to."

"I understand your reasoning but I still do not agree with it. No Emperor has ever done such a thing before."

"That's fine, you don't have to agree if you don't want to, but you still have to follow my orders."

The tactician scowled.

I don't know if I like that…

"Listen, keep an eye on him," Roger said. "Obviously we don't want him accessing any of our computer systems or touching the panels. If we have to discuss anything sensitive we can kick him out, but for the most part I want him there. I want to see his reactions to the battle and hear his comments. If we survive then I want him tracked, when this mess is all over with, just in case he reports to anyone."

"I understand," the tactician said. "It will be as you say, but I still think it is dangerous."

"So noted. I respect your opinion."

Suddenly there was a tremendous ragged explosion outside which violently shook the floor beneath them. The tactician stumbled and fell.

Roger stumbled as well but kept his footing. For a few seconds the floor seemed to be tilted, but it quickly leveled itself.

"That was multiple warheads at once," the tactician said as he got back up on his feet.

Roger looked out the window toward the edge of the city, and he saw that the forcefield surrounding the city was still crackling with energy. Beyond the forcefield he could see that much of the forest below was ablaze, which Roger surmised was probably from the energy released against Leonus.

"We have no more time," Roger said.

CHAPTER 33

Hydroponics

"**I**S SHE DEAD?" DEMEKUS ASKED as he stood next to Aneme and looked on the motionless form of the soke woman.

"I don't know," Aneme said.

"Don't sokes have an energy form?"

"Yes."

"Maybe she just abandoned her physical body?"

"No way of knowing. There is no breathing, and no pulse that I can detect. She could have abandoned her body but she expended so much energy that maybe…"

Aneme was not prepared to say what she was thinking.

Maybe she burnt up so much of her energy that her matrix was depleted…

"She will be remembered with honor," Demekus said.

"Yes," Aneme replied.

She reflected that she did not know how Nirin would take the news. He might decide to withdraw his support for the war, or he might become enraged and put more energy into the war effort.

Aneme looked up at the overcast sky. It was late in the day and the sun was in the process of setting. There would be no way for Sasha's body to collect energy from the sun, assuming that there was any life left in her body.

"Put her in the vehicle, we will take her with us to the command center," Aneme said.

"What do you want me to do?" Demekus asked.

"Take the men who are still in fighting condition and sweep the area around the Temple. Then I want you to return to the Temple and wait for my orders. I will call you from the command center."

"Understood."

Two of the men picked up Sasha and carried her over to the vehicle. As they were putting her inside Aneme heard the sound of air vehicles shooting overhead. One of them struck against the forcefield protecting the Temple and ricocheted off. It spun around once in the air before righting itself.

"They stole so many aircraft," Demekus complained.

"Or perhaps they were given aircraft," Aneme speculated.

"The pilots that we have are doing good, but they are outnumbered, and there are simply not enough freeze warheads to go around. If only we could get more aircraft from the front."

"It was a well-played war. We must rise to the occasion. Let's get to the command center."

Aneme sat back in the driver's seat and told Aderos to get in next to her. They were joined by a group of guards.

"I will connect with you 30 minutes from now, Demekus," Aneme said.

A portion of the forcefield was lowered so that Aneme could drive her vehicle off into the street. On the way to the command center they saw very few live Kaarumites. Since the Imperial citizens were free to own weapons they did not make easy targets for hostile invaders. Although they lacked the training of the Imperial soldiers, and the quality of weaponry which northerners possessed, they were still on equal footing in terms of training and weaponry to the invading Kaarumites. In some places normal citizens could be seen fighting off the invaders.

But while there did seem to be a lull in the numbers and activity of enemy ground troops, the damage they had done to Randar was apparent in every direction Aneme looked. There were places where entire buildings had been destroyed, and in many places there were smoldering fires and varying degrees of structural damage.

"What have they done to our city?" Aderos said. "Thousands of years of history just… destroyed."

When they neared the command center Aneme abandoned the vehicle and led them there by a roundabout path just in case any hostiles were following. They entered through an alternative passage that began in the basement of another building. Aneme entered her passcode and a wall slid open, revealing an elevator behind it.

"Who is there?" said a voice over the intercom once they were inside the elevator.

"Commander-General Vaila Maxelis," Aneme said. "Who is this?"

"It's me, Raynold," the voice replied.

"Good to hear that you are still alive, Raynold. Bring us down please."

"Very well."

The doors slid shut and the elevator began to descend.

"Who else is with you?" Raynold asked.

"The Imperial heir, Aderos, some guards, and Sasha, the wife of Nirin," Aneme said. "She's hurt."

"Understood," Aderos said.

A minute later the elevator came to a stop, but the doors did not open.

Aneme tapped the communications panel and said, "What's going on, Raynold?"

"Technical difficulties, madam, we should have it resolved shortly," Raynold replied.

"What sort of difficulties?"

"Well, this isn't one of the usual entrances, so it doesn't get the same level of attention and maintenance that the other shafts do. I'm not sure exactly what is wrong, but for some reason it's stuck. We are troubleshooting right now."

Aneme waited for a few minutes but nothing happened. One by one the guards sat down. Aneme tried to call Raynold again but there was no response.

More time passed. Aneme began to breathe more deeply but with slightly diminishing results. Then a thought occurred to her.

"Troubleshooting indeed!" she said.

She took out her sword and rammed it through the floor of the elevator. The abrupt loudness of it startled everyone that was in the elevator with her, except for of course the still and possibly lifeless form of Sasha.

With both hands Aneme vigorously pushed and pulled on her sword cutting a line through the bottom of the elevator. It made a horrible grating noise of metal on metal. Some of the men ground their teeth while Aderos covered his ears.

"Must you do that?" he asked.

Aneme stopped what she was doing to look him in the eyes.

"I'm sorry, did you say something?" Aneme asked.

"I said must you do that?" Aderos said.

"Yes," Aneme replied, and resumed her work.

Occasionally sparks shot out as she cut through the floor.

Once she had completed a jagged circle she pulled her sword free and stomped on the circle twice until it fell through. Then she sheathed her sword and removed a dagger, also of northern design, but also not a recent design.

"What are you going to do?" Aderos asked.

"Well, as my husband would say, I am going to get to the bottom of this, both literally and figuratively," Aneme said.

She held the dangerous blade between her teeth and lowered herself through the hole until she hung from the rim by nothing but her hands. She removed her left hand and activated the soke implant in order to ascertain how far away the walls of the shaft were, as well as the bottom.

Once she saw where the walls were she carefully removed the dagger from between her teeth, careful not to let the blade touch either her lips or cheeks as she grasped the hilt firmly in her hand. She uttered a short prayer and began to swing back and forth with her one hand that remained on the rim of the hole in the elevator floor. When she felt she had sufficient momentum she let go and fell toward the wall.

She swung her dagger so that the blade sunk into the wall running horizontal to the ground, ensuring that it would not cut downward through the wall, and thus cause her slide down too rapidly. She was safe for the time being.

She braced her legs against the wall and removed her sword. With her other hand she jabbed the sword into the synthetic stone wall of the elevator shaft and pounded the pommel twice with her free hand just to make it go in a bit further. Once she was satisfied she grasped the sword hilt firmly and began to test how easily the dagger could cut through the material that composed the walls.

One of the soldiers stuck his head through the hole in the elevator floor and looked around until he saw Aneme.

"Do you need any help there, madam?" he asked.

"I'll be fine," she said. "Just be ready."

Aneme removed her sword from the wall and sheathed it. Then she gripped the dagger with both hands, turned the blade to face toward the ground, and began her descent. A horrible screeching sound permeated the elevator shaft as her dagger cut through the synthetic stone of the walls, but the sparks it created provided her with illumination.

She slowed her descent by bracing her feet against the walls of the shaft. When she was about ten feet from the floor of the elevator shaft the blade could no longer cut through the material of the walls, and it came loose.

Aneme kicked off the wall with both feet and flipped through the air. She landed at the bottom of the shaft on her feet in a crouching position in order to absorb the shock, and her thoroughly blunted dagger clattered to the floor nearby.

"Are you alright madam?" one of the men shouted from the elevator above.

"Yes!" she replied. "But I can't say the same for the dagger. Sad old thing… quite outdated."

Aneme shined her soke light around the base of the elevator shaft. One of the walls consisted of a large metal door. She looked around the structure for hinges or latching mechanisms, but could find nothing. She decided to try cutting through the door, in hopes that the old northern sword she wielded was still more recent than the door, or at least the technology that went into making the door.

Cutting through the door proved more difficult than she had anticipated. Before she assailed the door she leaned her ear against it and tapped it with the hilt of her sword. She repeated that process in five different places until she triangulated a soft spot, but even so it was still quite difficult. The door was thick, and her sword was a bit out of date. If she had only the strength of a regular woman she never would have been able to force the blade through the door, but she was a northern woman in peak physical condition, which made her stronger than the strongest of men among most of the other races.

Using all her strength she made a foot long incision through the door, then two feet, then suddenly the door sunk in and began to pull to the side. Aneme quickly withdrew her sword and stepped back as the door slid aside. She was greeted by a wall of Imperial soldiers, fully armored, with weapons drawn. When they recognized Aneme they immediately lowered their weapons and saluted.

Aneme saluted back.

"What's going on here?" she asked.

"With respect, madam, we were going to ask you the same thing," one of the soldiers said.

"What do you mean? We were stuck in that elevator. Raynold said that there was an equipment malfunction and that they had to trouble shoot it."

The soldiers looked confused.

"I was passing by when I heard you attacking the door from the other side," the soldier said. "I saw your blade run through the door. I didn't know who you were, but I called it in and summoned some help."

"You mean… you weren't expecting me?" Aneme asked.

"No, madam."

"You did the right thing soldier. Now let's bring the rest of them down. Is the problem with the elevator fixed?"

"I didn't know there was any problem, or that anyone was coming down this way."

"Get the elevator down, and take me to Raynold in the meantime."

"I shall tell him you are here."

"No! No… just take me to him."

"As you wish, Commander-General."

Two of the soldiers escorted Aneme to the command center. Upon entering the room Aneme saw Raynold talking with an officer carrying a data crystal. His back was turned toward her and the door through which she came in.

She walked into the room until she was close behind him.

"Raynold!" she said a bit louder than necessary.

The man jumped, clearly startled.

"Commander-General Vaila!" Raynold said. "It is good to see you. I trust that… you arrived safely?"

"No thanks to you," Aneme said. "I tried calling you from inside of the elevator multiple times, but there was never any response on the other end. What teams do you have working on the problem in the elevator? I want to talk with them at once."

"Uh… Just give me a moment and I will call them for you…"

"No, tell me their names and I will call them myself."

"I… Really I don't think they are near any communication panels, but I will go to them directly right now and…"

"Save it," Aneme said. "Guards! Disarm this man and take him to a holding cell for interrogation."

Raynold's eyes grew wide. He attempted to run but Aneme chased him down and put him in a painful leverage. The guards took him by the arms, and forced him out of the room.

"Unbelievable!" one of the tacticians said.

"I wish I could say the same, but we have found other traitors in Leonus," Aneme said. "Now, about that elevator. Is there really any malfunction?"

"No evidence of a malfunction madam," said an officer as he poured over a set of glowing readouts.

"So he just halted the elevator?" Aneme asked.

"Apparently he used his access codes to lockdown the elevator while you were in it, and to cut off all communications going to and from."

"Can you get around it?"

"We can, just give me a few minutes here."

"Please hurry. My friend Sasha is not well."

"I understand."

"In the meantime let's find out what else he may have hidden. Can you go over the long distance and extra-Imperial communications? I want to see if we have heard back from the northerners."

"Understood madam," said a technician. "We will work continuously."

"I just don't understand why Raynold was a traitor," one of the officers stated.

"A thorough interrogation should reveal that," Aneme said.

"Yes but how?" the officer said. "We don't allow the Brotherhood in, or Kaarumites, and we always screen out people who show signs of disloyalty for military and intelligence jobs…"

"That is something to investigate," Aneme said. "I will interrogate him shortly, but first we need to secure the Imperial heir and Sasha."

"The elevator is moving," one of the technicians said.

"Let's go, and bring a stretcher," Aneme said.

Aneme returned to the bottom of the elevator shaft with four guards and a stretcher. Aderos and the soldiers that were in the elevator were stepping off as she arrived, and one of the soldiers was carrying the limp and unmoving form of Sasha.

"What happened?" Aderos asked.

"We had another traitor," Aneme said.

"Who was it?"

"Raynold."

"I don't know him. But I wonder how many more there will be."

"I intend to find out. But first let's put Sasha on the stretcher."

"What do you think you can do for her?"

"Isn't there a hydroponics section down here?" Aneme asked.

"Several," one of the officers said. "These tunnels were designed to support the Imperial family and the staff here for at least ten years in case the need arose. The hydroponics bays are kept at the ready."

"Good," Aneme said. "I want to take her to the largest one and set her under one of those bright plant lights."

"To what end?" Aderos asked. "She's not even breathing."

"Sokes are different," Aneme said. "We don't know what the exact relationship is between the energy form and the physical body."

Aderos shrugged.

"I think it would be best if you stayed with me sir, at least until I am able to interrogate Raynold and determine whether or not there are any other traitors here," Aneme said.

"Alright," Aderos said. "I'm also interested to know."

Aderos followed Aneme and the guards as they moved off with the seemingly lifeless form of Sasha on a stretcher.

They went down one long hallway, then another, and another, until they reached a large gleaming metal door with guards on either side. One of the guards tapped at a panel next to the door and the door sunk back and slid to the side. A bright light with a slightly greenish tint flooded out into the hallway.

The hydroponics room stretched on ahead of them for hundreds of feet, while the ceiling arched overhead at such a height that it almost reminded Aneme of being outside. Rows of fruit trees ran down the center of the room where the ceiling was at its highest, and radiating outward from that was row upon row of nutritious plants, all of which were nourished by artificial chemicals and artificial light.

Reminds me of my old den in the Northern Wastes…

"Do you know what you're doing?" Aderos asked.

"I have some theories," Aneme said.

The body of Sasha was placed beneath a particularly bright plant light, while Aneme began browsing through some of the equipment cabinets.

"What is it you expect to accomplish?" Aderos asked.

"I am attempting to revive her," Aneme said.

"But her heart stopped beating some time ago, how do you expect to revive her?"

"Sokes are not like humans. Their knowledge and consciousness are stored in their energy form, not the physical brain. The physical brain is just the main interface device that links their energy form to the physical form. Their nervous system is also more simplistic than ours, and is not fully interconnected, because the energy form connects with it at different anchor points. So it doesn't mean the same thing for a soke if the breathing and heartbeat have stopped as it would for a human or an animal. The chemical processes may still be going on. If the energy form is badly drained it may still be in the body, but too weak to restart the heart and lungs without first replenishing itself a little."

"I didn't know you were such an expert in soke physiology."

"I'm not. I just know a few the basics because I have spent a good deal of time with them."

"So why not plant her in the ground and water her? There are some places here where actual soil is used."

"Because, sokes are not actually plants, they just have some plant like properties. They are photosynthetic, but they ingest physical nutrients by eating, they do not have roots like actual plants."

"I see… I guess they don't."

"So I have already put her under a bright lamp, and what I am going to do next is give her some intravenous injections of chemical nutrients, like these plants are getting."

"But her heart is not beating, how will it disperse through her system?"

"I am going to set up some pumps to start her blood moving artificially."

About ten minutes later Sasha was hooked up to a series of tubes, and an artificial pump was connected as a way to get her blood circulating.

"So you are just going to run raw artificial fertilizer through her system? Is that safe?"

"I just want to give her body the nutrients it needs to rebuild itself and carry on the photosynthetic reactions. If her energy form is still trapped in that body and too weak to migrate then this body is the only way her energy form can be recharged. It's important that we nurture whatever chemical reactions might still be going on. Hopefully the energy form will be re-energized before the body decays too much to recover."

"Well I hope your efforts are met with success."

"So do I."

Once Aneme was satisfied that everything was working properly she ordered some of the men to stay behind and watch over Sasha. She also called for a medic to keep an eye on the equipment, and to notify her of any problems.

Then she turned to Aderos and said, "Now we have a traitor to interrogate, come."

The Traitor

RAYNOLD DRUMMED HIS FINGERS ON the armrests of the chair, which his arms were actually strapped to. His upper arms were also strapped, as was his torso, and his legs. The guards said nothing as they strapped him in. He had tried to fight his way to freedom, using the escape route he had prepared for just such an emergency, but the guards were too well trained thanks to Vaila Maxelis.

They kicked his legs from underneath him and knocked him out before he knew what was happening, and when he woke up he was being strapped into a chair in an empty white room. His heart beat rapidly, and his mood alternated between fear and frustration. He felt fear when he wondered what they would do to them, and frustration when he thought about the time that was passing.

Eventually the Imperial forces must triumph over the Kaarumite invasion. Even though most of the forces had left the Empire, the sokes stationed in the north combined with the northern style combat training of the remaining soldiers, and the fact that many of the citizens were armed meant that the invaders would inevitably be stamped out.

Even the air support would be destroyed, because they had no protection against the Imperial ice weapons, as they were all stolen western aircraft. It was true that they had the numerical advantage but the Imperials were significantly more intelligent and cunning than Kaarumites.

Therefore, the more time that elapsed the smaller his chances of escape were, even if he could get out of the chair and make a successful dash for his escape route from the underground complex.

Raynold did not particularly hate the Empire, he just did not care about it and felt no loyalty towards it, or any other group for that matter. He was told that the people who recruited him deliberately avoided people who openly or outwardly hated the Empire, as they were not only obvious suspects for treason, but were also less capable of concealing their emotions. Instead they typically chose people who were ambivalent toward the Empire, and who were also opportunistic. If they did hire someone who hated the Empire it was always one who hated it in secret.

Raynold still was not certain who exactly the people who hired him were, only that they were rich and foreign, and that they would shelter him once his job was done. For years he had worked as an agent for them, receiving pay from the Empire and from the foreigners who wanted to see it destroyed. But the big pay day would come, or would have come, when he returned to them after having aided in the destruction of the Empire.

The plan was for the Kaarumites to take the Empire and destroy it beyond all recognition and hope of recovery, while he would receive his pay and live a life of luxury in the Western Lands. His employers called it "world demographic restructuring" and said that it was essential to the future prosperity of the world.

They said that it would provide the western countries easier access to large numbers of unskilled migrant workers to fill farming and manual labor positions. Raynold did not see how letting the Kaarumites take another portion of the world would increase prosperity, but he did not care either. He just wanted his prosperity, and the people he worked for assured him that the Kaarumites would not receive dominion over any territory in the Western Lands.

Raynold debated inwardly on whether or not it would be better to tell everything he knew or to refuse to cooperate.

If I refuse to cooperate they will probably give me drugs, but they still might not learn everything. If I cooperate they might soften my sentence. But then... I am a traitor.

Raynold had attempted to kill the Imperial heir by suffocating him to death in an elevator, and he had hidden the call he received from the northerners offering to come to their aid. The best he could hope for was a life sentence of hard labor, but usually when one attempted to assassinate the Emperor or the Imperial heir they were executed.

As he sat there pondering these things Vaila entered the room accompanied by a medic. He clenched his jaw as he looked at her. He had always found her extremely attractive. Even though she had white skin, she was not like a typical western woman. She had a more athletic build which looked like an idealized concept made real.

Her facial features are definitely northern, and I've always found that attractive even though they never seem to find me attractive. If she had blue skin she'd look exactly like a northerner.

All of the northerners Raynold had seen appeared to be physically flawless.

Thanks to all the genetic engineering their ancestors did, where they perfected the human form! If only our race would do that!

Imperials also used genetic engineering but only to correct genetic mistakes. They did not believe that it was proper to tamper with the Great Maker's design by adding anything new.

Stupid religious nonsense getting in the way of science and progress…

As Vaila leaned forward to scrutinize Raynold his heart began to beat faster, and in spite of his better judgment he found himself licking his lips.

Perfection!

Then a thought occurred to Raynold which he had not considered before.

Vaila is northern! That's why she looks the way she does, and how she's so familiar with the Northern Arts! Her real name must be something other than Vaila Maxelis. But she was attempting to hide it all for some reason. If only I could get this information back to my superiors…

"I will ask you questions and you will answer them," Vaila said. "If you fail to answer one question, no matter how small, then I will have you drugged and you will answer anyway."

She was talking to him now, and he still had not resolved his internal debate on whether or not it would be in his best interest to cooperate with them. He considered playing for time.

"Do not attempt to stall for time or mislead me, or I will have you drugged right away," Vaila said.

Adimnor's blood!

Then a thought occurred to Raynold.

"Can we speak privately?" he asked.

"For what reason?" Vaila asked.

"I think we could come to a better understanding."

"Denied. I can give you drugs, and I will understand everything. Everything that you say is going on record as it is."

"Even so, I guarantee I will be more forthcoming if I can talk to you alone. But if you don't talk to me alone you will never know."

"Drug him," Vaila said to one of the medics nearby.

"No wait!" Raynold said. "Wait! I'll cooperate!"

It was too late, the doctor approached with a needle and swathed at his arm with a disinfectant.

"Northerner!" Raynold shouted. "I know you're a northerner! Why are you here? How did you get so high in the ranks?"

The medic cast an awkward glance back at Vaila and paused what he was doing. One of the guards also looked uneasy and favored her with a curious glance.

"Go ahead and drug him," Vaila said.

"But maybe you don't want to have everything I know shared with all the guards?" Raynold asked.

Raynold was convinced that he was being clever up until the needle pierced his skin and he began to enter a dreamlike state. What happened next was difficult for him to recall with precision, but he was dimly aware of one voice asking questions, and another which sounded very much like his own answering them.

He gave away locations, meeting places, contacts, and what he knew of the about the agenda for demographic restructuring.

"Easy access to unskilled labor," he responded to some question he could not recall. "Unrestricted flow of goods, services, and ideas... unrestricted travel... free trade... greater economic union..."

After an indeterminable amount of time had elapsed Raynold woke slowly. He found it difficult to focus his eyes for some time, but he was definitely aware of drool running down his chin.

As he lifted his head and looked around the room he noticed that some guards were still there, but Vaila was gone. He was not hooked up to any lie detector, so it occurred to him that the interrogation must be over, and he probably told them the majority of what he knew.

"Am I going to be killed?" he asked one of the guards.

"That is not for me to say," the guard said.

"If it were up to you would you kill me?" Raynold asked.

"That is not for me to say," the guard replied.

"Don't even talk to him," another guard said.

"So neither of you is troubled that you're taking orders from a northerner, and especially one who is fresh from the glacier?" Raynold asked.

Raynold felt his desperation escalate. He had been caught, interrogated, and now they were probably going to kill him. But the guards said nothing, and their faces remained expressionless.

"For the love of heavenly ministers!" Raynold shouted. "She's a northerner, and it's obvious! You seriously cannot tell?"

The guards said nothing.

I am most certainly dead.

"If you are going to kill me then just get it over with!" Raynold exclaimed. "All this waiting is irritating me!"

CHAPTER 35

The Heat of Battle

THE BATTLE RAGED ALL NIGHT, and as it continued Roger felt continually more irritated. There was nothing he could do, but sleep escaped him. He paced back and forth in the command center of Leonus, and drank energy drinks periodically throughout the night.

The explosions continued throughout the night, and frequently sent tremors through the floating city.

"It's like a thunderstorm on steroids," Roger muttered in English.

"Sir?" one of the officers asked.

"Nothing, nothing… I was just… Nevermind."

"Sir," the officer acknowledged.

"Shields at 80%" one of the technicians said.

An hour later the same technician announced that shields were at 70%.

"At that rate we'll be dead by the morning for certain," Roger said. "See if you can do anything to bolster the shields."

"Yes sir," the technician replied.

"And see what the progress is on nullifying their devices that keep us from using our freeze weapons."

"Yes sir."

"Make them go faster."

"Yes sir."

The rate of depletion slowed, due to the best efforts of the engineers, but two hours later they were down to 60%, then 50%...

"Is there anyone we can call for help?" Roger asked. "What is the status in the Empire?"

"Sir!" an engineer said as he burst into the room.

A few seconds later he was followed by a soke.

"What is it?" Roger asked.

"Sir, we have found a way to circumvent the technology that is blocking our freeze warheads!" the engineer said. "We couldn't have done it without the help of the soke scientists you sent us."

"Very good," Roger said. "Now what is it?"

"Well," the soke began. "To express it in human terms, it is a resonating energy wave of the frequency--"

Roger held up his hand.

"I don't need to hear the technical explanation," Roger said. "Just tell me how we can make it happen, in layman's terms."

"You can adjust the output of each of your flying machine's propulsion devices to emit this particular field of energy," the soke said. "It will nullify the field that the enemy is putting out."

"Unfortunately the power for the ships will deplete more quickly," the human engineer said. "The broader the field they generate, the faster the depletion, and we are going to need broad fields."

"I see," Roger said.

"The engines may burn out and have to be replaced," the engineer said.

"May?"

"If use is prolonged."

"How long is prolonged?"

The engineer opened his mouth to speak but Roger preempted him.

"Never mind," Roger said. "Just make it happen."

The engineer nodded and went to a console.

"I am uploading a computer program to the air fleet which will automatically adjust the output of their engines once activated," the Engineer said.

"Make sure you tell them what you told me about depletion," Roger said.

"Yes sir."

Roger watched and waited as the engineer worked away at the console. A few minutes later he announced that he was done.

"Is it working?" Roger asked.

"It has yet to be tested," the human engineer said. "We will know in a few minutes…"

Minutes passed by.

"It's working!" the engineer announced about ten minutes had elapsed.

"Finally we catch a break!" Roger said.

The attacks on Leonus began to abate as Kaarumite ships were being knocked out of the air.

Roger watched a set of monitors showing the battle from different vantage points. The night was frequently lit up by bright red flashes of the heat generating earth scorches, but there were also tiny white flashes of light, like sparks, where the Imperial freeze warheads were detonating. Those small flashes were often followed by a bigger flash as enemy ships short circuited and exploded or fell out of the air.

"Why don't we just target the big ships?" Roger asked.

"This time each of the ships has a built in suppressant device against our weapons, not just the big ones, which was why our ship's fields had to be set on the strongest possible setting," the engineer said.

"Understood," Roger replied.

Over the next hour the attacks on Leonus slowed to a crawl, but an incredible storm was raging just outside of the city's forcefield as a result of the heat and cold weapons being detonated in the skies. Then with one final strike of an incredible warhead against the shields, the enemy attack abated.

"What is going on?" Roger asked.

"It appears that they are focusing their attacks on the ground, clearing a wide path toward the Empire," the Engineer said.

"Put out a general order," Roger said. "I want any ships that are about to be depleted of energy to fire their final warheads and return to base, either in the Empire or in Leonus. Tell them to go to whichever they happen to be closest to at the time."

"Understood sir," an officer said.

Roger watched a set of schematics showing blue and red dots, which represented Imperial and Kaarumite aircraft. He also watched a computer simulated map showing the damage the Kaarumites were inflicting to the forest. They were cutting a wide swath, and in one place it came dangerously close to one of the tavlon cities which was being used as a base.

"Transfer these images to my office and bring me something to drink," Roger said.

He returned to his office and sat in his large cushiony chair as the surface of his desk lit up with a set of images. A few minutes later an officer came in carrying a warm stimulant which had properties similar to terrestrial coffee, but the taste was entirely different.

Tastes better, actually.

As Roger watched the images closely he saw red dots disappearing, but he also began to see blue dots either disappearing or leaving the battlefield. Still, the numbers favored his side. There was nothing he could do about the swath that was approaching the Empire, but as time went by the rate at which it advanced was slowed.

Roger began to feel extremely tired, in spite of his stimulant. His mind began to slow, and he could feel his head droop. Suddenly the line working its way through the forest toward the Empire shot forward rapidly, nearly to the edge of the Empire, then tapered off. As oddly sudden as it was, Roger somehow did not feel alarmed by it. He also became aware of the fact that there were no more red dots, and very few blue dots.

He snorted and woke up abruptly. It was morning outside and the clouds were beginning to clear. In spite of his stimulant Roger had fallen asleep. He looked down at the displays over his desk with a start and saw that what he had dreamed about actually happened.

He quickly rose up and ran out into the command center.

"Why didn't anyone wake me up!" he snarled at his chief tacticians.

"You have been up for over a day, and we thought you could use some sleep," one of the tacticians said. "Especially since there was nothing left for you to do at the time."

"I'll be the judge of that! What's the situation?"

"The situation is that the enemy fleet was decimated. We did lose some ships, but both the Empire and the contested area are clean of enemy ships."

"Well that's good, except for the lost pilots and their ships."

"The loss of a ship does not mean the pilot did not survive."

"Well, good. What else?"

"Most of our ships have returned to base, and some have landed in the Empire, but it will take some time before they are ready to fly again. We have exhausted all of the freeze missiles we had in Leonus."

"Well alright, but we won, right?"

"There is a massive amount of troops coming from the south, the largest army ever recorded in Imperial history, and they will be here in two hours. But we have no air support. This battle is going to have to be decided on the ground."

"Great…"

"Your wife called while you were resting, and said that the Imperial heir was safe and that they were nearly done cleaning the Kaarumites out of Randar, but there is severe damage there. She also said that they caught some more traitors, and that she wanted to speak with you on the matter when you have some time."

"I'll talk to her now then."

"Nirin called, and asked if you would like him to seal off the path the Kaarumites cut, which runs nearly all the way to the Empire."

"Have his people regrow the forest for two miles. Then tell them to eat something and sun themselves. I want them at full strength for when the Kaarumites arrive."

"Acknowledged."

"Now let me talk to my wife. Privately, in my office."

"As you wish sir."

Roger went back into his office and sat down in his large comfortable chair. He let out a deep breath and slouched. A few seconds later the visual displays on his desk disappeared and a large black rectangle appeared in the air over his desk with the word "connecting call" blinking in blue letters in the middle.

Roger reached out in an absent minded attempt to touch what looked like a solid flat screen, but his hand went right through it. Suddenly the screen lit up and a live image of his wife appeared. She was also in some sort of office.

"Mattis," she said.

Even on the private channel she was careful not to use his name.

"Vaila," he replied. "How is everything there?"

"We are cleaning up Randar and some of the other cities. There are a few small pockets of Kaarumites that are being stamped out, and we managed to defeat what was left with of their stolen airfleet, but if you could have sent ships earlier then the battle would have been over quicker."

"I know... I tried, but the Kaarumite fleet just started to follow the ships back north."

"It's alright, there was nothing you could do."

"You're sure of that?"

"If there was then you would have done it. As it was, the preparations you suggested were very helpful. I can only imagine how bad things would have been without the sokes and the Imperial forces that you did leave behind."

"Thanks."

"We found a handful of traitors in Randar."

"How many?"

"I don't want to say over the airways, even on a secure channel, but I believe we got all of them. It's not just Kaarumites who want the Empire dead, I have reason to believe that some major banks are involved."

"Sinister."

"I will give you a full report when I arrive."

"What about the northerners?"

"Apparently we did receive communications from them, but they were blocked and the traitors attempted to erase the records of their receipt. I was able to reach an outpost belonging to Kenna Den, you know, Marla's people. They said that an official representative from the Empire had formally declined their help, and that they would only reconsider our case if their elders could speak directly with me and a member of the royal family."

"What about our ambassadors we sent?"

"Raynold had them called back."

"That weasely bugger..."

"What?"

"Nothing... Take Demekus and get on the fastest airship you can to head north."

"Our fleet is badly depleted, if the northerners agree to come we may need to contract some help to transport them."

"Whatever needs to be done. Short of giving up any Imperial territory or sovereignty."

"Agreed."

"Let me know as soon as you have something. And be careful. You are the most important person in this world to me."

"I love you too."

Once the communication was over Roger returned to the command center and paced about nervously.

He bit his lip as he watched footage of the Kaarumite horde approaching. It was just like in his dream. There were hordes upon hordes of barbaric warriors, most were brown, some were white, but all were savagely tattooed and pierced. Among them were the tremendous sauropod sonolars, and the elephantine gulogs. Around the edges of the troop near the sides of the forest were hordes of mighty feline zangrons, which were shepherded by fierce Kaarumite women on swift reptilian mounts.

Included among the Kaarumites were large troops of theropod type dinosaurs, the dreaded sarathons, the very same creatures which had overpowered and captured Garek and Aneme. The sarathons were also equipped with light armor and some weapons. They seemed eager to burst forth at a much more rapid pace than their human escorts were moving, but were precariously restrained.

"I know we're out of freeze missiles here," Roger said. "But there should be more back in the Empire."

"All of our combative air vessels are still out of commission," one of the tacticians said. "Many of them will have to have their engines replaced."

Roger bit his lip and resumed staring at the monitors. There were vehicles moving along with the troops, probably mobile forcefield generators designed to shield them from air attack. Roger noted that he saw none of the devices designed to block their freeze weapons.

"What new game is this?" Roger muttered.

"A deadly one," said a smooth voice from behind.

It was Feren, the Haxian Kaarumite.

"Look," he said as he pointed to one of the monitors. "He comes…"

There was what appeared to be a large man of unbelievable size. He was at least twice as tall as Roger. He was standing on a large moving metal platform, which elevated him to a greater height than any of the troops. He was wearing some gold colored armor on his legs, and none on his chest. However, he did have a good deal of gold jewelry on his chest and arms. The combination of jewelry and armor went together rather well, but there was one item he wore which did not quite seem to fit.

"Zoom in on that man," Roger said.

The picture zoomed in to show a close up of the giant. In some places his skin shimmered in the sunlight, with the light of the sun glaring off of him similar to a reflective sheen on a metal surface. Then Roger saw what was incongruent.

Around his torso was a series of normal sized humanoid skulls strung together on a rope. The skulls were a lemon yellow color.

"Those are dried soke skulls," Roger said.

"I told you, there has never been a thing which could stand in the way of Atuskus-Var," Feren said.

"We are going to have to throw everything we have into this battle," Roger said. "Give the order for all the troops to start moving in. Especially the troops that are more distant. I want all the bases in the contested area emptied of everyone except for the minimal support staff necessary."

"Sending out the signal, sir," an officer said.

"Can we get audio on the enemy troops?" Roger asked.

"Yes sir, they are close enough now," one of the officer said.

A rhythmic beating of drums filled the command center, punctuated by the army shouting "Ooh! Ah!" in time with the beat of the base drums.

"Barbaric," one of the tacticians said.

"Barbaric splendor!" Feren said. "Now the moment of truth draws near!"

"Truth is absolute," Roger said.

As they listened the usual yelling and beating of the drums was occasionally interrupted by semi-melodic shouts in a garbled dialect.

"I have heard enough," Roger said. "Switch it off."

But just as the officer's hand was hovering over the panel a loud clear shout rang out over the battlefield, in a voice so deep that it did not sound human.

"Little man hiding in the air!" it shouted.

"The voice of Atuskus-Var!" Feren said.

"Wait!" Roger said. "Don't switch it off yet."

"I know you are there little man!" Atuskus-Var boomed. "You are hiding in your floating city! You cannot stay there long. I know you think you are a man of power, but you are not anything. I have seen you and tasted your fear. Come down now and surrender, and I will spare your life. There is no reason for you to die, horribly, for a people who have outlived their time."

"Interesting that he's not even asking me to convert," Roger said.

The officers and tacticians looked around uncomfortably. Two of them stepped close to Feren.

"I have not been in communication with him," Feren said.

"Little maa-an!" Atuskus-Var shouted in a mocking sing-song voice. "I know you are in there. If I have to pull you down I am going to rip off your arms and legs, one at a time, and I will inflict horrors and humiliations beyond your imagination on what is left of you!"

"Begin the battle," Roger said. "Plan two, modified, and shut off the audio."

The Outpost

Aneme, Demekus, and a group of twenty elite soldiers flew in a small transport vehicle over Randar. They would head north to the southern central region of the Northern Wastes, which was where the area controlled by Kenna Den could be found.

Much of Randar was still smoldering from the ferocious Kaarumite attack, but there were no longer any enemy aircraft in the air. Before Aneme left she gave orders stating that restoring the fighting aircraft to operational condition was to be the top priority.

As they cleared Randar they discovered that much of the Empire was badly damaged. Where there used to be farms and forests there was smoldering black ground. About half of the countryside they flew over was decimated, and all of the cities they passed over showed signs of damage.

"This is terrible," Aneme said.

"But it could have been much worse, if not for your husband," Demekus said. "I'm sure the sokes will help us repair the land."

"They will."

After they crossed the northern border of the Empire there were still some damaged spots where earth scorchers had been detonated, and smoke rose from a few small towns.

"They must have also attacked some of the other western nations on their way to the Empire," Aneme said.

"I call it poetic justice," Demekus said. "Or irony. Either one applies here."

"How could you wish the Kaarumites on anyone?"

"Well, technically they wished the Kaarumites on themselves, and they reaped the results."

"I cannot argue with that."

"That's right. A man who goes to bed with a snake shouldn't be surprised when he wakes up bitten, or when he doesn't wake up at all."

The plan was to fly north and cross into Hax. Since they had already been cleared for entry into Hax they would keep flying north until they reached a small town in northern Hax. From there they would proceed by ground vehicle until they reached a northern garrison peopled by warriors from Kenna Den.

"I wanted to thank you for letting me come," Demekus said.

"Well, depending on how we are received you may change your mind about that later," Aneme said.

"I can't imagine that they would be anything other than fair and honest with us."

The aircraft turned upwards and began to climb higher in the atmosphere. They were to fly at supersonic speeds in the upper atmosphere, which meant that they would arrive at their destination in a matter of hours rather than days.

Aneme looked out the window absent mindedly. This aircraft was different. Normally aircraft rose to the altitude they were going to cruise at before moving forward, like a bubble floating to the top of water, but this aircraft moved up and forward at the same time, going in a diagonal trajectory.

"Not all northerners are fair and honest," Aneme said.

"But they are all honest, and most of them are fair," Demekus said.

"They are mostly honest, but there are a few that are crooked. Have you forgotten what happened to my husband?"

"I haven't forgotten."

"They may not receive us with joy."

"But they already offered to help us. They just got confused by that traitor Raynold, who will be duly executed."

"Maybe."

"The northerners would execute such a traitor. Perhaps we should have executed him before we left as a show of good faith?"

"You're being childish, and executing anyone is serious business."

"I'm sorry, master."

"There is no need to call me master anymore, training is over."

"Yes, madam."

"That is better."

Demekus remained silent for a time and looked out the window.

"I feel like I am going to my destiny," he said after some time.

"Or a stop on the way to your destiny," Aneme said.

"I can sense her, out there, waiting…"

"Sense who?"

"Do you suppose we might formalize our relationship with an arranged marriage, perhaps between the house of Maxelis and whoever is chief there?"

"Unlikely. What they probably want to do is deal with the highest authorities they can talk to since Raynold dealt with them dishonestly. This is a show of good faith."

"Do you think…"

Demekus turned away from the window and faced Aneme.

"Do you think the northern women will find me attractive?" Demekus asked.

"Some may, but they will still not consider you as an option," Aneme replied. "Northerners very seldom marry out, especially those who live in the traditional way."

"Are you sure?"

"Yes."

"But you married Roger."

"Yes, but those were very special circumstances. For both of us."

"Sometimes northerners marry out."

"Yes, a few do, but those are migrants who have left the north, and even then it is rare."

"But—"

"Stop being ridiculous. We are on a serious mission and I want you to behave accordingly. You are a representative of the Empire and the Maxelis family. If I taught you all of the Northern Arts without teaching you responsibility then I have failed."

"Yes… I understand. I apologize. I will not say anything to embarrass you or the Empire while we are there. It's just that, I always had a strong impression that my wife would come from the north. Sometimes when I close my eyes I can see her face."

"Really?"

"Yes, I even had a dream about it once, and the impression was so strong that I just knew in my heart it was what I was supposed to do."

"Now that is interesting. Roger also had dreams about me back when he was on his native world."

"On the other hand it may just have been a really strong fantasy, after all, the dream was colorless. It was all in black and white, and shades of gray. I think if it were the forward sight it would be more realistic."

"I can't tell you how to interpret your dreams, but when you are interacting with my people you need to show restraint and dignity, and you need to be completely honest."

"I understand."

"Good."

Again Demekus was silent, and the pilot announced that they were approaching the border of Hax.

"Do you suppose that they will take us to their primary den?" Demekus asked.

"Maybe not this time, but eventually they must because they want technical help from the Empire," Aneme said.

"Why don't we fly all the way to the outpost?"

"As you know, navigational equipment does not work well over the Northern Wastes, at least, not when one is airborne. It has to do with the strong electromagnetic fields there, as well as some other types of radiation fields which wreak havoc with flight sensors."

"I can't help but wonder; what if we maintained our highest altitude possible and flew over the entire Northern Wastes until we came to the edge of the world?"

"Then, assuming we were above the range of the energy fields, we would entirely miss our target destination."

"But we would get to see the edge of the world, and we might learn something valuable about the north."

"It might be something to do, but it has been a long time since anyone tried that, because—"

"I know… I know… Because the ships and probes that were sent disappeared."

"Right. So if it is done then it needs to be done systematically, with a large fleet, and a way needs to be found to compensate for the electromagnetic fields."

"Hmmm… Something to think about."

As they flew over Hax to the distant north they experienced an odd sensation. The sun appeared to be setting in the south behind them. By the time they landed in the small town on the northern Haxian border it seemed like twilight, or early dawn, even though it was actually closer to the middle of the day.

"Fascinating," Demekus said as he stepped out of the ship and looked to the south.

The sun was low on the horizon, and appeared ruddy, while the sky along the southern horizon was pink. Overhead the sky was a dark blue, nearly black, and to the north the sky was black with stars clearly visible.

"At the edge of dawn…" Demekus commented as he stepped down the ramp.

A group of locals had gathered on the paved area beneath them. All of the men present had beards and they were wearing animal skins. Some of them also wore fur hats. Most of them had pale powder blue skin, but a handful of them were the same color as full blooded northerners, and a few of them even appeared to be but their demeanor gave them away as Haxians.

Beyond the paved landing area was a small tower, and beyond that were a few small buildings. Further south there appeared to be some farms, but to the north was nothing but pine forest right up to the edge of town.

A cool breeze blew across Demekus' face from the east as he stood on the ramp leading down from the aircraft. It was cool but not chilling. A few seconds later the direction of the wind changed and he felt a chilling breeze blow down from the north which stung his skin.

Demekus felt a hand on his back, and looking over his shoulder he saw Aneme standing in the doorway with a group of soldiers behind her.

"Of course," Demekus said.

Demekus walked down the ramp and stood among the Haxians. Some of them looked at him but most ignored him and kept looking at the vehicle and talking among themselves.

"Didn't know the Empire was still around," he heard one say.

"Oh yes, but it's much smaller now," another replied.

When Aneme came down she asked to speak with the authorities, which did not take long since the man in charge was also standing in the crowd. She began to explain to him why they were there but the man already knew. As Aneme was talking a rugged looking vehicle pulled up next to the landing pad, and a man got out of it. He came through the crowd and headed straight in her direction.

The crowd parted for him without making a sound. He had a powerful physique and medium blue skin. He was dressed in unusual blue-grey armor which was dented in a few places. He was unquestionably a northerner.

Aneme ended her conversation with the Haxian authority and turned to face the newcomer when he was still some distance away from her.

"Are you 'Vaila Maxelis'?" he asked.

The way he said her name implied that he knew it was only an alias name.

"I am," she replied.

"Hmm…" he said. "Do you have the Emperor's son with you?"

"I do."

"My name is Elias Karvak. I have been sent to take you to the nearest garrison to meet with the elders of Kenna Den. The vehicle is ready if you are through here."

"You mean that?" Aneme said gesturing toward the vehicle the man arrived in. "That won't contain much of my entourage."

"We didn't' ask for any entourage other than you and a son of the Emperor," Elias said.

"I understand," Aneme said. "My men will remain here and protect the ship."

"Then let us spend no more time here. The elders await."

Aneme ordered the men to lock down the ship and stand guard over it, then she turned and followed Elias back to his hovercraft. The front seat of the vehicle was wide enough for Aneme and Demekus to both sit there next to Elias as he drove.

In spite of the battered and worn look of the exterior of the vehicle the seats seemed to be in excellent condition, and showed no signs of wear and tear. The seats were surfaced with something that looked like black leather, but felt tougher and smoother to the touch.

"These are some nice leather seats," Demekus said as he slid into place.

"They aren't exactly leather," Elias said as he started up the vehicle.

"What are they then?"

"Skin torn from draenocks. We use what we can in the Northern Wastes."

"Oh…"

Demekus said little as they journeyed north, and Aneme said nothing. For the most part a path was cleared through the pine forest, but sometimes the road disappeared, and in those cases they had to drive slowly and carefully through the woods for a short time before they were on the road again. After an hour or so of driving the forest thinned, and then stopped altogether. They were in the open tundra, and off in the distance an object was jutting up from the rolling hills.

As they drew closer Aneme and Demekus were able to determine that it was a tall black tower of durable yet simple construction.

As they neared the tower Elias slowed down. It was surrounded by a black wall with rows of long spikes protruding out from the top in three different directions. A metal gate in the wall opened for them and Elias drove inside. There were a few other vehicles and northerners present.

A man and a woman dressed in the same kind of armor that Elias wore were standing in the back of a large flatbed vehicle behind a particularly hideous severed head. It was large and gray, with many spikes and a few tendrils. It had large black fangs and four eyes. The head was about the size of an entire horse, and it looked like its skin was made out of stone.

"Is that a… draenock?" Demekus asked.

"It's what is left of one," Elias said.

As they watched the two armored northerners pushed the head out of the vehicle and onto the ground. There was a group of northerners nearby, who then proceeded to approach the head. One of them kicked it so hard that one side of it briefly left the ground. He cocked his head toward the others behind him, and they approached the head with weapons drawn.

They took turns stabbing and slashing at the head, while dictating their results to a man holding something that was the size of a data entry pad, but which looked more like a printed book.

"What are they doing?" Demekus asked.

"Weapons testing," Aneme said.

"And that one with the book?" Demekus asked as he pointed to the man.

"He is taking notes," Aneme said.

"You mean, he is physically writing on non-electric media?"

"Yes, you're in the Northern Wastes now. Electronic data entry pads are at a premium."

"Come."

They walked toward the tower and Elias gave a hand signal as they approached. As they neared the building they heard a sound like stone scraping against stone, and a square portion of the wall sunk in and slid to the side.

"You have motion sensors that are activated by specific hand signals?" Demekus asked.

"No, that would be foolish," Elias said. "We have someone watching from a window."

"Oh…"

The interior of the building was finished with blue-grey stone of varying tones. There was no carpet, nor were there any relief carvings. The only attempt at decoration was the presence of mounted draenock skulls which had been stripped of skin and flesh. Stripped as they were, Aneme could still identify which species they had been from her childhood studies.

"Clatterfang," she said as they passed by a particularly large and hideous skull, which was a dull gray color and etched with lines that resembled circuitry.

"Is that what that thing is called?" Demekus asked.

"That's what we call it. Whatever names their creators may have assigned are unknown."

Aneme and Demekus were escorted into a round room with men sitting around the edge forming a circle. Most of them wore blue-grey armor like Elias, but a few had light form fitting armor which was black in color.

Some of them wore capes. They were all in excellent shape with powerful physiques, even those who appeared to be quite old.

"We are the heads of the leading families of Kenna Den and the associated guard stations and outposts," one of the men said. "My name is Arnas Kenna, head of the founding family of Kenna Den."

The man stood up and put his hand on Aneme's shoulder as he introduced himself. Aneme returned the gesture.

"I greet you in the name of the Great Maker," Aneme replied. "I am Aneme Strauss, formerly Aneme Kand. In the Empire I am officially called Vaila Maxelis. My companion is Demekus, son of the Emperor Adinis Maxelis."

When Aneme finished speaking they both dropped their arms.

"Marla gave us a full report when she returned, and we found the terms of an alliance agreeable, however, the encounter with a traitor within your ranks has caused us to reconsider. Some of the men here have very cogent concerns, which you must now allay if you wish to have any sort of alliance with us."

"I understand," Aneme replied.

"Why do you give your skin a false color?" one of the elders asked. "Do you not consider it wrong to deceive others?"

"I have told no lies," Aneme said.

"That does not answer the question," the elder said.

"I changed my skin and hair colors to protect my husband. Under those circumstances I do not consider it morally objectionable to alter my physical appearance. If someone were to ask me of my ethnic or racial origins I would either tell the truth or decline to answer."

"Yet your intent is to deceive."

"In this case, yes. But there is precedent for it. As you know on some occasions our people have temporarily changed their coloration for purposes of disguise. One of the men from your den who captured my husband was disguised in such a way."

"Irrelevant, they were not operating under our sanction when they captured your husband."

"My husband had to disguise himself, and I had to also disguise myself in order for us to avoid identification. If you examined the medical data on my husband you would know his skin color is not of this world."

"If he is the Mender of Ways, the one who was prophesied, then the Great Maker would protect him and there would be no need for him, or you, to result to trickery for protection. It is written that the Mender of Ways will overcome all things in this world that attempt to stand against him. I quote from the book of Elekon chapter four verses six through seven: 'He is sent of the Great Maker, and the Great Maker is behind him and ahead of him. There is no force in the world or of it which can stand against him, for the Great Maker has already made a way for him.'"

"You saw the medical data, so you know he is not of this world."

"I am not convinced of that. The medical data indicates that he has an anomalous genome, but he is still quite human. If he were from another world then how could he be so similar to human kind? We are not even genetically compatible with the sokes who share our world with us, it makes no sense for an alien to be so much like us."

"The Great Maker can use the same design as many times as he wants on as many worlds or universes as he wants."

"Yes he can, but that does not mean that he did."

"When my people examined him upon his initial arrival we found certain trace elements which are common to all things in our universe absent from him, and we found other elements which we previously had no record of in his system."

"But we have no way of viewing those results as the far western continent is under lockdown by the Tandorans."

"Are you saying there is something wrong with my word?"

"You are comfortable with deceit under certain circumstances."

"Sir, I find your accusation tasteless," Aneme said. "I do not lie, and you may connect me with a truth verifier and repeat your questions if you like."

"That will not be necessary," Arnas said.

"I relent, but I do not find her answers satisfactory on all points," the elder said.

"Next," Arnas said.

"Strauss is not a northern name," one of the other elders said.

"It is not. My husband says that in his world it is a 'jerr-men' name," Aneme said.

"Yes I know your husband is not one of us. My concern is that you may introduce out-marriage to our community. Not all of our people approve of out-marriage, and with the constant threat of draenock incursion we cannot afford to dilute our strength. What guarantees can you give us that an alliance with you will not result in out-marriage and dilution of our bloodlines with weaker men?"

Aneme was taken aback by the question. She remembered how she had initially disapproved of her brother choosing a soke woman for a mate, and how she argued with him. Now she was in a situation where someone disapproved of her, and he was not the only one.

"How can we protect the other peoples of the world if we consider them inferior?" Aneme asked.

"There is no logic in that statement, nor is it an answer to my question," the elder said.

"If we ally with other peoples then we, as northerners, will not have to rely only on ourselves to defend the world from evil. I recognized this basic fact when I met Roger. Don't look at it like we are losing strength, but like we are adding the strength of other people to our own."

"That is a subjective argument with no real merit, and you are not from our den."

"Very well, you have seen the package the Empire had to offer. You will have modern technology, including the technology of flight, and your numbers will be greatly increased."

"You speak of adding strength through numbers, but adding men of the white race will not increase our numbers because they are not northerners, nor can they be. You will increase the number of people here, but not OUR numbers. We are already pressed badly enough with draenocks, to add an alien population to our dens would create division and oppression, even if they do come as friends."

"No one is suggesting that you give up your sovereignty, we're just suggesting a military alliance where we each send forces to bolster each other militarily."

"Where would these Imperial soldiers stay while here?"

"We would have to work that out."

"So you admit that they cannot stay in our dens."

"No... Not necessarily."

"What is your plan, girl?"

"A mutual military alliance."

"It seems it's not complete. There are certain things which have to be enumerated, such as where the westerners would stay, and how we might prevent them from seeking courtship or marriage with our people. We cannot afford to introduce weakness into our tribe."

"If you're worried about out-marriage, then you don't have to grant citizenship or permanent residency to any foreigners, and that's not something the Empire asked for anyways. You have your lands and they have theirs."

"That's not enough. Even if we bar them from remaining among us, which of course we would do, they might still induce some of our women to leave with them, which would be a loss to our people."

"What do you suggest then?"

"If there is to be a treaty between us then it must be contingent upon there being no marriage between the Imperials and the people of Kenna Den."

"You cannot control people in that way, and it would be wrong to try. What would you do if someone did marry? Break the treaty? Then the Imperial government would still know where your den is."

"That is why I am against this alliance. I rest my case."

"Next," Arnas said.

"I have a question which I would like to direct at both of you," said another elder.

"By all means," Demekus said.

"I thank you," the elder said. "I am concerned that a traitor was able to infiltrate your government to such a high level. As you know, we northerners do not really have government beyond the council of elders, but we all keep the secrets of the den as if they were our very own. Now, while I for one am convinced of the validity of your offer, and the nobility of your intentions, I must ask, can you guarantee that there are no more traitors in your midst?"

Fire and Wrath

"THIS IS NOT GOING WELL," Roger muttered as he watched the battle unfold beneath him.

The plan was to avoid engaging the Kaarumites in the open as much as possible, and to lure them into the woods where they felt less confident and where the sokes could attack them with greater ease. Small numbers of Kaarumites often shot off into the woods, but the amount of troops they managed to lure away was a drop in a bucket compared with what remained of the forces in the cleared area.

Roger formed an ancillary plan to divide and conquer the Kaarumite forces. He instructed the sokes to send a rapid burst of plant growth, using all the plants available, right down the center of the Kaarumite ranks. He theorized that it would act like a wedge, causing the troops in front to split in half and run off into the woods on either side, and the troops further back would run back the way they came out of fear.

At first the plan seemed to work flawlessly. The Kaarumites were driven mad with fear as a wedge of dense writhing foliage rushed toward them and separated their ranks, but as the wedge neared Atuskus-Var he jumped down from his platform and stood directly in its path.

He assumed a peculiar stance with his hands extended toward the onrushing vegetation, and for a second he seemed to grow darker as if a shadow passed over him, or as if he were standing in a dark room and were difficult to make out, except that the light around him remained the same.

In the next second he lit up brightly, like a small sun in humanoid form, and before it reached him the groping vegetation began to wither.

At first the tips of the advancing vines and bushes grew black, but then the blackness spread up along the wedge, even encompassing the new trees that had grown, and all the plants withered and crumbled.

The Kaarumites behind Atuskus-Var cheered, and he led the advance on foot for some time, occasionally pausing to resume an odd stance which caused the vegetation to blacken and wilt in front of him.

The Kaarumites cheered so loudly that Roger could hear it even with the sound from all the live feeds switched off.

Roger immediately called the soke lieutenants on the ground.

"What happened?" Roger asked.

"He negated our efforts," they said.

"Obviously! But how?"

"We do not yet know precisely how, but he is some kind of energy manipulator. He has caused pain to some of us."

"Is he a soke?"

"The feeling is… different," one of the sokes said. "No, he is something else."

"He is the son of Kaarum," Feren said.

"See if you can figure out what he is," Roger said.

Roger then sent orders to all of his generals telling them to attack the Kaarumites from all sides, especially from behind. As a result the Kaarumites halted their advance and met the attack. At first the Kaarumites suffered heavy casualties from all sides, but the numbers were still massively in their favor. As the alliance soldiers grew weary they began to suffer more casualties. Roger then ordered them to fall back and for the sokes to cover their retreat.

Some Kaarumites followed the Imperial and Haxian soldiers into the woods, but they were ensnared by the sokes and killed off. After some time the Kaarumites renewed their march, and Roger let them go until they reached the fresh forest in front. The Kaarumites sent the Sarathons ahead, and put a line of mighty sonolars behind them. They advanced slowly in order to give the sonolars time to knock down most of the trees.

"So they are playing it slow and safe," Roger said.

Roger ordered a lightening attack on the sonolars, but before the men could reach the sonolars they were attacked by the vicious therapod sarathons. It was a fierce battle, and the sarathons took a higher toll on Imperial forces than did the Kaarumites.

We just don't have the numbers!

It did not help that the men were already tired when they had to fight the sarathons, or that there was no northern training specifically for sarathons, but the greatest difficulty was the fact that they kept having to move back to get away from the steady advance of the sonolars.

Roger quickly ordered more men to the front line when he saw what was happening, but then the Kaarumites released zangrons on them. The sokes helped by ensnaring as many zangrons and sarathons as they could, but there was nothing they could do to affect the mighty sonolars. It was a fierce battle, but after two hours of intense fighting most of the sarathons and zangrons were killed.

The Kaarumites decided to pull back. They brought the surviving sonolars back among them and halted their advance once more. When Roger saw that they had halted, he ordered most of his troops to also rest, but told them to continue small scale light attacks from all directions to keep the Kaarumites from moving on. When one group of attackers needed to rest, another would take their place, and for some time Roger was able to give most of his troops a rest.

But once the Kaarumites were able to discern what was going on they began to move forward again, ignoring the attackers.

"Will they walk all the way to the Empire?" Roger asked.

"They will have to rest at some point," one of the advisors said.

"And at that point our men will also have to rest, so it will do us no good," another advisor said.

"We should just have the sokes issue an all-out attack on them and overgrow them with forest," an advisor said. "We need to use the sokes more heavily"

Roger was silent.

"I agree," he said after some time. "Let's hit them from all sides. We will have a fifth of our men resting at all time, and we will cycle through them regularly so that at least some of them can get rest. That's what the Kaarumites are doing, whether they intend to or not. The people and animals near the edges of their formation are fighting us, while the bulk of them in the middle are not."

The advisors agreed, but they decided it would be best to whittle the number of men at rest down to one tenth and cycle more frequently. Roger consented.

The battle was renewed with full vigor, and again the Kaarumites stopped. Roger watched from above as the men fought desperately but vigorously against the much larger numbers of Kaarumites.

The sokes were able to overgrow some more of the battlefield, but not much more because as the growth approached the center Atuskus-Var flared up with bright light again and withered the plants. He also sent painful feedback to the sokes which put many of them out of commission for a few minutes.

"Tell the sokes to focus more on snaring than taking ground, and tell the soldiers not to bother with people the sokes have ensnared," Roger said. "Let them prioritize soldiers that are still fighting since the sokes can't snare everyone at once. The sokes are armed, they can also do some direct fighting or killing if need be."

The fighting below was intense, with Kaarumite casualties piled up so heavily that in some places there came to be walls of bodies.

"It's like Armageddon," Roger said.

"What, sir?" one of the advisors asked.

"It's this battle that… uh… never mind."

Unfortunately there were also allied casualties, and the Haxians experienced them more heavily as their training and equipment was less up to date than that of the Imperial forces.

"If only we had air support!" Roger said.

"They made sure that we didn't," one of the advisors grumbled.

"What is that being, Atuskus-Var?" Roger asked. "How do his powers work?"

"We don't know," one of the tacticians said. "From the scans all we have been able to tell is that he's not a soke, and that he is generating high levels of energy. It's hard to make out exact bio-readings because of the energy, but he is definitely human-like."

"I should be down there fighting with them," Roger said.

"What good would that do, sir?" an advisor asked. "You would be killed, and we would have to find another leader while the Emperor convalesces."

"It just seems wrong for me to stand up here and do nothing while our men are fighting and dying down there," Roger said.

"You cannot go. The Emperor put you in charge. You have other duties now."

Roger continued watching the intense battle below. The allies were putting up a staunch resistance, but if things continued the way they were going then the Imperials would probably lose.

"Put me through to Garek," he said.

The face of a Haxian officer appeared on the screen. The man looked like a regular westerner with no northern heritage whatsoever, but he wore a Haxian uniform.

"Where is Garek?" Roger asked.

"Fighting, sir," the officer said. "I am manning this communication post."

"Go get him now, I want to talk to him."

"But he is—"

"Get him now!"

"Yes sir…"

Almost 20 minutes elapsed before Garek finally appeared on the monitor. He had a crazed wild eyed look, and he was splattered with blood.

"Garek, are you alright?" Roger asked.

For a few seconds Garek said nothing, but stared blankly at the receiver on the other end with his wild dilated pupils. He was still breathing heavily. Then his breathing slowed and his eyes returned to a normal state.

"Yes I'm fine," Garek said. "No damage yet."

Roger frowned.

"Oh, the blood!" Garek said. "Yes… None of it is mine. I killed 50 of them… and then I gave up counting. Did you need something?"

"I think most of the Kaarumite men are here on the battlefield with us," Roger said.

"That does seem likely."

"I don't know if we can stop them from reaching the Empire, but we will whittle their numbers down as small as we can before they do."

"I was doing my best."

"I need you to do something else. Regardless of how this battle goes, we need to permanently end the threat of Kaarum or they will just come back to menace the world again later."

"I agree."

"Since the majority of them are blind to reason we will have to use force. I want you to take a thousand of your people and start heading for the Kaarumite holy cities right now. Take some of Nirin's people to provide you with cover the entire way. Maybe about 300 or 400, and take whatever equipment and provisions you need. Once you get there I want you to ransack the city and destroy all of their temples and religious structures. I want you to get going right away, and I want you to maintain communications silence no matter who calls you. I also don't want anyone, even me, to know what route you are taking. Understood?"

"Thank you… You are the truest friend I have ever known. You have made one of my greatest dreams come to reality. I shall personally destroy the lies of Kaarum."

The communication switched off, and the battle continued to rage below. About 15 minutes later Roger received a call from Nirin.

"Garek wants to take 400 of my people to Kaarum," Nirin said. "Did you clear that?"

"Yes," Roger said.

"I would like to go with him."

"No, I need you here coordinating."

"But Garek tends to get carried away. When that happens he will need someone to compensate for his lack of watchfulness."

"You mean you want to watch his back…"

"What purpose would be served by watching his back during a confrontation?"

"Forget about it. It's just an expression. I can't afford to send both of you at once, but pick the people you want to go with him."

"I understand."

After the communication switched off Roger began to reconsider whether sending Garek was the best thing to do, and the decision began to weigh heavily on him. The chances were good that he would be as brutal to the Kaarumites as they would be to Randar if they reached it. That was part of his logic in choosing Garek and the Haxians, but he also chose them over Imperial soldiers because he wanted it to appear that they were out of control. That way if the international community reacted negatively to the attack the Empire might not have to bear the blame.

But now that he thought about it, he realized that the city would mostly be full of women and children, and the odds that Garek would treat the women with any kind of mercy were low. The odds that he would restrict his rampage of destruction to religious structures were also low.

I have to fix this. Garek is going to go crazy unless he's given some better orders. I've got to be very specific with this guy…

He attempted to call Garek, but Garek did not answer. He then decided to call Nirin.

"Garek left 30 minutes ago," Nirin said. "Did you change your mind?"

"Perhaps…"

"You thought you might change your mind later, which is why you ordered Garek not to answer any calls. But you did the right thing. If the Kaarumites reach Randar they will destroy everything. They will ravage the women, and enslave the children, at least, those children they decide not to kill. Even Garek in all of his hate will not be so brutal."

"I hope not. But whatever he does down there will be my fault."

"It is only balancing the scales, as you humans would say."

"Either something is objectively wrong, or it is not. If it's wrong for the Kaarumites to destroy everything in Randar and kill women and children then it is wrong for Garek to do the same."

"You will just have to trust in Garek's judgment then. There is nothing you can do to stop him now. The battle grows more intense. I must go."

Roger returned his attention to the battle below, and saw that things had taken a turn for the worse. Atuskus-Var had once more stepped down from his platform and entered the battle.

Kaarum—by Ivor Kovac

CHAPTER 38

Showdown

WHEN ATUSKUS-VAR ENTERED AN AREA the other Kaarumites would fall back and give him a wide berth. He wielded a two foot long metal hammer on the end of a thick heavy chain. The chain looked like the sort of chain that was used back on Earth to hold the anchors for large ships. With one hand he slung the chain around, and with the other he gripped the chain further down and held the slack.

He swung the chain with such speed that it seemed to move like an active helicopter blade. When it struck against allied soldiers it was usually blocked by their forcefields, but the men were still sent flying off in all directions. Trees were instantly severed and splintered, as if his chain were a giant lawn trimmer. Nothing on the battlefield was able to stand in his way.

No one could charge Atuskus-Var or sneak up on him. He was an unquenchable whirlwind of destruction.

"As you can see, he is more than man," Feren said.

"Whose side are you on here?" Roger asked.

"Neither side right now. I must have a convincing argument."

Atuskus-Var was no longer glowing like a humanoid sun, but his body still shone with a golden sheen in places where there should have been shadow. When he slung his hammer around he seemed so impersonal, sending men sprawling through the air, but if one fell on the ground beneath him he took time to personally make certain that the man was dead. Sometimes he would stomp on their heads, or pick them up by a leg and dash them against the ground.

One time he kicked a man a man who was down and sent him soaring through the air like a football.

Roger felt sick as he watched the carnage. He began to feel light headed.

"He's not human," Roger mumbled.

"Of course he isn't," Feren said.

Atuskus-Var slung his hammer and took out a large clump of trees, but among the stumps were the legs of a soke along with the area just below the waist, and the tattered remnants of the entrails were visible hanging out. The soke was shorn in two at the same height as the freshly established tree stumps.

Nearby another soke lay sprawled on the ground, apparently knocked over by a broken tree and dazed by the force of the blow. A human soldier crawled on the ground not far from the soke. Judging by his armor he was an Imperial soldier. He also appeared to be dazed and struggling to get his bearings. He put his hands on a ragged tree stump and began to pull himself back up to his feet, but before he could stand up the rest of the way Atuskus-Var was on him.

Atuskus-Var put down his hammer and grabbed the man around the neck with one of his enormous hands. With his other hand he picked up the soke, who struggled and thrashed as soon as he realized what was happening.

Atuskus-Var lifted both men off the ground by their necks, and his arms began to glow with a brilliant yellow light. At first his victims began to thrash, then they smoked, and finally erupted into flames. Even with the sound muted Roger thought he could hear them screaming.

After a few seconds of writing in agony the forms went limp. Fragments of charred soke skeleton dropped down from beneath the giant's left hand, as the smoke and flames cleared. On the right the human's armor fell to the ground and a charred skull rolled out.

Roger felt light headed and dropped to his knees as the room spun around him.

"May God have mercy on us," he muttered in English as he struggled to his feet.

"If you react to situations like this with strong emotion then you may not be cut out for leadership," Feren said.

"Do you think it's a joke?" Roger asked.

He turned away from the table and headed toward the nearest door.

"Where are you going, sir?" asked one of the advisors.

But Roger said nothing.

I can't bear this any more!

Roger was so flustered by what he saw that he did not even bother to go to the armory and put on armor. His heart beat rapidly and his hands shook as he stumbled down the corridors at a rapid pace. He could hear the blood pumping in his ears, but the other sounds of the city became faint. He ran down to one of the bays where the aircraft were being refitted and jumped in one that appeared to have power running to the consoles.

"Commander-General, sir!" one of the technicians shouted. "You can't get in there. It's not fully operational! It's not safe! Sir!"

Roger did not listen. There was only one thing on his mind, and that was the thought that Atuskus-Var must be stopped. If Roger had been thinking about what he was doing he would have put on his armor which had braking thrusters that would allow him to descend safely to the ground without involving an unreliable vehicle which was in need of further repair.

Roger started up the aircraft and coasted to the hangar door. As he neared the forcefield around the edge of the city he called to the command center and ordered them to open a hole in the type one forcefield near him so that he could go out.

"I can't do that sir," replied an officer.

"You can and you will, or I will relieve you, and as many others as necessary, of their duty until either someone opens this forcefield or I have to do it myself," Roger said.

Some time passed before Roger heard an answer, and in the meantime he heard muttering on the other end which did not quite register to him. Finally they cleared him for departure and a circular opening appeared in the forcefield in front of him.

Roger sped through and descended toward the battlefield, heading in the general direction of Atuskus-Var, but before he reached him the vehicle quickly began to lose altitude. Roger did his best to pull it up but the most he was able to accomplish was a crash landing that caused him to skid through a group of Kaarumites.

For a few seconds Roger was dazed, but he quickly shook it off and opened the cockpit door of his small aircraft. He came out and stood on the back of his aircraft and looked in the direction of Atuskus-Var. Atuskus-Var was swinging his hammer around again, and at such a speed that hammer and chain looked like a semi-transparent grey disk.

Roger took out his sword and clenched his teeth. He was about to charge Atuskus-Var when he heard the sound of something else walking on the aircraft behind him. It was hard to distinguish exactly what was going on amidst the din of battle, but Roger definitely heard something behind him.

He swung his sword around just in time to slice off the head and shoulders of a charging zangron. He looked around and saw a few white Kaarumites trying to climb up onto his aircraft with leering eager expressions, but with one stroke he took them out.

The weapon he wielded was a 100 year old northern sword from the cache of old northern weapons on Leonus, which still made it more than a match for anything the Kaarumites had.

Roger jumped down from the aircraft and turned his attention back to Atuskus-Var, who was stooping over a wounded Haxian soldier and picking him up by the top portion of his breastplate. The man was dazed but still alive. However, Atuskus-Var was cocking back his other hand, balled into a fist and ready to deal the death blow.

"Atuskus-Var!" Roger shouted. "Put him down!"

Atuskus-Var turned to face Roger, but continued to firmly grasp the Haxian soldier.

"Ah, little man," Atuskus-Var said in his deep unnatural voice.

The giant picked up his hammer.

"I knew you would come down eventually, I hear the Emperor has taken ill," Atuskus-Var said with a crooked smile on his face. "Something to do with debilitating back pain."

Atuskus-Var released his grip on the Haxian soldier. The man fell to the ground and did not move.

"Are you prepared to worship my father?" Atuskus-Var asked.

"I don't believe in Kaarum," Roger said. "The sun is just the sun."

The Haxian man began to stir.

"I never said anything about Kaarum, I said 'my father'," Atuskus-Var said. "It is not for everyone to know, but I think you know who my father is."

The Haxian began to recover and push himself up off the ground but Atuskus-Var stepped down on his back and pinned him to the ground beneath his foot.

"The Kaarumites think I bring light to the world, but I bring darkness," Atuskus-Var said. "They have been in darkness for thousands of years, which is how we want it. Still, there are a privileged few who are permitted to know the truth of the world. I offer you this privilege. You can accept it or die."

"The truth of the world is that you are a vile criminal with much to pay for," Roger said. "I have come here to stop you."

"Oh have you?" Atuskus-Var said with a laugh. "Really now?"

He ground his foot harder into the Haxian's back until he stopped struggling.

"Let that man go," Roger said.

"Very well," Atuskus-Var said as he lifted his foot from the Haxian's back.

The Haxian soldier began to stir and made an effort to crawl away, but Atuskus-Var quickly brought his foot down on the man's head, crushing it as easily as the foot of a normal man might crush a chicken egg.

"Murderer!" Roger shouted and surged forward.

The hammer of Atuskus-Var instantly swung through the air, careening straight down toward where Roger was about to be, but Roger quickly changed his course.

When the hammer struck the ground the force of it sent Roger flying up into the air, but he flipped and landed on his feet. Atuskus-Var quickly jerked the chain so that the hammer flew up out of the ground and back to him, but before it came back to his hand Roger was able to slash at the chain, cutting through part of one of the links.

Atuskus-Var did not notice.

"Ha!" he said. "Too slow, little man!"

The hammer and chain were again whirling in the air, but Roger was able to dodge and run.

"What do you expect to accomplish, little man?" Atuskus-Var said. "I am faster and stronger than humanly possible. I am the most powerful life form in this world. Even the mighty sonolar is nothing next to me!"

Atuskus-Var was correct, but Roger managed to stay ahead of all of his blows. It was as if Roger saw the blows before they struck, or he already knew every place where the giant was going to strike in advance. It was difficult for Roger to say precisely which.

Atuskus-Var began to swing more wildly. Roger dodged, and once more he was able to cut the chain. Suddenly the hammer broke free of the chain and sailed through the air like an oversized bullet. It struck Roger's dormant aircraft and broke it in two.

Undaunted the giant took to slinging around his chain like a whip, but Roger knew where the whip was going to strike well before it struck, affording him time to get out of the way.

Atuskus-Var eventually noticed that his chain whip was becoming shorter and shorter. He cast it aside and drew a pair of tremendous ruby red swords from his back. For a normal man they would have been two handed swords, but for Atuskus-Var each was a one handed sword.

The blades were T shaped, like all Kaarumite swords, but they were clearly made out of a higher quality metal.

When Atuskus-Var swung his arms they moved so fast that most people could not even see the blades move. In the blink of an eye the blades were simply in another place. Most warriors would have been dead many times over by now, but in spite of the difficulties Roger was always a step ahead.

Sometimes Roger would flip out of the way in one direction or another, sometimes he would run, and sometimes he would dodge. At one point Roger simply fell down onto his back and quickly tumbled out of the way of the next strike, but in the process he managed to slash the front of the giant's legs.

The bottom portions of his golden shin guards fell off, and in a split second Roger observed something that his brain would process later. For the moment he had to keep moving and focus on staying alive.

Roger dodged another blow and cut the back of Atuskus-Var's legs. This time he drew a little blood.

Atuskus-Var roared, and the glowing gold sheen that glimmered on him where shadows should have been grew brighter. His forearms began to glow exceedingly bright, and the red swords began to heat up.

The giant took a double swing forward, which would have landed like a scissor blow cutting Roger in two had he not dodged. This time Roger lunged forward and slashed at the giant's chest. But in spite of his enormous size Atuskus-Var was inhumanly fast, and he managed to turn enough to avoid a killing blow, but not fast enough to get by unscathed.

Roger's slash managed to sever most of the gold jewelry that decorated the giant's chest, and as it fell away the glow left Atuskus-Var, and a streak of red appeared across his chest.

Atuskus-Var gasped, and took another double swing at Roger, but again Roger was already gone. He flipped to the side, sprung up from the ground using his hands, and landed on his feet behind Atuskus-Var. The giant turned around to swing but Roger was already in a crouching position and his sword was in motion.

He sliced off the giant's left foot, causing him to stumble backwards and fall, but Roger was still in motion. He rotated as he stood and maneuvered so that the giant fell back onto Roger's blade. The blade bit into the giant's back and came up through the front of his chest.

Atuskus-Var fell to the ground and gasped.

"I… know your face outsider," Atuskus-Var whispered as the life left his body. "They will never rest until they find you… This is… only… a… reprieve…"

Then the giant breathed his last breath and died, and Roger's legs suddenly felt like jelly. He fell to his knees, tired and somewhat delirious, and a troop of warriors dressed in blue-grey armor ran past him.

Someone put a hand on his shoulder, and when he turned to look he saw the face of his wife smiling down at him. In his tired and delirious state he thought he might be dreaming.

"It's all over now, my love," she said. "There are no words to express how proud of you I am, and how amazed."

"That was incredible!" said another voice.

Roger turned his head to see Demekus, and then he felt himself being carried away.

CHAPTER 39

Revealed

Chancellor Laena Skoranthor sat in her office with the lights off and watched the rain. She used to enjoy powerful rainstorms with thunder and lightning, but she derived little pleasure from them now. Her senses were a good deal more acute, and her cognitive processing speed better, but somehow everything seemed duller now than it had before she was augmented.

She tapped her long fingernails on the desk, and suddenly an idea occurred to her. She grabbed the end of one of her fingernails and suddenly jerked it back, tearing off the nail. There was a brief sharp pain, but the dull pain that followed was so insignificant that it barely registered.

"Eternal torment indeed," she muttered. "If only I could be so fortunate..."

Then suddenly she became aware of a familiar sensation, Olgrim was attempting to make contact with her.

"I hear and obey, master," Laena said.

"Wounding yourself again, Laena?" Olgrim asked.

"A little, master."

"If you perform well you will be rewarded with as much exquisite pain as you wish. Perhaps you will even beg me to stop."

"I hope so, master."

"You are aware that the forces of the Empire have defeated the Kaarumite army?"

"Of course, master. I follow everything."

"Then you are also aware that they had the help of sokes?"

"Yes master."

"Do you know why?"

"I have a theory."

"Does your theory include our quarry?"

The monitor on the wall lit up to show a newscast from an Imperial news station. It began to play footage of the duel in which Atuskus-Var was slain. When the footage zoomed in on the face of Atuskus-Var's opponent the image froze, and another image appeared showing the face of a pink skinned man with the exact same features.

"It is the one we are looking for," Olgrim said. "He is calling himself Mattis Maxelis now. Whoever released that footage to the Imperial news networks was a fool."

"Shall I have him assassinated, master?" Laena asked.

"Don't be ridiculously simple or I will have you chastised!"

"Master?"

"Do you think we cannot kill any individual in this world we wish at any time?"

"Forgive me, master."

"The death has to serve a constructive purpose."

"Of course, master."

"Our victory must be final, and absolute. In the past, the mistake that our side always made in the contest for this world was that we moved too quickly."

"But... we do intend to kill him eventually?"

"Killing is so... clean. The very word is clean. It implies a relatively swift finality. Nothing we do with this man, this creature... will be swift."

"What is it you want me to do?"

Roger Fights Atuskus Var
—by KTVL

After the Battle

ROGER WOKE UP WITH A start. He remembered a dream where he was tumbling around and becoming increasingly tired in order to avoid some peril, then the memory took on shape and definition. He remembered the giant with his chain whip hammer, and his deadly double swords.

When he sat up he saw the swords laid out across his dresser. He got up and walked towards them. They were enormous and ruby red, but when he flicked them with his finger they rang like metal, and they felt like metal to the touch.

"Atuskus-Var," Roger said.

"Is dead," said a female voice from across the room. "Thanks to you."

Roger looked and saw Aneme standing in the doorway leading to the bathroom. She was dressed in a sleek black gown, and her long black hair was loose.

"I have food if you are ready to eat," Aneme said.

Roger nodded.

Aneme brought a selection of fruits and meats and placed them on a small round table nearby, along with an assortment of beverages.

"So the battle is over?" Roger asked as he seated himself.

"Yes, and we won," Aneme said.

"Can you tell me what happened? Did the northerners ever come?"

"Do you want the long story or the short story?"

"I want to know everything that I missed."

"Well, as you know Demekus and I went to meet with the elders of Kenna Den in the Northern Waste. Some of the elders asked me hard questions, and Demekus was very concerned, but my answers satisfied most of the others, and it also helped that I offered them more than the original agreement."

"What did you offer them?"

"More land, and more aid in getting established. Right now they are carving out some territory on the coast, and south of what used to be the contested area. But most of the Kaarumites have already fled that area, so for the most part all they have to do is move in."

"Nice."

"The elders gave us 4,000 people, and we had to get the Haxians to transport them. The Empire owes the Haxian government some money now, but we should be able to pay them off, especially with the new resources we will be getting from Kaarum."

"Alright."

"We came back just as you began your fight with Atuskus-Var, which was recorded from multiple angles and at varying magnifications. We landed the troops just north of the battle and I led one of the charges. We charged in groups, and I took my group straight in your direction. I was so scared that Atuskus-Var would kill you, but by the time we got to you he was already dead. We pushed back the Kaarumites before they could attack you. But I don't know if they would have, they were so stunned over the death of their leader that most of them lost their will to fight."

"Is there footage of that?"

"Yes."

Aneme activated a monitor on the wall and the tremendous screen lit up, subdivided into smaller squares which showed the battle from a variety of angles. Again Roger saw the Imperial and Haxian forces struggling with the overwhelming numbers of Kaarumites, but this time he also saw large grey ships arriving from the north.

Thousands of warriors began dropping from the vessels like rain. When they landed they quickly organized and rushed at the Kaarumites. Although the number of northerners was a good deal smaller than the number of Kaarumites they washed upon them like a tide, leaving nothing but dead bodies behind them.

On the closer magnifications Roger could see them cutting through man, beast, and armor as if they were nothing but warm butter.

Although the Imperials had been trained in the Northern Arts, the northerners still had better equipment and years of experience. In addition, the northerners had superior physical strength and were fresh to the battle. But after the first five minutes the progress of the northerners began to slow, even though they suffered no casualties. Only one group did not slow in momentum, and it was the group led by Aneme personally, which cut a swath toward Roger.

Then suddenly the dynamics of the battle changed. The Kaarumites began to spread out, the northerners resumed their rapid progress, and the forest swiftly grew inward and swallowed up many of the combatants.

"This is where you killed Atuskus-Var," Aneme said. "The Kaarummites around him immediately began to panic, and the word spread. With him gone the sokes were able to use their powers more freely. Somehow he was able to manipulate energy on a massive scale. He didn't have the finesse of the sokes, but he wielded a lot more power than the average soke. Right now his body and his DNA are being analyzed by top Imperial scientists, and his equipment also."

"Oh yes," Roger said. "I remember that when I cut his leggings there was circuitry inside, and I think I saw the same thing when I cut the jewelry on his torso."

"Yes, they think that equipment was either giving him more power or helping him channel his natural abilities. So far all they know for certain is that the technology is not Kaarumite, or any other type of known technology. It was just made to look like Kaarumite jewelry."

Roger watched the battle continue, and he saw the forest completely swallow up the battlefield.

"The Kaarumites were insane with fear," Aneme said. "Some of them tried to fight, but usually they ran when the forest swallowed them. The sokes snared many of them. Most of the army was killed, but thousands of them still managed to retreat, and we allowed that."

"I don't think they will be a problem again," Roger said.

"Yes… I noticed that Garek and some of the sokes are unaccounted for…"

"I imagine we will be hearing about Garek soon enough, if not from him."

"Well… If you're done eating there is someone who would like to see you in the command center."

"Really? Does that mean you want me to go now?"

"Yes."

"Alright, I guess I'll go then."

Most of Roger's clothes had been removed before he was placed in the bed, so he quickly dressed himself in an officer's uniform, while Aneme put on one of her black outfits of light flexible armor.

She walked to stand next to the door and held her hand over the panel.

"After you," she said to Roger.

Roger shrugged and stood in front of the door. Aneme opened the door and they stepped out together, to face Imperial soldiers lined up in front of them. The soldiers immediately saluted.

Roger looked down the hall and saw that the walls on both sides were lined with Imperial soldiers in full armor standing at attention. As they passed each of the soldiers saluted and held his salute until they were gone. It was like that all the way to the command center.

Once they entered the command center everyone saluted, including the Emperor Adinis Maxelis, who was now fully recovered.

"My friends," the Emperor said. "There is no honor I can bestow upon you which will be worthy of the favor you have done for us."

"Adinis!" Roger said without thinking. "It's good to see you, sir! I was afraid you might be dead."

"Well, I am most certainly alive, and I have to say that this is the most pleasant awakening I have had in many years. I cannot thank you both enough for what you have done," the Emperor said.

"There is someone else who wants to see you," Aneme said. "Turn around."

Roger turned around and saw Nirin for the first time since he had arrived in the command center. Nirin was wearing a gold circlet on his head, a gold necklace, gold bands on his arms, and baggy blue pants which were translucent.

"What in the world are you wearing Nirin?" Roger asked.

"Actually that would be 'Emperor Nirin,'" he replied. "You are looking at the very first soke government in history since the time of Elrin."

"Seriously?" Roger asked. "Is that a good idea?"

"Well, as strange as this may sound, there were some Haxian soldiers who wanted to settle with my people. They were mostly soldiers that I worked with closely during the battle, and many of them took orders from me. They are going to bring their families and live under my authority. The Emperor Adinis suggested that I be crowned Emperor, and he gave me some artifacts to make me look more authoritative toward humans. I do not really understand how these artifacts will accomplish that, but I trust his judgment. Of course, no emperor is complete without an empress, therefore—"

"Uh, Nirin," Roger interrupted. "About Sasha…"

"What about me?" said a new female voice.

Roger turned around and saw Sasha approaching from another part of the command center.

"I would have been here sooner but I had to put on my things as well," Sasha said.

"Sasha?" Roger asked. "How are you… here?"

Sasha also wore a gold circlet, but hers was of a more delicate and intricate design. She wore gold necklaces, and bands on her upper arms and forearms. She also wore a long skirt of translucent blue material.

"I know you saw what happened, Roger," Sasha said. "Your wife told me. During the fight at the Temple I channeled and expended so much energy that my energy form was damaged and depleted. I could hear all the talk around me, but I could do nothing to communicate back. I nearly died, but Aneme knew enough about soke anatomy to put my body in a place where it could regenerate and begin to recharge my energy form. I recovered enough to walk and speak around the same time the battle ended here. I took a transport down here as soon as I could find one. Aneme has my special thanks, and my husband's."

"I can never thank you enough, Aneme," Nirin said. "If there is ever anything you need, please feel free to call on me. And, Roger, I want to thank you for everything you have done. What you have helped my people achieve is above and beyond our wildest hopes and dreams, but more importantly I want to thank you for restoring my faith."

Nirin held out his hand to Roger in an Earth-like fashion. Roger took his hand and shook it without hesitation, and then shook hands with Sasha.

"And now, there are some other people who would like to greet you Roger," the Emperor Adinis Maxelis said. "If you will follow me…"

"Alright," Roger replied.

Roger followed the Emperor down another set of hallways, which were also lined with soldiers who saluted as they passed. They came to a large round door with transparent slits in it. Roger could see open sky through the slits.

"Someone wants to meet me outside?" Roger asked.

The Emperor nodded and pressed the door panel. The door hissed and slid aside, revealing a balcony with a panoramic view of the city of Leonus.

When Roger stepped out onto the balcony he was greeted by a deafening roar. As far as the eye could see the streets and rooftops were crowded with soldiers standing shoulder to shoulder. They continued to cheer as Aneme came out to stand next to Roger. He took her by the hand and lifted their joined hands high into the air. The cheering grew even louder.

After a minute or so of cheering Roger began to wave his arms. It took nearly ten minutes for the cheering to die down, and when it did Roger was handed a small receiver so that his voice could be transmitted over the city's speakers.

"Well, by your cheering I take it that you consider me a hero of sorts," Roger said.

Another mad cheer broke out. When they were silent again Roger resumed his speech.

"The truth is, I killed one enemy and passed out," Roger said.

There was laughter.

"But every last one of you men are the real heroes here," Roger said. "You were on the ground fighting this battle from beginning to end. I could never have done anything without you. The victory belongs to all of you."

The cheering resumed at an even greater volume.

CHAPTER 41

Revealed

CHANCELLOR Laena Skoranthor sat in her office with the lights off and watched the rain. She used to enjoy powerful rainstorms with thunder and lightning, but she derived little pleasure from them now. Her senses were a good deal more acute, and her cognitive processing speed better, but somehow everything seemed duller now than it had before she was augmented.

She tapped her long fingernails on the desk, and suddenly an idea occurred to her. She grabbed the end of one of her fingernails and suddenly jerked it back, tearing off the nail. There was a brief sharp pain, but the dull pain that followed was so insignificant that it barely registered.

"Eternal torment indeed," she muttered. "If only I could be so fortunate…"

Then suddenly she became aware of a familiar sensation, Olgrim was attempting to make contact with her.

"I hear and obey, master," Laena said.

"Wounding yourself again, Laena?" Olgrim asked.

"A little, master."

"If you perform well you will be rewarded with as much exquisite pain as you wish. Perhaps you will even beg me to stop."

"I hope so, master."

"You are aware that the forces of the Empire have defeated the Kaarumite army?"

"Of course, master. I follow everything."

"Then you are also aware that they had the help of sokes?"

"Yes master."

"Do you know why?"

"I have a theory."

"Does your theory include our quarry?"

The monitor on the wall lit up to show a newscast from an Imperial news station. It began to play footage of the duel in which Atuskus-Var was slain. When the footage zoomed in on the face of Atuskus-Var's opponent the image froze, and another image appeared showing the face of a pink skinned man with the exact same features.

"It is the one we are looking for," Olgrim said. "He is calling himself Mattis Maxelis now. Whoever released that footage to the Imperial news networks was a fool."

"Shall I have him assassinated, master?" Laena asked.

"Don't be ridiculously simple or I will have you chastised!"

"Master?"

"Do you think we cannot kill any individual in this world we wish at any time?"

"Forgive me, master."

"The death has to serve a constructive purpose."

"Of course, master."

"Our victory must be final, and absolute. In the past, the mistake that our side always made in the contest for this world was that we moved too quickly."

"But... we do intend to kill him eventually?"

"Killing is so... clean. The very word is clean. It implies a relatively swift finality. Nothing we do with this man, this creature... will be swift."

"What is it you want me to do?"

ARIES

Before there was Kaarum, and before the Randaran Empire was founded, there was Alris.

--Commander Alons Bastilon,
Senior Researcher of the Northeast Province.

Though they say we drew breath at the same time, the soke called Alris was already a legend when I founded the city which bears my name, and I have seen nor heard nothing of him beyond rumor and conjecture. Among the southerners the name of Alris is a thing of fear and dread, and the story is used as an admonition and chastisement for their children. "Behave yourself or the sokes of the deep south will come for you," they say.

Another chastisement I have oft heard spoken among the women of the south is to say; "That was the way Landira used to act before the sokes came for her,"

When a child hears these words they often stop their behavior, but many of them come to fear that which is green and grows, save the crops they eat for nourishment.

--The Emperor Randar Maxelis, from
"Matters Concerning the South."

Landira is considered to be one of the most beautiful women in the history of the world, though no original images of her can be found among human populations, there is an abundance of descriptive imagery and paintings. It is well known that she was tall, possessed sharp features, and long black hair which flowed nearly to her feet. Those aspects of her physical appearance were quite common among the southern women, but unlike most southerners she had deep blue eyes. Though the ancestors of our contemporary races were more similar to one another in those early days than they have since become, even then blue eyes were a clear sign of foreign admixture among the southern population.

There is a theory which postulates that Manitar Skoranthor may not have been her actual father, though it is impossible to confirm since there is no record of her DNA on file, and after the incident with Alris, Landira's parents formally separated. Her mother failed to have more children after their divorce, and instead spent the remainder of her days working with Zangrons.

--From a lecture by Professor Demekus Maxelis,
the Scholar Prince.

The story of Alris and Landira begins in the southwest of the Central Lands during the time when the first "southerners" were ruthlessly expanding into the west. Though the cult of Kaarum had not yet been fabricated, the southerners were utterly merciless toward the ancient forests and their inhabitants, both soke and animal. Manitar Skoranthor, who was the ancestor of some stupid human politicians that would come later, was sent to the govern the new colony when it finally became stable enough to be counted as a province.

--Commentary by Nirin the First
(also known as the First Soke Emperor or Emperor Soke).

ALRIS AND LANDIRA

CHAPTER 1

Landira stared out through the narrow window in an attempt to catch sight of any interesting plants or animals they might pass as they made their journey. But much of her view remained obscured by the other vehicles of the protective convoy. Her father, Manitar Skoranthor, had been appointed prefect of the province shortly after her 21st birthday. After a brief but lavish celebration, they packed their belongings traveled west.

They had gone from one of the most advanced and well-ordered cities in the world, to a rugged wilderness where the roads were made of dirt. Landira was intrigued by the raw wilderness, but her mother, Nalana, was irritated preferred to glare at her father rather than look at the terrain.

"How much longer until we get there?" Nalana grumbled.

"We will get there when we get there," Manitar replied.

"This is awful," Nalana continued. "I don't see why we couldn't take an airship. The least they could have done is built a proper road! All this bumping around is making my head hurt."

"The world does not hinge upon you."

"But you're a prefect, right? What good is a promotion without the prestige and respect that are supposed to come with the position?"

"It is what it is."

"Stupid backwards place!" Nalana said. "Why couldn't they give you a good posting? What's the point in these savage backward lands?"

"I think I just saw a house," Landira interjected.

"This is a good posting, my love," Manitar replied. "I will be in charge of developing this place and overseeing expansion along the southern frontier. It is the biggest job I could ever have at this stage of my career, a huge opportunity."

"And there probably isn't a single shop!" Nalana shouted. "How am I to keep up with the latest fashions?"

"There will be clothes there, maybe not as fancy, but still adequate," said Manitar.

"Adequate for your purposes maybe," Nalana said.

"You already have far more clothing than you need. I had to requisition an extra transport just for your wardrobe. I didn't want to bring it all but you did, so I brought it to make you happy and all I get is complaining from you. If you hadn't brought so much junk with you then we could have gone in an airship instead of along the ground."

Manitar and Nalana continued to bicker as the vehicle rumbled along the jagged uneven ground. Eventually became smooth, but husband and wife were so caught up in their bickering that they failed to notice.

"Mother, the vehicle isn't bumping anymore," Landira said. "I think we are on a paved road."

"About time!" Nalana groused. "Maybe there might even be a grocery store when we get there."

"It will be better than that," Manitar said. "The region is heavily agrarian. You'll be able to get fresh fruits and vegetables straight from the farms if you want."

"Oh, how wonderful! I get to pick fruit, like a peasant!"

"Nalana—"

"Or better yet, maybe I can take the produce directly from the unwashed hands of the servants appointed to pick it!"

"Why don't you just shut your mouth for a while? If not for me you would be a servant. I'm the only reason you have anything at all."

"At your station you were extremely fortunate to get me! Who do you think you are, Manitar? Your only redeeming trait is your connections, and that's all it ever was."

"Mind yourself, woman! You still haven't borne me a son yet."

As her parents argued, Landira continued to stare out the window. The wilderness gave way to farms and plantations, which were farms on either side of the road, but beyond those the jungle still loomed. The trees of the jungle were of such height that it was almost like looking at mountains in the distance. The jungle had been cleared a great distance on either side of the road, but Landira wished that she could have seen it up close. She had often heard of the giant trees, tremendous reptiles, and strange fruits.

Suddenly they entered an area where trees grew close to the side of the road. They were not the massive trees Landira had heard about from the stories of the far south, but they were good sized and easily as large as the trees in the forests that grew in her native province.

"Father," Landira said. "Didn't you say that the trees were all cut down for at least half a mile on either side of the road?"

Manitar had not been paying attention to the landscape because he was focused on arguing with his wife, but now he looked out the window.

"I did, because all the trees were cleared," he said. "I don't understand how… Wait, those are not jungle trees, they are fruit trees. But I have never seen fruit trees so large. I know they were experimenting around with some alternative farming techniques but I have never seen a thing like that before."

After they cleared the orchard they passed by another which had smaller trees and workers moving about them. Landira pressed her face against the window and stared keenly at the workers. They appeared to be smaller than normal, for southerners, and they seemed to have yellow skin and brown hair.

"Father, are there any westerners this far south?" she asked.

"What?" Manitar said as he looked out the window. "No… and westerners have white skin not yellow, and those people are barely dressed. I know it's hot, but still… Hey, driver, what sort of people are those?"

"Those, sir, I believe are the forest people," the driver said. "Sokes. Some of the people around here use them for labor."

"Sokes!" Nalana exclaimed. "Here?"

"Don't look at them, Landira!" Nalana said. "Those creatures aren't human. Manitar, I don't want any sokes working on our estate. I don't want those things going near my dear sweet innocent daughter. And, Landira, you stay far away from those creatures."

The farms and plantations went right up to the edge of the city, which was not large but it was considerably more developed than Nalana's predictions. The vehicle pulled into a large estate near the western edge of town and stopped.

"We're here," the driver said.

Landira and her parents got out of the vehicle along with the driver, who on went to meet with the servants and inform them that the new master had arrived. The servants arrived in moments and began unloading the luggage.

"Hey," Nalana said to the servants as she took him firmly by the arm and dug her fingernails into his skin. "I don't want any sokes in my house for any reason."

"Why don't you go supervise while they move our stuff in?" Manitar said to Nalana.

"Hmph!" Nalana responded.

She walked off following the servants, giving them a multitude of orders as she went but not carrying a single item herself.

Manitar watched her go and then turned to speak with the servants.

"Well, are there any sokes working on this estate?" he asked them

"Just one, sir," they answered. "Would you like us to get more?"

"No, no… I just wonder if it's safe. What's his function?"

"It's a female soke, sir, and she just tends the garden. She never causes any problems or goes inside the house. She does what she's told and doesn't ask for anything except for meat. She never asks for money. She gets all the vegetables and fruits she wants from the garden so we just bring her meat. Sometimes she leaves for a few days but then she comes back. A lot of people around here use sokes for farming. They make the plants grow fast and healthy."

"So… is that how the trees in that orchard were so large?"

"Yes, sir. Sokes are very useful for farming, but usually not for anything else."

"Usually? Are there any exceptions?"

"There is that weird soke medicine man that lives in town. They call him Alris. Most of the sokes just sleep outside on the ground but this fellow lives in a house with a fence around it, and he wears clothes. He sells herbal remedies and makes skin and hair care products for the women. His stuff is pretty popular in town here, but he's the only soke that does anything besides farm. To be honest, sir, most of them don't seem very bright. When you get close to them they act like you aren't there, and if you try to get their attention they are slow to respond."

"Very well, I think we will retain her services for now, but if she causes any trouble she's gone."

"She won't. You probably will never see her, sir, and neither will your wife, unless she likes to garden."

"My wife would sooner have her hands cut off then dig into the dirt with them."

Landira smiled. She guessed that the servants were happy to keep the soke woman, since she saved them from having to work in the garden other than picking the fruits and vegetables to bring in the house.

No sooner had Manitar finished his discussion with the servants than another vehicle pulled into his estate. A man stepped out and walked hastily toward him. The stranger made a fist, placed it against his chest thumb first and bowed his head slightly. It was the traditional greeting among southerners.

"Sire, I apologize for my lateness but I was delayed by an emergency situation," he said. "I am Granadar, the overseer of this town. I bid you welcome."

"What was the emergency?" asked Manitar.

"One of the large reptiles of the jungle came into the city and damaged a shop before it could be driven off. I have given orders to improve the perimeter defenses."

"Very good. Now, if you don't mind, I would actually like a tour of the city before we discuss logistics."

"I will personally conduct you, sire," Granadar said. "We can take my vehicle if you like."

"I would," Manitar replied.

"Father, I would also like to come," Landira said.

"Very well," Manitar answered.

CHAPTER 2

S THEY DROVE THROUGH THE city, the overseer told them the history of the southwest province and of the current situation. The provincial capital actually began as a supply depot in the jungle. When explorers began to filter into the area they had need of a place to rest and resupply, yet there were none. There were no large natural clearings so one had to be made. Once a large enough clearing was made, then supplies could be flown into the heart of the jungle by airship.

Although the sokes caused no problems there were many difficulties with large reptiles and predatory cats. Because of that the area had to be fortified with a perimeter and a small troop of soldiers was permanently garrisoned there. Machinery was flown in to help accelerate the process of deforestation, and as more land was cleared up farms were established, making it unnecessary to have as much food brought in by air.

Even with heavy machinery clearing the forests it was still a hard and difficult process, but eventually other areas were cleared and other settlements created. The main industries of the province were farming, lumber, and mining, but the capital city already had a few factories.

Since wood was readily available all of the buildings in the province were made of it, at least in part. Making buildings out of wood was a considerable break in tradition for southerners, as typically the material of choice used in construction was stone. There were very few buildings over three floors tall in the city, but there were a few.

The streets were composed of some type of brown brick, which was also an unusual break with southern tradition. The overseer explained that the bricks were made from mud, which was also readily available. The population was growing and they needed to build, but it was still difficult to produce or to transport in the sorts of materials that were available further east.

"There is one issue that concerns me," Manitar said. "I have spoken with my household servants about this, but I would like to know what your position is on the sokes. Are they a threat and what role do they play in society here?"

"We don't get any problems from the sokes," Granadar replied. "As our people moved into this region they ignored and avoided us. When we cleared the land they just moved further south and west for the most part. In some places where we left patches of forest there are still some sokes. They are passive, quiet, and not very intelligent. Physically they are not very strong. Your wife could probably overpower their strongest individual. A lot of people use them to tend their farms and gardens, but that is all they do. As far as we have seen they never build anything on their own, and they don't even live indoors. They just sleep out on the ground in the woods, and they barely even wear clothing. They don't seem to have any art, music, government, or any civilization of any kind as far as we can tell. Regardless of what the old scriptures say, we have found the sokes to be little more than animals, and we would classify them as that except that the stuff that flows through their veins isn't blood."

"What flows through their veins?" asked Landira.

"Some strange pale yellow liquid," the Granadar answered. "We know this because old man Karkarus opened a few of them up one day. He keeps a lot of them as slaves. They don't seem to mind very much. I don't think they have the intellect to distinguish between freedom and slavery. He's got more sokes working for him than anyone in this province, and that's why the trees in his orchard are so huge."

"What laws have you made regarding the sokes?" asked Manitar.

"None yet," Granadar replied. "There hasn't been any occasion. The sokes just tend the plants without saying a word. The only type of payment they understand or accept is meat. I guess in nature they hunt their own meat but since we have driven off all the game they have to either leave or get meat from us if they want it. They never ask for anything else from us. We don't regulate their coming or going. They are free to go except for the ones old man Karkarus keeps. Some people abuse them and they just take it and say nothing in return."

"But there must be some laws regarding them, stipulating how they are treated," said Manitar.

"This is a new province, perhaps someday there will be laws governing the treatment of wildlife and livestock specific to this province but as of yet we have none," Granadar said.

"I would like to see this 'old man' Karkarus," Manitar said. "Unofficially, of course. I don't want to raise an issue of it."

"We can go now if you wish," said the overseer.

"I do," said Manitar. Then he turned to Landira and said, "Not a word of this to your mother."

"Old man Karkarus" turned out to be 900 years old, which meant that he was nearing the end of his life. However, he was still quite active. Manitar talked with Karkarus, asking him about how the sokes on his plantation behaved and how they added to productivity. He said that the sokes were of inestimable value to the agricultural industry, and that as workers they were very low maintenance.

"They work and say nothing," Karkarus said. "However, when I first began conscripting them into his plantation a few tried to run away. Some of them escaped but most were caught. I had most of them whipped, but I had to kill two of them."

"Why?" Manitar asked.

"Because they tried to fight back. I donated the bodies to a physician for dissection but there is still a great deal about their anatomy that the doctors couldn't understand..."

Based on everything Karkarus and Granadar told them, it seemed that the only intelligent soke was Alris, the medicine man who lived in the city. Karkarus explained that he was uneasy about Alris but he allowed him to visit the plantation in order to tend to any medical needs that his slaves might have. He wished for his work force to be healthy and productive, and as far as he could tell Alris did nothing to stir up the sokes on his plantation.

"That Alris fellow... he acts more like a man than a soke," Karkarus said. "I still don't like him, mind you, but I can't find any fault with him."

While they conversed, Landira looked out across the field. She was intrigued by the sokes.

They could almost be mistaken for human... I can't believe they're on a level with animals. That seems like an exaggeration to me.

They were seemed to be at the same average height as some of the other human races, but they were certainly shorter than Landira's people. They were also less muscular than her people although their physiques were still well defined and chiseled. About half of them had bright yellow skin while the rest had a yellowish-green or darker green tone. Most of them had light brown hair and all of them had long hair.

Some of them were tilling the ground and others were picking fruit, but it was impossible for Landira to tell what most of them were doing. Many were just standing and making gestures with their hands. They almost looked like they were manipulating invisible objects. Others stood with their hands placed against trees. Landira was intrigued, and she began to walk towards the sokes.

While Landira watched the sokes, from the other side of the field one of the sokes watched her.

CHAPTER 3

"I HAVE NEVER KNOWN TRUE BEAUTY, until today," said the soke to one of his fellows. "Have you ever seen such loveliness?"

"We are making good progress, Alris," the other soke replied. "We do everything you ask of us. The work is good, but the works we do in the deep forest are so much better. Will we go soon?"

"I wasn't talking about the work," said Alris. "I was talking about the young lady."

"You have never said that of any of the women here before," said the other.

"No, my friend. I am not talking about any of the soke women who are here. I am talking about the beautiful flower over yonder. Behold!"

Alris pointed across the field toward the woman who had caught his eye.

"You mean that human female?" said the other.

"Yes," Alris said. "Isn't she lovely?"

"She is human, she is not one of our kind."

"You cannot even evaluate her as a woman? Take another look!"

The other soke paused in his labors and took a moment to study Landira. While Alris was intrigued and absorbed her beautiful face and form, the other soke saw only the distance that separated her kind from his.

"Her colors are strange," he said.

"You have a limited mind," said Alris. "Can you not see that she has the look of one crafted by a master sculptor? She is a work of art, and if the kindness of her spirit matched the beauty of her form… Well… a man couldn't ask for anything better than that, nor dream of it."

"What difference does it make? She is human and you are soke. Would you know her as a man knows a woman?"

"Would you have a problem with that?"

"You are our leader. We do as you say because you are the wisest among us. If you can see a use for such a creature then there must be one. It is not my realm to question or understand everything you do, but you asked me what I thought. It is written that the Great Maker made the three kindreds as different as the substances that they were crafted from, but they are all of equal value in his sight. It is believed that in time he would have allowed us to share our essences with one another, had this world not fallen, but it is not done with us. They are humans we are sokes, the forest does not flow in their veins."

"Just because a thing hasn't been done, does not mean it can't be."

Alris began to walk toward the girl as she made her way into the field. The two of them locked eyes, hesitated, and began to move toward one another at an increased pace. But before they could meet, someone called to her and ordered her out of the field. The woman hesitated for a moment, then she turned and walked away. Alris watched as she returned to the vehicle and was taken away. Once the vehicle was out of site he returned to his friend.

"Well?" asked the other soke.

"Her beauty has touched my spirit, and I will have her," said Alris.

"How?"

"She lives in the city, I live in the city. We will make a beginning there. I will have her and no one can prevent me. But I believe that she will also seek me out, for as her lovely face is in my mind, mine is also in hers."

"How can you know that?"

"A saw it in her eyes. It's a worthwhile skill."

"What is?"

"To learn how to read humans."

"If you say so."

CHAPTER 4

O N THE WAY BACK TO her new home, Landira could think only of the soke she saw in the field. He was both like and unlike the other sokes. He had their usual appearance, the light yellow skin and the light brown hair, but he seemed more intelligent and purposeful.

He was coming towards me! What would have happened if my father hadn't called me back?

She understood the arguments that the overseer and Karkarus were making against the intelligence of the sokes, but the soke who approached her was dressed like a human, and when he looked at her she could see the intelligence in his eyes. She felt that the sokes were hiding a great deal, and she was determined to find out what it was.

But that soke I saw in the fields was special. Will I see him again? He seemed like more like the master of that place than that old Karkarus.

Landira was determined to make contact with the sokes, and especially the soke that caught her eye in the field. She decided to begin her investigation by meeting with the soke who worked in the garden on their estate but she allowed a few days to pass before doing so. She knew that her mother would not approve and she wanted to allow her parents to settle in before she began wandering the area on her own. Once she was ready she quietly approached one of the servants and inquired about the soke.

"I know that a soke works in our garden," Landira said. "Do you know where she lives?"

The servant shrugged.

"She works and when she isn't working she's not around," he said. "I have no idea where she stays."

Landira decided to try a different approach. She went into the galley and asked for the person who normally brought meat to the soke. Once she found the person who delivered the food she was able to determine that the soke usually took her food in the forest patch at the back of the estate where there was a shallow ravine through which a small stream flowed. Due to the presence of the stream and the fact that the terrain was not level, the trees and bushes were left in place around the stream. Landira had seen the trees before but thought nothing of it.

It was quite common for trees to be left around streams, or to be left in order to divide one property from another. Landira wanted to eventually step foot in one of the original and ancient jungles, but for now she would settle for exploring the patch of forest around the stream.

The wooded area behind her house was, at most, 30 feet across in the widest point, but as Landira approached it she could almost believe she was at the edge of an actual jungle because the trees and bushes were so thick she could not see through to the other side. She paused for a moment, then reaching out she pushed her way through the bushes and ferns and passed on into the depression.

It was almost like stepping into a different world. Once she finished struggling through the ferns and bushes, she found herself in a well shaded area with somewhat diminished undergrowth. Beneath the ferns and bushes the ground was covered with thick moss. The amount of sunlight that diffused through the heavy forest canopy was equivalent to that which would filter through the clouds on a stormy day. In the sunlight areas on the edge of the forest the undergrowth was so thick that it muffled many of the sounds from the open areas beyond. There were brightly colored flowers she had never seen the like of before, and large mushrooms which had probably burst up through the moss after the rain of the previous night.

Brightly colored frogs hopped out of her way and splashed into the stream as she walked. They gleamed like jewels when they caught a ray of sunlight. Aside from the noises of the stream, the only other sound was the songs of tropical birds with came in many different shapes, sizes, and colors. As Landira looked down the length of the stream it seemed to her that it flowed down a long green tunnel.

She could not see anything beyond the forest.

How beautiful! It feels like I have entered another world, and I could almost forget that there is another world just a few steps away…

"But how will I find the soke in all this?" she wondered.

She decided that the best way was to go to the left walking first to the northern edge of their property, but as she turned she saw a small female form reclining at the base of a large tree. The woman had yellow skin and light brown hair with a few streaks of gold. Her eyes were a light blue, almost white, which made her pupils stand out a great deal. Her legs were stretched out across the ground and her back was propped up against the trunk of the tree. Other than her eyes, the soke was as unmoving as the plants which surrounded her, and for a moment Landira entertained the notion that she was simply a plant which had grown into a humanoid shape.

At first Landira was startled and a bit disconcerted by the look of the woman's eyes. Although the woman had a humanoid shape, Landira could sense the inhumanity about her. For a second her skin crawled, and then she decided that she was being unfair and making judgments about this person before she knew anything about her.

"Hello," Landira said. "I was looking for you."

"Is there a need?" asked the soke woman.

"What?" Landira asked.

"You bring no meat," said the woman. "So there must be something new. I have already completed the growings of today."

Landira hesitated, wondering if Karkarus and Granadar were not correct about the sokes, and that their intelligence was not adequate for communication. But instead she dismissed the thought and considered what the soke woman had said. All the while the soke woman continued to look her in the eyes without blinking or moving.

"You mean you finished your work in the garden, and the only time anyone visits you is if they need something or are bringing you meat?" asked Landira.

"Yes," the soke woman said. "You do not come for these things?"

"No," said Landira. "I am new to this place and I have never seen any sokes before I came here. I just wanted to get to know you."

"Knowing is a new thing for us. Humans and sokes don't know each other. We don't talk unless there is need."

"Does it have to be that way?"

"I don't know if it has to be, but it is."

"What is your name?"

"Neela," the soke replied. "None of your people have ever asked my name."

"Well, Neela, my name is Landira and I would like to be your friend," Landira replied. "Do you have a place to stay?"

"Yes, I stay in this place. It is my home."

"You mean you just sleep outside here?"

"Yes."

"Why?"

"Why is the sun yellow? I stay here because this place is good."

"How long have you been here?"

"I have always been here."

"Where are all your belongings?"

"They are all around here."

Landira looked around and saw nothing but the plants and the stream. She looked back at Neela and saw that her eyes were still focused on Landira, as if she were awaiting another question.

"Would you like to stay in the house?" asked Landira.

"Stay?" Neela said. "I have never been in the structures that your people make. But the things I like are not there so I don't think I would like it."

"What things are those?"

"The soil, the growing plants, the light of the sun, and my..."

Neela paused and cocked her head slightly, then said; "It is different for us. I can't explain everything to you right now but maybe in the future there can be a better knowing."

"Have you ever listened to music before?" asked Landira.

"Yes, I listen to much."

"So sokes have music then?"

"Yes. I think everyone has music. Even the tavlons in their great closed places."

"There are people who say you don't have art or music."

"We have these things but humans don't see them. There are many things that humans don't see. Some of my people think that humans have no music, but I know the scriptures so I know that humans are capable of these things. They just do them in a different way."

"So you have art, music, and religion then? How come you don't share that information with humans? If you did then they would certainly treat you better."

"I told it to you."

"Yes but, I asked you first."

"If humans ask us we will tell, but they don't ask. Why don't humans ask?"

"I don't know… I asked."

"You seem good to me, better than the others."

"Thank you. You seem good to me also."

"I have never heard human music before, but I would like to."

"Well, there is a concert in town tonight. But you can't go like that. We are going to have to get you some clothes. Wait here, I'll be right back."

Landira went back into the house and shuffled through her belongings. Neela was considerably smaller than her so there would be no perfect fit. Although southern women typically wore tops with the waste cut out the only time they ever wore as little as Neela in public was if they were going swimming. It was considered lewd for women to not at least have some kind of wrap around their upper legs in public settings, aside from beaches or lakefronts. Landira had no tops that would fit Neela. Her skirts were also too long, but she did find a wrap that could be tied off to fit.

"That should be enough to get you into a clothing store," Landira said as she fastened the wrap around the Neela's waist. "After that we can get you something more complete."

As they walked off the estate the servants acted as though nothing worth noticing was going on. In those days servants and courtiers were trained not to notice questionable behavior on the part of their masters, which meant that nothing Landira did would be reported.

CHAPTER 5

"**H**UMANS LIKE TO MAKE THE ground hard around the places where they live," Neela commented as they entered the city.

"What?" Landira asked.

"The ground is hard like stone, but I see that you wear things on your feet to provide cushioning. Why not just leave the ground as it is and wear nothing on your feet?"

"Oh, you mean the paths and streets."

"I am sorry, I have a hard time using words the same way you do."

"You're fine. You know we have vehicles and animals that we ride, and the hard streets will not get ruts in them like a dirt road would. Also, there is less mud. We wear shoes to protect our feet from everything."

As they walked through the city they received a few curious glances. It was unusual to see humans and sokes walking together for any extended period of time, and the majority of citizens did not know that Landira was the daughter of the proconsul.

When they reached the store Neela hesitated to walk in.

"Never been in a human structure before," she said.

"It's all right," Landira said. "You can pick out whatever you want."

"I don't know anything about this. You can pick out the covers for me, I just want them to be green."

Once dressed Landira and the saleswoman took Neela to a mirror where she could see how she looked.

"Is this good?" Neela asked. "Do I look like one of you now?"

The saleswoman snickered for a moment but turned away quickly.

"Something funny?" Landira demanded.

"No," the saleswoman replied.

"Then why are you laughing?"

"I—"

"Just keep it to yourself."

Throughout the exchange Neela remained entirely focused on her image in the mirror.

"Yes," Landira said. "It's a good outfit, and you look great."

"Humans have some nice things, but so do the sokes," she said. "Since you are showing me human things maybe someday I will show you soke things."

From there they went straight to the music hall. Neela seemed to enjoy the concert, although for the most part her expressions were difficult to read.

"Well?" Landira asked when it was over.

"So this is human music?" Neela asked.

"One form of it."

"I will know the other forms as well," Neela said. "Maybe you have another that carries the trees and grasses in it."

"What do you mean?" Landira asked.

"The music was like this building, it was put together in a clever way, but it only reminds me of things that are like the building. There is nothing in it that carries the feeling of trees or grasses, or growing things at all. Soke music has these things."

"I would like to hear some in that case."

"Then I will take you to Alris. He is great and wise. I must have his permission to show you the hidden ways of the sokes. He said 'if a human asks after these things bring them to me first.' So I bring you to him."

Neela grabbed Landira by the wrist and pulled her away from the crowds of humans.

"He lives in the city?" Landira asked.

"In the city yes, and in a human structure. He lives like a human but he made the trees tall behind his house so that he could also live like a soke."

CHAPTER 6

Neela brought Landira into a residential area. The houses were built close together and surrounded by fences. One house was also surrounded by enormous trees, as many as could be fit into the small yard. Neela brought Landira to the front door and struck the knocker loudly against the door. The door was opened by a male soke with bright yellow skin, brown hair, and pale green eyes.

Landira immediately recognized him as the soke from the plantation who she had been prevented from approaching by her father. He was bit taller and more muscular than the other sokes she had seen from a distance, with his head coming up to the level of Landira's chin. He had sharp features and a long nose which reminded her of southern nobility.

"Alris, I have brought you my new friend," Neela said. "She is human but she wishes to know of the deep ways of the sokes. She asked of our music."

Alris was dressed like a human and his mannerisms were such that Landira could almost believe that he was human. He wore the long wide legged pants with an embroidered wrap going around his waist and legs, and had no shirt on, which was a very common style for southern men. But unlike the average southern man, he wore the necklaces, armbands, and accoutrements of a scholar or doctor.

"Well hello," he said looking at Landira and smiling.

He placed his fist over his heart thumb first and bowed.

"Greetings Neela," he said turning to the soke woman. "You have brought a very good friend indeed."

"I have seen you before," Landira said. "You were in the field of old man Karkarus. I was going in your direction before my father called."

"Yes, and so you have come to me," Alris said. "Do come in, and please be seated. Would you care for some tea?"

Landira and Neela stepped through the door and Alris shut it behind them. Landira and Neela seated themselves on a large green couch, which was situated just inside the door.

"I would love some tea," Landira said. "And I apologize for what you saw at old man Karkarus' place."

"What I saw? What I saw was the most beautiful woman ever to walk the face of Avramis. Your eyes called to me from across the field, searing me to the depths of my soul. From that day on, I knew that we would find each other again, because we must."

"That's…"

Intense!

Landira found that she could not talk. She had never heard a man speak to her before in such a bold and flirtatious fashion. As a member of the southern nobility, the purpose of marriage was to form alliances with other nobles. There was no love until after marriage, and sometimes not even then. If a normal man attempted to court or flirt with Landira her father would have had him flogged. But Alris showed no fear, and the words that he spoke lined up perfectly with what she had always wanted to hear a man say to her.

Her ideal man had always been the southern ideal; large strong, rough, and bearded with a hairy chest. But Alris was completely devoid of hair, save for his scalp and eyebrows, and he was also shorter than Landira and had long hair. No normal southern woman would even want to look at such a man, but he had the smoothest voice Landira had ever heard, and she wanted to hear more.

"You're clearly from an ancient and noble lineage," Alris said as he approached her. "I take it your father is the new prefect?"

When he reached Landira he stroked the side of her face with the back of his finger, then he lifted a strand of her hair. Landira bit her lip. Touching the hair of a southern noblewoman was an egregious legal offense for a man without status, much less one who was not even southern or human. Landira reached out and grabbed his hand, reacting instinctively. Alris clasped it firmly in return.

"You will try the tea," he said handing her a cup.

"Of-of course," Landira stammered.

"You look nice too, Neela," Alris said to the soke woman. "Your new outfit shows impeccable taste."

"I thank you, leader," Neela said.

"Listen," Landira said. "I wanted to see you again after I saw you in the field because I was curious about you."

"I was in your mind, as you were in mine," Alris said.

"Now see here—"

"Is it wrong?"

"No. You were on my mind, but I didn't know Neela would bring me to you tonight. I mean, I hoped I would find you eventually but I didn't expect to find you so soon."

"I thank you for coming."

"You're very sweet, but I wanted to apologize for what you saw happening to the sokes at Karkarus' place."

"What was happening to them?" Alris asked as he sat on the couch next to Landira and held her hand in both of his.

"Well, you know, being locked up and forced to work," Landira said.

Up until then Neela had been watching Landira intently, but now she now turned her attention toward Alris, and he turned to face her momentarily.

"No one is being forced," Alris said.

"Sokes are in fences, yes," Neela added. "But fences can't hold sokes."

"But how can they get away?" Landira asked. "I saw the guards and the whips and chains."

"And yet I tell you that no one is being forced. If I gave the word tonight all the sokes would be gone when you get up tomorrow."

"But, please don't take offense, sokes aren't as strong as humans."

"Physically humans are much stronger than sokes, but there are other types of strength."

"I don't understand."

"Don't let it distress you," said Alris as he stroked her hand. "Would you like to understand?"

"Yes," she answered.

"Then you will understand, come tomorrow and I will share our music with you. And after that you must come often."

"I don't know if I can do that."

"You will come, my sweet. You don't really have a choice anymore."

"Well that's a bold thing to say. You don't know that, maybe I won't ever come again."

Alris chuckled.

"You will come," he said. "Events have moved beyond the point of no return."

"Right," Landira said, trying to act nonchalant even though she knew she would come. "I do have one other question. What is all this equipment for?"

She pulled one of her hands free and gestured toward the machinery and laboratory equipment which filled the room. There were bottles, tubes, test tubes, microscopes, heating devices, and so on. Through the door to the next room she could see tables and shelves covered with supplies and equipment, and jars containing specimens of animals and plants. The walls were covered with diagrams and drawings.

"I'm a doctor," Alris answered. "I make people well."

"He is the most cunning doctor," Neela added.

"I don't know about that," Alris said. "But one of the reasons I came among humans was to learn their medical techniques and study human anatomy. I was already a healer among the sokes before I came. I help the people here with herbal remedies and skin and hair care products. But as of yet I have not been included in any operations on a human patient."

"I see," Landira said. "Well maybe you could show me some of your products."

"I would be glad to. Would you like dinner as well?"

"I would, thank you."

Dinner consisted of traditional soke dishes, all of which Landira greatly enjoyed. Although she felt a bit self-conscious because Neela and Alris each ate less than she did.

"Our bodies have a lower density than yours, and we also get energy from the sun," Alris said as if in answer to her thoughts. "If you had chlorophyll in your skin you would be as we are. That is also why we prefer not to wear a great deal of clothing normally. The sun gives us strength and energy."

After dinner Landira and Neela returned home.

***

420

Once Landira and Neela were out of the door Alris took the cup that Landira had been drinking from into his main laboratory. He carefully wiped the top and set to work isolating Landira's cells from the other items in the swab.

421

CHAPTER 7

L ANDIRA WAS CONSUMED WITH THOUGHTS of Alris, and wondered if there was a way he could fit into her life.

"Alris likes you," Neela said.

"I think I like him too," Landira replied.

"He is wise and good. All the single women among the sokes of this place like him, but he has always refused them saying that the woman of his destiny had not come yet. He said she would be unlike any soke woman who came before. I didn't think that she would be a human, but you are a good person and my friend, so I am happy that Alris would pick you. It is a great honor."

Landira said nothing in response. She knew that her parents would object strongly to the idea of her being with a soke, and was unsure of how to deal with the problems that would arise.

They would probably kill him slowly.

"Well," said Neela once they reached the estate. "I enjoyed that greatly. We will do it again?"

"Of course," Landira said.

Neela looked down at herself.

"I don't have a place to keep the coverings you gave me," she said. "Will you keep them in your place until we go into town again?"

"I certainly will," Landira replied.

***

The next day Landira overslept. When she came downstairs she found her mother sitting in the lounge waiting for her.

"You know, yesterday I thought I would go shopping for some new clothes," Nalana said. "Your father was in some dreary meeting and there was not a thing for me to do, so I decided to see if the shops in this town were any good. I went to this one shop, and I heard some of the sales associates talking about how a soke was in the store with a human girl. That sort of thing is important because I don't want to buy clothes from a place that was dirtied by one of those things. I'm not at all interested in trying on something that one of those monstrosities might have worn."

"What of it?" Landira asked.

"Well, I asked the sales associates for details, and, well, I guess they didn't know that I was the proconsul's wife, because if they had they certainly would not have been so bold. But do you know what she said? She said that the girl looked a lot like me in the face but had blue eyes. How many people have blue eyes around here?

"After that I went home and interrogated the servants. They were scared to talk but I still found out that my daughter went out into town with a soke. You even let that... that thing wear some of your clothes. I hope you didn't bring those dirty clothes back in the house. Do you know what my friends back home would say if they knew that my daughter had associated with a soke?

"Apparently this soke had been living on our estate this entire time and your father said nothing, so he is also in trouble."

Nalana turned her hand over and casually examined her frequently manicured fingernails, which were painted red.

"Anyways, that soke had to be punished," Nalana continued. "And if you ever do something like that again you will be punished too. I can't have you ruining our image."

"Punished!" Landira shouted. "For being my friend? Mother, what have you done?"

"That's right! Punished! This morning I said she would get 200 lashes, and after that... we'll see. And don't ever call a soke your friend again. They are inferior life forms, between man and animal, or animal and plant."

"I'll do whatever I want!"

Landira ran out of the house and slammed the door on her way. She knew that her mother would not have Neela brought inside of the house for anything, so the punishment would be executed outside. She saw nothing in the front yard so she ran around to the back of the house as quick as she could.

Behind the house she saw a small pitiful figure of a woman with her hands strapped to a pole. Her feet had collapsed beneath her so that she was only hanging by her hands. One of the male servants stood behind her with a whip poised and ready to lash.

"STOP!" Landira shouted as she ran towards the servant. "What are you doing? Are you crazy?"

The startled servant turned to face her.

"I am only following orders," he said. Your mother has ordered that this creature receive 200 lashes and she has only gotten 79, I still have over 100 to go before I can stop."

Landira looked around and found a shovel nearby. She picked it up and held it toward the servant in a menacing fashion.

"You'll stop now or I'll make you stop!" she said. "Now untie her!"

"If I untie her before I'm done, then your mother will have me flogged in her place," the servant said.

"But if you don't then I'll take your head off with this shovel right now!"

"Fine."

The servant walked over to the pillar and untied Neela's hands.

Neela's back was severely shredded by the lashes. The creamy yellow fluid that circulated through her veins was everywhere. Landira could see what appeared to be muscle tissue exposed. It was striated like human and animal muscle, but unlike human tissue it was an extremely light yellowish color. Landira felt sick. She caught Neela as she fell, and gently set her on the ground. She took off her sash and wrapped around Neela's back and chest.

"My new friend," Neela said weakly.

"I'm here, Neela," Landira said.

She lifted Neela to her feet and put one of Neela's arms around her.

"Can you walk, Neela?" she asked.

"I think I can move my legs," Neela answered.

They walked only a short distance off the estate, but as they walked Neela halted and dragged.

"I want to rest," she said.

"You can't walk anymore?" Landira asked.

Neela's head slumped for a moment and then abruptly raised.

"Where are we going?" she asked.

"We are going to Alris," Landira answered.

"Why? It doesn't hurt anymore," Neela said.

"We are going," Landira said firmly.

Neela took a few more steps and slumped. Landira reached one hand around her back and another beneath her legs and picked her up. Neela was small and petite, with her head only coming up to Landira's solar plexus when she stood to her full height, but she felt even lighter than she looked. Then Landira remembered her conversation with Alris the night before about how sokes had lower tissue density than humans. She was filled with rage when she thought about how weak and helpless Neela must have been when they came for her.

When Landira reached Alris' house she kicked the door loudly, rather than knocking, until he came.

"What has happened?" Alris asked when he saw Landira holding Neela's limp form and the yellow fluid leaking through the wrap.

"They tortured her Alris!" Landira shouted. "They did it to her just for being my friend!"

"Bring her this way," Alris said as he walked into his house.

He shut and bolted the door behind them once they were inside. Alris led Landira into another room where a table was set up with a cushioned top and some clean sheets. Landria placed Neela on the table and held her in a sitting position. Neela's head slumped forward and her arms remained limp. Alris gently unwrapped the sash from Neela.

"Hmm..," he muttered as he examined the wounds.

He brought out some herbs and passed them under Neela's nose. She snorted and raised her head.

"Alris..," she said weakly. "I don't think I can stay here anymore..."

"I understand, Neela," he replied.

He passed into another room and returned with a cup full of dark liquid which he held out for Neela to drink.

"Will that help her?" asked Landira.

"It will make her comfortable," Alris said. "That is the most we can do now. Let her lie down, easy now."

As Neela lay on the bed her breathing became increasingly laborious, until it stopped completely. Landira's eyes filled with tears until she could barely see. She sat down on a nearby couch and slumped forward, covering her face as the tears fell.

Out of the corner of her eye Landira saw a blur moving against the wall. It was nothing more than a distortion similar to what one would see during hot weather when heat rises, and when she looked up it was gone.

Alris came to Landira and placing his fingers beneath her chin he gently lifted her head.

"You shed tears for a soke?" he asked.

"It's all my fault," Landira sobbed. "I was just curious about sokes. I made friends with her so I could meet you and now she's dead. They killed her for being my friend. Just for being my friend!"

"You will see her again," Alris said.

"In Heaven?"

"Certainly in Heaven," Alris said as he put his arms around Landira.

"Landira," he said after a while. "You have a kind heart, but don't blame yourself for what happened. You did nothing wrong."

"I knew my mother hated sokes," Landira said.

"For every person who builds bridges there is another who tears them down," Alris said. "This is the way of things."

"Sometimes I wish I could run away," Landira said.

"There now," Alris said as he placed an arm around Landira's shoulder.

He hugged her for a time, and then kissed her on the cheek.

"Come now," Alris said. "I will show you things which will lift your spirit. I will teach you the ways of the sokes, in honor of our dear friend Neela who requested that I show you."

Alris took Landira by the hand and gently pulled her to her feet. He led her out the front door and locked the house behind them. As they passed through the city they received a few awkward glances but no trouble, until they got near the southern edge of town. Two men were leaning up against a wall outside of a bar, and as Alris and Landira drew near they began to stir.

"Hey, soke!" shouted one of the men. "Where are you going with that fine piece of woman."

"I don't see how that is any of your concern," Alris replied.

"You're taking something that doesn't belong to you freak," said the first drunk.

"That's right," said the second man who seemed to be less drunk. "No self respecting southern man would let a freak walk off with one of our pure and beautiful women."

Landira tensed with anger, but before she could speak Alris gave her hand a quick squeeze, communicating that he wished to deal with the situation. Landira deferred to him but she felt uneasy. Both of the men were quite large and Alris was smaller than she was, and at best Alris was as strong as she was, but he would not be stronger than one of the southern men alone, much less two.

"I don't suppose I could interest you in an exchange then?" Alris asked.

The men growled. One of them smashed the end his bottle against the side of the building and brandished the broken jagged edged remnant at Alris. Both stepped in front to block his path.

"Seriously?" Alris mocked. "You're so frightened of me that you think it will take both of you? I don't see how this encounter will make it any easier for you to get women of your own."

"Get... get back," the first drunk said to his friend as he pushed him back with his other hand.

The other drunk stepped back and stumbled against the wall.

"I'm going to mess you up freak," the first drunk said.

"I would think twice about that, or at least once in your case," Alris stated.

"You shut it! You aren't going to talk your way out of this!"

The charged Alris as soon as he finished speaking. Alris stood completely still, unflinching in the face of the onrushing danger. He made no move to brace for the attack, run, or assume a combative stance. At the very last second he dropped to the ground towards the left of his opponent and stretched his left leg across the ground in front of him. The drunk stumbled and fell forward. His face struck against the curb with a loud crack and he rolled into the gutter, unconscious. The broken glass bottle, which he had brandished against Alris, shattered beneath his chest when his body struck the ground, which caused him additional injuries.

The other drunk took a step forward. Alris raised his hand motioning for the other man to stop.

"I don't want a fight," Alris said. "You should be attending to your friend."

The second drunk paused and looked down at his friend.

"He had better recover," said the second drunk.

"He should, but if there are any problems you can bring him to my clinic and I will treat him free of charge. Is that fair?"

"But the woman…"

"Will make her own choices. In any case, the two of you cannot share one woman between you."

"That's true…"

The second drunk relaxed and walked past Alris towards his friend. Alris stood and watched for a moment and once he felt they had passed the danger point he turned to walk away.

The first drunk lifted his head and watched as they left.

"I'll, I'll get him," said the first drunk.

"Not by yourself I think," said the second.

"He didn't fight fair!"

"It wasn't exactly fair to begin with. You are three times his size and the rumor says that those soke people are supposed to be weak."

"Hey! Whose side are you on? Anyways we know where he lives, we can get him later. Right now I think I need a doctor."

CHAPTER 8

Alris led Landira across the empty fields that surrounded the city. The land had been cleared for miles and miles. Most of the land was now used for farming and grazing, but there were also empty fields between and beyond the farms and ranches which surrounded the city. They headed due south, and on the way they passed a few sokes who were engaged in farm work. Landira guessed that they probably lived in the narrow bands of forest which were allowed to remain around the streams and rivers. None of the sokes appeared to take any special notice of them.

"That was an amazing thing you did back in the city," said Landira.

"To what are you referring, my dear?" asked Alris.

"Those drunks," Landira said. "They were both so much bigger and stronger than you but you were able to beat them. Weren't you scared?"

"Not for myself, but I was a bit concerned for you," Alris said.

"I always carry a knife with me," said Landira as she tapped the knife case beneath the outer wrap which went around her skirt.

"As you know, we sokes do not engage in war and conflict. We were the first people to leave the old Eastern Lands because we did not care for how the humans and tavlons were changing the land."

"But why?"

"Sokes want only to be in the forests, and we have lost touch with the bonds we share with humans and tavlons. Most of us have believed that it is impossible to have relations with them, so we move when humans or tavlons enter an area. It is as though we walk in two different worlds, even though we share the same world. We have always acted as though the world were large enough to accommodate an unlimited number of retreats, but at some point we must stop retreating. I will tell you something which I have told no humans before. I chose to remain in your city in order to understand humans and to determine if there could be a relationship between your kind and mine."

"What did you decide?"

"I decided that I am happiest when I am with you," Alris said as he took her hand.

They walked for hours, so that by the time they reached the forest the sun had already begun to set and the white moon was rising in the east.

The forest towered before Landira. The trees were massive, taller than anything Landira had seen before, aside from mountains. They towered hundreds of feet into the air and their trunks were immensely wide. About the edge of the forest were trees that were broken and smashed. The larger trees were so massive that when they were cut down they broke and splintered against the ground creating a field of mulch and debris.

I guess they used the medium sized trees to make the new buildings here. Because these are kind of useless...

"They clear a bit more every now and again," said Alris noting the focus of Landira's attention.

She looked up to the forest once more. The edge had been cleared and already the secondary growth had taken root and grown thick. Beyond that the forest towered, and from the massive branches hung a great many tangled vines. She could hear the wind rustling the leaves of trees and vines, and beyond that she could hear an occasional animal noise. She took a step forward but froze as she heard a distant crash and the sound of splintering wood.

"He is a great deal off," said Alris.

"It's dark, Alris," she said.

"Don't be afraid, this is my home, and I am even better suited to protect you here than I was in the city."

Landira hesitated.

"Will you take the plunge with me?" Alris said as he turned to face her and extended his hand.

For a moment Landira hesitated, but then she remembered how Alris was able to defend her in the city even though it was not his habitat and he was overmatched.

And he is one of the people of the forest...

She also remembered how he once said that there were other kinds of strength besides physical. Landira took his hand, and he led her into the forest.

At first Landira was daunted by the tangled undergrowth around the edge of the forest, fearing that it would scratch her and that it would be extremely difficult to push through. But it was not. Alris went first and although he was shorter than Landira he somehow managed to prevent any of the underbrush from getting caught on her. She was touched by an occasional leaf but that was all.

As they passed further into the forest the undergrowth became less intense and more navigable. Still, there remained many opportunities to become snagged on something or trip, yet nothing of the sort happened.

Another thing which surprised Landira was that it did not seem to be as dark in the forest as it should have been at night. When they first passed into the forest it was quite dark, but in a short amount of time it grew lighter. It seemed as though the light of the moon skipped the forest canopy and shined down from the leaves, illuminating the ground below. It was not bright but there was enough light to make out the colors of flowers and the occasional fruits. There was easily enough light to see although not a great distance ahead of them. Sometimes Alris would pause and engage in some kind of motion with his free hand, which looked like he might be manipulating something even though nothing could be seen.

"It's all very beautiful, Alris," Landira said. "I can see why you like it here."

"It is beautiful, Landira, but none of it is as beautiful as you," Alris answered.

"Aww... I don't know about that."

"I have seen many wonders in the forests of my youth, brilliant flowers and fruits, the likes of which no human alive today has ever seen. Animals of terrible size and strength, vibrantly colored birds and amphibians, but none of them compare with your beauty. When I first laid eyes on you, your image was seared into my very soul. I knew in my heart that you were the companion I have waited for and longed for my entire life."

Landira felt her face grow warm.

"I don't know what to say," Landira said. "No one has ever talked to me like that before."

"Say that you will love me as I love you," Alris said, and he kissed her cheek.

"Alris," Landira began. "I—"

"Wait," Alris said as he halted.

He reached out to a bush and broke off a small branch which was full of small white flowers. He plucked another branch from a bush with yellow flowers and wove them together. Somehow he fastened the ends together without tying a knot. He held the wreath out for Landira to see and then placed it on her head.

"Now what were you saying?" Alris asked.

"I forgot," she answered.

"I have more to show you, my dear," Alris said, and taking her hand once more he led her on.

Alris took Landira to a place where thick leafy vines hung down and formed a curtain of sorts. With both hands he spread the vines creating an opening, which remained open after he removed his hands.

"After you, my dear," he said as he turned to face Landira.

The place beyond the vines was definitely darker than the forest they had passed through so far. Yet, Landira did not hesitate to step through this time as she had come to trust Alris thoroughly. She heard a rustling sound behind her and noticed that the opening in the vines had closed. Alris was not behind her.

"Alris?" she called.

As she looked about the area became a bit lighter. She could make out the structure of the place she found herself in. The trees were regularly spaced and had trunks of seemingly equal width, which gave off the impression of columns in a building. When Landira looked up she noticed that the branches of the trees formed arches as they came together overhead. Along the trunks of the trees grew vines in regular crisscrossing patterns, which bore small fruits and flowers. The ground was covered with moss in most places, while in some there seemed to be a growth of medium length grass in regular patterns.

"Here, Landira," she heard Alris say.

"Oh," she said as she turned to face the sound.

He stood near one of the column-like tree trunks off to her left, and towards the front of the room. He seemed to be manipulating something with his fingers but she could not see what it was.

"Behold," Alris said as he turned to face her and spread his arms.

The room grew lighter, and at the base of the trees patterns of green light emerged which were reminiscent of vines. They grew upwards through the air wrapping about the trunks of the trees in regular patterns, and when they reached a certain height they branched out and formed intricate patterns overhead, creating a ceiling of sorts. Alris motioned and smaller patterns in blue appeared among the green going along the tree trunks.

Landira began to hear music. It was like nothing she had ever heard before and it seemed to be coming from the patterns of blue light. She slowly reached her hand out to touch the pattern of light, and her fingers passed right through it. As the music played the lights changed, pulsating and shifting in patterns. In some places flowers of different colored light sprouted.

After a time, Alris took Landira by the arms and pulled her in close to him.

"I love you," he said and kissed her.

"I love you too," she responded.

"You are mine," he added and kissed her again.

As the night progressed Alris took her about the forest and showed her many gardens which his people had created. She saw bright flowers and fruits, and many of the bright energy patterns which seemed to run through the entire forest. However, the energy patterns only became visible after Alris made them appear so. In some places the energy was more concentrated than in others.

"You live in a wonderful world, Alris," Landira said. "I wish we never had to leave it."

"I appreciate that, my love, but I was thinking that perhaps we would live in your city as husband and wife," Alris said. "To live among us in our natural domain possible, but it will require trust, bravery, and sacrifice on your part."

"I'm brave," Landira said as she straitened to stand taller and lifted her chin.

"That you are, my dear."

"But, you had no problems or difficulties tonight because you were with me. If you had come to the forest on your own you would have been caught and snagged in the underbrush, and the forest would have been a dark place. The forest flows in our veins, and we are able to bend all the vegetation of the forest to our will. We draw strength and energy from the sun, and we sleep on the ground beneath the stars. Would you be willing to let go of some of what makes you what you are, in order to become a bit more as my people are?"

"You mean I could become a soke?"

"Not a soke, but more like us, and able to live in our kingdom with ease."

"Yes, that would be wonderful."

Alris smiled.

CHAPTER 9

L ANDIRA CAME HOME WELL AFTER midnight and shut the door behind her as quietly as possible, but it was of no use. No sooner had she shut the door than the lights turned on and she stood facing her mother.

"Where have you been?" her mother scolded.

"Out," Landira said and attempted to walk past her.

"Oh really?" her mother said, and reaching up she pulled the wreath off of Landira's head.

I forgot about the wreath!

"Out with a man you little hussy?" Nalana demanded. "Bringing disgrace to the family? Who is this fellow?"

Landira had been feeling elated when she first walked into the house but now her mood dropped by magnitudes.

"Not now," Landira said as she attempted to walk around her mother once more.

Her mother moved to stand in her way again.

"If you don't let me go back to my room then I'll just go back out," Landira said.

"What did you do with that dead soke this morning?" Nalana asked. "Are you cavorting with those freaks?"

With that the memory Neela's suffering and the emotions Landira felt at her passing came flooding back to her.

"What you did was sick, mother," Landira said. "It was murder, and I'm really not in the mood for any of your blind and endless hate tonight!"

"You foolish child!" Nalana shouted. "You have no right to sit in judgment over me, and killing an animal doesn't make one a murderer!"

"I'm done listening to this. Either move aside or I will leave this house right now and never come back!"

Nalana said nothing but her eyes narrowed and her nostrils flared. She grudgingly stepped aside but her fists clenched as Landira passed by.

"This isn't over, you rebellious tramp, I'm going to have words with your father," Nalana said.

Landira went straight to bed when she reached her chambers but had difficulty sleeping. Her mind alternated between thinking about Alris and her time with him in the forest, and the atrocity her mother had performed on Neela. She tossed and turned for much of the night, and did not fall asleep until the sun began to rise.

When she did finally fall asleep she experienced unusual dreams, consisting of disjointed imagery and odd physical sensations. Much of the imagery pertained to the forest. She saw plants growing rapidly at different times of the day and under different weather conditions. Vines were creeping through the forest at night. There were brightly colored flowers and fruits blossoming. The forest rushed by her, as if she were being pulled through it. Then she felt as though something were creeping through her body and growing through her veins.

At first the sensation was shocking and she resisted, but once she yielded to it she felt so better and more relaxed than ever before. Then there was Alris, she could feel his hand caressing the side of her face. She turned to face him and pulled him in close for a kiss.

At that moment she felt her mouth fill with cloth and the environment around her melted away. She was in bed turned sideways, and her arms were wrapped around her other pillow, which was pulled in close to her face and chest.

It was well beyond noon before Landira woke up. She showered, dressed, and went down to eat. Her father entered the kitchen while she ate and sat down next to her.

"Where did you go last night?" he asked.

"Do you really want to know?" Landira asked in return.

"Listen, whatever it is you are doing you need to be careful. I am occupying a very important position in this province, and my hold on that position could be upset if the reputation of my family becomes damaged in some way."

"I didn't do anything wrong."

"I never said you were. But you have been with sokes. Now honestly, I believe that your mother has made a much bigger issue out of this then necessary. In fact, she has probably caused a problem where there otherwise would not have been one. But I think it would be best if you stayed away from the sokes. We don't entirely understand them. Well… we don't really understand them at all. They have even less to do with us than the tavlons, and all the evidence is indicating that they are at least as far beneath us as we are beneath the tavlons. Probably further."

"But father, I don't believe that the tavlons are superior to us, they just live longer so they learn more. We all have different gifts. If you could see what the sokes can do—"

"I have seen them make the plants grow. They are a valuable natural resource, which we have to approach carefully so we can learn to harness them properly. But they are not human, and should not be mistaken as such. I would rather you leave it to me to deal with them. If you involve yourself with them people may talk."

"I understand, father."

"Grand," Manitar said as he patted her on the arm.

He rose up and walked away, leaving Landira alone with her meal and her thoughts.

He asked but he didn't make it a command.

When Landira was finished eating she idled about the house for some time. There was really nothing for her to do. Landira's father wanted her to go for schooling at a higher learning institute but her mother considered higher education to be irrelevant for Landira. The plan was for her to be married to one of the older ruling houses when her father was well established in his prefecture and started sending a significant amount of revenue back to the capital. It would elevate the status of the family, and in the meantime her parents would have other children in an attempt to produce a male heir so that the wealth could be kept within the family. But Landira had other plans.

She was in love with Alris. Even though she had only met him a short while ago, she felt she had always known him.

I'm an adult now, which gives me the right to make my own decision about who I'm going to marry, even if the law and customs say something else…

For ruling families the decision was typically made by the parents, but among the common people customs were less stringent. Most regular people often picked their own spouses, and even if they did not then they still had veto power over the matches their parents presented.

I didn't ask to be born into a noble family. I shouldn't have less freedom than the regular people just because of an accident of my birth… I'll pick my own man, and that will force people to accept that humans and sokes are equals.

Landira thought back to when Alris mentioned he was a leader among the native sokes.

The marriage will be the start of a new society. I guess I'll be the queen, but unlike the way things are back east, this new society will be based on understanding and compassion. Once everything is done, humans and sokes will combine their knowledge and achieve more together than they ever did before. I'll be the bridge between humanity and the sokes.

CHAPTER 10

L ANDIRA WAS EAGER TO DISCUSS her new ideas with Alris, but she did not go directly to his house after leaving hers. She wandered about the city first, to make certain she was not followed by anyone in the service of her mother. When she was satisfied that she was not being followed she meandered into the neighborhood where Alris lived and knocked on his door.

From behind the door Alris shouted, "Enter!"

When Landira went inside she found that Alris already had visitors, which consisted of a woman and a young boy who appeared to be in his pre-teens.

Alris handed the woman a small glass jar filled with the shredded remains of a dried out plant. The jar was stuffed to the brim with the substance.

"Just give him a pinch of this before bed until it is all gone," Alris said. "If you don't notice any improvement within four days then come and see me again. But he should be alright."

"Thank you Alris," the woman said. "May the Great Maker smile upon you."

The woman and the child left without giving Landira more than a passing glance.

"The human doctors were either unable or unwilling to do anything for her son," Alris said. "He has a bacterial infection in his lungs, but apparently it is a bacteria that human medical science is unfamiliar with. The doctors either misdiagnose the condition or focus primarily on treating the symptoms. Everything they have done has made her son worse, but the herbs I gave him are rich in a compound which is lethal to the bacteria."

"Your skills are amazing, Alris," Landira said.

"Today you have come earlier than I anticipated, but you are most welcome," Alris said. "Please, be seated. I will prepare tea for you."

Landira seated herself and waited on Alris to return. He presented her with a cup of tea and sat down next to her. He kissed her cheek as he put his arm around her.

"You have come to me with plans and ideas," Alris said after a moment of silence.

"Yes," Landira said.

She told him of the ideas she though up during lunch. As she spoke he listened intently.

"Similar ideas have been in my thoughts as well," Alris said. "You and I are of different flesh, but our souls are the same."

Then she told him of the dreams she had the night before. She tried to explain the strange sensations of rushing through the forest, as if she were being pulled, and the feeling of something growing through her body.

When Landira mentioned the growing sensation Alris raised an eyebrow.

"What does it mean?" Landira asked.

"I don't know," Alris said. "But I have some ideas,"

Before Landira could enquire further there was a loud banging noise, as if someone were hammering at the door.

"Come out of there freak!" someone shouted from beyond the door. "We know you're in there."

"Stay here, my love," Alris said. "I will deal with this."

Alris kissed Landira and rose from the couch. As he turned toward the door Landira grabbed him by the arm and held on tightly.

With his free hand Alris stroked the side of her face and said, "Do not be afraid, everything is under control. Please wait here."

Landira let go of his hand but her fear remained. The pounding on the door continued.

"If you don't come out we're going to wreck your house and come in!" shouted a man with a loud deep voice from the other side of the door.

"I come!" Alris shouted in return.

Before he opened the door he turned to face Landira.

"Landira, I want you to lock the door behind me once I step out, but don't let the men see you," Alris said.

"Alris don't!" Landira begged.

Her heart began to beat rapidly as fear and apprehension rose up within her.

"Just trust me, I am in no danger," Alris said.

Alris opened the door, stepped through, and shut it behind him. Landira felt a strong urge to run out and defend him but she trusted him enough to follow his instructions. With tear filled eyes she latched the door and stared through the peephole.

***

A crowd of about twenty large, angry, southern men had gathered outside of Alris' house. When he stepped out to face them they seemed to lose some of their bluster and backed away, giving him some space.

"Well," Alris began. "What do you want?"

One of the men was the drunk who had attacked Alris before.

"We know you're fooling around with human women and we want it to stop," said the man. "We want you to leave town."

"And if I refuse?" Alris asked.

"This isn't a choice. If you refuse we mash your head in and wreck your house. What's it going to be?"

"I refuse, of course," Alris said, undaunted by their bluster.

"Then we mash your head in!" said the man as he took a step forward.

As the crowd moved in Alris raised his hands and said, "Wait!"

They halted their advance and looked at Alris questioningly.

"If you try anything I can have you prosecuted," Alris said. "I am a citizen."

"You aren't a citizen," one of the men said. "You aren't even human."

"I am not human, but I am a citizen. According to the Charter of the Southwest Province, anyone who has permanent residency and engages in commerce and/or is employed for three years is automatically a citizen of the province. The requirements do not specify that the subject must be human. According to the laws, I am a citizen, and the penalty for attacking a citizen with the intent to do harm and destroy property is flogging and jail time. The penalty for killing a citizen is death. Your ruling class absolutely meticulous when it comes to the law, even when it's to their own hurt."

The men hesitated to move forward. They glanced at each other questioningly and muttered.

Finally one of them shouted, "He's lying!"

The men rushed forward as one. As they reached for Alris his hands seemed to flail upwards for a moment, just before he fell against the thick leafy shrubs, which lined the front wall of his house. Such shrubs were common in that neighborhood. It was a variety which grew thick with stiff branches and leaves, making it impossible for a man to walk through. But Alris was swallowed up by the bushes and hidden from view.

The men surged against the bushes, but could not push their way through. Some of them hammered and slashed at the bushes with weapons both blunt and sharp. As they grumbled and cursed, a yellowish mist began to fill the air around them. The men began to cough and gag and many rubbed their eyes. They fumbled around and bumped into one another as they attempted to get their bearings or run away.

"What is the meaning of all this?" a commanding voice boomed.

It was the voice of Landira's father. He was directly behind the troublemakers and surrounded by a group of armed soldiers.

"We were, uh… just leaving," one of the men said.

"Take them into custody," Manitar said to the officer next to him.

"Honestly, we weren't doing anything!"

"Shut up."

As the troublemakers were rounded up and herded into the police vehicle, Alris reappeared and stepped out into the yard.

"Well," Manitar said. "What is it you want with my daughter, soke?"

"I love her, I want her to become my wife," Alris said.

"Impossible."

"Not impossible. Might be improbable, but quite possible."

"Not at all. You aren't even of the same kind, and even if you were, I am the ruler of this region so Landira cannot just marry anyone. There are politics involved, and we have strict rules."

"You are a guest in this region, here at the sufferance of my people. A marriage between myself and Landira would help legitimize your presence here."

"The arrogance! It doesn't work that way, soke."

"How does it work?"

"In a way much different than what you suggested."

"So… you just move into an area, do whatever you want with it, and the native people just have to go along with whatever you do and get nothing in return?"

"I don't make the laws, I just follow them. I can't help being here any more than you can. In any case, Landira is off limits."

"Suppose we forget about your laws and deal one man to another."

"You're not a man."

"Then one sovereign to another."

"I don't have to justify myself to you, soke, but if you have half the intelligence they claim you do, then you know that our laws and customs are immutable."

"Can you make for why Landira and I shouldn't be joined without invoking your laws and customs?"

"I haven't come to bandy words with you, soke."

"Unfortunate."

"Landira!" Manitar shouted. "Come out of that house right now!"

No! You can't take my happiness away!

"Landira, you can come out now," Alris said.

Landira sighed, and after a moment's hesitation she opened the door and stepped out. Manitar scowled at Alris for a moment and then took a step toward his daughter.

"It's time to go, Landira," Manitar said.

"What if I don't want to go?" Landira asked.

"You have no choice," Manitar said as he raised a hand and motioned with it.

Two guards stepped forward and stood next to him facing Landira.

"You should really stop and reconsider what you are about to do, sir," Alris said.

"I don't think so, soke," Manitar said. "I tolerate you because you're useful and, until now, have caused no trouble. Cause trouble and that will change."

"If you do this, things will go in a bad way. You are ruining a good opportunity here. The best thing to do is allow us to marry and participate in the wedding. Either way the marriage is going to happen, but things will be better for our two peoples if you give your consent."

"Enough, you have no right to speak to me in such a way," Manitar said.
Landira looked at the guards, and then back at Alris.
Do I really have to go?
"Go with them for now my love," Alris said. "All will be well."

CHAPTER 11

Landira joined her father and was escorted back to the estate. Once home she was loudly scolded by her mother. When her mother was finished her father pronounced his sentence on her.

"You will be sent to a boarding school back east for higher education," he said. "It will be an all girls school. While you are there, we will find you a husband, and when you graduate you will be married. You will never see Alris or any other sokes again for the rest of your life. You will leave tomorrow with a military escort just in case you try to run away. Now go up to your room and pack your things."

Landira stormed off to her room in anger but said nothing. Once there she locked the door and lounged about on her bed reading. She did not pack a single item. Eventually she fell asleep lying backwards on her bed. Her head lay at the foot of the bed, partly over the edge, and her feet rested on her pillows. The book she was reading fell out of her hands onto the floor.

Eventually she was woken up by the sound of wind and rain beating against the side of the house. It was nighttime, and there was a storm outside. For some reason the window was cracked open, which allowed her to hear the full volume of the storm.

"Now why is that open?" Landira muttered.

She rolled off her bed and headed toward the window with every intention of shutting it.

"Landira," said a voice behind her.

She turned abruptly and as she did lightening flashed outside and bathed the entire room in brilliant white light, illuminating the face and form of Alris standing directly behind her.

"I apologize if I startled you, my love," Alris said. "You see, there are vines growing on the side of your house. I used them to get in."

"Can I get out that way?" Landira asked.

"I have not come to take you right now, I have come to tell you of my plan. My people are watching all the roads which lead out of this town, especially the roads going north and east. When you leave we will be ready… and waiting."

"How did you know they were sending me back east?"

"I did not know, but I suspected they would try to take you out of town in order to keep us apart."

"There will be a military escort."

"We will be ready. Do not worry, my love, my princess…"

Alris un-slung a canteen, which had been hanging over his shoulder, and offered it to Landira.

"What is it?" she asked.

"Something which will help you relax now, give you strength for tomorrow, and prepare you for what may come," Alris replied.

Landira took the canteen and opened it. She sat down on the edge of her bed and drank. Alris sat next to her and placed an arm around her shoulders. He looked at her with a wistful expression as she drank.

"What is it?" she asked.

"Nothing," Alris replied. "I had hoped to live among your people, but it seems that they are too intractable. Too grounded in rules and customs which serve no useful purpose, but which, by their nature, preclude questioning or revision… I cannot leave you, but the path that will unite is in marriage now together is the harder one."

"Why?"

"You will have to change."

"So what? Who cares as long as we are together?"

"Do you really want to be with me?"

"Of course."

"You will have to chose between being separated from me forever, or being separated from your people forever. One is the price of the other."

"I don't care! They made the choice for me. I will make any changes you want."

Landira finished drinking and handed the canteen back to Alris. She suddenly felt tired, as if she had eaten a large meal.

"Rest now," Alris said. "Tomorrow will come soon enough."

Alris helped her get into bed as she was about to pass out, then he was gone and she was fast asleep.

***

The next day Landira was woken abruptly by the sound of someone pounding on her door.

"Open up right now or I'll have the men break down the door!" Landira's mother screamed on the other side of the door.

Landira sat up and yawned and stretched. She stumbled out of bed and made her way in front of the mirror. Her hair and clothing were slightly rumpled, but not so much that it would have been noticeable from the other side of the room.

"I said open up, you rebellious little brat!" her mother shouted again.

Landira meandered slowly to the door and unlocked it. Her mother burst into the room, flanked by men in military uniforms.

"What?" Landira asked.

Her mother looked around the room and scowled.

"You aren't ready to go," her mother said. "You aren't even dressed, and look at your hair. You… you haven't packed a single thing? What's the matter with you child?"

"Maybe I don't want to go," Landira said.

"Now see here, you little freak loving hussy, I didn't ask what you wanted! Choice is for people who have sense, and you don't have any! Now you don't have time to pack, so I'm going to have to have your belongings shipped to you. Get dressed in some proper traveling cloting at once and be downstairs in ten minutes!"

Nalana left the room and returned 12 minutes later. Landira was dressed in a green outfit with hints of floral patterns in it.

"Get going!" her mother demanded.

Landira did not make a move in any direction. She tossed a lock of hair over her shoulder, then crossed her arms over her chest and yawned loudly. One of the men laughed, then quickly bit his lips, but Nalana still noticed. She struck him across the face and spat on him, then turned her attention back toward Landira.

"I said get going!" Nalana shouted. "You are just a daughter and I can always have another child!"

Nalana motioned with her hand and two huge men in military uniforms entered the room. They seized Landira by the arms and began to drag her. When she reached the door she broke free of them and began walking on her own, but at a slow pace. One of the guards pushed her from behind.

"GO!" her mother screamed.

There were five armored vehicles with large durable tires waiting at the end of the estate. They were parked in a diamond formation, with one in the middle. There were guards standing outside each of the vehicles. The guards were armored and equipped with personal forcefield generators and weapons.

Landira was taken to the vehicle in the center of the formation and loaded into the back seat. A guard was seated on either side of her. Once all the soldiers were inside their vehicles, they started them up and began to move. Landira looked out of the small windows in back as much as she could, but they were positioned rather high and she had to look around the guards at either side of her. But even with those difficulties it was not long before Landira could determine that they were out of town.

After driving for about an hour the vehicle stopped abruptly. Minutes passed by and still nothing happened. Landira smiled, she assumed that Alris had something to do with the delay.

I wonder what he's doing?

The door to the side of the vehicle opened and a solder peered in.

"There is a problem up ahead," the soldier said.

"What sort of problem?" asked one of the guards next to Landira.

"The road up ahead is blocked by some large broken trees. They are broken as if they were knocked over by the storm, but they seem to have been stacked next to each other. We are going to try to move them out of the way. Stay here and guard the girl and don't let her out for anything. I'm placing additional men outside of this vehicle just in case anything problematic is going on."

"Understood."

The door was shut again. Landira thought she could hear faint sounds of shouting from beyond the vehicle, but for the most part sound was muffled. A short time later the doors on either side of the vehicle opened again and a white mist began to pour inside.

The guards were startled. It was not normal for a thick fog to appear in the middle of the day without a storm. Sokes appeared out of the mist on either side of the vehicle and rapidly shoved something in the faces of both the guards. The guards squirmed for a second and then slumped over. The sokes pulled the unconscious guards out of the vehicle and stood aside. Another soke appeared out of the mist and offered his hand to Landira. It was Alris.

Landira took his hand and stepped outside. She hugged him and kissed him, pulling him in close. After about half a minute Alris gripped her by the arms and gently pushed her back.

"We need to go now, my love, before they wake up," he said. "I have no wish to kill anyone."

"You're right," she answered.

Alris took her by the hand and led her away from the road and into the forest. They were surrounded by a group of about 100 sokes, mostly male, but with some women interspersed among them. They passed through forest and skirted open fields from time to time, through the narrow bands of forest which divided the human farms. Eventually they reached a deep unbroken forest, a wilderness which was untouched by humans. The other sokes dissipated away as they traveled further in, until it was just Alris and Landira.

CHAPTER 12

A S THE SUN BEGAN TO set, they came to a place deep in the forest where leafy vines grew across the ground and up the trunks of some of the trees. Alris motioned with his hand and with a soft rustling sound a large patch of vines moved aside as if blown by a sudden gust of wind, revealing what appeared to be a wooden door with a metal handle on the ground.

Alris lifted the handle revealing a staircase of carved grey stone or perhaps concrete leading down into the ground. He smiled and motioned for Landira to enter.

"What is it, Alris?" Landira asked. "Did your people build this?"

"Alas no, my love," he answered. "As you know, my people have difficulties with solid construction, especially with metal and stone. But there are others who owe me favors and have done work for me in the past. For the time being this will be more comfortable for you than sleeping out in the forest."

Landira went down the stairs, and Alris followed closing the door behind them. When she reached the bottom of the stairs Landira hesitated to go further. There was no light. Alris came behind her and put a hand on her back, and a short time later the room began to light up.

The walls were of the same grey stone material as the stairway, and at the other end of the room was a doorway. Alris placed his hand on the doorway and leaned his head against it. His fingers, which were on the door occasionally twitched, and then with a push the door swung open.

In the chamber beyond a laboratory filled with scientific equipment, as well as some chairs and tables.

"This is one of my deep forest laboratories, I have many such shelters hidden throughout my land," Alris said.

"Your land?" Landira asked.

"Oh yes," Alris said. "I was the lord of these lands before humans came, and still am. They are here at my sufferance. I allowed them to come and do as they pleased for a time so that I could study them. All of the sokes who are supposedly enslaved by them are actually conducting observations, as per my instructions. I wanted to see if we could live together but it does not look as though that is possible. So now, for you and I to be together we must utilize my backup plan."

"Which is what?"

"You will change and become more like us, and perhaps through you some essence of humanity will enter into the sokes."

"Bring on the change."

"Very well, if you would be seated over there," Alris said as he motioned toward a large round chair shaped like a bowl mounted on a wooden base.

Landira seated herself. The chair was comfortable and had a thick cushion. Alris took Landira by the arm and swabbed the area near her joint with a disinfectant. Then he went back into another room and brought out a clear container with a small transparent hose attached. The container was full of a clear yellow liquid with a slight green tint to it. Alris hung the container from a pole and inserted an attachment with a long needle into the other end of the hose.

"I must insert this into one of your large blood vessels," Alris said.

"What is it?" Landira asked.

"It is a series of retroviral compounds which I have created to alter your DNA specifically. The change will be complete in a few days, but it will begin to manifest within a day because your system is already saturated with the nutrients the compounds require, and primed for the change."

"How?"

"Every time I gave you something to drink it was actually the nutrient compound. My original plan was to keep you fully human and live in the city with you, but I prepared my backup plan in the event that your people were too intractable to suffer one of their own to marry a soke."

"You really do plan ahead don't you?"

"I do. Now with your permission..."

Landira nodded.

Alris slowly inserted the needle into the large vein near the joint in her arm. She looked away as the needle penetrated her skin and clenched the side of the chair with her other hand.

When she looked back Alris was done. He loosened a clamp near the top of the transparent hose and the yellowish greenish liquid began to slowly trickle down the hose, closer and closer to her arm. At any time before it reached her she could jerk out the hose and abort the process, but once that liquid reached her veins there would be no going back. Her heart pounded as the liquid neared her arm.

She was about to tear the hose loose in a final moment of fear but, but the image of her mother slapping and spitting on the soldier who had come to escort her boiled up in her mind. That image was followed by the memory of Neela's tattered form after she had been mercilessly flogged.

It's not that I just don't want to go back, I don't want to even have the option to go back!

"Will you still love me and be with me if this goes wrong?" Landira asked as she looked toward Alris.

"Of course," he said. "But it won't go wrong. I've calculated this down to the last base pair…"

Landira returned her attention to the tube connected to her arm. She bit her lip and gripped the armrests of the chair as the yellow liquid neared the needle, then connected with it.

Well… that's the end of that…

She relaxed and leaned back into her chair, feeling fully content with the knowledge that she was now passed the point of no return.

Alris stroked the side of her face and kissed her.

"You bore that well," he said.

He then left the room and returned with a tall glass that looked very much like a beaker.

"Drink, my love," he said as he held the glass out to her.

She drank, and when she was done her body began to tingle. She began to feel drowsy. As she lost consciousness it felt as though something were growing through her body, beneath the skin.

CHAPTER 13

Landira woke up feeling stiff and groggy. She looked up and noticed that the clear container to which she was connected was now completely drained. Alris entered the room and withdrew the needle from her arm. Landira stood up and stretched.

"It is done," he said. "Come, it is time for you to go out and experience the forest."

Landira stood up stiffly and stretched.

"But first, you must dress as the sokes do," Alris handed her a simple top and bottom, which would leave most of her skin exposed.

"Since we are not yet married, I will give you some privacy," Alris said. "When you are finished come find me in the other room."

Alris left the room and closed the door behind him. Landira took off her clothes and threw them in the chair. Then she put on the traditional soke clothing which Alris gave her. Once she was finished she walked around the room until she found a mirror. To Landira the outfit looked like swimming wear.

"Alris!" she called.

The door at the other end of the room opened and Alris peered in.

"Is there a problem, my love?" he asked.

"No problem," she answered. "I am ready to experience the forest."

Alris came into the room and examined her. He gave her a wistful look just before he embraced her.

"What's wrong?" she asked.

"I like your black hair and brown skin," Alris said.

"Well thank you, I like your yellow and brown," Landira said. "Now let's go out and experience the forest."

Alris led Landira back up the stairs and out into the forest. Once they were out, he motioned with his hand and the vines swept back over the door on the ground. But this time when Alris made the motion Landira felt something. She let out a startled gasp as she felt the new sensation. Alris looked at her thoughtfully.

"The change has already begun," he said.

"What will I become, Alris?" she asked.

"You have become part plant, and you will soon manifest features similar to those of my people. You will be able to draw nutrients from the sun, and move through tangled undergrowth without any difficulties. You will feel the forest, sense the growth, and be one with it. When I commanded those plants to move it resonated with the floral nature inside of you."

Alris walked behind Landira and tied up her long hair so that her back and legs were fully exposed to the sun. Once he was finished he took her by the hand.

"We will go to the Precipice of Shantir, and you will stand in the full light of the sun and survey your new kingdom," he said.

"My new kingdom?" Landira asked.

"Yes, my love, you will be my queen, and we will rule these lands. Come."

Alris led Landira deeper into the forest.

"Before we go to the Precipice of Shantir we must make one small detour," Alris said.

Alris led her to a small bowl in the ground, out of which grew an enormous tree surrounded by ferns.

"There is someone down there who wants to see you," Alris said.

Landira had no idea who it might be, but she decided that it was best to follow Alris. She headed down into the bowl, and as she passed by the ferns and vines she noticed that none of them snagged on her or impeded her progress. The most thorny and disagreeable of plants felt only like bed sheets brushing against her skin as she slept at night.

The serum Alris gave me is working fast! But how far will this change really go?

When she reached the bottom of the depression she saw two yellow legs protruding from around the other side of the tree. Landira walked around the tree to see who it was, her curiosity was piqued.

When she reached the other side of the tree and saw who it was, she could scarcely believe her eyes.

"Neela?" she asked.

"Landira!" Neela said. "It is good to see you, my human friend. What are you doing so far in the woods?"

"Alris brought me here," Landira replied. "We are going to get married. But how are you alive?"

"I never died," Neela said. "Only the solid body was destroyed, but I fled to the forest and wove a new one."

"We sokes have an energy form that exists along with the physical, and we can exist outside of our physical bodies for a time if they are destroyed," Alris said from behind Landira. "We then utilize plant material to create a new one."

She did not hear Alris following but she did sense a disturbance in the ferns behind her, like wind passing through them.

"Will I have that ability?" Landira asked.

"No," Alris said. "If you become separated from your body you will die. You will remain human for the most part."

"Why are you dressed as a soke?" Neela asked. "And why is your hair tied up?"

"Landira is joining us," Alris said. "She will live like one of us. I have put the forest in her veins. Her hair is tied up to expose more of her skin to the sun."

"Oh, the forest is in her veins now!" Neela exclaimed.

She stood up and walked to Landira. She reached out and held her hands close to Landira's chest, which caused Landira to feel a tingling sensation.

"I can sense the growing in her!" Neela said. "How wonderful, she will a woman of the forest now."

"She will," Alris said. "We go now to the Precipice of Shantir. While we are gone, I would like you to make preparations for a soke wedding."

"The white flower of Serall will grow on her?" Neela asked.

"It will very soon, but I would also like you to prepare the flowers of T'shar," Alris said. "We will start a new tradition."

"It will be so," Neela said as she bowed slightly and walked away.

Alris took Landira by the hand once more and led her away. An hour later they reached a steep rocky incline, which required Landira to bend over and sometimes use her hands as well as her feet. Eventually they reached a spot where it was too rocky for any trees to grow, and a short time later the ground leveled off. Alris walked forward to the edge of a steep drop off. It was as if half of the mountain had been cut away by a tremendous knife.

Landira walked to the edge and looked over. They were facing south, and as far as the eye could see there were vast rolling forests, punctuated by occasional mountains and lakes. Off in the distance where the air grew hazy she could make out what appeared to be a jagged mountain range.

"Further south the land becomes increasingly jagged, and the jungle even more dense," Alris said. "Along the coast the land breaks up into a series of islands before it completely gives way to the southern ocean."

"It's beautiful," Landira said. "This is probably the most amazing view I have ever seen."

"For now, most of what you see is ours, and everything leading up to the edge of those mountains is under my sphere of influence."

"For now?"

"We may choose to expand the area we control later."

As they made their way along the ridge of the mountain, Landira began to feel an unusual sensation. It felt similar to taking a shower, but not quite the same. She lifted her hands to see if there was anything on her skin, and she noticed that her skin was a different color. It had grown lighter, and there was a definite green tone to it.

"Alris, my skin is changing colors," Landira said.

"Your body is producing chloroplasts now instead of human pigment," Alris said. "In time your human pigment will dissipate completely and you will become more green."

"Chloroplasts… Is that why my skin feels like it's being showered with something?"

"Yes. You are feeling the energy of the sun. It is giving new life to your body."

"I like it."

"I would have preferred to keep you the way you were, but there are definite advantages to your new form."

"I think this way is better, Alris. It brings us closer together by making us more alike."

"That is true."

"Be happy! Come on, let's go explore along the mountain ridge."

They walked along the edge of the precipice, which in time dropped down into the forest again but rose above it later as they neared a different peak. This time Landira led the way. She felt more energized than ever before due to the new strength her body was drawing from photosynthesis.

As they walked along the next precipice and took in the views Landira observed a speck moving off in the distance. At first Landira thought it might be a bird but it soon became apparent that the object was moving too swiftly and two straight through the air. The object turned and began to head in their direction.

With a sudden surge of adrenaline, Landira bolted down the side of the mountain and pulled Alris along with her. She tumbled down the opposite side of the incline, and Alris slid down after her. She continued her pace well after reaching the forest again.

"A human air vessel," Alris said once they stopped running.

"Yes," Landira said. "They are looking for me."

"Of course they are, but not for long. Look at your hands."

Landira looked at her hands. Her skin was now an olive green color, whereas before it just had a green tone to it.

"When they see what you have become they will not want you in their society anymore," Alris said.

"What will you do Alris?" Landira asked. "If they never see me again they will continue to look, but if they do see me then they might try to retaliate."

"I know, but even as we speak my people are making preparations. I've compiled enough data on them to start preparing countermeasures. For now, let us return to my lab."

"Are you going to do some more work on me?"

"No. I just want to give you dinner. So far you have been sustained by the compounds I had you drink, but you must be craving some solid food."

When they returned to the below ground laboratory Alris brought Landira a warm meal, which tasted good enough, but was lacking in one area.

"There is no meat?" Landira asked.

"Alas no, my people don't hunt because most of us have extreme difficulties in fashioning material objects, and photosynthesis provides us with the extra nutrients we can't get from our diet of plants and fungi."

"But you like meat. I know you do because that was what they gave Neela in exchange for the work she did at my parents estate."

"Yes, we like it when we can have it, but we don't need it."

"Well, you don't need to fashion a cattle killer or anything that sophisticated, but you could probably learn to make bows and arrows. I used to practice archery as a girl. I could teach you and your people, I mean, our people. If you show me the plants we can use for materials we can get started. Maybe we can find some flint to make arrowheads with?"

"I think we can do that much."

"And you have no difficulties working with material objects, your laboratories are full of them."

"I wouldn't say I have no difficulties, just less difficulty than most of my people. Or it might be better to say that my will and intellect allow me to overcome the natural deficiencies of my people."

"By the way, where do you get all your equipment from?"

"Some is purchased, and some comes from people who owed me favors."

CHAPTER 14

AFTER DINNER THEY WENT BACK outside and scouted for the materials Landira needed. Finding the type of wood needed for the bow and arrows presented no difficulty. Landira told Alris she needed something that was both strong and flexible, and he immediately knew which trees would work best. For the string a different sort of plant was utilized.

When it came to the arrowheads, things were a bit more difficult. Landira considered sharpening one end of the wood on each arrow but had no implements do to it with. Alris had some scalpels in his laboratory but whatever method she used had to be one that all sokes could utilize in order to be useful. She decided that stone arrowheads and stone knives were best for the time being.

She asked Alris to summon other sokes to help her look for the necessary materials, and when they came she described the sorts of stones she needed and asked them to search.

"From now on you will also take orders from her," Alris said to the other sokes.

They nodded and faded away into the forest and out of site. But their approach and departure were no longer hidden from Landira. She could sense them coming and going within a certain distance of herself, even if she could not see them. The effect their passing had on the foliage was palpable to her. No soke would ever sneak up on her again.

Once they were gone Alris turned to her and said, "I like the way your mind works, you will make an excellent queen, my love. I was right to choose you, because you will bring to us abilities and strengths which we did not have before."

"Thank you, Alris, I will do everything I can to help," she said.

After the sun set Alris took Landira to a part of the forest which was lit by the mysterious soke illumination. They visited a green skinned soke man who Alris said was an engineer.

"This is Ragon, he will put a bit of soke machinery in your hand which will allow you to interface with our technology, and with me," Alris said. "It will bond with your nervous system."

Ragon took her hand and manipulated what seemed to be invisible objects. As far as her eyes could see there was nothing there, but then small objects seemingly made of yellowish light appeared in the air and approached her hand from above and beneath. Once attached, other objects of light passed through her hand and connected the two objects. Once that was done she could definitely feel something, even though as she clenched and unclenched her hand there was nothing solid there.

Ragon performed the same procedure on her other hand.

"Which is your dominant hand?" Ragon asked her. "I know that humans typically have one hand that works better than the other."

"Oh," Landira said. "The left."

Alris nodded at Ragon and he proceeded to add more components to Landira's left hand and arm, going as far up as her shoulder. When he was done the light faded and the objects seemed to disappear, although Landira could sense that they were still there.

"The physical structure of your arm is uncompromised, but scope of your nervous system has been increased," Alris said.

"This should be enough to allow you to interface," Ragon said.

"Should be?" Landira asked. "You aren't sure?"

"It should work," Ragon said. "There is no reason why it should not, but it has yet to be tested."

"Is there anything you can do to make me more like a soke?" Landira asked.

"You want to be a soke?" Ragon asked.

"I have come this far," Landira said as she spread her arms out.

"You can't become a soke," Alris said. "We can change your body, but we can't create an energy form and transfer your consciousness to it."

"Wait," Ragon said. "We cannot do that, but I could apply more augmentations. We have fashioned artificial parts for sokes on the rare occasions when a part of our true form becomes lost or damaged. I could fashion a secondary system for her which could receive power from her skin, as ours does, and perhaps allow her to experience the world more like we do."

"Really?" Alris asked. "You're that confident?"

"To start with, I could put something around her heart and brain," Ragon said. "It would be heavily tied to her nervous system, and it might even allow her to perform some of the simpler energy manipulations…"

"You're that confident?" Alrisk asked.

"I am," he replied.

"I'm interested," Landira said.

"Very well, Ragon," Alris said. "Begin crafting the components, but remember, Landira is what I love more than anything, and I won't sacrifice one moment with her if it can be helped."

"I understand," Ragon said. "I would never harm you or she whom you chose."

"Then you may proceed."

"It will take me some time."

"Take all the time you need."

Ragon set to work on his new project, and Alris took Landira back to the laboratory again. He set up a cot for her with pillows and sheets.

"You are not yet ready to sleep as the sokes do," he said. "I will help you integrate one step at a time, my love. But rest now, tomorrow we will be married."

With that he left her and turned off the lights. Landira untied her hair and lay down on the cot, pulling the sheets up over her body.

***

When Landira woke the next day she wanted to examine herself in the mirror. Her hair was not at all mussed, in spite of how she slept, and it was now a dark blue rather than black. As she looked more closely at herself in the mirror she noticed something peculiar about her eyes, but was not certain if it were real or if she were just imagining it. The whites of her eyes seemed to have a slight bluish tone to them.

"Your have the hair and skin of the sokes," Alris said. "They will not require any attention from you, but…"

Alris sighed.

"What?" Landira asked.

"There was no way to preserve your original coloration," Alris said. "But I was able to steer the direction of the change by integrating sequences from the flowers of T'shar."

"Are you sad that I lost my original color?" Landira asked. "Are you saying that you find me less attractive now."

"Of course not! You are perfection, and as a result of this change you have become even more mine then you would have been otherwise."

"Huh."

"The flower of T'shar is my favorite blossom."

Alris turned her away from the mirror to face him.

"Are you ready for the wedding?" he asked.

"I can't think of anything I want more," Landira replied.

They ascended the stairs and left the laboratory behind. Neela was waiting for them outside. She took Landira by the hand and led her to a place where vines with small blue flowers were growing across the ground and up the sides of trees. She held her hands above the vines and Landira could sense the energy that passed between Neela and the plants.

One of the vines shot up and wrapped around Landira's right arm. It grew along her arm in a simple pattern, and from there it shot across part of her chest and thinned out before it stopped growing. One runner went up her neck as far as her jaw line. Neela severed the vine from the ground and placed the other end against Landira's arm, where it clung to her.

"Those are the flowers of T'shar," Neela said. "It is the new custom that Alris will start with your marriage."

Once more Neela took Landira by the hand and led her away. They came to a place where a different type of vine was growing. It had larger leaves and large flowers, which were pure white in color. There were also a few white fruits on the vine.

"This is the flower of Serall," Neela said. "It is a symbol of purity, and the fruits it makes also taste well. I will attach it to your arm as I did the blossoms of T'shar. It is an old custom of my people for the bride to wear the flower of Serall."

The process was repeated with the flower of Serall, and when it was done Landira had another vine growing on her arm, the same arm in fact. The vines of Serall crisscrossed the vines of T'shar on her arm, but only went up as far as her shoulder this time. It felt as though she were wearing a sleeve on her arm.

"You look beautiful," Neela said. "Alris will be pleased. I will take you to him."

On the way back to Alris, Neela informed Landira that the vines were bonded with her skin, and drawing nutrients from her body.

Neela left Landira in a grassy spot where there was a break in the forest canopy so that she would be bathed in the full light of the sun. She could feel the flowers growing on her arm, and she could feel herself growing stronger from the sun again.

Now I truly understand the dream I had before. The growing feeling is my new plant nature. I'm coming to full bloom, just like the flowers on my arm.

She looked at her arms, and found that both the flowers and her skin had become brighter and more vibrant in color. Her skin was now an emerald green. The olive color was completely gone which meant that the last vestiges of her human pigment were gone.

"You are the most beautiful site I have ever seen," Alris said as he entered the clearing to look at her.

He kissed her and held her hands.

"With the rising of the white moon tonight we will be married," Alris added. "Soke weddings are always conducted at night."

Suddenly a loud boom echoed overhead and resonated through the forest. Through the break in the forest canopy Landira witnessed a sleek aircraft shoot overhead.

"A sonic boom," She said. "They are still searching."

"Yes," Alris said. "They search in day and night without stopping. They have penetrated the woods to the north of us, and some of them are using dogs in an attempt to track your scent."

"I think my scent has probably changed as far as the dogs are concerned," Landira said.

"Shall we go to meet them?" Alris asked.

"Is that wise?"

"They must see what you have become."

"Alright, if you think it's for the best…"

They walked for a good distance, and in time they began to hear the voices of men shouting off in the distance. As they drew closer they could hear the men stumbling through the forest, their feet snagging on undergrowth and crunching on sticks. Some were hacking at the undergrowth with their swords. All of the wild animals in the vicinity were scampering away.

"They are so loud!" Landira observed.

"Yes," Alris said. "You are seeing them as a soke does, for the first time."

Soon Landira was able to actually see the men who were blundering through the forest. They were walking through a low area so Landira was able to observe every member of that particular expedition from above. Alris stopped walking and put his arm out in front of Landira to halt her.

"Wait here until I signal you," he said.

Without a sound Alris passed through a thicket and emerged on the other side, coming out very close to the humans. Landira was able to watch and hear everything that happened from where she stood.

"Where are you going?" Alris asked the human soldiers.

They seemed startled by his presence. They shouted and brandished their weapons in his direction.

"Hold it right there, you!" one of them said.

"That's the one!" one of the soldiers shouted. "The one who took the prefect's daughter. He's still wearing those pants!"

"Alright, you scum, where is the prefect's daughter?" another soldier asked. "If you cooperate with us we'll let you live."

"You will let ME live?" Alris said.

He laughed, which seemed to disconcert the soldiers a bit.

"You think it's funny?" the soldier said. "I'll take your stupid head off!"

"What will that do?" Alris asked.

"You'll be dead."

"Oh, will I? And if I'm dead then what information could you possibly get out of me?"

"Where is she?"

"She is close by. If you want to see her you can."

"That's better," said a soldier. "The prefect will be pleased with us."

"Landira, my love, come show yourself to these good people!" Alris shouted.

Landira was hesitant, but decided that Alris knew what he was doing. She headed down the side of the hill and passed through the thicket. She came out the other side of the bushes with barely a rustle, and the soldiers stood gaping in shocked silence when they saw her.

"Holy..," one of them began.

"By the suffering of Golomoth!" another said.

"Heaven protect us!" another shouted.

One of the soldiers grabbed Alris by the neck and slammed him up against the side of a large tree trunk. Landira flinched in his direction and inhaled sharply. She considered attacking one of the soldiers in an attempt to take his weapon but changed her mind as they were on guard against her as well. Those who faced her brandished their weapons and took a few steps back.

"What has happened to her?" the soldier asked as he pressed Alris against the tree with one hand and held a weapon at his face with the other.

Alris laughed.

"What is wrong?" Alris asked. "You don't like the new Landira? Even if you could take her out of the forest, you could never take the forest out of her."

"Can you reverse it?" the soldier asked.

"It was not made to be reversed, any attempt to do so would harm her greatly," Alris answered. "But, I am not holding her here. If she wants to go back with you then you can take her."

The soldier turned to face Landira and nodded at her.

"Are you ready to go back, Landira?" he asked.

"We can't bring that thing back with us?" said another.

"Right, she could be contagious," another soldier added.

"Well we have to report something back to the prefect," said the soldier who gripped Alris.

"Take some pictures," one of the men suggested.

One of the soldiers drew a small camera out of his pocket and took pictures of Landira.

"Maybe the scientists can figure out how to proceed from here after they see the pictures," the soldier said.

"We can't just leave her here," said another. "Our orders were to take her back at any cost."

"Not at the cost of contaminating the entire city with whatever disease she has," another said.

"None of you has asked me if I want to go back," Landira said.

"Do you want to go back?" one of them asked.

"No," she answered. "My life is here now."

"Well we can at least take this scoundrel back and maybe he can tell our scientists how to reverse whatever he's done to the prefect's daughter," said the soldier as he gripped Alris by the throat again.

"I cannot go with you either," Alris said. "I have to be at a wedding tonight. This was only a courtesy meeting."

"Why you arrogant little—"

The soldier was cut off as a large branch fell and struck the ground right next to him.

The soldier stepped aside and loosened his grip on Alris for a second. When he looked back Alris was gone. Landira backed away and was enfolded by the thick undergrowth. One of the soldiers stepped forward in pursuit but another grabbed his arm and pulled him back.

"Are you crazy?" he said. "There is no telling what you could get from her! You saw the way those plants were growing out of her skin, and how she was all green! We need to get back and report what happened."

***

From a distance Alris and Landira watched as the men turned and retraced their steps.

"Now it has started," Alris said.

"War?" Landira asked.

"War," Alris answered.

"I have never heard of war between humans and sokes before."

"For everything there is a first time."

Alris and Landira went deeper into the forest. Other sokes began to gather near a small hill for their wedding. As the day went on their numbers increased until there were hundreds, then there were thousands. As far as the eye could see and as far as her senses could tell the forest was brimming with sokes. Many of them greeted her and wished her well. They seemed to accept her as one of their own.

With the setting of the sun and the rising of the white moon the ceremony commenced. The wedding was performed by a spiritual leader who also happened to be the older brother of Alris. Traditionally the spiritual leader was the closest thing to government that the sokes had, but Alris had taken on the role of community leader through strength of personality and cunning.

When the wedding was over and the guests dissipated Alris took Landira to a secluded spot where there were fruit trees, and the ground was covered with thick moss and soft ferns. They spent the night in that spot, and the next day the flower of Serall came off of Landira's arm. Alris offered to remove the flowers of T'shar but Landira liked how they looked and decided to keep them for a few more days.

CHAPTER 15

When word of what happened to Landira reached Manitar, he was shocked into impotence. He sat in stunned silence as he stared in horror at the new pictures of Landira, and when he finally spoke, he ordered everyone out of his office. He was at a complete loss regarding how to proceed.

Hours passed, and finally an official barged into his office and asked him how he wished to proceed. Manitar said nothing but slumped down until his head lay on the desk.

"Leave me," he said.

"Sir, we have to respond to this!" the official said. "They abducted your daughter and altered her biology. Either one of those offences alone are more than enough to go to war over."

"I don't know what to do," Manitar said. "I can't think straight."

"I will take care of everything, sir," the official said. "Just give me your authorization."

"You have it. Do what you think is best."

The official walked out of Manitar's office and shut the door behind him.

***

"We go to war with the sokes," the official said to the others who were present. "I want troops stationed around the edge of the forest, and in each town. I want the forests cut down and cleared away, it's time for us to take full possession of this land. If the sokes retreat then we will let them go for now, but if any linger or resist the men are free to do whatever they want to them."

One of the other officials present snickered.

"I want that freak Alris brought in, dead or alive," the official said. "I want the prefect's daughter found and brought in for study. But, she is only to be handled by men in hazard suits."

***

Landira examined herself in the mirror. The transformation was now complete, but she still did not look completely like a soke. Sokes had pale eyes which were almost white, save for the pupils. Landira's irises were the same vibrant blue color they had always been, but the whites of her eyes were now a light blue color instead of white. Alris said that it was a side effect of the addition of soke DNA. Sokes had pigment producing cells throughout the entire eye which could produce more or less pigment, depending on the need, but the pigment was so light that it typically did not show up beyond the irises. In Landira's case her natural pigment was a dark blue.

The soke DNA Alris gave her was only part of the equation, since most of their genetic information existed strictly as energy patterns. He was compelled to borrow heavily from many of the local plants. He drew the chloroplasts that now served as pigment in her skin from a fern, and the genetic sequences he used to color her hair and eyes came from the flowers of T'shar.

Normally sokes did not use mirrors. If they wanted to see themselves they looked at their reflections in water, and since they wore little clothing and did nothing with their hair or skin the soke women were only seldom interested in viewing themselves, and the men less so. But Landira was still mostly human, and she liked to see how she looked at least every other day. Especially after she changed the flowers she wore. Since the wedding she often wore flowering vines on her arm, and sometimes on more of her body, with the flowers of T'shar being included in her ensemble more often than not.

Alris and Landira lived as both sokes and humans. Sometimes they spent the night out beneath the stars in a mossy or grassy place, and sometimes they slept in a bed in one of his underground laboratories. They alternated, but most of the time they lived out doors as sokes. Through the implants in her arm Landira learned how to interface with soke technology, and with Alris. Their minds would touch and they would share the feelings they had for one another.

Ragon came from time to time and added new soke technology to her, or tweaked existing technology. Eventually she was able to "see" all of the soke energy constructs, and she was able to perform crude manipulations of the plant life which allowed her to add and remove the vines and flowers she wore without the help of a soke. But her ability to manipulate energy was sluggish and meager compared with what the sokes could do.

I guess that's how it is for them when it comes to fashioning physical things. Sluggish and meager, with hands that don't work as fast as the brain…

Scouts came to her and informed her that they more found places where the type of stone she was looking for could be mined. She went out with the sokes and showed them how to create sharp arrowheads using flint. Few of them could master the art of fashioning arrowheads but most of them could learn to shoot. Since sokes could move through the forest without making a sound it was easy for them to hunt animals. Their recipes were soon adjusted to accommodate meat.

After a long day of work Landira reclined in a large wicker chair and sipped a creamy yellow soke confection from a clay mug. Because of Alris' status there was always someone on hand to bring her food or drink. While she relaxed and darnk, Alris was in the lab mixing chemicals with other sokes. Alris was experimenting with different compounds to create gas weapons for their war with the humans. Every other day a human air vessel shot overhead, and sonic booms reverberated through the forest day and night. Further to the north the humans had begun clearing the forest again.

The other sokes passed by behind Landira and left the compound. They were uncomfortable being in enclosed spaces.

Once they were in the forest they would begin mixing different compounds derived from plants, and contain them in bladders, which were also derived from plants.

Alris came up behind Landira and patted her on the shoulder.

"What now?" she asked.

"I am going to stop the humans from destroying our forest, and give them one last chance to be reasonable before we respond with violence," Alris said.

"Whatever you decide you will have my full support."

Alris tapped her on the arm and said, "come."

She followed him outside, where they came to face a group of sokes.

"I want all the deforestation stopped," Alris said. "Just as we planned."

The sokes shot off in all directions and were gone. Alris and Landira headed due north, and in time they were joined by a large group of sokes. For days they continued north, stopping only to sleep and eat. In time Landira could hear shouts and the sounds of machinery. She could hear the sound of blades cutting, trees breaking, and vehicles rolling over the smaller plants.

Many of the sokes present had strung together the bladders containing the reactive compounds and wore them as belts and sashes. Alris halted at a safe distance with Landira and motioned for his people to go ahead of him. The majority of sokes continued on but a group stayed behind to protect Landira.

The sokes crept up on the humans and began to throw the bladders as grenades. When the bladders ruptured the compounds inside reacted with the air to produce noxious gasses which rendered the humans unconscious. Some of the humans shouted but soon many of them were unconscious. Vines of varying sorts grew out of the woods and spread rapidly across the ground like rivers of green. The humans who remained conscious were in a panic. Some ran while others hacked at the vines. Those who did not run were swiftly entangled and left immobile. Vines grew up into the machinery from beneath and clogged their motors.

"Take this message back to your leaders," Alris said as he approached some of the humans. "I want all this equipment taken away, and I want no more attempts made to demolish our forests. If you can abide by this we will have peace, if not, then I will reclaim all of the land you have taken."

After the sokes withdrew the humans who were knocked out by the gas began to revive. They cut their fellows loose who had been entangled by the vines, but they were unable to restart any of the machinery. Vines and roots had grown through the machinery so that it would no longer function unless it was completely taken apart and put back together.

WHEN WORD OF WHAT HAPPENED reached the office of the prefect he did nothing, but the officer who had issued the orders for deforestation was in a fuming rage.

"'Withdraw the equipment from my forests' he says, but then he sabotages it so that it can't be moved," the official grumbled. "I want technicians sent down there to get as much of that equipment as possible operational again. Then I want all the military aircraft in this province to drop all the earth scorchers we have on that forest."

"But sir, we do not have enough earth scorchers on hand to put more than a few dents in that forest, and as you know land that gets blasted by earth scorchers is no good for a hundred years or so," one of the soldiers said. "The ground melts in the heat and becomes like stone."

"That's fine. At this point I just want to send them a clear warning. Drop all the earth scorchers we have on the forest. Then I want you to try to requisition additional men, air ships, and as many gas masks as we can get from the capital back east."

***

Alris and Landira were in their personal orchard when word came to them that a huge part of the forest had been scorched into oblivion. An air vessel shot overhead before a great ball of fire welled up from the ground and disintegrated everything within a 400 foot radius. Beyond that the plants were charred and some fires burned for a time before they died down naturally. The ground within the 400 foot area was turned solid, like fired clay.

By the end of the day word reached Alris that 200 other sections of the forest had been similarly obliterated. Some sokes were caught in the fires and their physical bodies were destroyed as a result.

"They are beginning to annoy me now," Alris said.

"How will we respond to this?" one of the sokes asked.

"We will repair the holes they have blown in the forest," Alris said. "I want it done immediately, the faster we restore our forest the more frightened our enemies will be. Use the roots of trees and mosses to break up the hard ground as soon as it cools. In the meantime I will go to the humans and tell them to vacate this area."

"I don't think they will listen to you," Landira said.

"I do not believe they will listen either, but I believe in fairness," Alris said. "I will give them a chance to leave our lands before we move on them in force. But be ready for my return."

Alris sent Landira to a cave further south in the event that the humans decided to drop more earth scorchers. Then he headed north until he reached the edge of the forest where a group of human soldiers were camped. Technicians were working to unclog the deforestation equipment and get it operational again.

Alris stepped out of the forest with his hands up, and as soon as he was spotted the human soldiers surrounded him.

"I come in peace," he said. "I wish to have words with your leaders."

"They wish to have words with you as well," one of the soldiers replied.

Alris was put in chains and brought back to the city where Landira's father held office. But before he could be taken to the prefect he was brought before an officer. In spite of his chains Alris was kept continually under guard. There were no less than five soldiers present at any given time.

"Well now, if it isn't the great Alris," the officer said. "Not so great anymore I think. Well, have your people learned their lesson yet? Are you ready to surrender?"

"I am not here to speak to an underling," Alris replied.

One of the guards raised his hand to strike Alris.

"Wait!" the officer said. "Let's take him before the prefect and see what he has to say."

Alris was taken into the office of the prefect where Manitar sat slumping in his chair. The prefect scowled when he saw Alris.

"What have you done to my daughter?" he asked.

"I have only done what you forced me to do," Alris answered.

"I 'forced' you!"

"Yes. I wanted to stay in the city and marry her, but you tried to keep us apart. I had to do what I did because there was no way we could live among your people and be together. As for what I have done to your daughter… I have put the forest in her veins. I did it with her consent, and she likes the change I have wrought in her."

"Can it be reversed?"

"No, but it can be done to others."

"Is that a threat?"

He rose from his desk and approached Alris. He picked him up by the shoulders and threw him across the room.

"You have taken my daughter from me and turned her into some kind of freak!" Manitar said. "I will kill you with my bare hands!"

"Wait!" Alris said. "Don't you want to hear what I came here to say before you kill me?"The officer stepped between Manitar and Alris.

"It would be best to hear what he has to say," he said.

Manitar growled but stepped back and returned to his chair.

"The majority of the lands which you have named the 'Southwest Province' belonged to my people for thousands of years," Alris said. "I am the current ruler of these lands. I allowed your people in as guests, to see if humans and sokes could live together and form an integrated society. However, you have been rude guests. You have attacked us and destroyed our homes. It is clear that we cannot live together. I have come to tell you that my people will no longer suffer your presence here. We are going to begin the process of reclaiming these lands in three days. I want your people to vacate the Southwest Province. We will work our way up slowly from the south. If we come to a city and your people are making honest efforts to leave we will allow them the time they need, but if you resist us we will respond with lethal force."

"Is that all?"

"Not quite. If any humans wish to remain here after I have reclaimed my land they must undergo the same process Landira has, and assimilate to our culture as much as science and psychology allows. That is all."

When Alris finished speaking Manitar unsheathed his sword and severed his head. The lifeless body tumbled to the ground.

"What are your orders, sir," the officer asked Manitar.

"Put his head on display in the middle of town," Manitar said. "Once that is done I want you to wipe out the sokes."

CHAPTER 17

Wɪᴛʜᴏᴜᴛ ʜɪꜱ ᴘʜʏꜱɪᴄᴀʟ ʙᴏᴅʏ, Aʟʀɪꜱ was able to move quickly across the land. He performed some reconnaissance throughout the human occupied territories before he sped back deep into the forest and fabricated a new body for himself. Once finished he sought out Landira.

He found her bathing in a spring fed river, which flowed out of a cave they occupied. The water was nearly as blue as her eyes. As per his orders there were many sokes in the vicinity acting as guards for her.

"Landira," he said.

"What news, my love?" she asked.

"It is time," Alriis said. "Summon the troops."

Landira clapped her hands and three of her attendants came running.

"Summon the troop commanders," she said.

They bowed and ran off.

When the commanders arrived Alris discussed plans with them and gave them each a different assignment. They would start from the edge of their great forest and move north, causing plants to begin to grow as they moved. Others would follow along behind the troops, mostly women, who would cause the plants to grow at an accelerated pace and they would reclaim the land for the forest as they went. Alris and Landira would move with the troops, but Landira would stay behind the lines, as she could not generate a new body should hers be destroyed.

"Here is a breakdown of the tactical situation," Alris said. "The humans have metal armor and weapons, superior physical strength, and superior combat training. They also have air supremacy due to their flying machines, and we have nothing to counter that at this time. Our advantage is in numbers, and the fact that they can only harm our physical bodies. As long as we have the forest we can generate new bodies for ourselves. The forest is our most important resource in this conflict, which is why we must immediately replenish it if they humans attack it again."

"It is important that we move quickly," Landira said. "We have the numerical advantage right now, but if we take our time the humans may send for more men and more aircraft from back east. If they do that then it will be extremely difficult for us to win. My father has probably already sent messages asking for help, and if not then he will once the attack starts."

"Yes," Alris said. "We must be cunning and swift if we are going to win this. We need to make them think they are fighting a force of nature rather than mortal beings who are simply utilizing abilities and technology that they do not possess."

Each troop commander summoned the men under his command and deployed them all across the length of the Southwest Province, forming a line which ran for miles.

***

By noon the forest began to creep ahead of the advancing sokes. Ferns, vines, and small trees began growing up along the edge of the forest. Every time people passed by the forest seemed a little closer. Farmers began to notice wild plants growing in their fields. It was not long before humans began to notice that the plants were growing at an observable rate, rising and writhing up out of the ground. Rivers of vines flowed across fields and streets.

People panicked and ran. Those who had vehicles or animals they could ride immediately boarded or mounted them and headed north and east away from the strange growth.

Commanders at the edge of the forest ordered their men to stand their ground. They hacked at the spreading plants but to no avail. Some soldiers dove into the strange growth looking for whatever was behind it, in an attempt to find an enemy that could be killed, but found no enemy other than the rapidly growing foliage which swiftly entangled them.

***

Throughout the initial onslaught the sokes remained out of sight. Landira hung back with a group of guards tasked with watching her.

The soke warriors were equipped with sashes and belts of the organic gas grenades which Alris invented, but in addition many of them had flint knives which Landira. They also had breastplates, gauntlets, and sometimes helmets made out of wood. Some wore breastplates made of bone strung together. Their crude weapons and armor were not nearly of the same quality as that which the humans had but Landira did the best she could with limited resources, and for the sake of efficiency whatever she taught them had to be something they could duplicate.

She also trained many of the generals in the martial arts she had learned in her self-defense classes, and they in turn taught their troops. It was not as extensive or effective as the training the human soldiers received, but it was more than what the sokes had before. They could build on the foundations she gave them later on.

Landira herself wore no armor, but she did carry a dagger. Unlike those which the troops carried, hers was made of metal and wrought by tavlon smiths. The sides of the blade were etched with detailed floral patterns, and the blade was sharp enough to cut through most types of human armor. She wore vines with purple and red flowers on her right arm and much of her right side for the occasion.

As the battle raged, the human soldiers were routed. Some were captured while a few were killed. A frightened looking human soldier crashed through the forest swinging his sword wildly and blundered right into Landira's guards. He slashed one of them in two but was quickly tangled by an eruption of undergrowth, which caught him up to his chest in bushes and ferns. He stumbled forward and was swiftly bound with vines.

The guards were about to kill him but Landira commanded them to halt. She walked to the fallen soldier and his eyes were wide with fear at her approach. He tried to squirm away but he was held fast, and one of the guards struck a blow to the back of his head.

"No!" he shouted. "Please!"

He cringed and closed his eyes as Landira bent down and removed his sword.

"A fine weapon," she said. "Do you mind if I keep it?"

"Keep it!" he shouted. "But just don't hurt me. Please! I'm not ready to die!"

"Why not? You're in the army aren't you?"

"I'm only 21. I come from a poor family. My father is dead and I have a girlfriend back home that I want to marry. I have to support my mother."

"I am also 21," Landira said. "Very well, remove your armor and weapons and you may go."

She nodded at the guards and they loosened his bonds.

"But if you try anything…"

Landira pointed at his face.

"Oh thank you!" he said as he unfastened his armor. "I won't forget you. What is your name?"

"Landira," she said.

The soldier's eyes grew wide with fear and he turned to run away at an incredible speed.

"They fear you, mistress," one of her guards said.

"They fear contamination," Landira said. "They think I am contagious. Maybe it is for the best. We can probably use that to our advantage."

***

The soke forces soon neared one of the larger towns. This town was protected by a wall, and had many soldiers to defend it. The settlement was surrounded by farms and ranches, and a river flowed nearby which was used for irrigation. As soldiers watched from the walls many of the farms turned a darker green and seemed to swell upward before their eyes. After a few hours of strange growth in the farms the river began to fog over, and the fog spread and surrounded the city.

The phenomenon was terrifying to them, as it was the wrong time of day for such a fog. To the already perturbed soldiers it seemed that the world had gone mad, and many questioned their sanity. But what the soldiers did not know was that Alris had sent a troop of chemists dump compounds in the water, which caused it to evaporate rapidly and re-condense as fog. Soldiers on the wall heard a soft rustling sound, and soon they noticed leafy vines protruding above the outer edge of the wall and creeping across the top.

They backed away in fear. Out of the fog near the edge of the wall sokes with war paint and crude armor of wood and bone climbed up over the edge. Some of the sokes had leafy vines growing on their bodies for added camouflage. The effect that all this had on the humans was that they experienced unbridled fear, and felt as though they had been overtaken by a living nightmare.

When faced with a threat the human reaction was to run or fight, but since they were at the top of the walls the only option available to most was to fight or jump to certain death. Most of the humans chose to fight, since the sokes presented them with a foe they could actually attack and visibly harm.

***

The bodies of many sokes were destroyed but more soon came to take their place, and the sokes were able to utilize their gas grenades. Eventually the defenders were worn down, and the city was taken.

The soldiers which were captured were disarmed and led to the center of town. Soke warriors flooded into the city and went from house to house confiscating whatever weapons were present and pulling the people out into the streets. Alris had many of the humans assemble in the center of town, under guard, and gave them a speech.

"Attention humans," he began. "I am Alris, rightful ruler of these lands. Your people were here at my sufferance as guests. But you have been poor guests. You have committed acts of aggression against the soke people, and we are taking back our lands. I want you all to leave. You may take anything with you that you wish, except for weapons, but the city is ours. You will leave the Southwest Province and never return. If you wish to stay, then you must become like my wife, Landira."

Upon concluding his speech Landira stepped into the town center with her personal guards and walked around the front of the human crowds. The people gasped when she appeared, and backed away when she approached.

Alris decided to make camp in the city. Within a day most of the humans were gone. In two days they were all gone. Alris left only one road heading northeast free of plants.

"Is it wise to let them all go, leader?" asked one of his generals. "Would it not be better to kill them all."

"You have become drunk with power," Alris answered. "I never wanted to kill anyone, so if we can drive them out without killing them then it is all the better. From a purely tactical perspective it is also good to let them run. They will spread the fear of us among their fellows and make it easier for us to win."

"We should arm our people with their weapons and personal forcefield generators," Landira said. "They have been using projectile weapons to dispatch some of our warriors but we have not been able to use our bow and arrows on them because of their armor."

"You are correct, my love," Alris said. "See to it that our people are equipped with the personal forcefield generators, and I want as many of our men as possible armed with their weapons."

"Yes, husband, but in time we must also learn to make weapons of steal."

"That will be extremely hard for my people… in their present state."

"What are you thinking? Are you planning something?"

"I'm always planning something… I'll share the details of my thought later."

Alris slowed the advance for two days in order to regroup and focus on making the new trees grow to full size in the lands they had taken so far. He also had his chemists working overtime to produce new chemical weapons. In the meantime, the forest expanded slowly northward.

Once they resumed their rapid expansion they encountered little resistance. Most of the southern part of the province had been abandoned. They continued to advance to the north without issues, and then suddenly they encountered a fortified barricade. There were many large vehicles parked behind the barrier and in front of it, and beyond that many trenches were dug.

"What is this?" Alris wondered out loud.

"It looks like a last stand to me," Landira said.

"Onward!" Alris shouted to his men.

The forest crept on. Vines and creepers first, followed by ferns, bushes, and small trees. The women held back behind the men and focused their entire energy on making the plants grow. Then something happened.

The sound of a sonic boom split the air and a multitude of aircraft flew overhead leaving trails in the sky. Others crisscrossed over the forest closer to the ground and sprayed it with something from the air. The vehicles parked in front of the barricade also began to spray the forest with something.

"This is bad," Landira said.

"I want everyone to fall back!" Alris commanded. "Especially you, Landira! I can't let anything happen to you."

Landira and her guards began to run back further into the forest. Shortly after that objects were shot into the forest from over the human barricade, which burst into flame upon impact. Much of the forest immediately burst into flame.

Everyone broke into a run, but many of the soke warriors were consumed by the flames. Landira could hear the men screaming who were caught in the blaze. She knew that they could re-body later but in the meantime they would suffer greatly.

The forest was burned and blackened within roughly a mile of the human barricade, for the entire width of the southwest province. Fortunately for the sokes all the land they had taken beneath the barrier, and the burnt area, was not completely forested. So they had plenty of room to retreat and regroup, and they had good cover.

Deeper in the forest Alris and Landira met with their generals to discuss tactics. About one fourth of their troops had been burned, but those men who were incinerated were now in the process of forming new bodies. The humans made no move since they burned the forest other than continuing to fortify their barricade and sending a few scouts into the charred area.

"They have already used up their earth scorchers and have probably used up their flammable chemicals as well," Landira said. "My guess is that they will focus on fortifying their position until they can receive reinforcements, or more chemicals."

"You don't think they have more?" one of the generals asked.

"I think they would have used everything that they had, but more is probably on the way," Landira replied.

"Which is why we need to resume our momentum," Alris said. "Tomorrow we take that barricade and penetrate to the capital city of their so-called Southwest Province"

The next day the forest began to grow again. The ashes from the previous day's burning acted as fertilizer for the new growth. The human soldiers were in a state of panic. Many of the soldiers rebelled and abandoned their post. In time the wall was overwhelmed and sokes were moving beyond, destroying any vehicles they encountered and causing the forest to grow.

The humans continued to retreat before them.

CHAPTER 18

I N THE CAPITAL CITY OF the Southwest Province a high ranking official from the ruling families back east met with Manitar.

"What have you done Manitar?" the official asked. "You have single handedly lost the Southwest Province. Don't you have anything to say?"

"I'm doing everything I can," Manitar said. "What about the reinforcements?"

"There will be no reinforcements."

"Sir, with respect," said Manitar's first in command, the man to whom Manitar had delegated the responsibility of confronting the sokes. "We have obliterated parts of their forest with earth scorchers, and fires. After the fires died down we even found skeletons of sokes among the ashes. We can put a dent in their advances, we just need more men and more equipment."

"Exactly," the official from the capital said. "All you can do is put a dent in their efforts, and if you haven't noticed the forest grows right back after you obliterate part of it. You have awakened a force of nature, and trying to put a hole in this enemy is like trying to dig a hole in water. Now, this being called Alris has said he only wants back the Southwest Province. We will parley with him and sign an official treaty. We do not want to look weak but we cannot fight a force of nature. You would not try to stop a tornado with a sword, or turn the sky from blue to red with threatening words. Our situation here is no different. I want you to send a messenger to this Alris creature to tell him that we would like to meet and discuss terms."

"Alris is dead!" Manitar shouted. "I killed him myself. His head was put on display for days in the center of town."

"Obviously you are mistaken," the official said. "There have been many sightings of him on the warfront," the official said.

"Maybe... maybe these things cannot be killed," Manitar suggested.

"Who will be brave enough to go meet with Alris?" Manitar's first officer asked.

***

As the humans continued to retreat, the forces of Alris drew closer to the capital city of the Southwest Province, but with reduced momentum. It would be at least two days before the sokes who were obliterated in the fire attack would be finished crafting their new bodies.

One day when Alris and Landira were in counsel with their generals they were approached by a messenger.

"Leader, we have taken a runner of the humans," the messenger said.

"Bring him to me at once," Alris replied.

A large human soldier was brought before Alris and his generals. He was guarded by ten soke warriors, who brandished human weapons which they had acquired earlier during the campaign.

"Well?" Alris said. "What have you come to say?"

"You are Alris?" the warrior asked.

He cast a glance at Landira and his eyes narrowed, but he said nothing and showed no sign of fear. There seemed to be an air of indignation about the man, as if he were put upon by having to speak with sokes.

"I am Alris, as you probably already knew due to the fact that my image was heavily circulated amongst your people," Alris replied.

"My superiors want to meet with you in the provincial capital to discuss terms for a ceasefire and negotiate a treaty."

"I will be there in two days. In the meantime, tell your superiors to begin evacuating their people from the capital city and the rest of the Southwest Province."

The soldier remained immobile. Alris casually rose from the log he was seated on and saluted the messenger in the traditional southern fashion.

"Dismissed," Alris said. "Guards, see to it that he gets back safely."

***

Two days after the messenger returned from the sokes, Manitar and the official representative from the leading families watched the farms and fields beyond the city darken and swell with green as the sun set. Manitar had already sent his wife back east, but the way the farms were swallowed up brought to mind the last conversation he had with Nalana before she left.

"Our daughter has been swallowed by the forest," Nalana said as she glared at the images of Landira in her new form. "We have no daughter anymore. That thing is no child of mine."

"You drove her to it!" Manitar said.

"I did no such thing, it was your fault for raising her wrong!"

"Enough! You always blame me for everything you don't like! I'm tired of listening to you. I have work to do. You will go back east with the rest of the civilians."

By the time the sun set the forest had grown right to the edge of the city, and creeping vines lay across some of the streets near the edge, while ferns and bushes sprouted in some of the yards. Manitar looked on the spectacle with a mixture of awe and fear. He could almost hear the forest growing, the sounds of leaves rustling and trees creaking and groaning wafted in on the evening breeze, along with the smells of flowering plants.

The trees loomed up as dark shadows in the moonlight, but beneath the forest canopy glowing lights occasionally appeared in varying colors.

"What is going on in there?" the official from back east asked.

"How should I know?" Manitar asked.

Moments later soke warriors surged into the city. They searched each building and confiscated the weapons from the few human soldiers who remained.

"You asked to see Alris?" said a voice from behind.

Manitar and the official turned to see Alris standing behind them with an entourage of sokes behind him, both male and female.

"But this is impossible!" Manitar exclaimed. "I killed you myself."

"Obviously you did not," Alris replied.

"Would you care to step into our office?" the official asked Alris.

"Who are you?" Alris asked.

"I am Menekar, official representative of the ruling oligarchy back east," the official said. "I have been sent here to reach an understanding with you. I'm authorized to speak on behalf of my government."

"Lead the way," Alris answered.

Alris and his followers entered the government building, and the remaining human officials entered as well.

"I don't know what exactly caused this," Menekar began once they were all seated. "But rest assured—"

"Your people attacked us," Alris said. "They attempted to destroy our homes and take our lives."

"Very well," Menekar answered. "But now we would like for the hostilities to stop. Surely we can reach some sort of a settlement. What is it you want?"

"As I told your people before, I want back the entire area which you call the Southwest Province vacated. All of your people are to leave, and you will not attempt to reclaim it."

"I think perhaps we can agree to that."

"I was not finished yet. There is more. When I started my campain the Southwest Province was all I wanted, but now I want all of the great southern forest going as far east as the Tavlon Delta."

"Well, that land is notoriously difficult with the mountainous terrain and heavy forests, but that is a great deal of land to claim jurisdiction over."

"It is land that belongs to sokes, and you know there are sokes there. I want no more human aggression against my people. The forests are not to be cut, burned, bombed, or in any way harmed, and no human is to enter our territories without explicit permission from soke authorities. I want only to protect my people, if you can agree to these terms then there need not be any more war between us."

"You ask a great deal. Many humans have made their homes in the territory you describe."

"Only in the Southwest Province, the other areas are pure forest."

"Very well, but the evacuation of the Southwest Province is causing us some logistical difficulties. We ask for understanding. If perhaps you would be willing to cede to us two cities in the north…"

"Negative, the Southwest Province is ours. But I will make this offer: Any humans who wish to stay here may, but they must live as the sokes do and accept our rule. That means that they must change as Landira has changed."

Many of the humans gasped and Manitar groaned. Menekar said nothing.

"I do not understand why you are trying to be clever and trick me into ceding land which belongs to my people," Alris said. "Your people have lost this conflict, if you want peace you must agree to our terms."

"Now see here," Menekar said. "If you'll just—"

"Someone bring me a map," Alris said. "I want a good map in full color which is composed of actual photographs of the region, and bring me a red pen."

The map was brought before Alris and he was handed a red felt tipped pen by a human officer. Alris put the map down on the table. The southernmost regions were a deep dark green, which was all jungle. Further north the green tone was lighter but with dark patches interspersed, and north of that was an area of light yellowish green and yellow, signifying grassy plains and occasional deserts. Beyond that was the Great Central Lake, and another area of green but that was as far north as the composite map showed.

Alris took his red pen and traced around the dark green areas of the deep south which represented jungle. He drew his lines as far east as the Tavlon Delta. He took extra care to include the entire territory of the Southwest Province, which did not show up as pure jungle on the map since much of it had been cleared before the pictures were taken. He then wrote "Soke Country" in the area he outlined on the map.

"No humans are to enter the Soke Country without our permission, and no damage is to be done to our forest," Alris said. "If you can agree to that then we will have peace."

"That is quite a lot of territory," Menekar said.

"Not nearly as much as your people have."

"I will have to discuss it with my superiors."

"You said that you were authorized to speak on behalf of your government. Were you lying to me then, or are you lying to me now?"

"Excuse me?"

"Do you think I'm stupid?"

"Of course not."

"You're lying again. You do think I'm stupid, but now you're beginning to see that you were wrong about me. Yes… I can see the fear creeping into your eyes. It's a frightening thing to be fully under the power of an enemy who knows it."

"That's an indecorous thing to say."

"As indecorous as lying? I won't wait for a response from your government. What do you say to my terms?

Menekar hesitated for a minute, as if he were thinking over the offer.

"And what if a human goes into your territory?" Menekar asked.

"They will be dealt with on an individual basis as we see fit, unless we determine that your government is behind the incursion, in which case there will be war again," Alris replied.

"What if a soke comes into our territory?"

"We have no interest in your territory as long as you leave us alone."

"You will not try to take more?"

"I have outlined what I want. We sokes are not an aggressive people. We will not try to take any of your land if you do not provoke us."

"And what about transforming humans into…"

Alris smiled.

"You will have your territory, and we will have ours," he said. "Beyond that there need be no more interactions between us."

"The terms are agreeable," Menekar replied. "We will draft up a treaty immediately."

"And both parties will sign in the presence of witnesses," Alris said.

"Agreed."

After the treaty was signed the crowds dissipated and the remaining humans began to evacuate the city.

"Is it possible for me to see my daughter before I go?" Manitar asked Alris as they vacated the government building.

"Yes," Alris said. "Go to your estate, she waits there."

MANITAR RETURNED TO THE ESTATE and found the gate guarded by soke warriors. They motioned for him to go through when they saw him. As he entered the estate a cloud obscured the moons, making it difficult to see. Up ahead he was able to discern the figure of a woman, who was too tall to be a soke. Her left arm was wreathed in a pattern of glowing yellow light, which included occasional protrusions of light. The patterns looked almost like a form of machinery, and seemed to pulsate slightly.

When the cloud moved aside the patterns of light faded away and the figure of the woman became more than a silhouette. It took a moment for Manitar to recognize his daughter. She was dressed as a soke, her skin was a deep emerald green color, and her hair a dark blue. There were flowering vines clinging to her right arm and parts of her torso, and to his greater horror the fibrous roots seemed to be bonded with her skin.

"Father," she said.

"Landira!" Manitar exclaimed. "What has he done to you?"

"Only what I allowed him to do, so that we could be together. If you and mother had not tried to separate us this would never have happened. But I forgive you."

"You forgive me!" Manitar exclaimed with a bit of incredulity.

"I forgive you," Landira responded nonchalantly. "The sokes have a wonderful lifestyle, and Alris is a fine husband. I have managed to marry aristocracy, which was what you intended."

"Even though he has changed you like this you don't have to stay with him. You can come back east with me."

"No father, I am of the forest now. What would happen to me if I went back east? I can never live among humans again, but you are free to visit me any time you wish. Alris has agreed to leave the estate intact. Any time you wish to see me you have only to come back to it. He's granted that dispensation for you."

"And what about your mother?"

"I don't think mother will want to see me ever again, but she is welcome to come visit as well if she wishes," Landira said. "I do not want us to part on bad terms, father."

EPILOGUE

Landira stood on the Precipice of Shantir, overlooking the vast rolling forests. The sun bathed her skin and gave her strength, while the wind gently stirred her dark blue hair and the flowers which clung to her arm. All of the humans were gone and the Southwest Province was successfully reforested. Alris put an arm around Landira and stroked her cheek with his hand.

"All of this is ours," he said. "Today begins a new age for our people."

"It is more than I hoped for in all my dreams," Landira said.

"I would do anything for you, my love, and for our legacy as well."

"Yes, I suppose they will speak of us for thousands of years."

"So will our children and their descendants."

Landira was stunned. Although she had been genetically altered by Alris, she was still not a soke biologically. Humans and tavlons could occasionally produce children together, which were sterile, but she was told that neither humans nor tavlons were genetically compatible with sokes.

"That would be wonderful, Alris, but I thought it was impossible?" Landira said.

"Naturally it is, but with the aid of science I believe I can find a way," Alris replied. "Together, you and I shall give birth to a new race of sokes who contain the essence of humanity as well. My dream of creating a combined human-soke society will still come true, but in a different form."

Landira smiled, and they kissed.

Alris Concept—by Ivor Kovac

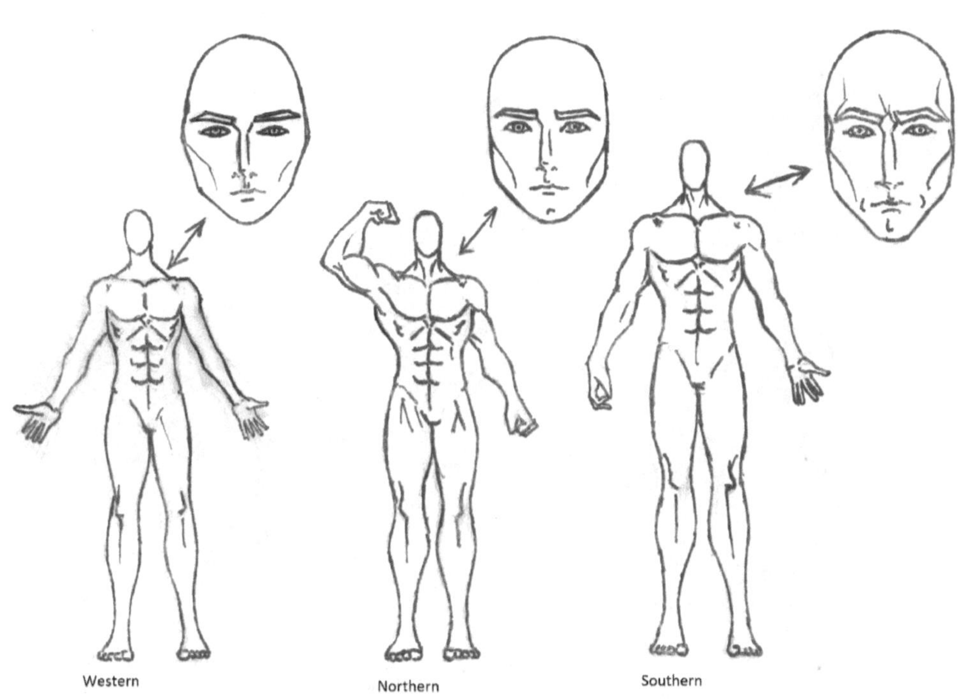

Racial Phenotypes—by Ivor Kovac

Randar Maxelis—by Ivor Kovac

Aneme Concepts—by Ivor Kovac